The Widows of Danford

A Novel by

JAN THACKER

BRIDGE LOGOS
FOUNDATION

Alachua, Florida 32615

The Widows of Danford

A *Novel* by

Jan Thacker

Bridge-Logos
Alachua, FL 32615 USA

The Widows of Danford
by Jan Thacker

Printed in the United States of America.

Library of Congress Control Number: 2011926425
International Standard Book Number: 978-0-88270-602-3

Photo on back cover: Kiana McCrackin Photography

Scripture quotations taken from the *King James Version* of the Bible.

DEDICATION

I dedicate this book to my wonderful husband, Troy, who is my best friend, my lover, my life. You are God's gift to me and I cherish our 46 years together.

Also, to my children:
For Janelle, who has always believed in me and given endless loving support.

For Lisa, who has read all the words I've written, critiqued them with honesty, and cheered me on.

And for my dear Scott, who was always so proud of "my mom the writer" and is waiting for us in Heaven.

Finally, for my magnificent grandchildren and great-grandkids: Christopher, Amanda, Kiana, Cody, Keenan, Troy, Alex, Scooter, Gianna, Andra, Benjamin, Kevin, and Owen. You bring a sense of wonder to my life and make it whole and beautiful.

I love you all!

ACKNOWLEDGEMENTS

Writing a book is a monumental task and there is so much more involved than the author, an idea, and a good computer. There are great crowds of behind-the-scenes people who help to make it happen.

The Lord has to be thanked first and foremost for allowing me to pursue my dream of writing and for blessing me so profoundly. Also, thanks to my incredibly patient husband, Troy, who encouraged me at least three times to quit perfectly good jobs so I could stay home and write—and really didn't mind that the dishes weren't done or clothes washed.

I can't say enough about the encouragement I've always gotten from our daughters, Janelle McCrackin, Lisa Boorman, and, before his death, from our son Scott. They are the ones I used to filter ideas and thoughts, and the what-ifs and plots. And when the grandkids started growing up, they joined the band of avid supporters and are also used as soundings boards. My fabulous sisters, Judy Harmon and Becky O'Donnell, are also to be thanked for their unending love and encouragement.

I am blessed to have a professional photographer in the family. Kiana McCrackin scheduled our photo shoot in San Diego, and took the photo for the back cover.

As a longtime journalist and newspaper columnist I have been blessed with a treasure-trove of support from readers and I'm so thankful for them. I also have a small tribe of friends who bless me greatly. In addition, three cheers to all my Facebook buddies who are always there with a kind word.

Two years ago I took my hands off this book, *The Widows of Danford*, and I simply gave it to God. I was ending the frustrating quest for a publisher and agent. Two days later a wonderful woman named Peggy Hildebrand, who was the acquisitions editor for Bridge-Logos Publishing, discovered the synopsis on an obscure website I'd forgotten about. She requested the manuscript and became a champion of the widows and their story. Before long I had a signed contract.

It has been a pleasure working with the team at Bridge-Logos, including Shawn Myers, who is my go-to person when I have questions. I can't say enough about the incredibly talented Elizabeth Nason who created the marvelous cover. When I saw the cover for the first time I put my head in my hands and wept. The contract was nice but it was the cover that brought home the fact that it was really happening.

Susan Parr and her sister Jackie Van Hauen, are to be thanked for their help in taking my words and putting them in "book form," and then making all the changes I wanted.

All of you who are reading *The Widows of Danford* are also to be thanked. I am truly humbled. And I ask you to stay tuned. There are a lot more stories coming out of Danford soon.

PROLOGUE

Simeon Quest pushed an errant hank of silvery hair back into place as he opened the car door for Katherine O'Malley. Once she was seated, he leaned inside.

"This isn't exactly my idea of a date," he grumbled as he watched Katherine place her purse properly on her lap. Unbeknownst to her, the skirt she was wearing had pulled up on the side, displaying a full twelve inches of shapely leg above the knee. Simeon gazed in admiration, marveling that someone in her seventies could have such fabulous legs. But then, to him, Katherine was simply fabulous all the way around.

"Going to court isn't exactly my idea of a date, either," she retorted, "but we have to do this for Letty. The poor girl is convinced she's going to prison. What are you staring at?"

He grinned a crooked grin. "Your skirt's all hiked up there, you brazen hussy. I can almost see your underwear."

"Oh! Oh, for heaven's sake," Katherine said, leaning to the side and pulling it down to a more seemly level. "Quit gawking and get in and drive."

"You're easy to gawk at," he said, still smiling. "You're still a looker, Katherine O'Malley."

"And you're still an old goat," she said with mock severity before giving in to laughter. Then she sobered.

"Seriously, I'm thankful that you're coming with me and I know Letty will be comforted seeing us in the courtroom. She must be a nervous wreck this morning. I know I am. I was praying most of the night. This whole thing is just crazy."

"Everything will be fine," Simeon said, reaching over to pat her hand.

If it wasn't such a somber occasion, Katherine would have enjoyed the ride with Simeon. She enjoyed every instant of time she spent with him.

Pulling into the courthouse parking lot they found a parking spot and walked toward the handsome brick building. Once inside they made their way to Courtroom A and found seats.

Not far away, the defendant, Letty Vanesse, was also making her way into the courtroom.

As she walked along the hallway, Letty thought she was going to throw up. The public defender, who looked to be anywhere from twenty to thirty-two with a homely unadorned face and lank brown hair, glanced at the young girl's clenched fists and assured her everything would work out fine. Don't worry, she said. The charges are minimal, she said. It was absurd the case even made it to court, she declared.

Easy for her to say, Letty thought, this earthy girl-woman who displayed bulging, naked, unshaved legs under a wrinkled blue cotton skirt with a safety pin where the button should be. She was on the right side of the law. She wasn't a thief.

Letty's hands were shaking and her stomach threatened to erupt.

"But what if I get sick?" Letty said, hugging her arms to her abdomen.

"Oh, you won't," Carol Blister said confidently, as if barfing in front of the judge wasn't allowed and, therefore, simply wouldn't happen.

She opened the heavy steel side door and stepped aside for Letty to enter first. Letty knew from the briefing that she and her defender would sit at the table just beyond the door. She also knew that there were a dozen cases to be presented in this courtroom. There could be just a few onlookers in the gallery, she had been told, or it could be overflowing with citizens: victims, supportive family and friends of defendants, and the curious public.

Letty knew her parents wouldn't be there. Her tiny mother had declared herself fragile after giving birth to eleven-pound Letty eighteen years before and used the excuse to get out of life itself. Her father chose to ignore anything that was upsetting, and that included his wife and daughter. Except for Carol Blister, Letty doubted anyone would be there for her. Certainly not her so-called friends who had taken off running the minute she grabbed the cake. That stupid cake.

Without looking up, Letty cautiously settled into the chair next to Carol. She sat on her hands so she wouldn't have to watch them shake. Lifting her head she noted the judge wasn't yet seated. It was quiet in the courtroom. Hushed. Terrifying. She lowered her head and closed her eyes.

"Letty!" The voice calling her name was barely audible. She turned.

The sight brought tears to her eyes. Old Lillian Dip was there, right behind her and a bit to the right, wearing an audacious pink and white polka-dotted hat emblazoned with "Let's Party!" and whispering her name. Lillian gaily waved a crocheted strip of afghan that was tethered to a skein of yarn hidden in the depths of a bag at her feet. Next to her was Katherine O'Malley, dear Mrs. O'Malley, looking so proper with gloves and not a single white hair out of place. Simeon Quest, the elderly groundskeeper at the mansion was also there, looking handsome and dignified in a sports jacket.

Simeon winked at her and Katherine conveyed nothing but love and assurance in her gracious smile.

Josephine Grimm was also there, sitting on the other side of Lillian. Letty knew her victim would be on hand to testify and seeing her brought an incredible sadness for what she had done. She turned away before Josephine could meet her eyes.

After everyone stood for the Honorable Judge Peter Wilkins, her case, the first on the docket, got underway. Letty's head buzzed with the legal jargon and Carol's halitosic whispers might as well have been in Swahili for all the sense they made.

Snatches of the prosecuting attorney's lengthy comments reached her brain. Thief... Disgraceful... Costly damage to the bakery... Untold mental damage... Fines... Retribution...

Letty sunk lower in her seat and bowed her head and prayed. Her long blond hair shielded her face. She could feel the gazes of the townspeople behind her. She sneaked a peek at the judge, whose bearded face was impassive. He'd obviously seen his share of thieves.

Suddenly there was a flurry of activity in the gallery.

Katherine O'Malley stood up, shaking her head in disbelief. This fiasco had gone on long enough.

"Oh, for heaven's sake, Pete, it was just a cake," she said to the judge. Heads all over the room swung around to stare at her.

Simeon looked amused and Josephine Grimm was shocked. Lillian gaped, her hands holding orange yarn and a crochet hook frozen in midair.

"Oh, my," Lillian said under her breath. Just last month she had seen this very same thing happen during one of her afternoon shows. That person had been escorted, dragged, from the courtroom and thrown in the clink.

"Objection, your honor!" Tanner Cartwright exclaimed, jumping to his feet. He was the youngest prosecuting attorney in the state, and in his glaringly white shirt and skewed tie, he looked like a kid in a junior high play—acting the part of a lawyer and not doing that great a job of it.

"She didn't break into Fort Knox or hold up a bank," Katherine continued, ignoring him. "It was a childish prank. A silly dare."

"Objection! Objection!" Cartwright said more loudly, holding out his hands pleadingly to the judge. Katherine and Judge Wilkins both ignored him.

"Josephine didn't even want to file charges and she wouldn't have if he..." Katherine motioned dismissingly toward a scrawny uniformed deputy sitting in the back of the room—"Freddie Kirby, Deputy Freddie Kirby, wasn't angry with

Letty's dad for complaining about his barking dogs." Deputy Kirby sputtered and turned alarmingly red.

Tanner Cartwright was beside himself, almost jumping up and down. "You can't do that! You're giving evidence. Your honor, I object!"

"Oh, pipe down, Tanner," Katherine said, acknowledging him for the first time. "You're becoming very annoying."

The young man threw up his hands. "Your honor...please," he pleaded.

"Take a seat Mr. Cartwright, and, by the way, that's what you get when you practice law in your hometown," Judge Wilkins said. "Most of us here have known you since you were in Pampers."

After the young man reluctantly perched at the edge of his chair and put his head in his hands, the judge looked straight at Katherine O'Malley. His eyes twinkled almost unnoticeably.

"So, Katherine—Mrs. O'Malley—what is your interest in this case?" he asked with curiosity.

"Letty works for me. She cleans and is helping me catalogue antiques and other items in O'Malley House. Letty is a perfect employee, and I assure you that I have never had anything but the utter respect for her. I trust her implicitly."

"Still, she went into the Danford Bakery and stole a very large cake," the judge said. "Plus, there was a horrendous mess made when the owner, Josephine Grimm, tried to stop her."

"Well, I know that. The whole town knows that. Higley Brown even had a photo on the front page of the Danford News, for crying out loud. It was all anyone talked about for a week, and that should be punishment enough."

Judge Wilkins turned to Josephine Grimm. "Is that true? That you really didn't want to press charges?"

Josephine glanced at the deputy. She looked uneasy. "Well, I thought we could just work it out between us, Letty Vanesse and me. But the officer said she needed punished so she wouldn't do it again. He said that's how it starts, with small stuff, and the next thing you know they're in prison."

"Oh, for heaven's sake," Katherine said, shaking her head. "That's utterly ridiculous. I could tell you the names of a dozen prominent people in this town who have done silly pranks and none of them ended up in prison. Why, I remember one fellow who, with a cohort, took a can of spray paint and painted all the lights on Main Street red." She looked pointedly at Judge Wilkins. "The entire town looked like a bordello and those culprits..."

"I remember that incident," the judge interrupted before she could reveal names, "and you're right; he turned out to be a fairly respectable citizen."

He turned to Carol Blister. "Do you have anything to add?"

The attorney smoothed her skirt but the wrinkles popped back up when she lifted her hands. She grinned. "Nope. Mrs. O'Malley has pretty much summed it up. But I would request leniency, your honor, since Letty's barely eighteen and has never before been in any trouble. You should have a pile of letters vouching for her character in front of you."

He glanced down and nodded and then turned to Letty. "How about you, Miss Vanesse? Do you have anything to say for yourself?"

Letty lifted her head and a tear rolled down her cheek. Her words were so soft they were barely heard. Everyone in the courtroom automatically leaned forward.

"I just want to say I'm sorry for all the trouble I caused Mrs. Grimm," she said.

"Let's take a fifteen minute recess and then we'll meet for sentencing," Judge Wilkins said.

The gavel pounded and everyone rose. Letty was terrified. In fifteen minutes she would know her fate.

Chapter One

Letty Vanesse could hear the lively accordion music when she got out of her car. Her heart leaped and a smile slid up her face. She wondered if there was another twenty-two-year-old in the whole state of Montana who, right this very minute, was as thrilled as she was to hear a fumbling version of the Beer Barrel Polka.

The music meant that old Fletcher O'Dell was back and his funeral plans could be put on hold. She mentally braced herself for how he would look. She knew he'd be pale and wasted and weak. But he was alive. That was all that mattered. Fletcher was alive and he had recovered to the point that he could gather with the rest of his cronies at the Danford Senior Center.

Barely glancing both ways before she sprinted across the street, Letty yanked open the bright red door on the old brick building and walked in. Fletcher was the center of attention, and Adeline Gunn, sitting in a chair close by and sporting a tight new perm, looked at him in rapt delight. Her right fist nestled against her heart, as if it would convey her feelings.

Everyone knew Addie had a thing for Fletcher. But then, so did most of the women who came to socialize at the Center every day.

It had been a scary ordeal, his last heart attack. They thought for sure they'd lost him that time. But Fletcher kept bouncing back, one heart attack after another. He was like one of those grinning plastic five-foot-tall blow-up clowns with the weighted feet....punch them and they plunge to the ground and linger there a scant second before popping back up. That was Fletcher.

Except for old squatty Henry Riggins, who was always a grump, the Center today exuded happiness and excitement. Letty knew that such days were rare. Everyone except Henry was singing along to the polka, the men mumbling the words and the women—most of them anyway—bellowing with nerve-shattering tinny voices.

The music and chaos assaulted her senses and Letty stood in the doorway a few seconds to get her bearings.

"Hey Letty, come and dance!" hollered Lizzy and Delmar Grant, in unison. The Grants imagined themselves gifted versions of Fred and Ginger and were bouncing out energetic traditional quick-quick-slow steps to the music, dipping and hopping and twirling about. At the edge of the group Galen and Justine Dow, who couldn't hear worth beans but loved to dance, were slowly waltzing and not even close to matching the rhythm of the music. Their steps were graceful and elegant and perfectly coordinated—the moves of a couple who were so in tune and so practiced with each other that they danced with pure instinct and memory. The sight was so intimate, so almost-sacred, that Letty looked away.

"Letty!" Lillian Dip shouted over the din and Fletcher, looking gray as a rainy sky, faltered and missed three notes in a row. He turned his head and winked at Letty and her heart swelled. She loved this man. She loved all of them.

There were about twenty of them today. Felicity, Galen, Lawrence, Wilton, Dora, and all the rest whose names she knew as well as her own. In the past few years a half dozen of the group had died off and for a time it seemed as if all she did was attend one funeral after another. A part of her died with each burial of the precious old people.

She had come to them in a roundabout way.

Now, in a way, they were her family. It all started with a bit of trouble with the local police when she was barely eighteen. A group of her friends were going to the lake to swim. On a dare Letty walked into the Danford Bakery and simply picked up a beautifully decorated birthday cake and walked out. On her way through the doorway she swiped her finger across the ANK in "Happy Birthday Frank" and poked the blob of green icing in her mouth.

Of course, all hell broke loose when Josephine Grimm, owner of the bakery, spotted her from the back of the shop.

"What are you doing?" Josephine Grimm had screamed in disbelief. Despite her enormous bulk, the shop owner plunged through the bakery, sending éclairs and truffles flying and knocking cakes and donuts to the floor. The decorating bag in her floury hand left a line of blue icing in her wake and her buttocks surged like giant pistons as Josephine ran clumsily down the sidewalk behind Letty, screaming at the top of her lungs: "Thief! Robber!"

When Letty tripped, Josephine landed on top of her, the cake between them. After that it got to be a real mess with what seemed like half the town showing up to watch the spectacle.

"You little brat! You robber! You ruined my cake!" Josephine yelled as she used her bag to squiggle blue all over Letty's face and blond hair. Letty's friends, of course, were long gone. But the police weren't.

The judge sentenced her to work at the bakery and pay off ten times the price of the stolen cake and also pay for the other damage created during Josephine's tear through the store. In addition, she was sentenced to serve six months of community service at the Danford Senior Center.

Now here she was, four years later, standing in the middle of them and tapping her foot to the Beer Barrel Polka. Letty knew that her punishment was the best thing that had ever happened to her. Even Josephine the baker, whom Letty had come to love as she worked off the fine, agreed.

Chapter Two

Setting aside her crocheting—today she was creating a neon green hat—Lillian Dip maneuvered her way through the folding chairs and plastic tables and her fellow oldsters and gave Letty a hug. Lillian was very proud that she had known Letty as a child—before the crime.

"This place is pretty crazy today," Letty said, loud enough to be heard over the music.

"It's a day to celebrate. We don't get enough of those," Lillian said with a lopsided grin. Lillian was an odd-looking person, shaped like a pear. She sometimes covered her short wispy iron gray hair with hats, usually baseball caps but sometimes more festive wear. But she couldn't seem to make the connection between the event and the hat and was often seen wearing an elegant, flowered, broad-rimmed bonnet festooned with gossamer ribbons with overalls, or a plaid skirt and jacket with a tight-fitting baseball cap.

Lillian dressed for comfort, not for beauty, and since the arrival of polyester stretch pants on the fashion scene in the 1970s she was rarely seen wearing anything else.

Today she wore a black and purple jogging suit and a bright yellow baseball cap with "Hot Stuff" scripted across the front.

"He looks good, doesn't he?" Letty yelled, motioning to Fletcher. "A lot better than the last time."

Lillian leaned in and shook her head. "I thought for sure Violet and me were going to be doing a funeral last week."

Lillian and Violet Lemke had become fast friends because of a similar love of a ceremony. The two attended nearly every wedding and funeral in Danford, and in a slow season, ventured to nearby communities. It didn't matter that they didn't know the deceased, or the couple about to repeat wedding vows. They just dressed up and went anyway. It was a bizarre hobby but after so many years no one in Danford thought it was strange at all.

Henry Riggins cleared his throat so loudly it was heard over the rollicking chorus of the music. He looked pointedly at Letty. She knew it was a summons and broke away from Lillian after giving her a pat on her chubby arm. She walked to where Henry sat in the corner. He was a funny little man, as round as he was tall, and he wore his pants just below his armpits. He reminded her of a fat little toad.

Letty grabbed a folding chair, put it in front of him and sat down. Henry watched her, frowning.

"Damn awful music. Wish he'd leave that thing here one night. I'd throw it in the nearest Dumpster."

"Oh, Henry, you would not. I'll bet deep down you like Fletcher's polkas."

"Ha. I know one thing. They won't allow that thing into Heaven. He'd scare off God himself, with that awful caterwauling. The only reason they all sing along is to drown out that blasted accordion. Don't know what's worse, that accordion or that singing. Makes a body cringe to hear them together. There are some things that a person shouldn't have to hear."

Letty's eyes danced. She was madly in love with this old fellow and admired his spunk and even his cantankerousness. "Henry, you are a curmudgeon," she declared.

"And damn proud of it," he said with a humph. "Now go away and let me sleep."

Letty got up and leaned forward and kissed him on the cheek. "I love you, Henry Riggins," she declared and she was rewarded by the smallest of smiles.

She worried about Henry. His three children lived within a ten mile radius and never visited him in his shabby little apartment. He was even alone last Christmas when they all took off on cruises and vacations. He'd spent Christmas by himself, choosing to turn down an invitation to join the other lonely seniors at the center, where they passed out little gifts and tried to pretend that it was a delightful day.

Letty ached for her people. She fretted over them and she kept thinking that there must be something—something that hadn't come to her yet—that she could do to make their lives valuable and worthwhile. Too many of them were simply wasting away...waiting to die. And many of them were dying long before they should because they simply didn't have anything to live for.

Walking away from Henry she sent up a prayer. God, please don't abandon your people. Please help me think of a way to help these precious souls find life worth living.

The reply came instantly:

Look and you will find the answer.

Chapter Three

After eating two hefty wedges of Fletcher's "Welcome Back" cake, Lillian Dip looked up to see Katherine walking through the door. She was surprised since Katherine usually was too busy with meetings and what she called "community responsibilities" to spend any time at the center. Truthfully, she really wasn't that fond of the place.

Katherine approached Fletcher and gave him a one-armed hug so she wouldn't interfere with his music. His grin warmed her heart. He knew it was an honor to have her here.

"Here, I brought you some cake," Lillian said, approaching Katherine and thrusting a plate toward her. Katherine looked at it dubiously but accepted it graciously. It was a huge piece of cheap supermarket chocolate cake slathered with over an inch of shortening and sugar frosting.

"Thanks. I can't stay long. Letty and I are doing some work on the house tomorrow, and I need to get organized."

"She's in the kitchen."

"I figured she was around here somewhere," Katherine said with a laugh. She put a small polite forkful of cake in her mouth and looked up in surprise. "This is really good," she said, digging her fork in for a bigger bite.

Lillian looked yearningly at the remains of the cake on a nearby table. "Maybe I'll get another piece," she said to herself and then looked at Katherine. "It's so good because Marianne Slocum's sister's mother-in-law works in the bakery down at the supermarket and she makes them special for us—more eggs and real butter and she even melts real chocolate to throw in."

"Marianne's Slocum's sister's mother-in-law...I'll have to remember that next time I need a great cake."

People lined up to visit with Katherine, but after a time she and Lillian stole away and drifted to the kitchen to help Letty wash cake plates and forks. It was a tribute to Fletcher that real dishes were used, rather than the usual paper plates.

After the racket in the main room, the kitchen was quiet and peaceful. Letty was wrist-deep in soapy water and absentmindedly washing a plate. Normally vibrant and fun, it was strange to see her in such a pensive mood, Lillian thought as she came through the double doors.

"You're going to scrub the flowers right off that plate," Lillian declared, chuckling.

Letty straightened and smiled at her. "I didn't hear you come in. Katherine! How wonderful that you came for Fletcher's party."

"I couldn't miss this one. Considering what he's been through he looks pretty darn good."

"He sure does. It's an answer to a lot of prayers," Letty said with a wan smile.

"So, what's going on?" Lillian asked, reaching for a dish towel and fishing a stack of plates from the rinse water. "You were so deep in thought a train could have barreled through here and you wouldn't have noticed. Are you okay?"

"I guess," Letty said and then she pulled her hands from the water, dried them off, and leaned her back against the sink.

"Do you think most of the people who come here are desperately lonely?"

Lillian laughed merrily. "Well, of course, that's why they spend so much time hanging around the place."

"I'm worried about Henry. He just seems so...so lost. And angry."

"He is lost and angry. His wife up and died and those kids of his moved him from his house to that crummy apartment. And to make it even worse, to get to town he has to drive by the old house he and Dora lived in for fifty-some years and see what those people have done to it. Flowers and lawn all dead and the front window broken. It must just break his heart."

"It's a plight many of these people are in. In Henry's case, it's particularly sad. His whole life has been turned upside down, and he probably doesn't have much hope of things changing," Katherine added as she opened a drawer in search of a towel.

Letty shook her head, as if to keep Henry's sad description from settling in there. "He reminds me of Hoyt Blackstone. Not in looks, but in the way he is just letting go. A week before he died I visited Hoyt. I thought I could convince him to go back on the chemo since there was a good chance his cancer could be cured. Know what he told me?"

Lillian set the stack of dried plates on the counter and stilled her dish towel. She shook her head. She had harbored a special fondness for Hoyt, who, inch by inch, just faded away.

"He said it might gain him a few more lonely years but he'd rather just get it over with. His kids had moved away, wife was dead, and the only thing he looked forward to each day was reading the obituaries and Dear Abby in the paper. 'I'm just a good for nothing old man,' he told me. I still can't get those words—good for nothing—out of my head. I know that's how Henry feels, too, and I don't want him to do the same thing as Hoyt."

Lillian shook her head in dismissal. "Henry would never just give up and die, he's too ornery," she said.

"I hope not. Katherine, answer me this, why is it that some of the old people are happy and content and others just sort of fold into themselves?" Letty asked the older woman.

"We women have it easier," Katherine said thoughtfully as she selected a dish towel adorned with faded roosters. "We seem to adapt better. I think it's because we do so many things. A man sort of gauges his self-worth by his job. When the job goes, who he is, at least in his own mind, sometimes goes with it. Women have more hobbies and probably more friends. They are generally closer to their kids and grandkids. It's awful to say, but for some of the widows who come here to the Center, this could well be the most social and happiest time they've ever had. Especially the farm wives who moved to town after their husbands died."

"I never thought of that," Letty said.

Lillian opened a cupboard door and noisily settled a stack of plates on a pile. "We're all of us darned thankful we have the Center where we can gather," she said. "I keep busy, but for a lot of the others this is the only time they see people. A lot of us still go to church, but for most of us the years of being active there have ended. The young people automatically take over all the church work. They have more energy."

"I guess," Letty said. "It sort of makes sense." She was thinking of her own church, which had a senior citizen Sunday School class. During services the seniors all sort of huddled in the back. A few people, like her, hugged on them and fussed over them, but most of the congregation simply ignored them. In her mind Letty thought of them as "the invisibles."

"Everyone has to cope with life and their situation their own way," Katherine said. "And what makes more sense, sweet Letty, is that you don't have to worry your pretty little head about it. You bless these people tremendously just by being here with them."

"Besides, today is a happy day. Just listen to that accordion music!" Lillian added, swatting Letty with the dish towel and then reaching into the water for more dishes to dry.

Letty laughed and her smile broadened as she heard Fletcher heading into the chorus of yet another polka. But inside she was rebelling against the idea of just sitting back and watching all her old friends wither away. God had a plan. She just knew it.

Chapter Four

Shortly after Letty and Katherine left the Center, Lillian made her farewells, took a plate of tinfoil-wrapped cake "for the road," and got on her bicycle and headed home. It was just a few blocks away from the Center, and it was a great day to be on a bike. The spring weather was perfect, the sky a heady blue, and there was a feeling of euphoria in the air. The weather was so invigorating she pedaled heartily.

"Good morning, Beanie," she hollered cheerfully to Beanie Hollingsworth, who was sweeping the sidewalk in front of her house. "Beautiful day, isn't it?"

"Sure is!" Beanie yelled back, waving her broom triumphantly.

Turning her bike down Fourth Avenue, she passed O'Malley House, the magnificent twenty-six-room mansion that, along with the nearby Whitmore Mansion and the Conrad Mansion in Kalispell, was known throughout the northwest for its beauty.

Looking over her shoulder she spotted the quaint caretaker's cottage that was, in its own way, as exquisite as the mansion itself.

Her friend, Katherine, was the sole resident of the mansion, and Simeon Quest occupied the cottage and looked after the grounds.

Besides Violet Lemke, Katherine was Lillian's best friend. The two were total opposites. Monetarily, one was poor, the other rich. Katherine dressed exquisitely, and Lillian took pride in being "interesting." Katherine dressed up even if she was staying in for the day and the only person she was likely to see was herself, in a mirror.

Lillian had been a regular in Katherine's life for over twenty years. The two had met shortly after a leisure-suited character purchased two acres of land a block from O'Malley House and marked off plots for mobile homes. No one quite knew how it happened that a trailer park had sprouted up in the plush neighborhood. It had reared its ugly head like a dandelion in a perfect lawn, and before anyone could react there were a half dozen mobile homes squatting on the land. Legally, nothing could be done about the interlopers, so everyone just learned to live together peaceably.

Lillian and her mild-mannered husband, Del, were among the first occupants of Eagle Wing Mobile Home Park, having dragged in a used, faded pink and white 12 x 57 Lancelot Luxury Home and happily setting up housekeeping. Although they were older, they were newlyweds. Lillian had two grown children who sneered at their flighty mother and her new husband, whose only claim to fame was that he was that he had been the top selling Fuller Brush Man in the state.

Before her geraniums had begun to flower in the new window boxes at the front of the trailer, Lillian had knocked on the broad front door of O'Malley House.

When Katherine opened the heavy door and her eyes took in the woman standing before her, the smile she offered her impromptu visitor was broad and genuine. She quickly learned that no one could be around Lillian Dip and not feel joyous.

"Good morning," Katherine had said on that morning so long ago, "can I help you?"

Lillian had grinned. "You sure can. I'm new here. Actually, my husband and I are new here. We're the Dips, Lillian and

Del. We're part of the trailer trash down yonder." She motioned down the street to the mishmash of trailers that were being set up. We're in the Lancelot with the geraniums in the window boxes. Del built the boxes for me and I got the geraniums from the flower shop."

"Anyway," she continued, looking pointedly at Katherine, "I decided today that I would make a friend and here I am. I had a leftover geranium and thought to myself, 'I'll bet there's a woman living in that big old house who just loves bright red geraniums, just like I do.'"

"I do love bright red geraniums," Katherine said, "and this is a beauty. So, Lillian Dip, do you have time for a cup of tea?"

The pair spent the better part of two hours chatting as if they'd known each other from birth. Katherine was so taken by the colorful Lillian that she told John about her over dinner and even brought her name up as they lay in bed that night. Katherine had never met anyone quite as down-home comfortable and quirkily interesting Lillian. Lillian had never met anyone as sophisticated and wealthy as Katherine. Both women felt they were doomed to be lifelong friends.

From their first meeting, Katherine and Lillian formed a bond of instant and true friendship. Lillian was one of the few people that Katherine would allow herself to be honest with. She let Lillian see her for who she was, not for who she was expected to be. She didn't bare her soul to Lillian, because of Lillian's unintentional tendency toward gossip, but she was able to converse without hesitation and without weighing the intent and importance of her conversation. Raised to be careful and cautious while conversing, she was free to blurt any old thing to Lillian. She could be as flippant as she liked with no one telling her to act her age and to use more decorum. Lillian, true friend, delighted in the rare times when Katherine let loose with some silliness.

Most people, who didn't explore past her clothes and figure, didn't discover that Lillian was actually brilliant and a fascinating conversationalist. She had a wealth of information on thousands of subjects. In her lifetime Lillian had been a flower arranger, obituary writer for a weekly newspaper, artist, square dancer, freelance photographer, and wife and mother. She had dabbled in everything from kick boxing to ceramics and had even learned to shoe horses when she was a teenager.

Their bond of friendship deepened when their husbands died within weeks of each other. Lillian's husband, Del had died an excruciating death from bone cancer, and Lillian had cared for him untiringly, setting up a hospital bed where the dining room table had been and sleeping, herself, on the couch in the living room so she could hear him at night. She had started mourning him long before he was reduced to the hospital bed in the living room; sometimes she wondered if she started mourning the day the doctor had given him his death sentence.

His death came just a few weeks after John O'Malley's fatal heart attack. It was to her credit that Lillian didn't find it upsetting that literally hundreds of people, including the governor, attended the O'Malley funeral but less than thirty attended Del Dip's.

After his death Lillian went back to work, not falling back on any of her past careers. This time she was a driver for the Bluebell Cab Company, ferrying people—usually drunks on Friday and Saturday night—around Danford.

Lillian liked the job. She was a good driver, adept at inane chatter, fearless, and had a nurturing compassion that endeared her to many a fare who'd had too many at the local pub.

Some she'd actually coaxed off the bottle, at first giving them pamphlets about Alcoholics Anonymous and meeting times and telling them about Del's "dark period" before he and Lillian were married. Del had been a twenty-year recovering alcoholic and devoted to bringing others out of the dark abyss which sucked away his life for years.

Now Lillian just drove for Blue Bell when they needed an extra driver. She managed, however, to keep her life brimming with activity.

As she biked past the mansion, Lillian thought about turning into Katherine's driveway but decided she had to get home and let out her dog. Petunia would be pacing with impatience by now.

"Hello, O'Malley House," she bellowed as she sped by the mansion, its windows winking in the bright sun. "I'll come visit you soon. Promise!"

Her smile turned to a worried frown as she coasted past Margery Reynolds's house, the house just past the mansion. No one had seen Marge for months and months. They knew she was there because the newspaper disappeared from the box next to the door each morning and there were lights at night. Still, the house looked so empty and sad. Maybe one of these days she'd try again to get Marge to answer the door.

"Hello, Margery Reynolds," she yelled in a softer tone as she passed the house. "If you can hear me I want you to know that Katherine and I miss you."

It was so strange, she thought to herself as she pedaled to pick up speed, that not that many years ago the three of them still had husbands.

Chapter Five

Margery Reynolds watched her neighbor speed by and even noticed when she gave a small wave in the direction of the house. Margery Reynolds saw everything that happened along the street. She spent most of her day sitting on the couch in the living room where she could see all the traffic—the life—moving steadfastly and happily along. She knew full well it made her more miserable but she was as drawn to that window as hornets to a bloated carcass.

Anyone looking at her wouldn't have guessed Marge Reynolds was the bony bag of troubles that she was. A slim woman with a figure that would be the envy of many 40-year-olds, she kept her once-blonde hair in an attractive shoulder-length pageboy that she trimmed herself and wore makeup every day, even if she never ventured anywhere but from one room to the next.

Marjorie Reynolds lived in a pool of despair. She was seventy-two and it seemed she had been in the pool for decades, maybe all her life. She couldn't recall what happiness, or joy, or contentment, felt like. Sometimes she lingered in a shallow pond of self-loathing, other times she wallowed in the desolate deep waters of self-pity and misery. Sometimes she dangled in just a foot or an arm; other times she immersed herself until it covered her body and then her head until her whole body was lying pathetically on the murky green bottom, waiting for itself to come completely undone.

Her bleak life was drowned in anguish and despondent hopelessness. Prone to bouts of sickness, depression and panic attacks, she hadn't left the house in nearly four years. Sometimes, on good days, she could make it to the front porch but then, after a few breathless minutes, she'd scuttle back inside to safety.

This, though, wasn't a good day, and there would be no attempt to conquer her agoraphobia. Today she would just settle in and suffer.

A gust of wind sent a collection of debris skittering across the lawn and brought her to her feet. Parting the curtains on the side window facing O'Malley House, her lips narrowed to mere slits.

"I knew it. I just knew it," she hissed as a small branch tumbled from the mansion grounds onto Marge's side lawn. "You would think with all that help she has the woman could keep her trees on her own side of the yard," she said to herself. Then she noticed the cat.

She sucked in her breath in disbelief as the big tomcat that lived at the mansion strode across the lawn as if he owned every blade of grass.

Rapping angrily on the window, Marge yelled hoarsely, "Get away! Get away from here!"

The cat paid her no heed. He marched to within six feet of the house to a flower bed, turned his rump toward Marge, dug a hole in the earth, shook his behind to settle into position, and squatted purposefully to do his business.

"Stop that! Stop! You flea-bitten beast!" Her fingers were red and hurting from banging on the window.

Swatting the curtain back into place, she stomped to the phone and pushed speed-dial to the Sheriff's Department.

"This is Margery Reynolds," she said before the dispatcher could answer. "I have a complaint. You know where I live—next to O'Malley House. Her tree branches are in my yard and her cat just came over here, right next to my house, right under my very nose, and pooped in my yard."

The dispatcher sighed. "Mrs. Reynolds, this is the third call this month. These aren't legitimate complaints. Last week it was because her mail was in your box. The week before you thought you could smell her cooking. Those just aren't things the Sheriff's Department deals with."

"Well, what do you deal with? That Letty person who speeds? That Simeon person who uses manure? I can smell that stinking manure when he uses it, and she's going to kill someone. You have to do something. I pay taxes."

There was a long pause. "Mrs. Reynolds, have you ever considered moving?" The words were gentle and silence on the other end convinced the dispatcher to continue. "You really aren't happy where you are. Maybe you should consider finding another place to live."

Marge's voice was an emotional squeak. "My home? You expect me to give up my home when those people are the ones who are making my life miserable?"

"But your complaints simply aren't rational. Your complaints are simply those little irritating things that happen in life."

Marge didn't answer and hung up the phone with a sob. "You don't understand," she said, looking at the receiver. "No one understands."

Chapter Six

As Lillian zipped by the mansion on her bike, Katherine O'Malley was sitting restlessly in her favorite chair. She sighed and for the third time looked at the expensive gold watch on her slim, liver-spotted wrist. It was still early afternoon. She really should haul herself out of the chair and get something accomplished. The only thing she had done so far was visit the Center, chat with friends, and eat cake. Maybe it was the talk with Letty and Lillian that got her feeling so discombobulated.

"Maybe I'll redo my nails," she said to herself, studying her fingernails that really didn't need new polish at all. She sighed. She was so bored. Not really bored. Just tired. Listless. Maybe lifeless. Life seemed to be sluggish, as still and unmoving as stagnant water in a pond. She knew from experience that these lulls in life meant two things: she had to change things and bring vibrancy into her existence, or that something was about to happen to turn everything topsy-turvy. God had a way, sometimes, of turning things upside down and changing the most carefully laid plans.

So, she sat. And sighed. And listened. Far away in the kitchen the refrigerator gave that familiar shuddering cough before quieting down and she could hear the melodic murmur from the radio Letty had left on the afternoon before. On the stair landing came the soft rhythmic sound of the massive grandfather clock that had held reign over the comings and goings of O'Malleys for over a century.

As the sole heir to the O'Malley throne, she had inherited the clock, along with the mansion and grounds and a scattering of businesses and real estate, when John died.

"OK, Katherine O'Malley, you have to get something done today," she said to herself, but instead of getting up from her chair she leaned her head back on the rose-colored brocade rocker and plotted out the rest of her week. Letty usually did the shopping, but tomorrow she, herself, would brave the crowds at Polsky's Market and buy real food. No frozen pizzas and none of that canned spaghetti and meatballs or lard-laden hash that college students like Letty seemed to love. She would buy rib eye steak and fresh vegetables and fruit.

Letty, bless her heart, threw any old thing into a cart. She didn't thump watermelon or smell the ends of cantaloupe or turn tomatoes to see if the underside looked as good as the displayed side. Letty tossed things into a cart helter-skelter, giving no heed to nutrition or quality. Given her way, Letty would fill the house with Twinkies and HoHos, boxed fried chicken and pretzels. And bubble gum. The girl was forever popping and snapping a mouthful of bubble gum. Once she even took a box of it to the Senior Center and passed it out. More than one person had to retreat to the bathroom to remove strands of it from their dentures.

Tomorrow she could pick up her prescription at Tompkins Pharmacy and, perhaps, visit the library. Katherine loved the library. She loved the smells, the hushed quiet, the far-off jingle of a phone she didn't have to answer, and the drowsy peace that came over her and settled clear down to her toes. She wondered how many other people, besides herself, went to the library and didn't read a word. She studied the fresh-faced children in the kids' section. Or she sat in the atrium lobby and watched the populace come and go through the glass doors. On nice days, she sat on the bench outside and breathed deeply of fresh air and life. The library was such a friendly, peaceful place to visit.

She was glad she had forced herself to go to the Danford Senior Center and help welcome back Fletcher, even though she was so tired. She didn't seem to have any gumption.

She really should be excited. She and Letty were going to go into the ballroom tomorrow and she hadn't been up there in years.

Chapter Seven

Still buoyant over the good news of Fletcher O'Dell's recovery, Letty had a light heart the next morning as she folded herself into her old beat-up car and headed to O'Malley House. She had learned to juggle community college classes, spend time at the Danford Senior Center, and still help out Katherine O'Malley. Several times a week she made her way to the mansion in order to help Katherine catalog items in the huge old house and help her restore rooms to their former glory. Katherine had twice-weekly maid service, but Letty was doing most of the cleaning in the rooms they were restoring.

The work was hard at times, moving grand old pieces of furniture and combing through the attic to find accessories for the rooms. She and Katherine had unearthed untold treasure in the attic rooms, including turn-of-the century ball gowns and trunks and crates full of ancient vases and paintings and housewares. They had a few rooms finished, but there were over a dozen to go. Cataloging items was a tedious task and they hadn't even started in the library. The thought of all those old dusty books made her cringe.

Simeon Quest helped when he could but he would much rather tend the gardens and lawns than putter through old trunks in the attic. She loved Simeon, who was an extremely handsome seventy-something. For years, after John O'Malley died, the citizenry of Danford thought Simeon and Katherine would get together, and that they were even destined to be together, but it never seemed to come to pass. Sometimes, though, Letty saw Katherine's yearning look when she gazed after Simeon. It mirrored the same look she observed in Simeon's eyes when he watched Katherine. Letty wished she could just lock them in a room and leave them there long enough to sort out their feelings.

This morning she and Katherine were going to open the ballroom. Letty hadn't been in the ballroom yet and looked forward to it. She had heard about it since she was a child. Every kid in Danford, well, every girl anyway, had dreams of dancing in the O'Malley ballroom.

Simeon was working in one of the beds by the ornate wrought iron fence when Letty drove up the driveway. He stopped and looked at her, shaking his head and grinning.

"You should retire that poor old thing—put it out of its misery," he said when she got out of her car. To open the door she had to roll down the window, reach through it, and use the outside handle. She had no idea what happened to the inside door handle.

Letty stood to her full six-foot length and pushed her blond hair back with all the grace of the Queen of England. "You're just jealous," she said. "Anyone can drive a new pickup but I have the rare privilege—granted to only a few of the truly blessed—to drive a 1979 Mercury Comet. This, my friend, is a classic."

"What is that you've got there holding up the side mirror? A rope? I don't believe it. A rope?! Tied to the antenna?"

"I wouldn't call it rope. Rope is thicker. This is more like baling twine. Actually, it is baling twine. I found it along the road—over by the stockyards."

"How many rolls of duct tape you got on that thing, anyway?"

"A few, a few," she admitted proudly, slapping the rump of the old car fondly.

The vehicle was dented and bashed and had once been a sort of moss green until Letty painted it with white house paint. Now it was white with green patches where the paint flaked off. It sported Band-Aids over some of the smaller rust spots and both back taillight shields had been long broken and had been painted over with reddish maroon fingernail polish. A bevy of stuffed animals lived in the back window and a grubby Garfield tail swayed from the trunk lid.

"So, what are you and Katherine up to today?" Simeon asked.

"We're opening the ballroom. I've never been in there and I have to admit I'm pretty darned excited."

"The ballroom..." Simeon said, shaking his head as memories flooded in and settled comfortably. "There certainly have been some good times in there."

"You should come up and join us," Letty said. "Bring a machete to fight through the cobwebs.

"I might do that," he said. "I'll stop by and talk to Kate in a bit."

Letty turned to head toward the house and then turned around.

"Simeon, do you remember Henry Riggins?"

"Sure. He is a great guy. He worked on the railroad but his passion was gardening. The guy grew the most beautiful roses and peonies. I used to stop by and get tips from him when something around here was bug-infested or not thriving like it should. What about him? He didn't die, did he? I know his house was sold a few years back."

"His kids put him in a dinky little apartment and he evidently just hid out there for a time. Recently he started coming to the Senior Center. He's having a hard time and he's fading fast. Driving up here and watching you in the flowers got me to thinking. Do you think he could come over sometimes and tag along and help you? He's a little feeble and uses a cane but I think that's just from being so inactive. His mind is alert—even if he is an old grouch."

"Henry? Here, helping me? Letty, that would be great! The man is a walking gardening encyclopedia. I sort of picked it up as I went, but I think Henry was born knowing things about plants. Let's clear it with Katherine, but I think that's a great idea."

"I don't think it was mine," Letty said, laughing. "It just sort of clicked when I saw you."

Leaving his side, Letty made her way up the sidewalk, tripping over a small rock along the way. Regaining her balance, she turned back to Simeon.

"If you see Lillian go by on her bike, will you send her in the house?" she asked him. "She said a while back she'd like to see the ballroom again. I figure since we're going in there this is her chance."

"I'll keep my eye out," Simeon said. He watched as Letty stumbled over the first wide step that led to the massive doors of the mansion. He had never seen anyone who was so prone to stumbling, falling, tripping, lurching, slipping, and faltering. Luckily, she rarely sported anything more serious than a Band-Aid or a bruise. And her heart, which was as big as she was, never lurched or faltered but was always centered on the wellbeing of others. It was just like Letty to give purpose to old Henry's life.

Chapter Eight

Just down the block, Lillian Dip wasn't even close to being out on her bike. Instead, she was carefully, and reluctantly, getting herself out of bed. "Getting old is heck," she muttered to herself as she sat on the edge and tested her feet. Moving them up and down, she felt the left one, the one with the chipped pink toenail, crack and pop. She stretched her back, moving gingerly and pivoting from one side to the other. Not bad. Unless she met with misfortune, which wasn't out of the realm of possibilities, she was going to have a great day. A marvelous day.

"Sorry about saying 'heck,' because you know I was thinking of the double-L word when I said it," she muttered to God and gazing heavenward—which was somewhere beyond her gold painted ceiling. "But, Lord, getting old just can't be described by the word "heck." It really is that double-L word. And most of the time it hurts. No one ever told me about that part of it. My mother warned me about strangers and put that little book from Kotex on my bed when I was twelve and said that vinegar would make my hair shine and that coloring gray hair was a trap, but she never once said, 'Lillian, I have to warn you, honey, that getting old is really quite painful.'"

Rotating her head in a careful circle, she happened to notice the big blue plastic backscratcher hanging from the doorknob. She frowned and tried to remember why it was there.

Hanging things from doorknobs and cupboard knobs was Lillian's way of reminding herself of things. Reminder items could be anything—dish towels, necklaces, a bell on a string, a plastic flower with a bent wire and, once, a pair of her husband's boxer shorts. Somehow draping something over a door handle to remind her to water the roses or put out the garbage was easier than writing a note to herself.

The problem was that sometimes she couldn't, for the life of her, remember what she was supposed to remember. She would spend a good part of a day glancing at the odd item hanging from a handle and wondering what hidden meaning it had.

The secret of the back scratcher popped into her head immediately.

"Oh no," Lillian groaned as she remembered. She flopped back down on her bed. It was lip wax day. Today, for the first time in her sixty seven years, she was going to get her upper lip waxed.

It had all come about the day before when she'd ridden home from a funeral with her friend Violet Lemke and they were chatting about how well the deceased looked in his blue pin-striped suit. Mid-conversation Violet suddenly declared she was going to treat Lillian to something special.

Making a U-turn, Violet drove to the Shear Perfection Beauty Salon, zipped into the parking lot and declared she was going to buy Lillian a lip wax. Her treat.

"A lip wax," Lillian had said in alarm as she pulled down the vanity mirror. "Why on earth would I need a lip wax?"

Violet had informed Lillian as she turned off the car that every well-groomed woman needed a periodic lip wax.

"It's sort of like the ritual of shaving your legs and under your arms to rid yourself of unsightly, unwanted hair," Violet told her. "It's like tweezing your eyebrows."

"I don't tweeze my eyebrows," Lillian confessed.

"I know and we'll get around to that little problem another time," Violet said cheerfully. "For now we'll just take care of that lip."

Lillian had moved her head this way and that, peering into the car mirror. She put on her 2.75-powered Wal-Mart reading glasses and still couldn't see any mustache. But then, even with glasses she could barely read the phone book.

What the heck, she thought, it might be one of those special moments that friends share. Besides, it was free.

They walked up the sidewalk and Violet threw open the big brass doors. The eye-watering stink of perm solution, hair spray, nail polish and ten dozen hair potions walloped their nostrils. Lillian discreetly covered her nose. Violet didn't seem to notice.

Violet was a regular. Rows of beauticians, all of them standing behind wet-headed customers and in various stages of cutting, rolling, coloring, drying, perming or curling hair, called out greetings to her as the pair entered the shop. They peered at Lillian curiously. Clearly, here was a "before" desperately in need of one of them to miraculously pull off a magnificent "after."

Unfortunately, the receptionist said, frowning and shaking her head sadly while thumbing through her well-worn appointment book, there were no openings that afternoon. But, good news, she added, looking up with a chipper smile; she could get them both in bright and early the next morning. Ten a.m. Sharp.

And here it was, four minutes after nine and Lillian was just getting up. Violet was never late. She'd be knocking at the door in forty-five minutes.

"Good grief, I'm going to have to skip breakfast and everything else," she said to herself. The "everything else" included reading her Bible. Six months earlier she had joined a program to read through the entire Bible in one year. She was already two months behind. At the rate she was going she might have to adopt the "Read the Bible in Your Lifetime" plan.

Then Lillian remembered something else that was happening that day. Today they were counting the votes at the Senior Center. Edith Snippel had convinced Lillian to run for Treasurer. She didn't really want the job but Edith could coax the bark off a pine tree. You didn't say no to Edith; she'd harangue until she got her way.

Lillian sat up, ran her fingers through her short, dark, graying hair and ruffled it vigorously. Then she slapped the bed.

"Petunia! Where are you?" she called in a sing-song voice, bouncing up and down. "Help me, Petunia. Help me get up! We've got to hurry."

The lump beneath the gold satin bedspread began to wiggle and worm its way toward the edge. Lillian lifted the covers and peered into the cozy cavern. "Petunia! There you are, you silly little rascal." Petunia bounced happily and shook the mop of white hair out of her face before jumping into Lillian's lap and nuzzling against her warm, flannel-covered belly.

"OK, little girl," she said, holding the scrappy little dog next to her cheek before putting her on the floor, "it's time to get going here. Violet will be here in less than an hour." Petunia raced up and down the hall, happily barking a greeting to the new day.

Lillian shook her head as she realized she wouldn't have time to even make her bed. As she walked from the bedroom she heard the muffled sound of a telephone.

"I do this every time," she said, throwing up her arms and turning around. "Every single doggone time!" Going back into the bedroom she thrust her arm under the pillows and fished out the portable phone. Lillian kept the phone under her pillow at night. Just in case. A woman never knew when she might need to call 911. Not that Lillian didn't feel perfectly capable of tackling some young punk burglar. Still, you never knew.

"Good morning!" she chirped into the phone while walking down the hall, Petunia frolicking ahead of her.

After talking a few minutes she grabbed her workbook and

pen from the kitchen counter, tucked the phone under her chin and scribbled a few notes before hanging up.

"Another survey, Petunia. We've got work. And that, my little sweetheart, means we can put more money toward that Moped," she said, opening the back door to let the dog out into the fenced yard. It was her dream to someday roar down Danford's Main Street on a bright pink Moped, a long scarf flapping in the wind behind her. Heck, if she made enough money maybe she'd buy one of those Harleys and get a leather jacket with a skull on the back. She'd love to see the faces of the people at the Center if she pulled up on that.

Petunia raced onto the deck and leaped to the lawn beyond, yapping ferociously to scare any lingering demons out of the yard. Watching her from the doorway, Lillian chuckled and muttered to herself.

"Silly dog. She weighs less than three pounds. She couldn't scare away a hungry flea."

Lillian stepped onto the deck, her bare feet instantly cold from the dew-kissed wood planks. She took a deep breath, savoring the crisp air and the earthy smells of early spring.

The lawn was greening up and the delphiniums were cautiously poking their heads out of the ground. The buds on the birch were swollen with new life and would soon burst and unfurl, revealing shiny spring-green leaves.

"Petunia. Hurry up!" Lillian was impatient to start the day. After starting the coffee maker Lillian headed off for her shower and stripped off a well-worn, tattered nightgown. It was as comfortable as the old sneakers she'd worn for thirty years. It was so faded now that the sprigs of green and the pink roses were barely visible and the ribbon bow was frayed to the knot.

Chapter Nine

Violet drove in the driveway just as Lillian finished slipping on her shoes. Her hair was still a little damp but it was tidy. She'd dismissed the comfort of stretch pants and wore a pair of tan slacks and a navy blouse. Now she wondered why. It wasn't like getting the mustache ripped off your lip was an Event.

"Ready for our beauty treatment?" Violet asked, as she and Lillian walked toward Violet's old Cadillac, which was as big as a boat and seemed to drive itself. Violet was so tiny that many people took a second look to make sure there was someone behind the wheel.

Any stranger in town watching the pair chatting together would be curious. Violet Lemke and Lillian Dip were about as different as oatmeal and granola. Lillian was chunky and big boned, steadfast and reliable, and didn't get overly excited about much of anything. Eccentric and a bit odd, she was also good and kind and definitely a town character. Everyone loved Lillian Dip.

Violet was about the size of a grasshopper and seemed to hop rather than to walk. Her movements were short and quick and precise. She didn't waste time, money, motion, or words. Her hair, clothes, house, car, and life were neat and tidy and organized. She was too common-sense to ever be considered a town character.

The fact that she and Lillian were fast friends was a surprise to anyone who knew both women. Each one thought the other was a bit strange but accepted the eccentricities and, in fact, found them rather humorous. Lillian felt Violet should be slowed down with a small dose of tranquilizer, while Violet wondered if there was anything on the market that could speed Lillian up a bit.

As they neared the beauty shop, Lillian began to have misgivings. "You're sure it doesn't hurt?" she asked. She was skeptical. How, after all, could it not hurt?

Violet took her hand off the steering wheel to give Lillian a reassuring pat on the knee. "I've been doing it for years and it doesn't bother me a bit," she said with a jolly laugh.

"Well, I don't know about this," Lillian said. "I've gone over sixty years with my lip just the way it is."

"I just think that with a little help in the beauty shop department you could be a handsome woman," Violet said. "Not that you aren't beautiful now but a girl can always use a little outside help," she added quickly. "My goodness, you'd be shocked if you knew everything I have to go through each month."

It only took a few minutes to drive to the salon. Inside, the same receptionist from the day before carefully noted in her book that Lillian and Violet had arrived and they were whisked to a pair of soft, black-leather reclining chairs by the sinks. Violet decided Lillian should go first—since it was her first time to undergo the procedure.

The hair removal person, who looked about twelve and wore a heavy purple plastic cape, took the lid off of a little pot and used a tiny spatula to dig out a glop of dark green wax. She troweled it over the left side of Lillian's upper lip. The wax was very warm and heavy.

Lillian sat up and looked in a mirror. Seeing the green worm resting on her lip, she hunkered back in the chair so no one else in the place would see that she was getting her mustache taken care of.

"Are you on any medications?" the hair removal person asked her. Lillian was feeling a bit giddy. She talked as best she could around her waxed lip.

"Vitamins and stuff for females," she slurred, "the stuff that keeps women my age from turning into men, or maybe it saves us from the Heartbreak of Psoriasis. I never can remember which."

The exfoliator didn't laugh. "We have to ask you that," she said, ignoring Lillian's brilliant humor, "because sometimes if you're taking certain medications when we pull off the wax your skin comes with it. It can be really bad."

"Say that again," Lillian asked.

The girl said it again.

"Don't you think you should ask that before you spread on the gunk?" Lillian asked. The girl didn't answer. She was busy testing an edge of the wax, picking at it with a blue fingernail. Then she gave a mighty jerk.

RIPPP!!

She yanked it off.

Lillian screamed.

The pain streaked from her lip to the top of her head, down to her big toe and back to her lip. Tears formed at the corners of her closed eyes. She thought of calling for her mother but the woman had been dead for years and Lillian doubted she'd show up.

Before Lillian could protest the girl had waxed up the other side. This time she knew what was coming and braced herself. The girl ripped off that side with just as much zeal as the first. This time Lillian stifled the scream.

Chapter Ten

Two hours later, Lillian was back home and facing her unmade bed. She pulled on a pair of sweatpants and a work shirt and studied her lip in the mirror before carefully pulling up satin sheets and bedspread and placing a bounty of elegant pillows where they belonged, nudging the ones in front into proper formation.

"All done, Petunia," she said as she smoothed the comforter. Petunia pranced on her hind feet and turned two perfect circles.

Picking up her old nightgown off the chair, Lillian folded it haphazardly and stuffed it in the top drawer of her dresser. Then she pulled it out again and held it in front of her and studied it carefully. She shook her head. It really was disgraceful, wearing such a ratty garment. What if she had a heart attack and the ambulance crew saw her wearing such a thing? She'd be the laughingstock of Danford.

"Petunia, I'm going to go to that new shop and look for a nightgown," she declared decisively, patting the dog on the head. Petunia trembled in excitement, thinking erroneously that the words meant she was getting a treat.

Lillian had spotted a gorgeous array of nightwear, including a gold satin nightgown that she coveted, in the window of Sandra's Sensual Lingerie and Candle Shoppe just off Main Street. The store was new in Danford, and Lillian, due to a dreadful case of the stomach flu, had missed the grand opening. New businesses in Danford were such a novelty that she was one of just a handful of the female residents who missed the event.

A few minutes later she was on her bike, peddling toward town. She wasn't really dressed for a fancy-pants store but she decided to pop in anyway. Leaning her bike, an ancient green Ladies Schwinn Hornet with high handlebars and a battered basket, against the brick wall, she wiped her hands on her sweat pants, patted her windblown hair in place, opened the pink door and entered a world unlike any she had ever imagined.

The building had previously been home to a myriad of failed ventures, the most recent being the All for a Buck store that contained heaps of cheap, plastic junk that no one evidently wanted.

Hard work and a lot of money had been spent to change the atmosphere dramatically. Music played. Soft, subtle, and romantic music. The air was lightly perfumed with an exotic mix of gardenia, lavender, sandalwood and eucalyptus. Lillian lifted her nose and pulled in a hefty chest full of the lovely scent. Silk flower arrangements abounded and tall, round, brass-ringed racks held sleepwear in all sizes and colors and styles. Some were satin, some were silk and some looked as wispy and fragile as spider webs. There were tidy stacks of luxurious underwear, some that caused her eyes to widen.

"My word!" she said to herself.

Lillian looked around and determined she was the sole customer in the shop. She spotted a small middle-aged blond woman standing behind a counter. Inwardly, Lillian groaned and felt herself falling into the trap these women always managed to set out to capture their prey.

She felt like she'd been thrust back to junior high and she could almost feel the pimples exploding on her face and classmates snickering at her clothes and hair that, no matter what she did, never turned out like the Teen Magazine photos.

The proprietor of the sexy underwear shoppe, with the PE at the end, was one of those perfect women, the kind who has elegant nails, perfectly fitted clothing, sophisticated hair, tiny ankles, and a confidence that is bestowed at birth.

Lillian felt huge and awkward and homely, and her first impulse was to apologize.

"I'm sorry," she would say with a hearty laugh. "I must have come in the wrong door. Thought this was the thrift store."

It was obvious the Sensual Shoppe had few clients who were pushing seventy. And, catching a look at herself in a full-length mirror, Lillian had to admit she looked more like a thrift shop customer than one looking for a satin negligee.

The woman was frowning. Moving swiftly, she appeared to be maneuvering Lillian toward the door. Lillian flashed back to a television show featuring border collies herding sheep. She hoped the woman wouldn't nip her heels.

Lillian mentally jerked and twisted a bit and pulled herself free of the imaginary trap. She sucked in her stomach, stood up to her full five-foot, seven-inch height and adopted her sophisticated-but-aloof stance.

"Hello there," she said, affecting a bit of an English accent she'd picked up from a bit part in a high school play, "I was riding by and noticed that gold nightgown in your window. I'm wondering if you have it in a size sixteen, maybe size eighteen. And if you have something like it in cotton or flannel that would really be great."

The woman raised a perfectly arched eyebrow and stared. Then she laughed. The sound tinkled down like tiny icicles falling to frozen ground. "Flannel! Honey, you need to go to the mall. I carry nothing but satin and silk in my shop. A size sixteen or eighteen?"

"Yup,'" Lillian said, laughing merrily. "So, are you Sandra?"

"Yes, I'm Sandra Farris. I own the store."

"Hi. I'm Lillian Dip."

"Dip?"

"Yup. Dip. It's a silly last name but it's mine. And if you think Lillian Dip sounds bad...my husband's name, God bless him, was Delaware Dooley Dip. I never met his folks but they must have had a chuckle over that. His sister's name was Daisy. Daisy Dip. And the crazy thing is, when she married she kept her maiden name. Can you beat that?"

Lillian stuck out her hand. "Anyway, Sandra, it's nice to meet you."

Sandra reluctantly placed the tips of her long elegant fingers into a large hand that boasted chipped nails and work-roughened palms. After pulling free from Lillian's hearty shake, she discreetly wiped her palm on her thigh.

Lillian noticed that Sandra kept staring at her newly-waxed lip.

"Lip wax," she said in explanation. "I've never had one before. It was an experience."

Sandra didn't comment.

"So," Lillian said brightly, looking around the store. Somewhere along the way she'd lost the British accent and her eyes twinkled mischievously. "Do I need a note from someone to purchase one of your expensive frilly nightgowns? I know I'm probably not your usual customer but I promise you I have money to spend. Or is this is one of those exclusive stores where you have to be a size eight and wear designer clothes before entering? The only thing designer I have is a toothbrush. It says Designer Pro right on the side. But I could bring it in if I need to."

Sandra arched her perfectly curved eyebrows and her nose flared just slightly as she worked to suppress a smile. She was thinking there was more to this woman than met the eye. It might be one of those don't-judge-a-book-by-its-cover situations. She pursed her lips and then gave up the pretense and smiled.

"Miss Dip, you make it sound like I have a very snooty store. It's really not. I have clients from all walks of life. If you follow me I think I have the gold chemise in your size."

Lillian plodded behind as Sandra sashayed smartly to a nearby rack and expertly flipped through the padded hangers to the section marked 2X. Lillian watched, wide-eyed.

"Holy cow! Back in the '60s I thought shorty pajamas were racy!" Lillian commented to herself. The woman snorted softly and chuckled.

Sandra found the gown and held it up for Lillian to see and then put it in her arms. It was gorgeous. Lillian had never dreamed of owning anything as beautiful or that felt as luscious. It was like holding a piece of something fluid that wasn't wet. Like holding quicksilver. If it slipped through her fingers it would probably puddle on the floor in a pool of gold.

"I'll take it!" Lillian declared.

The nightgown purchase took her mind off of her lip for awhile, but back home it felt very swollen and she looked in the mirror to confirm. She got an ice cube out of the freezer, wrapped it in a washcloth and held it to her traumatized face. When the phone rang she thought about not answering it, but she never had been able to ignore a ringing phone.

It was Katherine. "I was just wondering about your beauty shop experience this morning. How was it?"

"I don't know how you and Violet do that lip thing every month or two," Lillian said. "That girl gave absolutely no warning. She grabbed onto that baby and pretended she was husking corn. Husking corn while suffering from PMS, having just opened a black-banded letter from the IRS and learning the night before her boyfriend left her."

"Surely it wasn't that bad, was it?" Katherine asked, laughing.

"Maybe it's easier for you because you do it all the time," Lillian said. "I had virgin hair on my lip and it hurt like heck. And that's not all. For the first hour my lip was white—a sure sign of severe lip-shock. Then it puffed up and turned fire red and it's still that way. And all swollen. I look ridiculous. Violet had to go to Polsky's Market for something important. We kept our hands over our mouths but I still could feel people looking at us. And that's not all. Next week she has me signed up for a brow job."

"Maybe you could get a bikini wax, too," Katherine said, trying to sound serious.

"It gives me the chills to even think about that," Lillian said. "It's one of the reasons I don't wear a bikini."

Chapter Eleven

Earlier that day, from her perch at the front window Marge Reynolds had used her binoculars to watch Violet Lemke pull up into Lillian's driveway. Violet honked and, just a minute later, Lillian pranced out the door like she was something special and shoved her bulk into the car.

Margery felt her lips move downward and the frown lines form between her eyes. It was hateful the way those two gallivanted all over creation. And it was despicable the way they felt it was their obligation to attend every funeral and every wedding within forty miles. What must the families think—these two doddering old women, strangers no less, showing up and shoving cake and punch into their bellies? She'd never heard of anything so rude in her life.

"I've never heard of anything so rude in my life," Marge muttered, echoing her own thoughts.

When Violet zoomed out of the driveway Marge moved to the side bedroom and focused her binoculars on O'Malley House. Just the week before she had hired that Dawes kid, Hogie Dawes—and if that isn't an awful name for a kid—to cut back the lilac bushes between her house and the mansion so she could have a better view. The kid, who had shaved his lumpy head, wasn't too bright and couldn't seem to understand what she wanted. She couldn't very well just go outside and show him—so she had to haul him into the bedroom and put it to him simply.

She led him to the window and pointed. "I want to see Katherine's house. See? The mansion, right there? It's simple. Just get out there and cut the bushes down so I can see."

Hogie saw. And slashed the bushes right down to the ground.

Now she was back at the window, peering over the mangled bushes toward O'Malley House. "Stupid dunce," she said about the poor fellow who cut them, as she settled in to watch Simeon.

Simeon was poking around in his flower beds and Marjorie choked back a gob of bitterness that she couldn't be in her own flower beds. It wasn't fair that she was kept prisoner in her own home. It was so sad that she had been reduced to this.

Tears threatened to overtake her when she heard the atrocious sound of that girl's car make its way up the block. She hated Letty's car, which she thought should be outlawed from the highway. She had, in fact, tried to do just that—called the sheriff's department and complained about the junker. After they checked out her complaint, the nasty officer declared that the vehicle was road-worthy and there was no reason to issue Miss Letty Vanesse a citation or, as Mrs. Reynolds requested, "haul the heap to the landfill."

She hated the sheriff's department and the way they dismissed her complaints like she was some sort of common troublemaker or something.

Letty was speeding. She knew she was. She was going at least five miles over the limit and maybe more like twenty miles over. Maybe thirty. If she knew it would do any good she'd call the authorities and file a complaint.

Marge jumped back as Letty got out of the car and stood beside it and stared right at the bedroom window. Right at Marge. Standing motionless, Marge hoped that she was invisible, that Letty couldn't make her out in the dim room. Her eyes widened in horror when Letty grinned and waved. Then Letty said something to Simeon and he turned and waved, too.

"Why, those nosy busybodies!" she declared to herself in anger. "I can't believe a woman can't even live in peace in her own home."

Turning from the window and hugging the binoculars to her bony chest, she slid along the wall so she wouldn't be seen and made her way to the kitchen. She'd fix a cup of tea. Chamomile tea. Maybe that would settle her down.

Then she'd call that Danford Christian Center and hope that someone there would take her grocery order. She didn't know why it was so hard to get someone to just help her. They knew she couldn't leave her house. How was she supposed to get food? And things like shampoo and toilet paper? You'd think people would be more caring and considerate.

Sighing, she put her head in her hands and hoped she wasn't tumbling into one of those moods.

Chapter Twelve

After wandering through the lower rooms of the mansion, Letty found Katherine in the library, digging through the large mahogany desk that sat in front of a bank of mullioned windows. The library was huge and yet had a coziness that came from old, worn, red leather couches and chairs and an oversized Oriental carpet over maple plank floors. Floor to ceiling bookshelves held thousands of books, none of them looking any newer than 1940. Katherine, Letty knew, kept her personal books in a small study off her bedroom suite.

Letty knew that there were probably priceless books in the collection, and Katherine had told her there were also family mementoes and paperwork that reached back to the 1600s. Letty wasn't much of a reader but she knew enough to realize that anyone who valued books would think this room was a bit of heaven on earth.

"Having fun?" Letty asked from where she leaned against the door frame. Katherine looked up and rolled her eyes. An errant piece of hair had pulled loose from the bun she wore at the nape of her neck and was floating in newfound freedom.

"I can't find the key to the ballroom," Katherine complained. "I know it is in here somewhere. John kept all the keys to the closed-off rooms in this top drawer. I've gone through it a dozen times."

"Did you try the other drawers?"

"Mmm-hmm. I even crawled around on the floor, thinking they might have fallen down there."

"How about one of the pieces in the desk set? Maybe it's in one of those or the humidor."

Katherine stood up from the desk. "I checked the little jars and inkwells in the desk set but I didn't check this," she said, pulling the humidor closer to her. Peering into the empty void, which still smelled of John's cherry tobacco, she pulled out a ring of keys. "Aha!" she declared triumphantly.

She tossed the keys to Letty, who quickly noticed that many of them were so old they'd be worth a fortune in an antique shop. Then Katherine pulled one of the pipes, a handsome briar pipe, from its resting place at the side of the humidor. Holding the bowl to her nose she smelled the sweet smoky scent of tobacco and then she rubbed her fingers across John's teeth marks on the stem. There were so many things in this library that reminded her of him. It was so odd to think he had been dead for so many years.

Lifting her head and giving Letty a quick smile, she came out from behind the desk. "Letty, is that what you are wearing to the ball?" she teased.

"Just think of me as Cinderella," Letty said with a grin as she pulled her sweatshirt out from her chest, "I'm still waiting for my gown...and my prince charming."

Together they went through the main floor of the mansion until they reached the stairway that led to the third floor ballroom. The ballroom took up nearly the whole floor. Letty had been in all the other rooms in the mansion but had never been in this one. Maybe today Katherine would tell her why it was locked.

Other rooms on the third floor consisted of the nursery suite, the sewing room, two maid rooms and the old laundry.

Letty had spent hours in the laundry, marveling that anyone could actually have utilized the behemoth copper pots and scrubbing boards and hand-wringers mounted on well-worn wooden mounts. An ingenious tubing system made of copper obviously drained water from the room to the outside of the house somewhere, but Letty figured someone still had to haul it up three flights of stairs. She hadn't found any sort of a hand pump and never thought to ask Katherine. The cupboards in the room still contained bars of Fels-Naptha soap and a tin of soap chips and stacks of crisply ironed aprons and linens. It was as if one of the O'Malley ancestors had purchased a brand new electric washing machine and no one ever came back to the laundry room.

The nursery was a delight, with delicate flower-sprigged wallpaper and vintage rugs over hardwood floors painted dark green. Packed shelves of ancient toys and children's books would have been an antique dealer's dream. There were old cradles and rocking chairs and ornate iron cribs. The windows were low in this room with window seats just begging for someone to settle in and read. Wardrobes and closets contained quaint little dresses and suits and dozens of turn-of-the-century shoes, all lined up and covered with decades of dust.

The three small rooms for the maids were under the eaves and had sloping ceilings. The rooms were comfortable, furnished with iron beds with rolled-up and tied mattresses at the end. Each room had a glass-fronted bookshelf with a few books, an oak rocking chair, and there was a small desk under the window. A bouquet of ancient dried flowers with a small Valentine stuck in the stems still remained in a dusty vase in the middle room, giving rise to questions about the recipient.

Letty and Katherine made their way to the double French doors that led into the ballroom. Standing in front of the doors, Katherine fanned open the set of keys like a deck of cards and then selected one that was large and black and very elegant. Lifting the key, the others fell into place below it with a jingle.

Chapter Thirteen

If Letty had been asked later what her first thought was of the ballroom her answer would have been the smell. It was the smell of time. And of dust, and the faint smell of floor polish. But more than that. It was the smell of memories and excitement—of French-perfumed ladies and Macassar-haired men, of leather and silk and satin and even the resin smell of violin strings and the fruity smell of punch. It was the smell of candles and tea cakes and coffee from Africa and oranges and nectarines from far off lands. It was the smell of contentment.

There were sounds there, too, lingering in the dusty gloom... sounds of an orchestra and beautiful music, and tinkling laughter and the clink of forks to plates and crystal goblets to other crystal goblets. There were echoes of swishing gowns and the tap-tap-tapping of feet on the dance floor and the scrape of chairs moving and the shuffling sound of people shifting and, over it all, the buzzing hum of soft chatter. It was the sound of happiness.

The room was massive, with incredibly high ceilings. Light filtered through the long wall of windows and Katherine watched Letty carefully. When the young girl lifted her arms and moved her body in a quick sweeping circle, Katherine smiled. Rarely did anyone enter this room without lifting arms and doing some sort of graceful dance move. It was a room that beckoned and invited and enveloped.

Letty tiptoed back to Katherine's side. "It's beautiful," she whispered. "It's stunning!"

"Why are you whispering?" Katherine whispered back, leaning toward her young friend.

Letty laughed. "It's just so....so...amazing!" she exclaimed, throwing her arms wide.

Together they walked to the middle of the room and then turned right and headed toward the stage. Letty had turned a complete circle several times during the short walk, trying to absorb the magnificence of the room.

There were tables and chairs stacked at one end, and the ballroom, except for the fellow who tuned the grand piano every so often, had obviously not been opened for years.

"When was the last time you used the ballroom?" Letty asked. Katherine looked at her with a small smile.

"Just before John died. We had a wonderful Christmas party up here. After that I just didn't want to be reminded of the memories, I guess, so I've sort of kept away from it."

"I can understand that," Letty said. "Sometimes memories, even happy ones, are too hard to bear. I see that in the people at the Center. They'll be recalling some happy event and the memory will sort of bring a cloud over their day."

"To be honest with you," Katherine said, "I don't have the faintest idea why we are up here today. It was just something God has put on my heart. I feel he wants us to tackle the ballroom next. Why, I don't know, but he evidently has something in mind. Maybe it's nothing more than what we've been doing... renovating the rooms and getting them ready."

"But we don't even know why we're doing that—getting them ready. Ready for what?" Letty said, laughing. The sound chimed like a thousand tiny crystals.

The two of them had been under a conviction for quite

some time that the Mansion, like an old dress lingering in a closet, was supposed to be lifted up, shaken off, and prepared for something exciting. It was up to God to provide them with the reason—to provide the "something exciting."

Within a short time Simeon joined them, and for the next hour they surveyed the room and took stock of the incredible effort it would be to get it back into the shape it was in its heyday. They wouldn't tackle the floors or most of the cleaning, however. Simeon said he would call the company they were already using to do that part of the work, and they could probably start tomorrow. He would supervise the heavy cleaning and Katherine and Letty could organize the back room behind the stage and do things like dust off the grand piano and wash vases and table decorations that were wrapped in paper and nestled in crates. Together the three of them, with a lot help by professionals, could get it done in no time.

As Letty rummaged around on stage, Katherine and Simeon walked toward the windows overlooking the grounds of O'Malley House.

"You've done some marvelous things here, Simeon," she said, motioning to the lush, sweeping lawns and the flower beds.

"You've done some pretty marvelous things inside the old place," he said, returning the compliment.

"We make a pretty good team," she declared and he looked at her and smiled.

"I guess we do," he agreed.

"What do you think this is all about? Getting this place all fixed up?"

"I haven't got the foggiest but it's been a lot of fun. Maybe it's just to keep two old people moving."

"What old people?" Katherine asked mischievously. "Oh! You mean us. You and me. Old? No way. You're only as young as you feel and I feel about thirty-two."

"Thirty-two…I remember what you looked like when you

were that age. I have to say, Kate, you are as beautiful now as you were then."

"My, that's a wonderful compliment," she said, touching his hand lightly. Simeon turned red with embarrassment, and it only deepened when she leaned forward and said softly, "and I have to tell you that you are as handsome as you were the first day I saw you."

Chapter Fourteen

There was a newcomer to the Danford Senior Center the next afternoon when Letty arrived. Pauline Oakes was the mother of Sandra, the owner of Sandra's Sensual Lingerie and Candle Shoppe. Lillian had befriended Pauline the day after she visited the store. Meeting her was really quite easy. Lillian simply figured out that the pair lived above the shop, and after closing time she climbed the stairs behind the building and knocked on the door.

Pauline was a very pretty seventy-four-year-old but she was so shy that no one noticed her beauty. Lillian hoped that her friends at the Center would bring her out of her shell.

When Letty got to the Center the men were sitting in front of a television watching a rerun of "Walker, Texas Ranger." The women, who were chatting and laughing, were busy making place mats out of old greeting cards.

"How was school?" Adeline Gunn called across the room when Letty walked through the door. Lillian, who was feeding the cards and plastic sheets through a laminator, waved a hand before quickly going back to her task.

How was school? Letty wondered how many times she had been asked that question. You'd think by the time a woman started college it would have subsided. But not with this bunch.

"I learned a lot," she declared, "but Billy Joe Simpson knocked me down at recess and then I fell off the monkey bars. But I forgot all about that when Professor Smith lectured on the division of economics among the southern states."

"You are such a teaser," Adeline laughed.

Lillian was done laminating by then and she reached down and grabbed Pauline's hand and hauled the poor woman to her feet.

"This is Letty, the girl I was telling you about" she told Pauline. Then she turned to Letty. "Remember Sandra from the new store? This is her mother, Pauline. We're hoping she'll join up with the Danford seniors."

"Like you'll give her a choice," Letty said laughing. She reached out her hand, and the embarrassed older woman ducked her head before cautiously extending her own. Then she noticed the big bag in Letty's left hand. It was overflowing with books. Not just paperbacks, but also hardbacks. As quick as a petal falling off a faded rose, Pauline shed her shyness.

"Books!" she declared, reaching for the bag. "May I look?" Letty handed over the bag. Hugging it close to her heart Pauline made her way to an empty table and carefully removed them, one by one. She studied the fronts, and the backs, and thumbed through the middles. One old book, a collection of Walt Whitman poetry, she held to her nose. After taking a deep breath, she sighed in sheer delight.

Lillian had been watching with wide eyes. This was a new version of the Pauline Oakes she had met earlier. "So, you like books?" Lillian asked with a hint of sarcasm.

"I love books. I adore books," Pauline declared loudly, causing Kingston Phillips to swing his head from the television and then sit up. Bracing himself by putting his hands on the sides of the chair, he stood up and then made his way to the table. He was an elegant man, tall and slim, with a full head of white hair and every one of his own teeth.

"Mind if I check them out?" he asked Pauline before reaching his hand out to shuffle through the pile. She noticed he had a healthy tan and wondered if he golfed. She'd never tried the sport but heard it had great health benefits.

"Be my guest," Pauline answered, leaving Letty wondering in amusement when she had relinquished ownership of the bag and its contents.

"Look at this," Pauline told him, "An old copy of Leaves of Grass—the wonderful poems of Walt Whitman."

Closing her eyes and lifting her head she quoted eloquently, "*Goodbye my Fancy. Farewell dear mate, dear love...*" and paused in rapt silence.

"You got any Louis L'Amour in this pile?" Kingston asked, jarring her out of her reverie. She didn't notice the glint of humor in his eyes and became flustered. She helped him paw through the books.

"I'm sorry, sir, but it doesn't look like it," she finally said.

"Kingston. My name is Kingston Phillips, but everyone calls me King," he said.

"How do you do," Pauline said.

"I do just fine."

"Oh. Well, then. So do I—do just fine. I'm Pauline Oakes."

"Pauline," he acknowledged with a short bow. Then he picked up another book.

"So, what do you think of this one," he said, displaying a sordid romance paperback. The cover showed a half-naked pirate and his busty captive in the throes of unbridled passion.

Pauline frowned. "I'd stick to Louis L'Amour," she said quietly. She could feel her face redden. She didn't know that he thought it was very becoming. She really was quite an attractive woman, he thought.

"I agree," he said, laughing. Then he turned to go back to join the other men. Halfway there, he turned back. "Pauline?" he called and she turned her head.

"I'm going away, I know not where, Or to what fortune, or whether I may ever see you again, So Good-bye my Fancy," he quoted, finishing Whitman's poem.

Before she could consider a response he had returned to his chair and plopped back down. Her heart thundered in her chest so fast and hard she worried that it might simply stop from the excitement.

"Don't let him fool you," Lillian said in a loud whisper. "He's a retired professor from the university at Missoula and he's sharp as a whip."

"A professor. And he loves books. Oh, my," Pauline said in awe. She hoped she didn't die of a heart attack right then and there...before she got to know him better.

Chapter Fifteen

Marge Reynolds had gone from window to window, assessing the weather, the traffic on the road, the set of the sun in the sky, the wind velocity, and every other measure she could think of. She changed jackets three times and then pulled on a sweater and then went back to the closet and pulled down the same jacket she had put on in the first place.

Pulling a scarf over her head and tying it under her chin she closed her eyes and held her breath so long she became light-headed.

Then she walked with quick determined steps to the front door, turned the knob, and before she could back out took two steps onto the porch.

She stood there as still as a squirrel in a tree, keeping her eyes straight ahead and not peering from left to right. Her heart raced and she felt ill but, damn it, she was going to stay here. She was not, she vowed, going to scuttle back in like some shivering monkey. She was strong. She was well. She was healthy.

And then it happened. The sound of a squeaky bicycle seat and that grating "Yoo-hoo" she had been hearing for years. Lillian Dip.

Marge opened her eyes only to see the horrifying sight of Lillian veering off the main road and zipping up her driveway. She was grinning like an ape with every tooth in her head in plain sight.

"Margery! It's just grand to see you out and about," Lillian exclaimed, letting her bike fall to the ground as she rushed toward the porch.

Giving a strangled sound of utter terror, Marge lurched awkwardly and rushed through the open door. Slamming it behind her and quickly locking it, she leaned against it and breathed heavily.

Lillian, encouraged by the sight of her neighbor and alarmed by her look of fear, knocked heartily on the door. "Marge! Let me in. Are you all right? Marge?"

"Get away from here or I'll call the police!" Marge screamed. "Get off my porch and leave me alone."

A few minutes later she gathered enough courage to look out the window. The bike was gone. Her friend—ex-friend—Lillian was gone. She was left in her agony, knowing that she had been defeated again.

Chapter Sixteen

If Lillian was dismayed at Marge's response it wasn't because she felt rebuffed but because she was truly worried about her friend. Marge didn't have anything to do with any of them anymore.

Oh well, she'd worry about that later, she thought as she punched in a familiar number on the telephone. Right now there was a wedding she and Violet needed to attend.

"Miz Lillian Dip here for Miz Violet Lemke," Lillian said in a high lilting voice when the call was answered. She plugged her nose with her fingers to disguise her voice.

"Lillian, you are such a hoot," Violet said, laughing.

"So, are we still on for the Bradway and Smith wedding tonight?"

"I'd like to," Violet said. "I've heard rumors there may be trouble and I feel we should be there."

Lillian leaned in. "Trouble? What kind of trouble?"

Violet sighed. "Well, I really shouldn't say anything but Meg from down at Polsky's Market just phoned and asked if we were going and then she said that her sister told her that she'd heard there may be relative problems. Out-of-town relative problems."

"Oh, I hope not. I hate relative problems," Lillian said. "It can make the nicest wedding so nasty when the family gets involved. I don't know why they can't just keep their mouths shut and just smile for two hours. After all, it isn't their ceremony."

"I know, I know," Violet said, clucking her tongue. "But maybe we can be of help. I'm going to take the full bag of gear tonight, just in case."

"I'll get mine ready, too," Lillian said. "Actually, I've been thinking we should always carry full bags. Remember the Jarvis funeral? We didn't foresee anything unusual that time and then that kid slammed the door into the widow's head."

"You're probably right," Violet agreed. "If we hadn't had full bags that night it would have been a real mess. I've never seen so much blood from such a tiny head wound and it looked worse since her hair was so blond."

Twisting the phone cord, Lillian chuckled. "I still can't believe that incredible hat thing you made out of that black ribbon and a bit of black netting. No one ever knew the back of the poor woman's head was caked with blood."

After deciding when they would leave for the festivities Violet clicked off her phone, shook her head and bounced up from where she was perched on a kitchen stool. Over the years she and Lillian had seen every calamity under the sun—fleeing brides, split gowns, heels broken off of dyed satin shoes, lost rings, missing organists, throwing-up flower girls, bawling ring bearers, and toppling cakes.

They had learned to be emergency workers in such situations. Violet taught herself the Wedding March and a few somber funeral tunes on the piano, Lillian could repair any cake catastrophe, and they could both fix a broken shoe or an off-the-track zipper, and run a quick stitch through a ripped dress.

Their emergency bags—white brocade for weddings and black for funerals—contained first aid items, smelling salts, sewing kits, coloring books and crayons for disruptive youngsters, tissues and paper towels, a hot glue gun, safety pins, makeup, eye drops, tubs of white frosting, tiny boxes with fake rings, and even a small battery-operated sewing machine.

They had been known to send eye-to-eye warnings to bratty ring bearers, to counsel sobbing, reluctant brides into marching up the aisle, and to sober up many a groom with an evil concoction Violet called "The Colossal Cold Feet Cure."

Seeing the names "Violet Lemke" and "Lillian Dip" signed in the guest book was something every couple, and every mourning family, desired. Even families that had never met either woman considered it a great honor to have their presence at a wedding or funeral. A wedding seemed more official and the deceased more important when family members observed the pair sitting quietly and respectfully in a pew.

Now Violet shook her head over what she had learned about tonight's wedding. Young people these days just had it so tough compared to when she was that age. Why, back in the 1940s no one would have dreamed of interfering with the sacredness of a wedding. Quickly crossing the kitchen floor she headed to the bathroom to start applying fresh makeup.

On the other side of town Lillian was deep in her closet, rummaging for her burgundy pantsuit. She wanted to be comfortable in case there was Trouble with a capital T. She pulled the pantsuit out of the closet, slapped the dust off the shoulders, and draped it over a chair. Then she got on her hands and knees to find her black pumps. Crossing the room, she pulled a pair of panty hose out of the dresser drawer.

Panty hose. She hated panty hose. It was an invention of the devil himself. Who else would decree that a properly dressed American female should stuff her fifty-two-inch butt into a six-inch wide tube that was so delicate you could shove your whole thumb through the material? By the time she got them on she'd be sweating like a pig and out of breath and feel like an overstuffed bratwurst. Forget the panty hose. She'd just tug on her old stretched-out girdle and pull on a pair of knee hose. Unless they drooped down around her ankles, no one would ever know.

Chapter Seventeen

Lillian and Violet always arrived at their weddings early in order to secure the proper seating—not too close to the front and not too far from the back and they had to be on the aisle in order to assist in case of an emergency.

They knew the bride in this wedding, Penny Bradway, so they would sit on the bride's side of the church. Of all the churches in the area they liked this one best. Mainly it was because of Danford Worship Center's vibrant pastor, Mike Warren, who treated them like long lost family when they decided to attend regularly. Since then they had come to love and admire their young bachelor pastor. Their dream was to someday attend his wedding.

There were only a few cars in the parking lot when they pulled up but the suited young ushers were at their stations and they dutifully led Violet and Lillian into the sanctuary where they quickly selected their seats. The poor young men looked uncomfortable in formal wear. One wore a suit that was too small, exposing a good five inches of white shirt sleeve, and the other wore what appeared to be something salvaged from his father's closet and was many sizes too large.

After thanking the fellows graciously they opened their bags and took out the "This Seat Reserved" placards and placed them on the chairs. Out of experience they had learned that oftentimes the cards were ignored and stuck underneath or into the seat back of the chair ahead so they then took out a personal item—Lillian put down a pair of gloves and Violet draped a scarf over the back of her chair. A card was one thing but people were hesitant to remove personal items.

"Ready?" Violet asked, as she hefted her bag. She was dressed in a magnificent turquoise silk frock and looked fit to kill.

"After you, ma'am," Lillian said, grabbing her bag. She wasn't jealous; well, except for Violet's slim ankles with that dainty tendon running up the back. Lillian's ankles were thick and sturdy.

The two headed to the side rooms, where they knew the bride's party would be. They were ready to put their expertise to work and help ensure the perfect ceremony.

Knocking discreetly on the door of the bride's room, Violet then just walked in, followed by Lillian. The bride wasn't there. However, there was a huddle of hand-wringing females who were obviously distressed. Before long Violet and Lillian learned that there was, indeed, a problem. Penny, the bride, was off trying to settle a battle between her father and her stepfather. Each had arrived thinking he would escort the bride down the aisle. Penny was under the misunderstanding that her real father wouldn't be able to attend. It was a real mess. They were, right now, in Pastor Mike's office, trying to straighten it all out.

In two minutes flat Violet and Lillian were at the pastor's office door. They put their ears close and listened.

"Well, you have never really been there for her since the divorce," a male voice bellowed loudly.

"That's because you and my ex-wife wouldn't let me be there for her," came the loud retort.

"Please don't argue," pleaded the bride.

"Everyone needs to settle down. This isn't an insurmountable problem," Pastor Mike put in.

Straightening up, Lillian and Violet looked at each other and nodded. Then they simply walked in.

The conversation stopped as the foursome in the office stared at the interlopers. Actually, there was a fifth person in attendance—the bride's mother, who was huddled in a chair in the corner and crying quietly.

"Pardon us," Violet said, "but we understand what is going on and there is a solution."

"We ran into this same thing at the Steele and Heffle wedding a few years back," Lillian assured them.

No one said anything. They just gaped. Only the bride's mother recognized the pair. She'd heard about them fixing things at weddings and funerals. She dearly hoped they could fix this one.

Quickly setting her huge bag on an empty chair, Violet reached in and rummaged around and then extracted a large plastic bag from the bottom. Opening the top she removed a long length of soft, thick, white velvet rope.

"Unless you rearrange the chairs, and there isn't time now since people are arriving, the aisle isn't wide enough for both of her fathers to escort Penny. And it isn't really a matter of which one, because both of them are so precious and loved by her. They both need to be there for her today. And they can be if each father takes an end of this velvet rope and Penny carries the middle of it behind her bouquet," Violet said.

"The two fathers walk side by side, about ten feet ahead," Lillian interjected. "That way they are both involved and they are both leading her into her new life."

Everyone in the room looked at everyone else and there was a glimmer of hope. This might work.

"When they all get to the front," Lillian concluded, "the fathers, still holding their ends, can take the rope from Penny and carefully lift it up and over her head and drape it over her shoulders and then the three of them stand close, within the circle of rope. The rope, that way, symbolizes that they will always be together; that they will always be in a circle of love."

"What happens then?" Penny's mother asked, sitting up. Violet answered.

"Penny's real father takes the rope and folds it—he doesn't wad it, mind you—he folds it and places it near where the wedding party will be. This symbolizes that in her new life Penny must make her own circle."

"That's beautiful," Penny declared, reaching out and grabbing the rope that would solve this awful problem.

The fathers looked relieved that there was a solution.

"Thank you," the mother of the bride said gratefully.

From his chair, it was all Pastor Mike could do to keep from bursting into laughter. That was the hokiest bunch of malarkey he had ever heard. The circle of rope. Leading her down the aisle like a pet cow. But, still, these two had managed, once again, to save a wedding from disaster. They were really quite remarkable.

After practicing a few times the fathers got the hang of it and the bride scuttled back to her entourage.

On their way out the door Lillian turned to the mother of the bride. "I hate to be critical, dear," she said, patting the woman on the shoulder, "but you have mascara running clear to your chin. Violet and I have just the solution for those puffy eyes and that red nose and we can get you fixed up in no time."

The woman clung to her in gratitude and Lillian caught Violet's eye and smiled. They'd done it again. My, how they loved their weddings and funerals.

Chapter Eighteen

The idea came to her in the middle of the night and Letty was so struck by it she sat straight up in bed. She tried to go back to sleep and couldn't. Instead she got up, threw on her robe, and went into the kitchen. The apartment was so small that this journey consisted of fewer than six steps. Grabbing a notebook and two pens off of the corner of her tiny computer desk, Letty started writing.

First she made a list of all the regulars who came almost daily to the Danford Senior Center. Not the ones who lived full and busy lives and were supported by tons of family members, but those who were lonely and had no purpose. People like Adeline Gunn and Lillian and Violet were so busy they didn't need an extra boost in life, but so many others did.

The idea was so perfect and so simple she was astounded that she hadn't seen it before. Then she thought, maybe God just hadn't allowed her to see it before.

Katherine O'Malley had a huge mansion that they were working to put in perfect repair. The Center was full of people who had skills but no way to utilize them. Her idea—God's idea, actually—of having Henry Riggins help Simeon with the flowers and the rest of the grounds was just a start. There were tasks for all of them.

She tried to remember her conversations with them and what they had done in the past as far as vocations and avocations.

Henry Riggins topped the list, and Letty wrote "gardener" next to his name, followed by a check mark. She had a job for Henry.

He was followed by Burl Sands, who had been a mechanic. Letty remembered the day she had gone to the center and found the old fellow in a slump. When she asked him what was wrong he lifted his hands. "They're clean," he said sadly. "It's the first time since I was a toddler that I haven't had grease under my fingernails." Somehow, even though she was so young, she understood. His life's work had been taken away.

Burl could do all sorts of things around the mansion. There were always tractors and lawnmowers and all sorts of mechanical things that needed attention. And Simeon, bless his heart, wasn't too sharp at that sort of thing.

Mick Hogel had been an accountant and owned his own firm until heart problems forced him to retire. Maybe there wasn't much for him to do at the Mansion, but she bet she could get him connected with Sandra Farris at the new boutique. She had heard from Pauline, Sandra's mother, that Sandra hated all the book work that came from owning a business.

Henry Knutson. Henry was an old rancher who had spent more time on a horse than anyone she knew. His two daughters lived in another part of the state, and she knew that since his wife had died he was very lonely. Maybe he could come to the Mansion and give the horses some exercise and restore the tack that was piled up in the barn.

Virgie Cramer, seamstress. She had owned her own little sewing business until she got too old to handle a six-day-a-week work schedule. Virgie, along with Lulu Chin, who was also an avid seamstress, were always discussing patterns and sewing machines and remembering the dresses they had created in the past. Maybe they could look at all the trunks and closets and wardrobes that were filled with ancient gowns and other clothes. They could be in charge of any repairs.

The list was long but between the Mansion and her connections around town Letty thought she had found something for everyone to do. None of it would probably pay much, if anything, but it would give them something to do to get them back into the stream of life.

Pauline Oakes was at the bottom of the list. Actually, it was Pauline who triggered her nighttime revelation. The scraps of conversation she had overheard as Pauline chatted to Kingston suddenly added up. The day before she had talked about cataloguing and suddenly Letty realized it wasn't a catalog of merchandise. Pauline was talking about library cataloguing. She was a librarian! She could tackle that horrendous job of taking stock of everything in the O'Malley House library. Letty knew she would be delighted at the opportunity. In fact, she might just drop to the floor in a faint when she saw the library for the first time. It was truly a treasure trove of ancient tomes.

After thinking about it, Letty added Kingston Phillips's name beside Pauline's. They could both work in the library. It would be perfect.

As she completed the list she pondered whether to go back to bed or just stay up. She decided to go back to bed. As she drifted off, she thought that she couldn't wait to talk to Katherine in the morning.

Chapter Nineteen

Over the next few weeks Letty put her plan into action. Katherine was more than excited—not so much about getting such splendid help in the mansion, but in being able to help others. Both of them wondered aloud many times why they hadn't thought of it before.

"I guess it was just not the right time and God had to get everything in place first," Katherine finally concluded.

Letty was discreet about asking people to lend a hand in the restoration work. She didn't want to ask those who already had active lives, focusing instead on those who were at loose ends now that their productive years had ended.

Instead of announcing her plan in front of the whole group, she visited people in their homes. Her visit with Henry Riggins, who was the first she approached, would always remain a fond memory.

Henry's apartment building was shabby and in need of a coat of paint. Each tiny apartment had a wee balcony and she smiled when she spotted Henry's. Even though it was barely past spring, his little balcony was overflowing with flowers and plants.

He opened the door almost instantly and he looked startled and somewhat frightened. She knew he probably had few visitors. He invited her in and fluttered around the small living room and adjoining kitchen, asking her if she'd like tea or water or he could make a pot of coffee. When she refused he started tidying, picking up a stray sock and straightening magazines and newspapers. Finally she stood up, took him by the hand and led him to what she knew, from the dip in the middle, was his favorite chair.

"What I really want," she said with a smile, "is to talk to you. I need your opinion on something, plus I want to see if you'd like a project."

She quickly outlined her plan and asked Henry if he thought it was good and the people she had selected for certain jobs were good choices and would make use of their skills.

"It's a perfect fit for everyone," he said. "Especially Pauline and Kingston. I've never been inside O'Malley House but I can't imagine anyone else who would be so perfect for a library. I do have one idea. Dora Hoffman. Her only daughter just died so she has no one. She and her daughter were very close and I know she's just lost without her. You probably don't know this, but Dora graduated from college with a degree in art history. She'd be perfect for researching and cataloguing any paintings that there might be in the mansion."

"That would be wonderful. I know there is a fortune in paintings there and many are original works. I really appreciate any other ideas you might have, Henry."

"Glad to help. It's pretty terrific, what you're doing here, Letty—you and Mrs. O'Malley."

"It really isn't us at all. It's something I think God is putting together." She leaned forward. "Well, we do have one other job and I have someone in mind for it. Henry, how would you like to help Simeon Quest in the gardens?"

He didn't answer. He just looked at her in stunned silence. Then he shook his head and looked down.

"You don't want to?" she asked him. Letty was dismayed. She thought he'd jump at the chance. Then he looked up and she saw the glint of tears in his eyes. He quickly swiped them away. She knew then that he wasn't shaking his head to indicate he wasn't interested; he was shaking his head in wonderment at the chance of working on the beautiful grounds.

"Are you serious?" he asked quietly. His voice was rough, like it was traveling over sandpaper.

"Simeon is chomping at the bit, he's so excited to have you help. He says you're a walking encyclopedia when it comes to gardening. And Katherine? She wanted to come over here with me but then remembered she had a prior appointment. So, are you interested?"

"Can I start tomorrow?" he asked.

Since then, things were humming along smoothly. Virgie and Lulu set up sewing machines in the sewing room and were using one of the maid rooms as a staging area to carefully go through all the clothing. They were also cataloguing every piece. Virgie, they found out, was a history buff and had great knowledge of fabrics and costumes of the past. She and Lulu were astounded at what they were finding in trunks and in the attic rooms and declared it should be in a museum. There were gowns dating back to the 1700s and, amazingly, they were in almost perfect condition. Once they got everything sorted and cataloged, Katherine said they would bring in an antique specialist to determine just what they had.

It was through Lulu that they learned about old Peter Chervis, who was a jeweler. Peter was sorting through the amazing array of old jewelry in the mansion and making any repairs that were needed. Some of the pieces were so unique he thought they could be replicated and sold.

Beyond the mansion walls, in the outside buildings, things were equally as busy. Henry was sorting through a century's collection of saddles, tack and even old buggies and buckboards. He was being helped by an old cowboy buddy and they were cleaning and repairing and delighting in riding the few remaining horses.

Next door, Burl Sands, the mechanic, was repairing everything from an old Model A Ford to a 1945 John Deere tractor. When Letty visited him the second day he was out in the big outbuilding that served as his shop, he looked ten years younger. He held up his black hands and grinned and said one word: "Grease!"

Across town, at Sandra's Sensual Lingerie and Candle Shoppe, seventy-six-year-old Mike Hogel was happily crunching numbers and jotting them down in a ledger. Sandra had even promised him a computer with an accounting program. He was back to his numbers and felt like he was in heaven.

Conrad Moyers, who loved to bake since he retired, was helping Josephine at the Danford Bakery and Polly Long, who was a retired music teacher, had started a citywide singing group. She was so enthused she had even roped in Katherine, Simeon, Lillian and old Henry Riggins, who, it turned out to the surprise of everyone, had a beautiful voice.

Letty had also talked Pastor Mike Warren at Danford Worship Center into starting a unique "family" Sunday School class which was comprised of every age group—from kindergartners to junior high and high school students, adults, and the elderly. The one rule for being in the class was that everyone had to agree to share. The class was proving to be a phenomenal success and the adults were getting surprising insight from the youngsters.

As far as work in the mansion, there were, of course, some people at the Center who were miffed at not being asked to help but when Letty carefully explained to them how their lives were full and productive, they understood. At Katherine's suggestion, all of the Danford Seniors had been invited to the mansion for tea and cookies and a tour so they could see it firsthand. They were all delighted with the experience. Katherine promised another visit soon, so they could see the progress.

All in all, Letty's project had gotten off to a phenomenal start and she and Katherine were thrilled at the progress that they could see on a daily basis. She wished she'd hurry up and finish college so she could devote full time to "her people."

"What do you think God has in mind next?" Letty asked Katherine one afternoon, as they sat in the kitchen after checking on all their helpers. The work, of course, would someday come to an end.

"I don't have the foggiest," Katherine said, reaching for a slice of banana bread. "But I know he has a plan."

They both smiled. For now they were just content watching lives change.

Chapter Twenty

Lillian Dip spent as much time at the mansion as she could, but some days she was too busy to visit her friend Katherine and check on things. Maybe it was all the work happening down the street that got her thinking about her own humble abode. After getting Petunia settled with a chew bone, she stood in the hallway of her trailer and squinted and contemplated the living room.

Lillian often thought she should go to school to become a decorator. She loved changing and fixing and improving things. Sometimes when she visited her friends' homes she had to fight to keep from fixing awkward furniture arrangements, switching out paintings, and popping to the store to buy a gallon or two of paint.

She was most proud of her bedroom and had dragged her friends into the room, one by one, and basked in their admiration and compliments. But it wasn't as if you could haul an everyday visitor to the bedroom. The scrawny, somber meter man who trudged through the house once a month to read the meter dials in the back bathroom would keel over if she invited him to check out her bedroom. She could imagine how his eyes would bug out at the suggestion, and fear would jiggle the elaborate comb-over held down with a gob of hardened gel.

Lillian had leaped headlong into her bedroom project, scraping and painting and refurbishing the old bedroom set and haunting garage sales and flea markets to find proper accessories. She had stripped the headboard, dressers and night stands and painted them white and added gold flourishes and gold knobs. The walls were covered in what were originally king-sized flat sheets. Pale yellow and shot with gold, Lillian had carefully stapled them to the walls and then nailed gilded molding around the top and bottom to hide the edges.

When she couldn't afford massive paintings of elegant women, Lillian simply bought some acrylic paints and a few canvasses and frames and painted her own. Then she dumped a dab of watered-down brown stain onto a cloth and patted it onto the dried paintings, making them look like old heirlooms. They looked, well, to her they looked magnificent.

Now she squinted and assessed the living room. It was a dismal room with dark brown paneled walls and stuffed with furniture she and Del—may he rest in peace—had purchased over twenty years ago. Green with turquoise flecks, the uncomfortable living room set was ugly even back then. Her cluttering problem didn't help. Piles of magazines and newspapers and books were stacked on the floor and spilled into the kitchen. Her crocheting bag and a colorful stack of yarn skeins huddled next to her chair.

Bright and light, she thought. She'd paint the paneling something airy and cheerful, maybe a soft green or a buttery yellow. Then, a few paintings, some new furniture and, viola!, it would be beautiful.

She thought about starting the project right then and there, but then decided she needed to start on the latest survey as soon as the fax machine delivered the questions. She'd make a few calls this morning but save most of her calling for later. She had learned through experience that the best time to make survey calls was early evening.

Lillian had stumbled upon the survey job while in line at Safeway. The woman ahead of her who owned the company was having a small crisis since two of her employees had up and quit without notice. The woman asked her friend, the store clerk, if she could recommend someone. Anyone. Lillian, not embarrassed at listening in, cleared her throat and said maybe she could help.

The Stevens Research Company, Lillian learned over coffee with the frazzled owner Bette Stevens, had been in existence for over ten years. Among other things, the company's freelance interviewers collected data by doing public opinion and customer satisfaction surveys, did market research, and performed those cursed polling interviews during election season. All that was required was a cheerful, friendly attitude, a telephone, fax machine or computer, and the desire to perform quality work and to be honest. Depending on the number and intensity of the questions, Bette paid from $2 to $6.50 per survey.

While she had her Social Security and a small pension from Del, Lillian decided she could use the extra money and this job was ideal. She could work as much as she wanted and name her own hours. Best of all, she enjoyed chatting with people.

Lillian heard the fax machine come to life and went into the kitchen. Depending on the number of questions, she should be able to get fifteen surveys done in no time.

Grabbing a fresh cup of coffee, she picked up the survey papers off the fax machine and settled into her rocking chair. Next to her on a TV tray were the tools of her trade: a notebook, an antique vase full of pens and pencils, box of tissues, and a glass of water. Petunia jumped up daintily and nestled next to her.

"This is going to be an easy one," she told Petunia. "Only ten questions." People liked the short surveys. They were quick, easy, and people felt their opinions were being documented. The fifty-plus question surveys were harder to sell. If they were on a highly controversial subject, such as illegal immigration or abortion or gun control, they took twice as long due to the long tirades Lillian was forced to listen to.

This survey was a political investigation to appraise the pre-election waters. Lillian wiggled herself to comfort, put the clipboard with the phone list on her lap and adjusted the headphones that plugged into her phone. She punched in the first number and after a few rings hung up. Putting a tiny "AM" for "answering machine" next to the number, she dialed the second number, which rang ten times before she disconnected. After writing NA for "no answer" she dialed the third number. A female voice answered.

"Good morning," Lillian said cheerfully. "I hate to bother you on such a gorgeous spring morning and I'm hoping we can chat for a few minutes. My name is Gretchen and I'm from Stevens Research and we're conducting a poll. It's just a few questions and I guarantee it won't take more than a few minutes of your time."

"Well, I don't know. I really don't like these surveys." Probably older. A bit of a Southern accent. The woman wasn't exactly eager and Lillian strived to reassure her.

"I promise it will be very quick," she declared. "No more than a minute and a half." Lillian smiled as she said the words. She had read recently that people can hear you smile.

"I'm really busy. Washing clothes, you know, and breakfast dishes to do up."

Lillian was encouraged. She'd be able to reel this one in. It was a good sign that the woman was talking and hadn't slammed down the phone like so many did. Lillian had heard thousands of slammed phones. And obscene words. Sometimes she thought she should wash out her ears with soap. She had learned to be quick at clicking off her headset.

"I know what you mean," she said, joining the woman's team, "my dishes are still in my sink from last night and I'm dying to get out there and plant some flowers. Tell you what, you answer my questions and then we can both go outside!"

"Well, maybe, if you promise it's a quick survey."

"I promise. Here's the first question: 'If you were voting for governor today would you vote Republican or Democrat?'"

"Does it have to be one or the other? I sort of lean toward the Green Party."

"I'm sorry," said Lillian, "but this is just to get a broad view so they're just giving the choice of the two major parties."

"Well, then, I guess Democrat. No. Wait. Which one was President Reagan? Republican. Change that to Republican. Definitely Republican."

Lillian marked the "Republican" box on the survey form. She had learned never to make a sound after a question since it could invite comment, sometimes an intolerably lengthy—endlessly lengthy—horribly lengthy—comment.

"Answers for the following two questions are yes, no, or I don't know. Here is the first question: "Do you feel the Democrats are in touch with the concerns and needs of the American public?"

"No. Well, maybe. But then... No. I'm going to say no."

"Do you feel the Republicans are in touch with the concerns and needs of the American public?"

"Yes. I'm going to say yes. But sometimes I think they don't have a clue either."

"OK. We're almost done. 'Do you think illegal immigrants should be given amnesty and allowed to live legally in the United States?'"

"Do I just answer yes, or no?"

"I'm sorry, I should have said that. Yup. Just a yes or no."

"No. Well, maybe. Hmm. This is complicated." The woman laughed. "There's no "it depends" category?"

"Sorry. Just a yes or no," Lillian said, shaking her head. She knew the question was too complicated to be categorized by a yes or no.

"No. I guess I have to say no," the woman said firmly. Then she sighed in frustration.

Lillian checked off the box and quickly asked the remaining questions and then set aside the survey sheets and settled back in her chair. Petunia opened one eye at the disturbance, then wiggled a bit and went back to sleep.

"OK," Lillian said. "We're all finished with the official survey but I do have a bonus question that's just for fun."

"You weren't kidding. That was quick! What's the bonus question?"

Lillian loved her bonus questions. She had started asking them just about six months before. She didn't ask them every time, just often enough to make the surveys more interesting.

She made the questions up and they covered a myriad of topics: Have you ever visited a foreign country? How many times have you been married? Has a member of your family ever been in jail? Growing up, did you have a pet? Do you watch daytime television?

She had gotten wonderful answers that led to fascinating conversations. While she would have loved to pursue friendships with some of her questionees, she didn't. She was very careful to protect her anonymity, and always used a pseudonym rather than her real name.

"The question is, 'Have you ever met anyone famous?'"

Lillian sat back and waited for the response.

"Hmmm. Does being related count?" the woman asked.

"Sure."

"I'm supposed to be related by marriage to the Kennedys but I never understood how. We weren't even Catholic. Or Democrat. And I never met any of them in person. But I did meet someone famous once. Ringo Starr. At this charity wine tasting thing. He gave me a hug and said I looked just like Sophia Loren. I think he'd had way too much wine."

Lillian laughed. "The only famous person I ever met was the Maytag man," she admitted. A few minutes later she was dialing the next number on her list.

Chapter Twenty-One

After two hours of surveys, Lillian's ears were ringing. Besides getting opinions on her specific questions, she had heard three hours of diatribe on global warming, terrorism, the judicial system, the plight of the honeybees and wheat crops, and a dozen other subjects. It was time for a break. And it was almost time for her favorite afternoon television shows.

She tried to call Katherine to ask about paint colors for the living room since she was still thinking about redecorating it, but the line was busy.

The phone rang just before three o'clock and she knew it was news about the election for officers at the Center. When the voice on the other end of the phone was Bill Fester, outgoing president of the Danford Seniors Group, she had a deep foreboding that it wasn't good news. She was right. Edith Snipell was the new treasurer. Edith, the one who insisted Lillian throw her name in the hat. "Just throw your name in the hat. You'd be perfect," Edith had said. Then she decided to run herself? That didn't make a lick of sense, but then, a lot about Edith didn't make sense.

Lillian knew that in the grand scheme of things losing the election was a small defeat, but it was still unsettling. It would be difficult to go back to the center, knowing she was a loser.

A half hour later, just before 3:30 in the afternoon, when she was still reeling from the humiliation of losing the election, there was more bad news. Lillian heard the report that Vinnie Biedeck was dead. Murdered. She was shocked. She fell back into her chair and felt the horror of the news seep into her soul.

She felt dazed but she had to admit that everyone knew it was coming. After all, you can't act as immoral as Vinnie and not anticipate being pumped full of bullets. Vinnie was not a nice man. People were lined up to shoot him: ex-wives, husbands of ex-wives, betrayed business partners, disillusioned family members, and a good portion of the community at large.

First the treasurer job and now the bad news about Vinnie. Lillian was stunned. She had known Vinnie since, what? The late 1960s? Oh, he had his problems, but deep down he wasn't all bad, he had done some good in his life. And he was very handsome, despite his age.

Covering her face with her hands, Lillian started to cry. Petunia lifted her head and joined in with pitiful warbling yowls. Lillian hugged the small dog and together they shed months of pent up emotion.

After a time she blew her nose and shook off any remnants of misery. "OK, Lillian Dip, this is crazy. You've got to pull yourself together," she said out loud.

Then she went to the cupboard and pulled down the mug with the faded Mickey Mouse logo, fixed herself a cup of hot chocolate and plopped in marshmallows. She liked the Mickey Mouse mug because it was big enough to float four marshmallows.

Taking the lid off the Garfield cookie jar Lillian stacked four store-bought chocolate chip cookies on a napkin, pulled all four corners to a peak in the middle and carried it and the hot chocolate to the yellow Formica-topped table in the dining room.

Sitting down with a heavy sigh, Lillian stared at the cocoa and cookies. Using her pointer finger she bobbed a marshmallow up and down. Since the table was in front of the bow window that stretched along the entire width of the trailer, she could see up the tree-lined street, a view she usually enjoyed. She could see the porch of cranky Marge's house, and, beyond, the curving drive of O'Malley House. Above the trees she could see the third floor ballroom of O'Malley House with its rows of windows. Three homes. Three widows.

Chapter Twenty-Two

Standing up from the table, Lillian adjusted the waistband of her sweatpants and yanked the gray Danford Bulldogs sweatshirt over her ample hips. Then she dialed Katherine's number.

Katherine answered on the fourth ring.

"I just wondered what you were doing," Lillian said. She could envision Katherine nestled in her rose-colored velvet chair, the ivory and gold receiver up to her dainty ear and the expanse of the mansion grounds just outside the broad windows. She would be impeccably dressed right down to panty hose and chic shoes and jewelry. Katherine was as close to perfect as Lillian had ever been around. Yet she didn't make anyone feel uncomfortable or under-dressed, and she wasn't arrogant or haughty. It was just Katherine's style, just as sweatpants and sweatshirts and hats were Lillian's style.

"Well, I just finished eating leftover meatloaf and got the dishwasher started. I figured you'd be getting all dolled up for a wedding tonight."

"I'm not sure if I'm going. Probably not. It's at seven and I haven't even thought about it. I need to call Violet."

"Well, I hope you go. I know how much you like your weddings and funerals. You sound all stuffed up. You getting a cold?"

"No," Lillian said, her voice quavering.

"You're crying! What's wrong? Are the kids all right?"

"They're fine. I guess. I haven't talked to either one of them for a month. Miserable kids. It's really nothing. I'm just feeling sorry for myself."

"I'm sorry you're upset. Do you want to talk about it?"

"Oh, it's not important. It's stupid, really. I just wanted to talk a minute."

"Well, it is important if it has you in tears. Tell me what's wrong, Lillian."

Lillian gasped out a sob and then chokingly let it all out in one long string, "Oh, that Edith Snipell," she said, her voice rising. "I am so upset. Remember I told you she talked me into running for treasurer for the Center? Well, then, after talking me into it, she went and decided to run herself. You know she flirts with any man who'll look at her twice. But the women don't like her all that well. Anyone who still has a husband hangs onto him with both fists when Edith's in the room. I thought for sure I'd get the female vote. Well, I guess not because do you know what she did? She went and baked all these cookies. Chocolate chip, sugar cookies all decorated up, brownies, chocolate nut rolls. That's all they talked about for two hours at the Center yesterday. She even made sugar-free cookies for the diabetics and people who are on diets."

Lillian suddenly quit talking and, except for some sniffing noises, there was a long silence.

"Lillian? What happened?" Katherine asked. "Did she win?"

"Did she win?! I got two votes. Two votes, Katherine! And one of the buggers was mine! I don't know who the other fool was."

"Well, she won by bribery so that shouldn't break your heart," Katherine said firmly. "There are probably laws against that. You know that by next week everyone will forget all about it. Besides, why on earth would you want to be treasurer? You hate even balancing your checkbook, for heaven's sake."

Then she paused. "I do feel badly for you and if you really wanted the treasurer job I wish you would have gotten it. I know you would have been a great treasurer." Katherine's words were soothing and full of tenderness. She knew that Lillian, bless her heart, sometimes needed some mature guidance and affirmation that she was loved and she was important.

"Oh, it's not just the treasurer job," Lillian said with a long sigh. "I really didn't want it anyway and I was hoping I wouldn't win. It's just that I didn't want to lose by that much. The awful thing is that Vinnie died today."

"Vinnie died! Vinnie Parsons? Oh no!" Katherine was horrified. She felt her body sag into a slump. Vinnie Parsons was in his early forties and owned the Chevron station at the corner of Main and Fifth. He had at least six children.

"Not that Vinnie. He's okay. I just saw him yesterday when I had my bike tire pumped up. Vinnie Biedeck died. You know, Vinnie Biedeck." Lillian said, her voice rising in tearful distress.

Katherine snorted with spontaneous unleashed laughter and in a split second clapped her hand over her mouth so Lillian wouldn't hear. Then she pulled the phone receiver tight to her chest and bent over, convulsing in choked-back laughter. Digging her fingernail painfully into her palm, she closed her eyes and brought the phone receiver back. She willed herself, with everything she had in her, not to laugh.

"I don't know what to say," Katherine said so softly Lillian could hardly hear.

"What did you say?" Lillian said through a Kleenex.

"I said I don't know what to say," Katherine said, her fingernails digging into her wrist to keep from howling.

"It was just awful," Lillian wailed. "He was shot. There was blood all over. I know it was wrong for him to be with Sabrina Whitfield but they were soul mates. They were made for each other. They were going to get married years before, but on the way to the wedding he crashed his plane and had amnesia and wandered in the woods and ended up being taken in by those hillbilly swamp people who wanted him to marry their daughter. Sabrina thought he was dead so she married Bruce Pentland and then there was that yacht fire and the diamonds went missing and she was sent to prison...Katherine, I don't think it's funny."

"I'm sorry, I really am," Katherine said through her snickers just before she burst into full-fledged belly laughs.

"Fine! Laugh all you want. But my afternoon shows are important to me," Lillian said indignantly.

Katherine's laughter ended as suddenly as it started. She mentally berated herself for being so unsympathetic.

"I know. But, sweetheart, you sometimes let them become too important."

"I know, I know," Lillian said with a sigh. "Sometimes I think I watch those afternoon shows too much. But I've been doing it for forty years. It's hard for me to just sit and crochet and it's hard to just sit and watch TV. The two just go together, sort of like coffee and cream."

"Fred and Ginger," said Katherine, trying to perk up her friend.

"Dean Martin and Jerry Lewis," said Lillian, catching the spirit.

"Robin Hood and Maid Marian," said Katherine, chuckling.

"Bobbi Jo and Miles," declared Lillian fervently.

"Who?" Katherine asked.

"Never mind."

"Who are Bobbi Jo and Miles?" demanded Katherine.

"A couple. Okay. They aren't real," Lillian admitted.

"What show?" asked Katherine.

"Generations of Love. It's on from two to three," Lillian said with a weak giggle.

"Lillian," Katherine teased, "you need rehab!"

"I feel better, Katherine. Thanks for talking to me. You're a good friend," Lillian said.

"Anytime. I suppose there are worse things than watching

soaps. I'll see you tomorrow, okay? And I'll pray for you tonight—that God helps you put this treasurer job into perspective and see that, in the grand scheme of things, it isn't all that important."

Suddenly, Lillian felt her world falling back into orbit and revolving the way it should be, with rhythm and focus and planned purpose.

"Now that you got me in a better mood, want to hear something funny?"

"Sure."

"Remember that satin nightgown I got from that fancy store? I wore it to bed last night. Just to see how it would feel. I took a long bath and put it on and I felt like a lady—an elegant, genuine, beautiful lady. I wondered what Del would have thought if I'd come to bed wearing something as seductive as that thing. Heck, Del thought sleeveless was racy."

"You are a beautiful lady and he would have told you so," Katherine said, laughing. "So, then what?"

"I figured out that satin sheets, satin comforters and satin nightgowns don't work together. I slipped and slithered and the comforter kept sliding off the bed. When I finally did fall asleep I woke up an hour later, hot and wet and suffering from the queen mother of all night sweats. I ended up putting on my old faithful flannel nightgown and slept like a baby."

Katherine laughed heartily, imagining the scene. "So, what are you going to do with it? You paid a fortune for that thing," she asked.

"I figure I might get my money's worth someday," Lillian said. "I'm putting in my "hope" drawer. I'm too old for a hope chest but I reckon maybe someday I'll have another husband to love. And if that happens I just hope that sexy gold satin won't give the poor fellow a heart attack."

Chapter Twenty-Three

Up the street from Lillian's mobile home the ebbing spring sun was sitting low on the horizon, sending shafts of gold and bronze through Marjorie Reynolds' spacious backyard. Had she been at all observant, she would have marveled at the way the setting sun poured its vibrant colors over everything—changing dead white roses on overblown bushes to a pale orange and making a decrepit gazebo in a corner look almost elegant.

Oblivious to the spring beauty just outside her kitchen window, Marge sighed and put the last of her waning energy into rinsing a delicately flowered Windsor plate, a matching teacup and saucer, and a variety of silverware. No matter how bad things got, no matter how much she cried, or how much she fought against her life, there was something lodged deep within her that forced her to keep up the dishes. If she died, a month later, when the stench reached the sidewalk and someone investigated, they would remark that, by Jove, the house was tidy and the dishes were done.

There were other rules that had to be adhered to. Her bed had to be made every morning. Breakfast and lunch might be eaten in the breakfast nook, but evening meals required a more proper setting. Marge ate dinner at the old oversized mahogany table in the formal dining room, used a linen napkin, fine china, and said a grace that was as canned as her nightly vegetable. Sometimes it was adhering to a routine that kept her as sane as she was.

Tonight her meal had been a frozen box of meatloaf, mashed potatoes and gravy. A little corner square was supposed to be cherry cobbler but tasted more like flavored glue. Once she had accidentally missed cleaning up a dab of "dessert" off the table, and the next day she had to use a knife to pick it off.

Over four dollars and it was barely edible. There should be a law against selling such rotten slop, she muttered to herself. The stuff is probably killing me, clogging my arteries and jamming up my bowels. Tomorrow I'll cook up a chicken. Flattening the cardboard box the dinner came in, she moved to the pantry and tossed it in the garbage.

Moving to the sink Marge drained the water and used the sprayer to send tufts of soap froth down the drain. A ray of sunshine stabbed through the window, hitting her in the eye, and she pulled a faded green shade to block it.

Then she went into the bathroom and used the mirror to freshen her lipstick. The image that looked back at her wasn't scary. She didn't look crazy. She was simply an elderly woman wearing a pair of tan slacks and polyester flowered blouse with graying hair pulled back into a ponytail. For most of her grown life she had enjoyed a weekly appointment at the Golden Mirror, but it had been years now since she had been able to do that—to allow herself to be trapped in a chair and surrounded by commotion and sharp smells that plunged her into panic.

At first she tried to cut her hair herself and had coaxed the woman at the beauty supply shop, for a ridiculous $20 delivery fee, to drop off tiny bottles of hair dye and crème developer. Somehow, the colors were never right and, besides, Marge couldn't see the back of her head to do an adequate job. Sometimes her hair, when she rinsed out the residue dye, was nearly black; other times it was light brown and streaked with whatever color had been there before. After a year of home beauty shop misery she decided to go natural. Who, after all, would know? Who, after all, would even care?

She blotted her lips and sighed. There. Done for another night. And now what? Television? Do my nails?

Marge didn't feel like doing her nails. Maybe she'd work on the puzzle.

She had found the puzzle in the attic the year before and had completed it twice already. It was a 1,000-piecer, an idyllic fall scene with orange and yellow trees and a pond with a rowboat and a smiling, happily-ever-after couple. Marge really wanted another puzzle but Nate from the church had forgotten repeatedly, even though she marked it carefully on her weekly list. She hated being so dependent on Nate, but what could she do? Call that church and ask for someone else? What if they got huffy and Nate found out and refused to come? Then what would she do? Starve?

Maybe that would be the best. Just go away. No one would miss me. God, do you hear that? No one would miss me. Not one person.

There was no answer.

Chapter Twenty-Four

The daytime bustle of the day was winding down in Danford, Montana, when the dark green Rent-a-Wreck van with dusty Washington state plates wheezed up to the first of only three street lights. A small coughing backfire accompanied the squeal of aging brakes and caused the heads of a few pedestrians to bob toward the roadway.

Inside the van were four adults and four children in various stages of that numb disarray that comes from traveling great distances. It was obviously a family on vacation.

Two youngsters pestered each other with stealthy pokes, while the other pair gazed out the window with vapid curiosity. The adults looked weary. Only the old fellow in the second row of seats looked as if he was having a good time. He was gleeful, sitting straight as a flagpole and staring out the window and grinning as if he'd just popped over the hill and entered the Promised Land. Even the tufts of snow white hair that had escaped the morning slick-down with a comb seemed to be standing in excitement.

"Slow down a bit, Dan," Connie implored as her brother started through the green light. She craned her neck to look at the massive glass and steel building on the corner and then shut her eyes and shook her head, as if the action would fix things; make them the way they were supposed to be.

She had looked forward to this day for years and now everything was wrong. Nothing was where it should be. The landmarks she had stowed in her memory were gone, taken over by strange edifices that had apparently lumbered into town and squatted heavily on top of buildings that had been there since the turn of the century. Buildings she had grown up with.

"I don't like this," she muttered. "Not one bit. I think I'm going to cry. Look at that. That glitzy building isn't the First National Bank of Danford. The First National is over on Second Avenue. And the dry cleaners! What the heck did they do with the dry cleaners?"

"You really going to cry?" Dan asked, glancing at her as he slowed the vehicle. He had as much fondness for his hometown as his sister, but he was puzzled over why she would bawl over a new bank building and the disappearance of the Danford Dry Cleaners. True, the red brick bank building had been there since the turn of the century, but the dry cleaners had been an ugly narrow little building sandwiched between the Whistle Stop Bar and the Hometown Furniture Store. The place's sole claim to fame, besides a brand of starch that scraped tender skin raw, was the row of massive thick-leafed bromeliads that groped perpetually steamy, weeping, windows.

Behind her, Miranda, Dan's wife, reached forward and patted Connie's shoulder. "I'm sorry," she said in a whisper, her voice choked with sympathy. Connie wouldn't have been surprised, had she turned around, to find Miranda also shedding tears. Miranda internalized the feelings of everyone around her, as if her own delicate thoughts weren't enough to take on.

"I wondered why there were so many people here," Dan said, ducking his head to look up at the Visitor's Center sign they were driving past. "They've got a Soroptimist Convention, the Danford High School prom, and a Global Energy Symposium going on this weekend. A Global Energy Symposium...in

Danford, Montana? Now that's hoot!"

He glanced at Connie and smiled. "I'm sure glad you got us room reservations and a place for Dad's party, Con, or we'd be pitching tents and having Safeway cupcakes," he said.

His grin quickly changed to alarm when his sister made a choking sound. Connie, no longer looking at the Danford scenery, was staring at him with unveiled distress. "No, Dan," she said, shaking her head. Her voice was high pitched and tinged with a trace of hysteria. "I made the room reservations. You and Nora. Remember our little sister? You and Nora were supposed to get the place for the party. Remember? I distinctly remember the conference call. I'd get the rooms and you or Nora would find a place for the party."

"Not me. You girls do this stuff. Not me."

Connie rummaged in her purse for her cell phone, flipped it open, punched up the menu, thumbed a number and put the phone to her ear. "I'm sure it's not a problem," she said as she waited for the call to go through, "Nora must have done it." Her head started bobbing, keeping time to the seriousness of the potential crisis. Dan could only pray that the whole thing would be solved easily and quickly and without him having to hear the endless details.

"We got a problem?" old Patrick O'Reilly asked loudly learning forward in his seat. He couldn't hear well enough to take in any of Connie's conversation but knew from her facial expressions and the increasing speed of the head-bob that something was wrong.

"No problem, Dad," Dan bellowed loudly, flashing a white-toothed grin. "Just a mix-up in some of the birthday party plans."

"Okay," Patrick said as settled back into his seat and he turned his focus back to his old hometown. He had a broad smile on his face as his eyes roamed eagerly.

The van continued down the once-familiar street as Connie's voice took on more alarm. Then, her conversation with her sister Nora finished, she folded her phone slowly and deliberately. Gripping it tightly, she shut it with a snap of finality. She looked at Dan and shook her head.

They had planned for six months for the ten of them to hold Patrick's eightieth birthday party in this place where he was born and raised his children. Connie and Dan and their families and old Patrick had driven from Washington. Nora and her husband were flying in from Cleveland. And now the sleepy little town of Danford was so packed with visitors and events there probably wasn't even a church basement available in which to hold the festivities.

"Where did you say we could buy those cupcakes?" Connie asked, trying valiantly not to burst into tears.

Chapter Twenty-Five

Katherine O'Malley was deep into a new novel when the shrill ring of the telephone next to her brought a startled jump. She looked at her watch. It was nine o'clock at night. Who on earth would be calling so late?

Katherine smiled. Probably Letty, who could never remember her schedule. Or maybe one of the crew of seniors who were helping in the Mansion. Or, she frowned, maybe the police chief again, calling to inform her of the latest complaint from Margery Reynolds. Marge called the police frequently, complaining about Katherine's lights shining on her property, missing newspapers and mail, car tracks on her lawn, and, once, even about Katherine's barking dog. Katherine didn't even own a dog.

Before she could verbalize a greeting the voice on the other end began speaking.

"I need to make reservations," declared the agitated female. The blare of an insistent TV could be heard in the background.

"I'm sorry; you must have the wrong..." Katherine began.

"Oh, please, please listen," said the cultured, beseeching voice on the other end. "We thought we had reservations at Rocco's but found out that there was a misunderstanding and no one had made them. Since then we've tried everywhere and because of proms and conventions and whatever else is taking place here, virtually every restaurant in Danford is booked solid. Please, can't you fit us in somewhere? It's not until Saturday night, day after tomorrow. My father is turning eighty and we've come in from all over the country. This is such a special time and I can't find a single place in town for us to eat. I just..."

"I'm really very sorry," broke in Katherine when the woman paused to catch her breath, "but you..."

"Wait! Before you say no let me tell you this," pleaded the woman. "My father was born right here in Danford and spent most of his life here. We just came back here to Montana to celebrate his birthday. There are ten of us. Please don't say no."

"I'm sorry but I really can't help you. You have the wrong number. This is a private residence, not a restaurant. I'm really very sorry I can't help you."

For a time there was just the television noise, gunshots and sirens wailing and shrill music, on the other end of the line. Katherine couldn't determine if it was the news or one of those shoot-'em-up action movies. Then a quiet, woeful voice said, "This isn't the Simpatico Mexican Restaurant?"

"No, it isn't."

"Oh. I didn't realize. I'm sorry I messed up your evening with my ranting."

"That's all right, dear," Katherine said with a chuckle. "I was just sitting here reading. I'm just sorry I can't help. I hope you find a place."

"Thanks. We'll figure out something."

After placing the receiver back in its cradle, Katherine ran a slim hand over her smooth, shoulder-length white hair and pondered the oddness of the whole phone call. What a nice person she had just talked to. A little desperate, perhaps, but that was understandable under the circumstances. Shaking her head and smiling a thin, small smile, Katherine wondered if the woman knew how wonderfully blessed she was to have not only a father still living but all those other relatives. She hoped the woman on the phone never had to go through the sad loneliness that comes from having no one left in the world save yourself.

Still in her reverie, Katherine jumped when the phone rang again. It was the same woman.

"Please forgive me for bothering you again. I pushed redial to get you. I'm wondering if you would have any ideas on what we should do. I gather that you have lived in Danford for awhile and you might know of some new place that I don't know about. I left right out of school and the place has grown so much and my memory seems to have collapsed somewhere along the way. The only place I really remember was the Tip Top Café with a huge Styrofoam cowboy hat on top of the building and car hops on roller skates and I can't even remember the street that was on."

"It was on Elm Street, just off of Fifth. It was torn down years ago, not long after the owner was discovered serving more than greasy hamburgers out of the back room. Drugs, you know," Katherine said absently.

Her mind was whirling. "I might have an idea. Let me think for one minute," she said. Closing her eyes she held the receiver to her forehead and said a quick prayer. She couldn't just dismiss this phone call. Why couldn't she provide a place and a little nourishment for a birthday party for an old man?

Okay, Lord, what would you do?

Invite them.

"All right, Mrs...."

"Ames. My name is Connie Ames and my father is Patrick O'Reilly. Please call me Connie. Thank you so very much for your help. I can't begin to tell you how much this means to me. If you can give me any idea where we can celebrate Dad's birthday, it would be wonderful."

"All right, Connie. I think I have a solution. You probably won't find a place in town to hold the festivities. I am surprised you found a place to stay. This might be a crazy idea. I live in one of the big old homes in Danford that you and your father should remember. O'Malley House. It's been standing right on this corner for over 100 years and sometimes I feel like I've been here that long myself. I would be delighted to have his party here. I'll serve more than appetizers, too. And I would be honored to make the birthday cake."

"O'Malley House? You're Katherine O'Malley? Oh, wow. I can't believe this. Of course I remember it. I walked by the mansion every day on my way to and from school. We lived over on Park. I used to daydream I was a princess and I lived there and my room was at the very top, the one with the rounded turret. One time I was so caught up in my after-school daydream I walked right up the sidewalk, climbed the stairs, crossed the porch and opened the front door. Then I came to my senses and was horrified by what I'd done. I ran all the way home and waited for three days for the police to come and get me."

Katherine was delighted with the tale. When she was a new bride, fresh to Danford and hanging onto the arm of her handsome bridegroom, she felt the same way about the immense, stately edifice. She felt like a princess, too, finally coming home to her castle.

"You should have rung the doorbell," she told Connie Ames, "I'd have taken you on a tour."

"I would have loved that," said Connie, then she sobered with the thought of what had been offered. "Wow! Well, my goodness. I don't know what to say. But, why would you do a thing like this for total strangers?" Connie asked.

"It just seems like the right thing to do," Katherine said, shrugging her shoulders. "It should be a lot of fun for all of us."

After deciding the time and going over the guest list, Connie paused. Then she asked conspiratorially. "Mrs. O'Malley, do you believe in fate and that things happen for a reason? I know a woman who lost the diamond out of her wedding ring—a big diamond, too—and she searched all over the house and had her nose to the ground all over the yard. That night she went to bed and dreamed she should get up and sweep the kitchen floor. She swept the floor and there was the diamond, right there in the dustpan.

"And then there was this man who used to go to our church and he won a trip to Europe. He was standing in the Louvre looking at the Mona Lisa and someone came up and stood next to him. Gazing at the painting, he said, 'It's beautiful, isn't it?' and the man turned to him and said, 'Mike?! What the heck are you doing here?'" Turns out it was his brother he hadn't seen in three years. There they were, the both of them, standing right in front of the Mona Lisa. Mrs. O'Malley, I've got to admit, I'm a great believer in fate and coincidences. Well, and Godly intervention, of course."

Kate laughed merrily. "Well, I am, too, and that, Connie, is exactly why I have agreed to be hostess for your party," she said cheerfully. "You just leave it all to me and I think we will have a fine time. I'll even show you the turret room."

Chapter Twenty-Six

Connie Ames placed the telephone receiver in its place and gave a wild whoop. "We're going to O'Malley House!" she yelled, bouncing up and down on the hotel bed. "O'Malley House! Do you know how incredible this is? I've always wanted to get inside that place."

"You're making me seasick," exclaimed Brent, who was propped up with pillows and supposedly watching a movie, although his siblings on the next bed kept accusing him of channel surfing. Eleanor, his twelve-year-old sister, sat up and swung her legs over the edge of the bed and faced her mother. She was in the process of peeling the dark purple polish off her fingernails and had a small pile on the night stand between the beds. She lifted her pinkie to her teeth and chewed at a reluctant bit of paint on the end of the nail.

"So, what's so great about O'Malley House?" she asked, sawing her fingernail between her teeth.

"Just wait until you see it, El," her mother replied. "It is a grand old house, a mansion really, or a castle. It is the dream house every little girl envisions living in. When I was a little girl I walked by it every day on my way to and from school and I began to feel it was MY castle. Then, when I was in high school

I realized I'd never probably live in such a place. But I never lost the yearning to go inside."

"It's a real castle? With dragons and everything and moats? I wish Dad could see it." Six-year-old Donny had come from his cuddle-point next to Eleanor and plopped beside his mother on the bed. His interest, for the next few seconds at least, was piqued. Connie reached over and mushed up his silky blond hair.

"I wish Daddy could see it too, but he had to work. It's not a real castle because in America we don't have kings and queens but if we did, they might choose it to live in. It's huge. Huge! You will love it Donny. Even if it doesn't have a moat or a dragon. But what it does is have turrets and I heard there is a ballroom and a garden room and dozens of other rooms, all of them filled with all sorts of wonderful things."

"Did you hear that, Brent?" Donny exclaimed. "It has turrets and everything." Leaning toward his mother he whispered, "What's a turret?"

"It's a sort of rounded tower. There are two of them," she whispered back.

"Big whoopee. I'd rather stay here and order pizza," said Brent, his eyes not moving from the television. While he and Eleanor were both teenagers, she, for the most part, was sweet and malleable. Brent had entered the black hole of teendom and had donned the robes of disrespect, sullenness and insolence. His mother, young enough to remember those difficult years, tolerated it for the most part. His father, who was raised on a farm and was worked too hard to indulge the deep feelings of a teenager, reacted with discipline and yelling. Sometimes their battles progressed to the point where Connie thought Mitch was actually going back in time and becoming a fourteen-year-old himself.

A timid knock sounded on the door.

"Open the door please, Brent," Connie said. She had reached over and grabbed her Monet bag and was fishing for a notebook and pen. Along with her purse, she seemed to carry the Monet bag, which featured the artist's painting of lily pads, everywhere, despite the fact that the water was starting to shred at the corners and the lily pads were scuffed and frayed.

"Make Eleanor do it. She's not doing anything," Brent said as he restuffed the pillows under his head.

"I'm doing my nails," Eleanor said.

"Brent, please open the door," Connie asked again, more firmly. "Now."

"Fine!" he said as he jerked from the bed and stomped to the door. "You know I didn't want to come on this stupid trip anyway and now I have to do everything. I should have stayed home with Dad." The quiet knock sounded again just as Brent threw open the door. Without uttering a word of acknowledgement to the meek little woman standing before him, he turned and flopped back on the bed.

"Can I come in? Am I interrupting? Am I here too early?"

Miranda Ames is way too shy for this family, Connie thought to herself as she watched the tiny woman's eyes dart from mother to son and back to mother. Sometimes it was hard for Connie to imagine her brother, a successful athlete and scholar in high school who was very popular, settling on this gentle brown bird of a woman. In high school and college he could have had his pick of any one of a number of eligible females, and when he brought Miranda home to meet the family it surprised everyone. Nora, at dinner that night, had decided it was a joke and laughed rudely. Miranda seemed to fold into herself and never really came back out. Now she was alternately wringing her hands and running her thin bony fingers through her mouse-colored hair. Her eyes were the color of milk chocolate and wavered in a sort of suppressed fear. She looked as if she wanted to dart back out the door.

"I apologize for my rude son," Connie said. Turning to Brent she said, "Please turn off the television. You can either sit here and listen to the plans or you can turn off the TV and go in and take a shower. Whichever you do, I expect it to be done quietly and with respect." Brent grabbed the in-room magazine which detailed the wonders—not many of them, he thought sneeringly—of Danford and northwest Montana. He opened the glossy pages and put it up as a shield between himself and his mother. Connie sighed and turned to her sister-in-law brightly.

"Miranda, come and sit at the table. I am so excited! Is Dan on his way?" Miranda perched at the edge of one of the four black faux-leather club chairs.

"He was in the bathroom but said he'd be right over. I left your door open so he can just come in. Connie, I have to tell you we've called our half of the restaurant yellow pages and there's nothing. I don't know what we're going to do." Miranda was a highly organized woman with keen sensitivity bordering on fluttering nervousness. She was visibly upset at the thought of ten family members gathered for a birthday bash that wasn't going to happen because there was no restaurant in which to have it.

Connie patted her hand. "Well, I have some good news," she said, "but we'll wait until Dan and the rest get here." She was grinning from ear to ear. Miranda pulled her hand away and looked at her with suspicious alarm. She knew her sister-in-law well enough to know that she might revert to something stupid and idiotic, like renting the party room at McDonalds and making everyone wear hats and blow up balloons and play Pin the Tail on the Donkey.

"She's got us a castle with a turret, whatever that is," Donny spouted.

"Oh, isn't that nice. A castle? Really?" Miranda said quietly. Her worry increased.

"Don't tell! We want to surprise them," Connie admonished gently.

Just then a ruckus started at the motel door. Dan O'Reilly was a giant of a man with a heart and a laugh just as big. He was a practical joker, a dishwater-blond, curly-haired teddy bear of a man who gained the love of everyone he encountered.

"Little Pig, Little Pig, let me come in!" he growled loudly from the hall as he jiggled the knob and pounded the door wildly. Miranda jumped to her feet and rushed to the door, flickering her hands on the way.

Opening it quickly, but carefully, because she was a careful person, she looked up and down the halls past her husband. "Shhh! Dan, you'll wake up everyone," she whispered, pulling him in and shutting the door.

"It's not that late, Sweetie Pie!" he said, jovially.

"It's nearly 10 o'clock," she said, frowning.

"Not by the hair of my chinny chin chin," he said, looking at his watch. "It's 10:30!"

"Guess what, Uncle Dan," Donny said, running up and leaping into his massive arms.

"What, my little pig?" he asked, nuzzling his whiskery chin into the boy's neck.

"Ouch! That hurts! And I'm not a pig!" Donny yelped.

"Don't tell. Don't you tell him!" Connie warned.

"Don't tell me what?" Dan demanded, holding Donny out and looking him keenly in the eye.

"Will you please be quiet. I'm trying to read here," Brent barked.

Connie and Dan looked at him and back and forth at each other and burst into laughter. *He's trying to read here?* Connie mouthed, feigning shock. Her firstborn son had never been known as a reader and had whined and groaned through every reading assignment since kindergarten's picture books.

"Like that's an interesting thing to read," Dan said. "You can discover the wonders of Danford in about three pages. So, don't tell me what?" he asked, turning back to Connie. She shook her head and grinned.

He looked at Miranda. She hunched her shoulders and gave an I-don't-know shrug.

"Can't tell you," Connie teased. "We have to wait for Nora and Stuart and the rest. Is Jessie Lou coming?"

"Jessie's watching the tube," Dan said. He had plopped Donny on the bed and rifled through the plastic grocery bags of items purchased for snacking. Settling on a handful of Oreos, two long, flat slabs of jerky and a jar of peanuts, he fell into a chair at the table and plopped up his feet on the fourth chair.

"Waiting for Nora might take the rest of the weekend," he said, chucking a palm full of peanuts into his mouth. "Hey, little buddy," he said to Donny, "come over here and let's see how strong you are." The youngster shrieked and leaped to the middle of the bed.

"Donny! Get off the bed! Mom, make him get off! Now look at what you made me do. Darn it." Eleanor had finished picking off the purple polish and was in the process of brushing on a bright blue. "Darn it, Donny, you made me blob it all over!"

"Donny, get off the bed. Eleanor, why don't you do that in the bathroom. You're smelling up the whole room," Connie turned from her offspring and scrunched up her face.

Brent pushed the magazine away long enough to give a disdainful look at his mother. "She can't use the bathroom. I might take a shower."

Eleanor cast him a hateful look. "The only reason you're even thinking of taking a shower is because Mom said I should do my nails in there. Sometimes I hate you."

"Hate is such a lovely word, a family word," Dan said, pulling apart an Oreo and scraping the frosting off with his front teeth. A flicker of annoyance crossed Eleanor's face as she turned to Brent.

"I only have one finger left to polish anyway, so go ahead and take your shower."

"Nah. Changed my mind."

"So, Connie," said Dan quietly, looking carefully at his little sister. "What gives with Mitch? You two okay?"

"I guess we're as okay as any couple could be when they're

starting a new business," she said, leaning forward and resting her elbows on the table, then settling her chin on her fists. "I shouldn't complain because this rental business has really taken off and we have some major contracts with big companies. The contracts are big enough that we were able to secure loans to purchase a lot of equipment...front-end loaders, Bobcats, Uniloaders, dozers, ditch diggers, and smaller stuff. I try to help but I don't know anything about machinery. I can answer the phones and that's about it.

"To tell you the truth," she admitted, lifting her head and putting her forearms on the table, "I threw a real hissy fit when he said he couldn't come with us to Danford. I yelled and screamed and cried and made him feel like a jerk. Afterwards, I was thoroughly ashamed but you just can't take away the words you say. 'I'm sorry' just doesn't cut it sometimes. I know I hurt Mitch terribly and I was unfair. He's doing it for the kids and me and I know he misses us as much as we miss him."

"Just be patient. It'll all come together soon. You really have a great guy there, you know," Dan said. He squeezed her outstretched hand.

Connie pulled loose and patted his face. "You're a good big brother," she said as she reached for an Oreo. "I hope they get here soon. We need to make plans! Doesn't it seem like we're always waiting for Nora to get beautiful?" She pulled the cookie apart and absently handed the unfrosted half to Dan, who popped it in his mouth. Since they were children, she had given Dan the plain half of dismantled Oreos.

Chapter Twenty-Seven

Dan and Connie's sister, Nora, had inherited, from who knew where, the sophistication gene. She looked like a model and dressed like one. She spent more time on her makeup on any given morning than Connie did in a month. She spent more on her clothes in a year than Connie did in ten years. Once, Connie had dragged her to Super Savers, a discount, "gently used-a-bit" clothing store that reeked with bargains. Nora had been horrified. They were out of the store within five minutes and once back at Connie's house Nora had stripped down and showered immediately. That night, Connie overheard her shuddering version of the venture as she whisperingly related it to Stuart over the phone.

That Christmas, Connie had deliberately picked out a perfectly beautiful white lacy Super Saver blouse and had it professionally wrapped, which cost ten times more than the blouse, which sported a stapled-on blue dollar tag the day she bought it. Nora was effusive in her gratitude for the gift. Connie still chuckled at her underhanded, deliberate, deception. The only person she had ever told was Dan, who understood and appreciated the gesture and had looked questioningly at Connie a few months later when Nora flounced into a restaurant for a family dinner wearing a white blouse, black velvet skirt and antique jet jewelry. Connie nodded her head ever so subtly and Dan had admirably praised a glowing Nora on her good taste in clothes.

Unlike Miranda and Dan, Nora and Stuart were soul mates and they should have been the siblings. Stuart seemed almost as fashionable as Nora. When he wasn't wearing a lawyerly suit he layered casual clothes: khaki pants with a checked shirt and a sweater sportily draped over his shoulders. Stuart and Nora were the darlings of their country club and God, in a bit of wisdom, had decided not to bless them with children. Connie had mixed feelings about this. On the one hand, it was good since neither of them would have been able to handle the delivery room, let alone a stinking baby diaper. On the other hand a kid throwing up in their all-white living room would have made Connie's day. Nora and Stuart seemed to look down their professionally sculpted noses at the rest of the family, especially Connie's boys, who were normally dingy with boyhood grime.

Connie was wishing for the tenth time that Nora and Stuart would hurry up and get there when the authoritative knock came at the door. Connie strode to the door and opened it.

Stuart and Nora Whitcomb looked like the Bobbsey Twins, all decked out in tan slacks, similar plaid shirts and red sweaters. Nora's hair, as usual, was hanging in frosted blond perfection and her ears glistened with diamonds. Nora didn't go out much without her diamonds.

She strode in majestically, Stuart following like an obedient puppy.

"Come in! We need to plan," Connie said, holding the door open for the pair. Dan moved his stocking feet from where they were sprawled on a chair and stood up. He pulled the table to the end of the bed, so one of the five party planners could sit at the edge. Stuart and Nora, paying no heed to who had previously laid claim to the comfortable chairs, promptly sat down in two of them. Nora pushed the jar of peanuts away in distaste.

"Do you have any Perrier?" she asked, turning to Connie.

Connie moved to the front of the mini refrigerator and kneeled. She began digging through sacks of food and bottles of drink.

"We have…let's see. Lukewarm grape soda, orange soda or root beer. No water. Sorry.

"I'll have a grape," Dan said.

"Hmph," said Nora with a raised eyebrow. She turned to Stuart and patted his leg. "Stuart, would you be a dear and go back to our room and grab a Perrier for me?"

Stuart dutifully got up and went to do her bidding. "Bring back the tray of hors d'oeuvres Rose packed, too," she said after him. Rose was their housekeeper and cook and had looked after their quirky needs for years. It was just like Nora to have her prepare a tray of hors d'oeuvres to bring on the plane.

Nora turned to Connie. "You know, Connie, a body needs water. You can't live on grape soda alone. How can your bowels work properly on grape soda?

"My bowels work fine," she said. "Dan, how're yours working?" Without waiting for a reply Connie called after Stuart, who was just headed out the door. "And hurry up Stuart! I'm about to burst with news here, if anyone has noticed. And you," she added, pointing a finger at Donny, "you keep your cute little mouth shut."

"You know there isn't any place in this town to hold the party," Nora said. "I told you it was an insane idea to try and hold anything in Danford. We should have just rented a small ballroom at the Wakefield in Chicago and called it good. But no. You two insist on traipsing all over the country to this dinky little nothing town. When I left here twenty-two years ago I vowed I'd never come back.

"And yet here I am," she added merrily. "And what a joy it has been."

"Is your room as nice as ours is?" Donny piped up, just as Stuart tapped on the door.

"Let Stuart in, Brent," Connie ordered.

"Why do I always have to be the doorman?" he grumbled

as he crawled off the bed. "I don't know why we don't just prop it open. Better yet. I have a great idea. Why don't you all just go out in the hall?"

"Don't get smart," his mother replied.

"We have a new room," Nora said, answering Donny's question just as Stuart placed the silver tray of hors d'oeuvres in the middle of the table. As Nora's words sunk in he stared at Connie and shook his head almost imperceptibly.

"I saw that, Stuart," Nora said. "Why shouldn't we be honest here?" Leaning toward Donny, she said fiercely and deliberately: "Let me tell you about our room. Well, first let's just talk about the overall disgust of this dismal, disgusting flea-bitten motel."

"I think it's nice," Donny said quietly. "The bedspreads are all slippery and the beds are humongous and there is soap and shampoo and shoe polisher things in the bathroom. Plus, it has movies on the TV and video games if you want to play."

"I suppose some people would consider this quite plush, but once you've stayed in a Hyatt Regency or the Fairmont or the Kensington in London you get a little spoiled. Maybe someday when you grow up you will be able to stay at one of the better hotels."

Connie was angry. Miranda looked bleak and upset. Dan was amused. Eleanor had stopped painting her nails and was staring. Donny looked threatened. Brent, oblivious to the world, continued hiding inside the covers of the magazine.

"You can be the most intolerant person," Connie sputtered. "I don't know how you ever came to be in this family. There is nothing wrong with this motel and you know it. The rooms are tidy and clean. The place is only four years old, for crying out loud."

Nora lifted her chin and pursed her lips in defensive arrogance. "Your room may be clean but ours wasn't."

"Ohhhh. Did you find a piece of lint on the floor? Was a magazine out of place? Did the pillowcase have a wrinkle?" Connie teased snidely.

"There was a hair in the bathtub," Nora declared, staring at her in defiance. Stuart rolled his eyes. The rest of the room broke into laughter.

"A hair in the bathtub?" Dan hooted.

Connie was shocked. "You made them change your room because of a hair in the bathtub?" she said in a hushed voice. "Why didn't you just wash it down the drain?"

"What's going on?" Brent asked, peeking over the top of the magazine. Everyone ignored him.

Dan and Connie looked at each other in disbelief and started howling.

"I don't think it's funny," Nora said. "Stop laughing or I'm leaving."

"What's going on?" Brent asked again.

"You had to have been here," Eleanor told him as she went back to her nail polish.

"You people are all crazy," he muttered.

"It isn't funny. And I am not arrogant and pompous," Nora said.

"So, what did the front desk people say when you called them and said there was a hair in the bathtub?" Connie asked. Nora shook her head.

"Oh just forget it. I don't want to talk about it anymore."

"Well, if I was them I'd be terrified word will get out and the health authorities will pay a visit to this place. I'd be getting me a lawyer, if I was them," Dan said with mock indignation as he reached for a smoked oyster and miniscule slice of Gruyere cheese from the tray.

"I said I don't want to talk about it anymore," Nora declared loudly.

"OK, then, let's get back to business," Connie said, impatient to tell her news. "It's late and I'm dying to tell you all something. You sure Jessie Lou's not coming over?" she asked, turning to Miranda. Jessie Lou was their sixteen-year-old daughter, who took after Dan in build and looks and, on the surface, seemed to have gotten Miranda's vanilla personality. To those who first met her, Jessie Lou was a big, quiet, mild girl who seemed to be hovering on the fringes of life. In actuality, once she got over her shyness, she was smart, funny, and quick-witted.

"She's staying with Papa O'Reilly. They're watching a John Wayne movie," Miranda said softly. Her voice was like thistledown. Sometimes you had to lean close to her to catch it before it floated off. Tonight it seemed to be an almost insurmountable effort for her to talk. Being in the middle of the whole family was overwhelming and disturbing to her—especially being around Nora and Stuart. Connie knew Dan had ordered her to take part in the birthday party and that Miranda would rather be in bed, reading one of her endless romance novels or in her laundry room "studio" painting a pallid, pastel scene in watercolors.

Somehow Brent had caught what Miranda said and tossed aside the magazine. "A John Wayne movie! Awesome! Can I go over there and get out of this madhouse?" Brent asked his mother.

"Go. Go!" Connie told him, "But you come back as soon as Dan and Miranda get back there. I don't want you up watching movies all night long.

"Now," she said, turning to the others, "I know some of you"—she looked pointedly at Nora—"thought it was crazy bringing Daddy here for his eightieth birthday, but I thought it was a great idea. This may be the last wonderful thing we will be able to do for him."

"Tell them about the moat," Donny said, yanking on her sleeve.

"There isn't a moat," she said to him as she hauled him on her lap. He was a gangly boy and his bony legs flopped awkwardly over her legs.

"But it is a castle, isn't it Mommy?"

"What castle?" Dan asked.

Connie grinned, her face glowing with the secret she was holding tight to.

Chapter Twenty-Eight

Connie kept them waiting in suspense for just a few seconds, relishing the full attention she got from everyone.

"Stuart and Miranda, you won't know anything about this but Nora and Dan will. Do you remember O'Malley House?"

"Who wouldn't remember O'Malley House?" Dan said.

"I used to dream I would grow up and live there," Nora admitted. Turning to Stuart she said, "It is the most gorgeous mansion you have ever seen. It is quite an anomaly for Montana and would look better in Upstate New York or someplace civilized. It was built well over a hundred years ago by a lumber baron."

Nora turned back to Connie. "So, what does O'Malley House have to do with anything?"

"You won't believe this," Connie said, relating how she happened to have a conversation with Katherine. "To make a long story short. Are you ready? We're having Daddy's birthday party at O'Malley House." Connie sat back and beamed triumphantly.

"What?" Dan was flabbergasted.

"I don't believe this!" Nora said, her eyes wide. "We get to go inside O'Malley House?"

"But wait! That's not all," Connie gloated dramatically. "Mrs. O'Malley is arranging for us to have dinner and be entertained. Oh, she's a wonderful, warm and friendly woman. I can't wait to meet her in person."

"Stuart!" Nora said in wonder, "we get to go to O'Malley House. Oh, I feel sick. I think I'm going to be sick."

"You look white as a sheet," Connie said, peering at her little sister closely. "Are you okay?"

"I think it's the excitement," Nora said.

"So, tell the rest," Dan demanded.

"There is no rest. That's it. We're supposed to be there at 7 p.m. Saturday night for dinner and a birthday party."

"Is this castle really that wonderful?" Eleanor asked. She had finished her fingernails and had pulled a knee to her chest and was painting her toenails. Her tawny hair fell in long straight sheets on either side of her petite face.

"You won't believe it," Dan said. "All our childhood we walked by it and dreamed of going inside. One Christmas it was opened to the public and the O'Malleys served cookies and hot cider. Your Mom had brought home the measles and she and Nora were in bed so we couldn't go. Our mama said there would be other years, but there weren't."

Connie jumped up and grabbed the visitor guide magazine from where Brent had thrown it and was riffling through the pages. "Here it is!" she exclaimed. "Look!"

The full color photo of O'Malley House took up nearly half the page. The soft early morning light captured the beauty of the old mansion. It was a huge edifice crafted of Montana rock and wood that had weathered until it looked as if it had grown up with the trees and mountains. A small black and white photo taken the year it was built was on the bottom of the page and showed the house surrounded by small, newly-planted trees and shrubs and nothing behind or beside it. It looked enormous and almost naked.

Turning the magazine back around, she said, "Listen to this: 'O'Malley House, while not open to the public, is the most extravagant and elegant of the Victorian homes in Montana and rivals the famous Conrad Mansion in Kalispell and the Whitmore Mansion, which is also in Danford. Built in 1895 by Franklin Eldridge O'Malley and his wife Beatrice Livingston O'Malley, it is a combination of styles to include Queen Anne and Stick, but is basically High Victorian in style and ornamentation. The two turreted corners add a castle-like look to the massive three-story private residence, while the broad veranda in front and sun room off the back give it an old Southern look. The mansion contains twelve bedrooms, three of them suites, an indoor fernery, billiard room, ballroom, nursery, laundry room, maid's quarters, and furniture that has been in the Livingston and O'Malley family for generations. O'Malley House is a landmark of High Victorian architecture, furniture, wallpapers, ceramics and stenciling. The home boasts the two original toilette rooms, on the second and third floors. A small fire in the early 1940s resulted in a minor remodel of the first floor that included updating the kitchen area and adding two spacious bathrooms. Wiring was updated for the second time in 1987.

" 'Franklin and Beatrice O'Malley had only one child, a son, Edward, who married a local girl, Sophia Bradley, in 1925 and brought his new bride to reside with him and his parents in O'Malley House. The couple had three children, one who died in childbirth and one who succumbed to pneumonia at an early age. The surviving child, John, resided in the house until his death in 1995. John and his wife, Katherine, had no children.

" 'O'Malley House is currently owned and maintained by Katherine O'Malley, who is well-known and much loved by the people of Danford. A philanthropist who is recognized for her charity and compassion, she and her husband in the early days hosted many extravagant parties and soirées, including a Christmas open house for the people of Danford.

" 'The original O'Malley ancestors, who were successful businessmen in Ohio, came to northwest Montana in the mid-1870s and added to their wealth through lumber and cattle and, later, holdings in the Great Northern Railroad. O'Malley Lumber Company, under the broad umbrella of OM Holding Company, is one of the largest enterprises in the valley and ships lumber all over the northwest and overseas.

" 'While the immediate grounds surrounding O'Malley House still boast over twelve acres, much of the adjacent land was sold off over time; it is said because gregarious Sophia O'Malley yearned for neighbors. There are many outbuildings on the grounds, including the carriage house, a barn, the stables (which still hold a few horses), and, near the mansion, an enchanting six-room caretaker's cottage that was built in 1924 and is in the same style as main house.

" 'In the early days, O'Malley greenhouses and the two-acre summer garden provided green and flowering plants and cut flowers to local churches and medical facilities as well as gifts for delighted residents. In its heyday, O'Malley House generated dozens of jobs for locals, to include grooms for the horses and employees to work in the gardens as well as the house.' "

Looking up from the magazine, Connie was wide-eyed, "And we get to go there for dinner!" she said. "Can you believe it?"

"I didn't have any idea the house had all that," Dan said.

"What do you suppose Daddy will say?" Nora asked softly, as if speaking to herself.

"I think he's going to be shocked," Connie said.

"One time when Dad and I were driving home in the winter we slid into the ditch right by the mansion," Dan said. "The snow was really deep that year. I must have been about Donny's age. Dad got out the shovel and started shoveling snow while I sat in the car and watched. The mansion was all decorated for Christmas with greenery all up and down the pillars and candle lights in every window. It looked like something from a fairy tale. There was a big red bow on the door. After about ten minutes of digging and trying to drive the car out, we were more stuck than ever. I looked up and here came Mr. O'Malley and that groundskeeper man who has lived there since the beginning of time. What was his name? Quent or something."

"Simeon Quest," Connie offered, and then gave a puzzled frown. "How did I ever remember that?"

"Right," continued Dan, "Simeon Quest. Mr. O'Malley was walking and Mr. Quest was on a big old John Deere tractor. 'Havin' some trouble?' Mr. O'Malley asked Dad. Dad said 'Yup, guess so,' They hooked a chain to the bumper of the car and pulled us out lickety split. Mr. O'Malley invited us into the house to warm up but Daddy said we needed to get on home to dinner. I always wished he'd said yes. But we had to get on home to dinner."

"I think we all have O'Malley House stories," Nora said. "I remember once in high school when a bunch of us decided we'd sneak down the driveway and look through the windows. Manny Selma was with us—remember him? Geeky guy with a giggle loud enough to raise the dead? Wore glasses with those big black frames? Anyway, we got closer and closer and just when we were about there Manny started to giggle. He always giggled when he was nervous. Then all the porch lights came on, and we ran like demons were chasing us."

"I told Mrs. O'Malley about my daydreams about living there when I talked to her tonight. I told her I always dreamed the turret room was mine," Connie said. "She said I should have just come right to the front door and asked to see it. The funny thing is, I believe if we had just done that—asked to see the house—she would have showed us. I can't wait for you to talk to her. What a grand person she is." She looked closely at Nora.

"You don't look much better. Do you want something to drink?"

"No, I'm fine."

Connie frowned and then changed the subject by asking Nora what she planned to wear to the party.

Chapter Twenty-Nine

Before he reached the motel door Brent could hear John Wayne's drawl. *I'll ask you one more time, Mister, and then you'll have to start answerin' to me or to your maker. It's your choice.* Brent knocked on the door. He could hear Jessie Lou lumbering across the room. She slid the chains off the latch, clicked off the lock and opened the door. "Oh, hey," she said, stepping aside and looking back at the TV. Brent followed her into the room.

"Why do you keep it all locked up and then just open it to anyone who knocks?" Brent asked as he sprawled next to his grandfather, who was propped up against the headboard. "I could be Jack the Ripper."

"Grandpa'd protect me. Wouldn't you Grandpa?"

"What?" Patrick O'Reilly reluctantly turned his eyes from the movie. The old man looked tired tonight, Brent thought, and his fine white hair was sort of messed up and his clothes were all wrinkled from lying on the bed. Brent looked at him and spoke loudly.

"I asked Jessie Lou why she locks up the door and then just opens it to anyone. I said I could be Jack the Ripper."

"And I said you'd protect me," said Jessie Lou, smiling shyly. She and her grandfather had a special bond, especially since Grandpa had moved into the tiny basement apartment in their house a year before.

His eyes twinkled. "I'd give him the old one-two. Knock him clear to kingdom come," Patrick said. "I don't remember this one at all. Thought I'd seen all the John Wayne movies but I don't remember this one. Old John sure does look young, doesn't he?" No one answered. Jessie Lou tossed Brent a half-empty family-sized bag of M&Ms.

"Thanks. You got anything to drink?"

"Diet Pepsi in the fridge," she said, and watched as he scooted off the bed. Holding up a cold can, he cleared his voice.

"Want one, Gramps?"

"Nope. Had enough junk food for one day." The movie had faded to a commercial. Patrick gave his attention to his oldest grandson and motioned him to mute the remote. Brent pushed the button and the room fell silent.

"So, what's happening with the birthday party?" Patrick asked.

"They're all over there talking now. Sorry, but I think maybe it's going to be Big Macs and fries. Just joking. But there's nothing much in this town and there's all sorts of proms and stuff going on but I think they found a place." Brent raised his head, lifted the bag of M&Ms six inches from his mouth and poured. The candy gave a soft clatter as it tumbled against his teeth. Brent was a handsome boy, with a mass of brown hair glinting with gold highlights. In the past year his pudginess had turned to muscle and he seemed to be put together with carved and sculpted angles. He was an athlete who, to his father's consternation, made mediocre grades—just high enough to keep his spot on the bench in football, basketball and lacrosse.

"It's changed some but much of Danford's the same as it was eighty years ago," Patrick O'Reilly said. "The old Town Hall's the same and the big clock in front of the bank building. Shame they took down all the old fancy streetlights and put up them ugly modern ones. Same with the Masonic Temple. Covered the whole dang front of it with those ugly sheets of plaster or something. Used to be really fancy. The odd thing is that there are lots of new buildings on Main Street and I can't remember what used to be there before. It's driving me crazy. The old Clack Service Station, for instance. Now it's a credit union. But the credit union building is twice as big as the service station was. What was on that lot next door to it? Wish I had a book to show me the way it used to be."

"Maybe the library would have one," Jessie Lou said. Jesse Lou was an advocate of libraries. She felt quiet joy when she was enveloped in the quiet atmosphere and surrounded by books. She loved books. When she grew up she was going to be a writer. She'd already had a poem published in the Letters to the Editor section of the Spokesman Review.

"Mom said maybe tomorrow we should go to the cemetery and visit the family graves. What do you think?" Brent asked, looking at his grandfather closely.

"Hmph. Maybe. It's been a long time since I've been there. Haven't seen my Edna's grave in over fifteen years. Sometimes it's hard to believe she's been dead for over twenty years. My folks are buried there, and my O'Reilly grandfather. Lots of friends. My grandmother died before they moved to Montana from the Dakotas. Last time I went to the Danford Cemetery was when my brother Frank died. Back in 1994. No, must have been 1995."

Brent twisted the top of the candy bag and tossed it to Jessie Lou. She opened it and poured a handful of M&Ms in her hand and carefully arranged them in rows before popping them, one by one, into her mouth. She tossed the last one to Brent, who tried to catch it in his mouth and missed.

"If he died in 1995 and Grandma O'Reilly has been dead over twenty years, that doesn't make sense," he said as he crawled under his chair to fetch it.

A look of regret and guilt passed the old man's whiskery face. "I didn't visit her grave after Frank's funeral," he said. "I don't know why. I was upset about Frank's passing and I walked away from the graveside and got in my car and drove off. I called the florist once I got home and had them put roses on her grave. I guess I just know she isn't there. She's still alive and up in heaven and waiting for me."

"That's sort of sad but sort of wonderful, Grampa," Jessie said, looking at Brent and imploring with her eyes that he say something to ease the delicate moment.

"You really believe that?" Brent asked bluntly. His grandfather cast him a quick look.

"Of course I believe it. Every bit of it.," he said.

Chapter Thirty

After settling on the time, 7 p.m., and agreeing to turn her home into an impromptu "restaurant," Katherine fell limply back into her armchair and stared wildly around her. What on earth have I gone and gotten myself into? she asked herself. Why, I don't even know these people. Oh, Lord, what have I done! I should call her back but I don't even know what motel she is in. Oh, Lord!

Jumping from her chair she dashed to the library and opened the top drawer of John's old secretary and pulled out a tablet and pen. Settling into his big leather chair, she reached for her wire-rimmed glasses and pulled them on. She looked like a frazzled schoolmarm, her mostly-white with an aura of reddish frizz framing her face, and complementing a khaki-colored linen pantsuit and sensible, though chic, shoes.

She sat and nibbled on the pen while thinking out the menu. Something simple, she thought. Good, hearty food that an eighty-year-old would enjoy. None of those fancy lattes or quiches. Roast beef, potatoes mashed with lots of butter and sour cream, brown sugared carrots with a sprinkle of mint, a green salad with her own special dressing and maybe a salad of fresh fruit. Crab or shrimp cocktail to start, maybe. Homemade rolls and home brewed coffee. Dessert, of course, would be cake but not just ordinary cake. Something special. Something lovely to look at and delicious to taste.

"No, maybe it's too plain of fare," she muttered to herself. "Maybe something a bit more exciting. Ham. Maybe ham. No, not ham. That's too Eastery. What AM I doing? This is insane. This is madness. I haven't entertained since, what...the early '90s? Since John's funeral when all those weeping people took over the house and sent me running all over looking for Kleenex? I was the widow and here I was traipsing around wiping up tears and patting arms as grown men snorted into hankies. You couldn't really call a funeral gathering 'entertaining,' but was it that long ago? Who do I call? Oh, Letty, I hope you're home and not off bowling or reading poetry in a coffee house or something."

Putting on her reading glasses, she reached for the phone and slowly dialed a number.

While Katherine waited for the phone call to go through she took stock of herself. Her heart was pounding and she hadn't felt so vibrant...so alive in years. When the phone on the other end was picked up she held her breath for a scant second before letting it out in a whoosh.

"Hey," said the bright familiar voice over the blast of some atrocious television music. Letty could recount amazing details on the lives and activities of countless television characters. For six months Katherine had thought the Biedeck clan, with their marriages and divorces and affairs and endless fighting, were Letty's family. It wasn't until one luckless soul named Myrna was kidnapped and held for six months in a tank submerged in the Mediterranean that she got suspicious. That and the fact that Lillian Dip also knew a lot about the Biedecks. Letty had slipped off her kitchen chair and rolled on the floor with laughter when she found out that Katherine thought the zany Biedecks were relatives.

"Oh, Letty, my goodness I was so busy here thinking I didn't realize the time. Please forgive me. I will call you back in the morning."

"Mrs. O? That you? I wasn't asleep. Just studying for an exam. What's up?'" Katherine chuckled and thought the sound came across as a little hysterical.

"The oddest thing has happened. I don't know where to begin." She related her conversation with Connie. "So, it seems that I'm hosting this big birthday party," she finished.

"No way! That's awesome! When?"

"In two nights. Which is why I called. I desperately need your help."

"Mrs. O, don't waste another word over the phone. I'll be there in a flash." Letty slammed down the phone so hard it bounced back up. "Dang!" she said, and slammed it down again. On her end, Katherine carefully replaced the heavy white and gold receiver and rubbed her ear, which still rang from Letty's enthusiastic hang-up.

Ten minutes later Katherine could hear Letty approaching the house. She always had a five-minute reprieve to get mentally ready for the girl, since she drove that belching, coughing old Mercury Comet that spewed a thin trail of blue smoke with every mile and left a hearty cloud at every stoplight. The car rattled and shook and roared with each gear change. Two blocks before reaching the O'Malley drive, Letty geared down to second, which made the poor vehicle growl piteously until it shuddered and sputtered to a stop.

When she was first hired, Katherine politely told Letty she could park the car out of sight around back. Then she caught a glimpse of whispered curtains next door and knew Marge was snooping again. Marching through the house, and through the kitchen to the back veranda, she told Letty she changed her mind and assigned her a privileged parking space as close to the busybody's house as she could get without infringing on her property. In fact, when the car's tail lights needed repainting, Katherine donned her gardening shirt and set to work with the nail polish brush, knowing full well that Marge was staring, thin-lipped and disapproving, from a shrouded window next door.

Now Katherine was so familiar with the old Mercury Comet's vocabulary she had actually become rather fond of it. She listened as the brakes squealed like tortured swine all the way up the driveway and then stopped. A second later the car door opened with a groan and then shut with a crash. Katherine could envision Letty unfolding herself from the old beater and emerging from its cocoon like some sort of strange butterfly.

Tall and gangly, Letty always seemed surprised at the arms and legs she'd been given. She always thought God had made a mistake. She was meant to be petite and compact with tiny bones and a diminutive, gently sloped nose. Instead she was six feet, one inch tall, wore size eleven shoes, and her arms and legs seemed to be out of control. She knocked into furniture and tripped over curbs and bumped into people on sidewalks. In bed, her feet hung over the edge, and coats and jackets were never long enough to cover her wrists.

She had weighed eleven pounds, two ounces at birth. Lorene, her diminutive mother, who stood barely four-feet eleven inches tall in stocking feet, had writhed in pain, she claimed, for sixty two and a half hours before her doctor finally gave in and performed a Caesarian section. Letty still held the record for the largest baby born in Danford.

Despite her shaky beginnings, Letty had turned into a delightful adult. She was even beautiful, in her own way, with her long silky hair and violet eyes. A warm-hearted, giving person who could befriend anyone from any walk of life, she had scores of friends. In her own way, Lorene was proud of her Amazon daughter, primarily her ability to attract and keep friends, since Lorene had no real friends. Everyone loved Letty, and Letty loved everyone in return.

In school she was the child everyone wanted to be with. She was friendly, helpful, compassionate, caring, full of heartfelt advice, giving, and, best of all, she wasn't competition. In high school none of her friends had to worry about their boyfriends being swept off their feet by Letty, despite her charms and the latent beauty that was slowly emerging but wouldn't be truly manifested until she was in her mid-twenties. To males and females alike, Letty was just Letty. Two years in a row she was elected Homecoming Queen, not because of her looks, but because she was beloved. In a way she was the mascot of Danville High.

Letty thrived on abnormal. If long hair was "in" she had hers clipped to the scalp. She might dress in a Jackie Kennedy sheath and pumps one day and a gypsy skirt, bandana and hoop earrings the next. Letty had the grand height and build to pull either of them off, a fact that was unnoticed by her peers, who embraced emaciated, petite, wispy females with tittering voices and brainless heads covered with perfect hair.

Like many of her classmates, Letty stayed in Danford and attended junior college. Like them, she was trying to figure out what she was going to do with life. So far, all she had discovered was that she might never know. She might muddle right through to the end and never figure it out. In a way, she sort of embraced that idea. She was an artsy girl who played trombone in the band and was gifted at collage and oil painting. She had a flair for the unusual and was confident enough to dress and act the way she wanted. And what she wanted was to live a sort of bohemian lifestyle, dressing in quirky clothes, embracing art and music and languages, and being abnormal.

At least that was what she'd always thought. But now she was organizing the Danford senior citizens, and she realized she loved what she was doing. She truly enjoyed helping others.

The summer she was a senior in high school Letty went to work helping Katherine O'Malley, at first washing windows on the outside and doing housecleaning and heavy work Katherine was unable to do. She continued after starting college and now worked her class schedule carefully around her O'Malley schedule. She was twenty-two-years-old and was excited about life and the future.

Chapter Thirty-One

Letty Vanesse cared deeply for Katherine O'Malley and, right now, was eager to find out what was going on. A restaurant? Is that really what she said?

Letty sprinted up the broad mansion steps and threw open the ancient ornate door. She slammed it shut behind her and the tiny beveled stained glass panes protested with chiming rings. Pulling herself to her full height, Letty pulled a heavy tattered white cable knit sweater over her head, revealing a skimpy T-shirt and a tiny gold ring in her navel. Black sweat pants hung low on her hips and she hiked them up as she tossed off the sandals from her long feet. A fringe of thick blond hair, saturated with static electricity from the sweater pulled over it, floated in a halo around her head. She flung the sweater toward the door that still seemed to be shuddering from her arrival. The sweater slid across the gleaming rosewood floor and piled against the door. It looked, oddly, like a dead dog that had just happened to end its life right there.

In a dozen steps Letty had crossed the huge foyer and reached the broad steps that led into the grandly furnished great room. Although there were many cozier rooms in the house, Katherine O'Malley preferred a quiet corner of the great room that was one of two turrets—large rounded outcroppings off the outside wall. Floor to ceiling windows—dozens of them—looked over the perennial garden and a small pond. One of the rounded turret rooms housed a glossy black grand piano, but her quiet nook was furnished beautifully with settees and chairs in soft roses and greens. From her lair she could look over the expanse of the great room, taking pleasure in the ancient oriental carpets held down by clusters of white overstuffed couches and chairs and the massive fireplace that, for the season, was banked with flowers.

"OK, Mrs. O, tell all," Letty demanded as she pulled a chair close to her employer and plopped down. Arms on her knees and chapped hands clasped so tightly her fingertips turned white, she leaned forward in anticipation. A tarnished gold heart pendant swayed in time to the tick-tock of the grandfather clock. Despite her beginnings, and the fact that her father had channeled her largeness into sports, which she wasn't good at because of her clumsiness, Letty had actually turned out to be a young woman of substance and strong feelings of self-worth. She might trip over a piece of lint, but she did it with a sort of grace and, always, with a sense of humor. Tonight, unlike herself, Letty sat quietly, expectantly.

Katherine related the odd phone call and subsequent invitation down to the tiniest detail. Twice during the telling she bopped up from her chair and trod nervously on the thick carpet. Watching her, Letty's eyes twinkled in delight and she pursed her lips to keep from grinning like an ape.

Truthfully, she had been increasingly anxious about the welfare of Katherine O'Malley. Over the months the elderly woman had seemed to lose her zest for life and only seemed to perk up when blabbermouth Marge next door did something to irk her. Letty would never admit it, but a few of the things that were attributed to Marge were actually perpetrated by Letty herself. Just last week Letty told Katherine that she had seen Marge frowning at the rock work. Maybe, she thought, Marge was thinking the rock work on Katherine's house needed a good cleaning.

Katherine had fumed and stomped and muttered under her breath for two days. But while she was stomping and fuming and muttering, she was also baking furiously. Every afternoon she and Letty loaded up the Lincoln with cakes and cookies and rolls and donuts and took them to the Rescue Mission. Walking briskly, she helped haul them inside and, at least twice, stopped to say a few words with the curious lounging men who wondered what such a stately older woman was doing at the Mission.

The Katherine O'Malley pacing before Letty tonight was someone new who fairly vibrated with excitement and energy. Letty imagined it was the Katherine O'Malley of the past and she could see why she had been the toast of Danford as a young woman, why she had been sought-after and treasured after her marriage to John O'Malley and why she was still revered and loved by so many hundreds of friends and admirers.

As Letty watched, Katherine's past beauty shone through, dimming the etched and wrinkled face and changing the gray of age to the peachy glow of youth. Letty shook her head as the two visions, one old and frail and one young and strong, twined and mingled and merged. The tale of the phone call ended and Katherine, again, was struck with what she had gotten herself into. Her eyes widened, giving her the look of a startled rabbit and she shook her head.

"Gracious me, Letty, there is so much to do! I don't even know what kind of cake to make and surely we need to call the florist and the silver probably needs polished, and what about entertainment. Great Heavens, what about entertainment? What have I gotten myself into?" Katherine declared as she wound up to a finish.

She sank into her chair and stared at Letty, waiting for her thoughts. The girl, however, seemed to be falling apart. Head down, she was shaking slightly, her back sort of convulsing.

Oddly, it reminded her of Letty's car. Katherine felt a shiver of alarm.

"Letty? Are you all right?" she asked, touching the girl's arm. Letty grabbed the small hand and lifted her head. Her laughter spilled out and cascaded in rich peals of utter delight.

"Mrs. O, things like this don't even happen on TV. Some woman in a hotel room dials the phone wrong, and the next thing you know we're having a big birthday bash for some old codger. This is funnier than the lap swimmer. This is funnier than the dog pound episode!"

Katherine failed to find the humor or the similarity.

"Letty, this is serious and I need your help," she said. She hated it when Letty brought up things like the pound and the swimmer. How was she to know that when she pledged two dollars a lap for the kid on the swim team the scrawny youngster would swim 342 laps? And when the local pound put that tear-jerking plea on the television and paraded all those sad dogs, what normal person could resist? Admittedly that dog incident was a disaster that still caused her to shudder. Four wild pound mutts in the house were a nightmare and after Letty helped her find them all good homes she had to call a professional cleaning team to mop up.

Chapter Thirty-Two

After a period of hearty laughter, during which Katherine joined in, Letty sat up and scooted herself to the edge of the chair.

"OK, serious time," she said, wiping tears of mirth from the corners of her eyes. She stood up and grabbed the pad and pen next to Katherine. Frowning in thought, she went over the menu Katherine had carefully written.

Katherine broke the silence. "No, Letty, we are not having cheeseburgers and curly fries and canned spaghetti. Or ordering pizza. And we're not shoving a candle into a Twinkie and calling it a birthday cake."

"Oh, you have no appreciation for the good things in life," Letty protested. "Actually, I think the menu is fine. Simple. It's the kind of food an old fellow would like. But I think we should add something really wild, something exotic, something that would make these people say 'Wow!' Something like fried goat ears or something. Also, birthday cake is okay but boring. You make the most awesome apple pie in the whole county, Mrs. O. Think you could find the time to whip up a couple?"

Katherine considered Letty's assessment and decided the girl had surprisingly good ideas. "Something exotic and apple pie...I think you're right. I haven't met a man in my life who didn't like apple pie," she said as her mind whirled with ideas for the added dish.

"The house is always spotless, thanks to me and the Merry Maid Service, of course," Letty continued with a grin, "but fresh flowers would be nice for the dining room. Lots of flowers so that runway of a table doesn't look so enormous. You know you could call that table an apartment and rent it out. And we'll drag out all your grand china and the silver and tablecloths. Do you think white damask or maybe pink, or we could even go with that green and rose plaid. And candles, lots of candles. Oh, isn't this fun!?"

"I've been thinking of calling in Maxie Bruce," Katherine said absently, drumming her fingers against her knee.

"Who's Maxie Bruce?" Letty asked and Katherine cocked her head and gave her a half-smile.

"How odd that you don't know Maxie Bruce," she said, shaking her head. "Maxie ran this house for years and is the best cook in the world. You think I make good apple pies; you should taste hers. I doubt they serve such pies in Heaven. We'll have her make the pies. Oh, we used to plan some terribly grand dinners, she and I. She's younger than me, must be all of seventy by now. I got a birthday card from her a while back. I'll call her first thing tomorrow morning and try to coax her into helping."

"Good idea. If she can't make it, I can pitch in."

"That's an awfully frightening thought. We want these people to leave healthy," Katherine joked.

"Hey, I make great macaroni and cheese. So, the food and the house are taken care of. Now we have to deal with entertainment, a small present for the birthday boy, and you."

"I don't know what you mean about 'you,' but I did think about a birthday gift and I have something perfect in mind. As for entertainment, I just don't know. Maybe just soft music from the stereo. My fingers are too stiff anymore to play the piano. I suppose we should do something to entertain. It's a party, after all. We can't just pass out Kazoos," Katherine frowned. Lifting her hand, she put the tip of her finger between her teeth.

Letty knitted her brows and thought for a few minutes before saying, "I have an idea for entertainment. Just leave it to me." Katherine felt a nudge of alarm. Letty could be a bizarre young woman.

"Letty, I will not have any voodoo hooligans or half naked tattooed, earring-wearing men pounding on drums and guitars in my house. I might be old but I know about acid rock. I think the stereo playing melodies like 'Moon River' will suffice."

Letty's bark of laughter shot through the room. Her dangling gold and silver earrings danced merrily as she threw back her head in merriment.

"Melodies? Moon River? Are you, like, serious? Moon River? Katherine O'Malley how long have you known me?

"Mmm. Two years?"

"Four years. And in all that time have I done anything crazy? Well, except for the way I dress and my car, I mean? You can't count that. I mean, like anything crazy as your assistant?"

"Not one thing. Except your idea of food is a bit strange and there was that time you put dishwashing liquid in the dishwasher and we had bubbles floating all over the kitchen, and then there was the time you sprayed all those windows with that spray vegetable oil for pans, thinking it was window cleaner, and remember when you killed all the plants when you…?" Letty waved her quiet.

"Those things don't count. I wasn't that familiar with the dishwasher and who'd of thought they'd put Crisco in a spray can? As for the plants, that was a mistake, pure and simple."

"I'm teasing. No, Letty, you have never done anything really crazy."

"Then trust me for getting entertainment. I promise you'll like it."

Katherine looked at her odd, quirky employee for a full minute, her lips pushed out in thought. Then she placed both hands on her chair and smiled.

"All right then," she said, taking a deep breath and blowing it out through puffed-out cheeks. "You are in charge of entertainment."

"Great!" Letty said, and then added, "I've been thinking and I know you're going to argue, but I feel strongly about this. You need to sit at the table with the guests. You need to be the hostess. You can't just wander around filling glasses and being a waitress. Even though you don't know these people, you need to sit at the head of the table and be in charge."

Katherine frowned. "I don't know, I think..." she started.

Letty interrupted. "You'd flutter. You know you would. You'd flutter around and make everyone nervous. If it would make you feel more comfortable, ask someone to join you as co-host.

"By the way," Letty added, "if I was you I'd hoist the flag tomorrow and let Simeon know what's happening. He'll get excited and come up here to find out what's going on if he sees a bunch of people running around the property."

"Simeon! My goodness, I need to make sure the walks are swept and the gardens are in good shape in case anyone wants to stroll the grounds. I'll hoist the flag right now so he sees it first thing tomorrow."

"No, you stay put. I'll do it," Letty said, as she took off toward the back door of the glassed-in fernery. Turning around and walking backwards, she hollered across the broad expanse of the great room, "Why don't you ask Simeon to sit beside you? You'd be the handsomest couple in Danford?"

"Simeon!? He'd rather go to the guillotine," Katherine yelled back.

Chapter Thirty-Three

The fernery, which was basically an indoor greenhouse off the great room, wasn't as grand as in the old days. The fountain still gurgled and the stream still flowed, but the tile floor, once vividly colored, was cracked and faded. Moss had settled in some of the cracks and the copper fountain had a green patina of age. The room, although still beautiful with its hundreds of tiny windows and a stained glass row across the top, held a wonderfully ornate, ancient white wicker patio set with modern, puffy, brightly-flowered cushions and an abundance of lush plants. It was one of Katherine's favorite places to sip tea in the morning. She loved the tinkle of the fountain and the fragrant steamy smell of flowers and greenery. Cages of zebra finches and cooing doves added to the idyllic peacefulness.

Letty opened the fernery's outside door and hoisted a white flag up an old brass flagpole next to the building. For decades it had been the means of summoning gardener and groundskeeper Simeon Quest to the mansion to give him additional instructions. Several times during the day Simeon turned his leathery face toward the house to see if Katherine needed him. Which she frequently did. Sometimes it was just for a donut and hot chocolate on a chilly morning, other times it was to root out a bird from the attic, or to get his advice on plantings and garden plots. Most times it was because she was lonely and just needed a chat with an old friend.

Simeon resided in the handsome caretaker's cottage not far from O'Malley House. It had been built the same time as the mansion and had been used by a succession of groundskeepers until Simeon came along and claimed the job as his for eternity. A few years before John O'Malley died, he and Katherine deeded the cottage and five acres to Simeon in gratefulness for his loyalty over the years. Simeon had fussed and fumed and ranted over "charity" and insisted on paying for the place. John and Katherine reluctantly agreed, but dedicated his monthly payments to a slush fund they used for such things as Bibles for people in Africa and to help students go on summer mission trips. They discovered there was no end to Godly causes.

The summer after Katherine and John were married, the happy couple spent many sunny weekend afternoons helping Simeon add a large room to the cottage. The three of them pounded nails and swilled lemonade and laughed. John paid for all the materials and Simeon was grateful for the contribution as well as the help. At the end, John surprised Simeon with all new kitchen appliances, and even helped haul out the old wood cook stove and the lead sink that had been there from the beginning. As they struggled to drag out the stove, a huge spider crawled out and sauntered across the top—first toward John and then toward Simeon.

"I think he's after you," John said.

"Nope, he's turning around. He thinks you're cute."

"I believe, looking close, that it's a female, and she's headed back to you," John said as he took a deep breath of air and blew the spider toward Simeon. The spider landed on Simeon's stomach.

"Kate! Get over here! We have an emergency," John yelled. Katherine scrambled from where she was painting the front door.

"Where? What?" she demanded.

"A spider. On my belly. Get him off," Simeon said.

"I don't like spiders," Katherine said, as she tried to flick him with her finger. The spider leaped on her hand and she shook it frantically, flinging it on Simeon's neck. Without thinking, she threw back her arm and with all her might slapped the spider with the paintbrush.

Simeon, blue paint dripping down his neck, dropped his end of the stove. John, in turn, dropped his end. Kate, looking from one to another, said, "You boys better quit the roughhousing and get back to work," she said, and strode off to finish her project.

Some weekday afternoons, when John was at his office at the lumber mill, Katherine would go to the cottage herself. She learned to plumb a straight line, to set in a window, and to shingle a roof. Mostly, she learned what it was to have a good friend. She and Simeon talked about everything under the sun, and even about the sun itself. He was one of the few people she could open up to, that she could be herself with. He called her Kate, or Katie, the way John did. John didn't seem to mind that he and Simeon were the only two people in the world who didn't call her Katherine.

There was no romance there, at least on Katherine's part. She was headily in love with John and didn't recognize the same thing in Simeon's eyes that she had in her own. Simeon had fallen head over heels in love with Katherine. He longed to be with her and, at the same time, when she came by, he hated being with her. In the end, he rushed through the construction of the new room, working like a madman to finish it and get her out of his life. He thought her absence would lessen the misery and heartsickness that engulfed him.

After the cottage was finished John and Katherine invited Simeon, time and again, to festivities at O'Malley House. He always, with weak contrived excuses, refused. After a while they quit asking. In time, John and Katherine assumed their roles in society and Simeon his self-imposed inferior role as gardener and employee. It was odd that where John and Katherine saw no division, Simeon saw a great divide.

After struggling with frustration that his life seemed meaningless and headed nowhere, Simeon joined the Army and fought in Viet Nam. He was the oldest man in his platoon, sharing meals and bunks with youngsters who were really just babies. He took them under his wing and protected them as best he could. Each time one of them died, a part of himself died. He begged God to spare them and take him. Some of them had wives and babies or parents who were aged and ill and needed help. Please God, take me and let them go home, was his nightly prayer.

He got out in the spring of 1967. He looked young and healthy but felt old and used and useless. His America had changed. He no longer fit in. He yearned to find a place to settle.

Simeon bought a used car from a dealership outside Fort Lewis in Washington State. He started driving down the coast through California, over through Texas to Louisiana and then north. He had planned to carefully skirt Montana and end up back near Fort Lewis but when driving the endless highway through Wyoming he gave in to his yearnings.

Simeon cried when he crossed the border. He was a Montanan. He always had been. He crossed the state and headed northwest toward Danford. It was dusk the next night when he entered the city limits. He drove slowly down Main Street. It hadn't changed. Through the grease-smeared window of the Daisy Belle Café, he could see old Mrs. Maple behind the counter. She was leaning against the ice cream freezer fingering a wash rag and chatting with Web Monk, who was in his policeman's uniform.

Simeon drove up and down every street of Danville that night until he finally checked into the Shady Grove Motel. Sally Benson was so glad to see him back home she called her husband out of the back room where they lived. Red Benson emerged shoeless in just his work pants and undershirt and shook Simeon's hand and clapped him on the back until Simeon wondered if he was being welcomed or thrashed. Through it all, Red kept up a dialogue of admiration for Simeon's service to his country, disgust for the "commie idiots" who were burning flags and apology that he wasn't over there in Nam doing his share. As delighted as they were to see him "back home right where you belong," the Bensons didn't offer a discount on the room, nor would have Simeon accepted one.

Within three days everyone knew he was back in Danford. On a Saturday morning John and Katherine O'Malley knocked on the motel room door and begged him to come back to them. The caretaker position, having been filled and refilled over the years, was conveniently open.

And that's how it was that Simeon stepped back into place as if he'd never been gone. The grounds of O'Malley House were the balm to his tortured soul. Planting flowers and trees and helping mares foal brought forth new life that helped shove out the death and destruction of Viet Nam. It took a year before he quit diving to the ground when a door slammed loudly or someone dropped something near him. Sometimes he thought it would take a lifetime before the nighttime images faded.

It was John and Simeon who contrived the flag solution. It was during a rainy spring in the late 1960s and rivers and creeks all over northwestern Montana were flooding. Bridges were swept away and livestock unaccounted for. At O'Malley House, water was oozing across the lawns and gardens and back pastures and splashing against the outbuildings. The horses, vehicles, and equipment had been moved to higher ground.

Simeon worked frantically, piling up sandbags to save the perennials and bushes and young trees. Together he and John and some help from the lumber mill worked to save the house's foundation. Both John and Simeon were finding themselves running either to the house or the cottage to seek each other's help or advice. Together, they came up with the flag as a solution.

A white flag flowing on the brass pole outside the fernery meant come quick!

Katherine had been aghast the first time she found John hoisting the flag. To her it was like summoning a servant, a slave. It was too demanding, too demeaning, she said. John pointed out there wasn't a phone in the cottage.

"Then install one!" she retorted.

"I plan to. But what if Simeon is outside? What if he's at the stables or in the rose garden or out on the far lawn? What if he's down in the gully chasing down a mare? He wouldn't hear the phone. But he can see the flag."

Katherine wasn't appeased. She slogged through the rain, mud slurping over the tops of her boots, to find Simeon. Her hair clung in wet tendrils around her face and her jacket was soaked through at the shoulders and the tops of her breasts. She found Simeon piling sandbags around the gazebo. His yellow slicker glistened and rain dripped from the bottom. His boots were slimy with mud. Hearing Katherine sloshing toward him, he looked up and grinned. Water streamed down his cheeks, his black curly hair was dripping, and a speck of mud was caked to his forehead. His blue eyes were alive with excitement and challenge. The noise from the rain was deafening and they had to nearly shout to be heard.

"Kate! What are you doing out here?" Simeon hollered. "You're getting soaked. You'd better get back to the house!"

"I came to talk to you about this idiotic flag idea," she yelled back.

"I told John you'd not like the flag."

"I don't. I think it's embarrassing. It's like whistling for a dog."

Simeon burst into laughter. "A dog, eh? Like whistling for a dog? Did John tell you it was my idea?"

"No. He said you both came up with it."

"Well, right now, with the flood, we're in a sort of crisis. John and I both tried to think of a way of communicating and

I thought of putting the flag up. Katherine, I don't think of it as a demand for my presence, like a king calling for his jesters. I think of it as a way to let me know I'm needed. If I'm outside no one has to try and find me. After the flood is over I think we should keep using the flag."

"I just don't like it."

"Well, I think it's ingenious. Let's make a deal, Katie. I won't ever look at it as a kingly summons if you won't. I will think of it as being needed by a friend, if you will also see it that way. I also need you to promise to use the flag if you need me. Promise?"

"I guess. But I'll only use if someone's bleeding to death."

"If someone's bleeding to death I'll bring bandages. Do we have a deal?" Pulling off his glove and wiping his hand on his jeans, he thrust it toward her. She grabbed on and was surprised at its warmth. Her own hands were freezing.

"It's a deal," she told Simeon. Turning away from him she slogged her way back to the house.

Chapter Thirty-Four

In all the years they had known each other, Katherine could never convince Simeon that he could just come to the house without being summoned. They had such good conversations and often laughed long and hard about the plights of humanity. Since John's death, Katherine had become braver about summoning Simeon and often found herself making up excuses to have him share a cup of coffee or a bit of lunch. She sometimes wished he could get past the fact that she was wealthy and his employer. It didn't matter beans to her and she wished it didn't for him, either. She didn't even write his monthly checks, which came out of the estate trust.

"There. Flag's all hoisted so Simeon'll be popping in here first thing in the morning," Letty said when she went back in to Katherine. Letty had heard the story of the flag and thought it was amusing that both Simeon and Katherine used it to keep up a sort of private form of communication. It was like long-marrieds who can converse through mere eye contact. Sometimes, in fact, Simeon had come to the house even though there hadn't been a phone call or the flag raised. He simply knew when Katherine needed him.

"Letty, you are a dear. Thank you."

"So, what time and when is dinner again?" Letty asked.

"Saturday night at seven o'clock. And there are ten of them. I think some of them are young people. I didn't think about that. Young people might need special care, don't you think? Hmm. This might be a challenge, taking care of all these people and making sure they are entertained."

"No problemo. Remember, I'm doing the entertainment. So, we have all day tomorrow and, in reality, all day Saturday, to get ready. This'll be a piece of cake."

"Oh my goodness! The cake! Even with the apple pie, we have to have a cake. I know! We'll order it from Josephine at the bakery. I hope she can make it at this late date," decided Katherine.

A few minutes later Letty excused herself, saying she'd better get busy on her entertainment assignment. After pulling on her sweater and opening the front door she turned quickly.

"What do you think of rap?" she blurted with a straight face. Katherine sputtered something unintelligible.

"I'm joking!" Letty said merrily as she bent over and scooted out the door backwards. Katherine followed her out, muttering that she didn't think it was funny and watched from the front porch as Letty folded her long body into her car. The pathetic vehicle whined and protested against being started and then roared to life, shivering and shaking in anticipation of the trip home.

Katherine glanced toward Marge's house and felt a small thrill when she saw a shadow in the busybody's upstairs window. The old bat was watching every move. Letty shot backwards out of the drive like a race car driver, then spun the car to the left and lurched to a stop. Gears ground piercingly as she fought them from reverse into first. Katherine cheered silently when Letty pounded the accelerator a few times before letting out the clutch. She knew Marge would be wild with curiosity, wondering what brought Letty out so late at night.

She turned to walk back into the house and lifted her fist in triumph when, behind her, Letty peeled out at the first turn, sending a shrill squeal through the dark of night.

Chapter Thirty-Five

Marge knew, from the living room light spilling out over the side lawn and creeping into her own living room side windows, that Katherine O'Malley was still up. Furthermore, she had heard that disgusting car disturbing whatever shred of peace might have been available. Curious, Marge peeked through the curtains and watched as that Letty girl galloped up the sidewalk. She heard the door slam and cringed. How could one person be so disruptive? She had all the grace of a blindfolded Clydesdale.

Marge stood at the window for nearly ten minutes, hoping that there wasn't anything wrong with Katherine. She peered down the street, watching carefully for any ambulance lights. She and Katherine, and Lillian for that matter, were all at the age where an ambulance in the middle of the night wouldn't be a surprise to anyone.

They used to be friends, she and Katherine, but that was long ago, back when Bud and John were both still alive. Sometimes they would play Pinochle into the wee hours. Bud was her strength. He gave her courage to go out in the world, to do things and go places. She felt safe when he was with her. Now that he was gone she panicked at the thought of leaving the house. She had decided that if she had a heart attack she wouldn't dial 911. She would just lie there until she died. The thought of being hauled out into an ambulance and taken to the hospital made her physically ill. Before making her decision, if she pondered being taken out of her home, she felt breathless and lightheaded and held her stomach, which threatened to erupt. It would be easier to die at home.

The corner cupboard in the kitchen gave a clue to her problems. Medicine for depression, anxiety, irritable bowel syndrome, high cholesterol, heart palpitations, back pain, leg pain, restless leg syndrome and a prescription renewed yearly for urinary tract infections, although she hadn't had one in sixteen years.

She missed Bud. If she was sick he would hold a cold compress on her forehead and cluck tenderly. He knew if she said, "I don't feel well," no matter where they were, it was up to him to make apologies, to gather coats and her purse, or to leave the shopping cart or movie, and get her home. He never complained. He loved her and, while he didn't understand her many maladies, he took care of her.

But six years ago Bud had left her. Up and died. Right in the garden among the tulips, which had just come up the week before. She had spotted him from the kitchen window and known instantly he was gone. She grabbed a jacket off the peg next to the back door, threw it over her shoulders, and went out to him. Cradling his head in her lap she wept, her tears dropping one by one onto his forehead and running in rivulets into his gray hair. He was a lovely man, a loving, dedicated man, who overlooked her neuroses and foibles and cherished her anyway.

The tears turned to a sort of wailing and Marge chanted, over and over, "What will I do? Please don't leave me. What will I do?"

When Katherine left her house next door to fetch some twine from the garage, she heard Margery's keening and came through the back gate. Her heart leapt into her throat as she took in the pathetic scene—two people, one dead and one sobbing, sprawled out in a bed of newborn tulips.

Katherine rushed to the couple, murmuring platitudes she wouldn't remember later. Carefully, she moved Marge's hand and felt for a pulse in Bud's neck, even thought she knew he was dead. Then she turned her attention to the distraught wife.

"Oh, Marge, I am so sorry. So very sorry," she said, cradling her friend and crooning into her ear. "Here. Let me cover him with my jacket and let's go in the house."

"No. I can't leave him. Please. Oh God. I can't let him go. I can't," Marge choked through her tears. Katherine hugged her head, feeling the tears on her cheek. Standing, she stripped off her jacket and put it over the body.

"OK, sweetheart, you stay with Bud. I'm going to make a phone call. I'll be right back."

Dashing into Marge's kitchen she turned off the pan of leftover stew that was bubbling on a back burner and went to the phone.

It took only five minutes for the ambulance to arrive. They gently, but firmly, forced Marge to give up her husband and then carefully handed her off into Katherine's care. Katherine held Marge close, shielding her eyes from the obscene reality of loading the sprawling body onto a gurney and trying to maneuver it through the soggy spring lawn. Within ten minutes it was over. Bud Reynolds, already cold and with dirt in his hair and the smell of smashed tulips on his jacket, was on his way to the mortuary, and Margery was on her way to life ever after.

In just a matter of weeks Katherine was also a widow.

There were differences in the way the two women reacted to the death of a husband, especially as time marched on. Katherine, although incredibly lonely at times, clung to wonderful memories and the knowledge that she and John would be together again. She and John had been extremely active in their church and were faithful in praying together and doing devotions together. She felt they were ambassadors of

Christ, meeting the challenge of being home missionaries. It wasn't until after John's death that she truly comprehended the Bible verse about "storing your treasures in Heaven." John was her treasure in Heaven. Their life together would go on through eternity.

Marge had no such security, no such promise. She thought Bud was surely in Heaven because he was a good man, a kind man. They hadn't belonged to a church but, if anyone would have asked, Marge would have laughingly claimed to be Methodist, which was her mother's claim. When it came to baptisms and burials, they turned to the Methodists.

Bud's death had destroyed Marge. She had no one to lean on, no one to talk to. She became bitter and frightened and angry.

Now, as she peered out the window wondering why Letty was next door so late, Marge brushed aside her initial concern for Katherine's well being. Her thoughts turned to acid.

Well, it sure would be nice having someone visit *me*, Marge thought now, after hearing Letty whistling down the sidewalk.

What would you do then? a dark thought prompted. *Get sick and hide in the bathroom? Panic and want to scream? Face it, you're a mess. No one wants to be friends with a mess.*

But I want friends; I want a life. I want to be normal again. Katherine thinks I hate her. She doesn't understand.

Marge was right about that part of her brooding thoughts. Katherine did think her next-door neighbor disliked her for some reason. After the funeral, she had tried to help Marge but she had nearly slammed the door in Katherine's face. Each time, Marge rebuffed her friendship and concern.

For a time, Katherine would see Marge periodically come and go. But then it stopped. Katherine couldn't remember the last time she saw Marge out of the house. Surely she must be just missing her in the store and other places throughout town.

After awhile, Katherine noticed that Nate Jorge from the Baptist church down the road started dropping by the

Reynolds house. He always came on Mondays, carrying in bags of groceries. He hauled out the garbage at the same time. A neighbor kid haphazardly mowed the lawn, sometimes ignoring it until it had gone to seed. The hydrangeas and phlox and other plants had died the first winter and the roses, after nearly four years, were sprawling and leggy and barely hanging on. The backyard, which Katherine could see if she nosed her way to a hole in the fence, was a shambles—an overgrown jumble of weeds and branches which had fallen from the unpruned flowering plum and birch and willows. In less than four years, it had simply come undone.

Katherine still cared and twice in the four months had attempted to visit Marge. She rang the doorbell and knocked and finally quietly went away. That Christmas she sent a card with a cheery "Let's get together. Come over for lunch!" message. She didn't get a card, or a phone call, in return.

Marge cringed when she heard Letty slam the car door. She closed her eyes and counted. One. Two. Three. Four. Five. Roar. Sputter, sputter. Roar. I know the sounds of that wretched car as well as my own heartbeat, she thought. Aiming the remote at the TV she turned it off. The silence was overwhelming. Just the furnace and the tick of the mantle clock. The far-off sound of Letty's car. Sighing, Marge pushed her aching bones from the chair, straightened the armrest covers, and walked to the bathroom. One more day over. Completed. Finished.

How many more days like this, God? How many more do I have to endure?

There was no answer.

Chapter Thirty-Six

In his cottage, seated well back on the twelve acres that comprised O'Malley House grounds, Simeon Quest had just gotten to sleep when he heard the squeal of the tires and recognized the roar of Letty's car. He glanced at the digital clock on his dresser. It was a little after eleven o'clock. Alarmed, Simeon quickly threw on a pair of jeans and pulled a sweatshirt over his head. He pulled on a pair of loafers, combed his fingers through his graying hair and headed quickly to the mansion. Just outside his door he saw the white flat fluttering on the flag pole. Something was clearly amiss.

Katherine was in the kitchen putting a tea bag into a mug when the automatic light at the edge of the patio came on and Simeon approached. She heard his quick steps on the back porch and opened the door before he could knock.

"Simeon! What's wrong?" Katherine asked in alarm, flinging her hand to her chest.

"Me, what's wrong? What's wrong with you? Why's Letty here so late?" Simeon demanded.

"Oh, you must have heard the white tornado take off down the driveway," Katherine chuckled, waving toward the driveway. "I swear that girl will never be incognito as long as she's driving that car! Simeon, come in and I'll fix you some tea. I'm just getting some for myself. It's been an amazing night and I figure a little chamomile will do just the trick. Chamomile calms the nerves, you know."

"I'm not really dressed for visiting. Don't even have socks on," Simeon said.

"Oh, for heaven's sake, Simeon, I've seen your naked feet before. Your sockless feet aren't going to bother me one bit. Besides, I can't tell you what's going on unless you come in. I'm not going to stand out there on the cold porch. Just come inside and sit down."

While Simeon settled himself into a chair, Katherine opened a cupboard door and took down a heavy blue mug and filled it with hot water from the teakettle. Opening the tea drawer she relayed the choices.

"Chamomile. Peppermint. Ginseng. Other choices are raspberry, black cherry, blackberry, licorice...."

"I don't care. Just pick one," said Simeon, looking exasperated.

"Well, you'd better not have ginseng or you'll never sleep. I'll give you a nice decaffeinated orange spice with some honey. I'm having honey in mine. Just a dollop, not much. Honey is amazing stuff. Did you know that honey..."

"Kate. You're rambling. It's nearly 11:15. Letty just left. You're so excited you have red cheeks and of course I know about honey because I have had twelve hives out in the back pasture for nearly two decades. The honey you're dolloping is the honey from those hives."

"Oh! I feel so stupid. Of course you know about honey," Katherine giggled as she finished dipping the tea bag up and down. Placing it on a saucer beside her chamomile tea bag, she handed the mug to Simeon and moved to sit down across from him. She brushed her hand through the wisps of hair that had escaped the bun. Despite her age she was still a beautiful woman, a woman of elegance and charm.

The table and chairs in the breakfast nook were old and painted white. The chairs had high backs and brightly colored cushions with lots of orange and blue. Holding his blue mug, Simeon waited patiently. Katherine bopped up from the table and moved to the pantry. She emerged with a Tupperware container. Placing it on the table she lifted the lid.

"Ginger creams. Your favorite. I made them just yesterday and I was going to bring you a plate but time just sort of got away from me. I had to go to the dry cleaners and that took forever since they lost my black coat. Do you know they must have had at least thirty black coats in there and they had to search through all of them to find mine? And then I had to go to the bank and sign some papers, and the library and return that dreadful book from that new author Norman something or other, and when I got back home it was almost time for dinner and I thought to myself, 'Well, Simeon will just have to wait until tomorrow.' And then tomorrow, which is today, came and Lillian called and you know how long that always takes, especially when one of her story people have had some bizarre thing happen..."

Simeon sat patiently looking at her, smiling broadly. She became flustered.

"Oh dear. I am rambling. Simeon, I guess I just don't know how to tell you what happened tonight without you thinking I'm an old mad woman ready for Shady Pines. "

"Try me," he said, reaching for another cookie and dipping it in his tea.

"Okay. Well, this is what happened. This lady called here and she had misdialed the phone. She was very sweet. Her name is Connie Ames. She and her family came to Danford to celebrate her father's eightieth birthday. He was born here. His name is Patrick O'Reilly. Well, as you very well know, what with all the conventions and everything in town, there is no place to have his party. After all, Danford is very limited in places for such things. You have the Masonic Temple, the

Danford Hotel, the Eagles Hall and that's about it, unless you want to use the high school gym and that's not good because it always smells like, well, it always smells like stinky socks and sweat and basketballs. Of course if it was nice and warm they could probably have a picnic at the park but...you're laughing." Leaning back, she folded her arms and glared at him.

"Katie! Settle down!" he chuckled, his blue eyes crinkling at the corners. "Let me guess. There was no room at the inn so you offered to throw the party."

"How did you know?" she asked in surprise.

"Because I know you. Remember the strays from the pound?"

"Why does everyone keep bring up that dog thing?"

"Because it's what you do. You take care of people. And dogs. And cats. I've seen you with that cat." He took two more cookies.

"Simeon, I haven't had a party for years. Maybe since John's funeral and that surely couldn't be considered a party. Do you know how scary that is?"

"You were born to have parties. You could do this blindfolded. How many people are coming?"

"Ten. Mr. O'Reilly, his children and some grandchildren. Letty was here helping me plan things."

"I think it's a great idea. You need to get back into the swing of life. It's been too long."

"Simeon, I need your help."

"Sure. I'll make sure the outside looks great and you and Letty take care of the inside."

"I'm going to call Maxie Bruce."

"Maxie Bruce." The smile faded from Simeon's face as he softly said the familiar name. "Kate, I think that's a good idea. I heard lately that she's not been doing well since her husband died. I saw her daughter, and she said Maxie's lonely and having a hard time. She's also had some health problems, but her daughter didn't say what. The two of you used to throw some great parties. I'm glad you're going to be back together. I think this will be just what she needs."

"Oh, poor Maxie," Katherine said, frowning. "I wish I'd kept better track of her. I attended the funeral when she lost her husband but I wonder why she didn't call and tell me her health was not good and she was not handling things well."

"You know why. Because she's from the old school She's black and you used to be the white employer in the big house."

"That's ridiculous. We were friends. We are friends. I'd trust Maxie Bruce with my life. We are equals in the eyes of God."

"She'd never think that. And you know it."

"But that's so wrong. I've always thought was wrong. It's limiting people. It's putting big roadblocks and barriers on relationships. It's building giant walls. It's wrong to do that. The fact that I have more money than some people or that I live in a bigger house has nothing to do with the 'me' and who I am as a person. I didn't build this house or make this money. I inherited it. I think it's prejudicial on her part that she can't accept me as I am. I don't care two hoots that she's black. That means nothing to me, nothing, except that she's a lot better dancer. Boy, can that woman dance! This whole thing hurts, Simeon, and it always has."

"Well, that's the way life is, sometimes, and you're right. There are prejudices in the world that make no sense. And I love Maxie as much as you do, but I respect her view of the world."

"But that's wrong, Simeon. Don't you see? If Maxie and I were in an orphanage together, if we were both dropped off there buck naked and no one had a claim on us, we would be perfectly equal, right? There would be none of this materialistic mumbo jumbo, who's got more than who. Or is it 'whom?' Do you want to know who's rich? She is! Maxie Bruce is! Simeon, she has four kids and probably forty grandkids by now, and she has a load of brothers and sisters. Now that's wealth.

Comparatively, I'm poorer than a church mouse."

"I agree with you that she's wealthy in family and love and, if you look at that, she has more than both of us put together. Let's get back to your party. Any special requests? Paint the tree trunks gold or line the walkways with red velvet?"

She looked at him and almost laughed.

Honey, you don't even want to know, she thought to herself as she pondered the way to ask him.

Chapter Thirty-Seven

She decided to just say it and get it over with. "Simon, I need you to do more than just the outside," Katherine said with a hint of apprehensive firmness. "I was going to talk to you about it tomorrow and that's why Letty hoisted the flag."

"What? Set the table? I wouldn't know what side the little fork goes on!" he exclaimed with a snort before reaching for another ginger cream.

Katherine took a deep breath, let it out, and leaned toward him. Looking him in the eye she reached a hand toward his but stopped just short of touching it.

"Simeon. The party is at seven o'clock Saturday night. I want you to be at my side. I will be the hostess and I want you to be the host," she said.

Simeon pulled his hands to his lap and leaned back in the chair, as if getting space between her and her request. Cocking his head to one side he moved slightly toward the table.

"Kate," he said softly. "You know I can't do that."

"Why?" she demanded, instantly angry. They had had this argument so many times before. She never won and she railed against his stubbornness and his pride. He, in turn, harangued her about her place in society and his not belonging there.

"You know why. We've been through this before."

"We've been through this since, when? 1950? When John and I asked you over and over again to come to our parties?"

"I didn't belong."

"You did belong. You were our friend."

"I was your employee."

"You're as bad as Maxie! You're as prejudiced as she is!"

"Kate..."

Before he could continue she had leaped to her feet. Standing spread-legged she placed her hands palm down on the table, bent over, and faced him with rage.

"You are! You are as hung up on this slave/master thing as she has always been. Well, I want to tell you something, Buster; there is more to life than who has money and who doesn't and who has power and who doesn't. There is love. Love should overcome every bit of it. And friendship. Friendship and caring and compassion should trump bank accounts anytime. And what about God? You go to church every Sunday. Do you think God looks at one person as better than another? Of course he doesn't. He says, right there in the Bible, that everyone is equal. None is better than any other. Well, I think we're supposed to emulate God. If he says one person isn't better than another it's a slap in his face for you to say otherwise. So there. And I'm not asking you to be with me because I am your employer—I don't feel like your employer anyway and I never have—but I am asking you as a friend. And friendship, you stubborn old fool, should be more important than anything. You are over seventy years old. Don't you think it's time you grow up?"

Standing up and turning away from him she strode to the counter and grabbed a Kleenex.

"And now look what you've done," she yelled, wiping her eyes and honking into the tissue. "You made me cry and I haven't cried in years."

Simeon Quest couldn't stand female tears. He'd fought in wars and watched men die, wrangled balky cattle, hunted wild animals and lived his life bravely with courage and strength. But crying females were his undoing. He got up and went to her side. He didn't know what to do and tentatively touched her shoulder.

"Ah, Kate," he said patting the air awkwardly. "Don't cry. Please don't cry."

"Leave me alone," she snarled, jerking away.

He patted her shoulder.

She cried harder, her tears plopping in the sink.

"Please don't cry," he begged.

"No. Don't stop me," she wailed, turning her head to glance at him with eyes that reflected heartbreak. "I need to do this. Just let me cry." Simeon rolled his eyes and pulled her toward his chest. He placed his hands on her quaking shoulders.

"Shhh. Don't cry. I'll do it. I'll come to your party and sit at the table. I'll sit wherever you want me to," he declared.

Katherine sobbed with added zeal. She pushed him away and stomped to the table where she pulled out her chair and sat heavily.

"I don't need your pity," she wailed with derision. "After all, I'm the rich person who isn't worthy of friends or loved ones unless they have money, too."

"OK, just quit crying and sit down, and let's talk." Kneeling before her, he held her loosely for a few minutes and then gently let her go. He got the box of Kleenex and plopped it in front of her. He grabbed both their mugs and fixed more tea. Then he sat quietly in his chair and waited.

"I'm sorry, Simeon," she said, mopping her face with a new tissue. "Whew! That felt good to just cry. And to get angry with you. You make me so angry. I know how this bothers you and I should never have brought it up again. But I just really dreaded having to sit with all those strangers. I thought maybe Lillian could be there but she's...well, you know Lillian."

"She's such a Dip," he said, laughing softly.

"Mmm-hmm. She'd start off talking about those awful Biedeck television people and I'd be mortified. Victor Biedeck died yesterday and Lillian's all upset about it. Letty could be with me but she's doing the entertaining. For a really fun time I suppose I could ask Marge. Now, she'd be delightful company. I know she's dying to know what Letty was doing here so late and she's probably crawled up to the kitchen window by now to find out what you're doing over here."

"Maybe we should give her something to talk about," he mused.

"Oh sure. Like that's what you want to do."

"Kate. While you were crying I thought about what you said. You're right. I've always had this problem with your money. It's like a barrier between us that shouldn't be there. It shouldn't matter one whit. I guess it's a man thing—worrying about what people are going to say about an old handyman and gardener chasing after the town's wealthiest widow."

"They'd say, 'Well, finally the old codger asked her out.' That's what they'd say," Katherine retorted.

"Probably they would. Kate, you're right. But there's more to it than that. And I'm just not ready to talk about that right now. But I will come and play host to your hostess role Saturday night and I will continue to be your friend. Right now that's all I can offer you," he said sadly. Katherine sighed and smiled a pathetically tragic smile.

"You'll still come by sometimes and have coffee if I ask you?" she asked.

"You won't be able to keep me away," he said. "Especially as long as you keep making ginger creams and banana bread."

A few minutes later she walked out on the porch with him. The sky was dark, with no moon to lighten his path. A million stars glittered overhead and they looked at them quietly. Katherine shivered and Simeon put his arm over her shoulders.

"Do you want a flashlight?" she asked. He laughed.

"You could spin me around twenty times, blindfold me and

tie up one leg and I could make it home without one stumble. I know, personally, every blade of grass and bush on the place. Kate, you get on inside before you freeze." He pushed her gently to the door.

"Sweet dreams," he said softly.

"You, too," she said. Going inside, she shut the door quietly, carefully, and listened to his feet as they quickly maneuvered down the walkway and to the path leading to his cottage. She sighed with yearning.

It was nearly 12:30 p.m. before Katherine climbed the wide, ornate staircase to the second floor, walked through the gauntlet of ancestors, and entered the trio of rooms –sitting room, bedroom, bathroom—that comprised her quarters. She was exhausted, emotionally and physically.

Past the patio and the horse stables, Simeon lay wide awake in his bedroom, staring out at the moonlit sky and pondering his life and what he'd made of it.

God, what should I do?

Do you love her?

Yes, but is that enough?

Trust me.

Chapter Thirty-Eight

On Friday morning Katherine was out of the house before the *Danford News* thudded on the porch. Two hours later, she pulled slowly back into driveway. She took great pride in her driving ability. She planned to be driving well into her nineties.

Lillian Dip was sitting on the top step of the back veranda when Katherine arrived back home. Katherine drove carefully around the back of the house, holding the wheel with both hands and sitting up alertly while looking at Lillian on the porch step. Lillian had obviously been there awhile and had been crocheting up a storm. A puddle of blue and orange yarn filled her broad lap. Next to her was the faded canvas crocheting bag that had seen her through births and deaths, hurricanes and tornadoes and every bad-luck and good-luck event that had studded her life. The bag was frayed and duct taped at the seams. The handles had been replaced at least six times over the years. Lillian Dip's crocheting bag was as important to her as her purse. She would no more consider leaving the house without it than she would consider leaving the house without clothes.

"Katherine!" she hollered from the porch before Katherine was even out of the car. "Where have you been? It's past coffee hour. I've been sitting here for a half hour. I hollered all through the house and couldn't find hide nor hair of you. Finally I checked the garage and, sure enough, the car was gone. Where have you been so early in the morning? Darn it, now look what I've done." Lillian, who had become so agitated she lost count, was quickly tearing out a row of orange. Katherine laughed merrily.

"Good morning, Lillian, and what a beautiful morning it is. I've been to Polsky's. Where's Petunia?"

"Home. I didn't know what I'd be doing this morning after coffee. You've been grocery shopping? So early? Today's the wedding, you know. Beth's marrying Brett for the third time."

"Who?"

"Beth and Brett. After he woke up from that coma and discovered that the jewels had really been stolen by Mariah and Beth had been falsely accused, he found out she had been hiding in a convent and he went to fetch her. Her hair was a mess, all cut off, and she was singing a lonely little song in the chapel and she heard a noise and there he was, standing in the doorway. It was the most romantic thing. I cried and cried. Anyway, today's the wedding. You aren't going to miss it, are you? It's at 2:30."

"What happened to Vinnie? I thought he died yesterday. I figured they'd be getting ready for a funeral," Katherine said, puzzled.

"Well, it turns out that maybe it wasn't him. It might all be just a big mistake. I hope so. I can't imagine the show without Vinnie. Anyway, right now everyone's all excited about the wedding. If you wanted you could watch it with me. Maybe then you'd see why I like these shows."

"I'm sorry, Lillian, but you know I think those afternoon shows are a waste of time. I'd rather take a course in tax collecting. But you almost had me fooled. For a minute there I thought that Beth and Brett were real people, but the coma and convent made me realize they were some of your afternoon people."

Katherine pulled two bags of groceries from the trunk of her car and walked briskly to the back door. Balancing one on her raised knee, she opened the door and started in the house, saying over her shoulder, "Besides, I'm busy."

Lillian, who had lost count again, put down her crocheting, marched to the car and heaved a deceptively heavy bag from the trunk. She followed Katherine across the veranda and through the back door to the kitchen, peering in the bag as she went.

"My goodness, Katherine, this hunk of beef is big enough to feed half the poor in India, except that they don't eat cows. Did you know there are something like ten million cows in India? Cows, cows, everywhere and not a steak to eat. Get it? It's supposed to be water, water, everywhere and not a drop to drink. But I said, cows, cows. What are you doing, anyway?" She plopped her bag next to the two Katherine had placed on the counter.

"You can be very quick-witted," Katherine said with a laugh. "I'm having a party. It's a long story." Katherine shook her head and headed out the door to get more groceries. Lillian trotted along behind.

"What kind of party? Tupperware?"

Katherine handed Lillian two bags and took the remaining two out of the trunk. Placing one on the ground, she slammed the trunk shut, smacked her hands together to clean off the dust, hiked the bag on the ground up to her arms, and turned to face her friend.

"Nope. This is a birthday party. For an old fellow, Patrick O'Reilly, who used to reside in Danford. His family has all gathered here to celebrate his eightieth birthday and, through circumstances that are too strange and time-consuming to relate right now, they are having the party here at O'Malley House."

Climbing back up the porch steps with bags of groceries, Lillian huffing along behind, Katherine noticed the stray cat at the door. Using her foot she shoved the big gray brute gently out of the way. "Shoo, cat, get along with you now. I don't know how long that stray cat is going to stay around," she said.

"A cat isn't really a stray if he's been living here for four years and you've been feeding him all that time," Lillian Dip said. Putting down her bags she called softly, "Here, kitty, kitty; come here, kitty." The plush gray cat came shyly forward, stopping just outside of touching range.

"As long as he doesn't have a name, I believe he's a stray. 'Cat' isn't a name, Lillian. It's a recognition of his species."

"I say he's a part of your home if you feed him," Lillian protested as she made little mewing noises and coaxed him close enough to scratch behind his ears. "Oh, look, he likes this!"

"Don't be playing with that cat, Lillian, or he'll never leave," Katherine said as the cat sauntered off the porch and Lillian picked up the grocery bags.

"Katherine, you've been feeding this cat for years and he's not leaving. I say he's your cat. And he needs a proper name. Serenity is a nice name for a cat. Or Dimples."

"Serenity doesn't quite suit a rugged fellow like him. Nor does Dimples. It's a male cat, Lillian. How could you miss seeing that? That cat's got the biggest...oh for heaven's sake. I don't have time right now to name a cat. Besides, I'm not really a cat person."

Inside the kitchen, Katherine quickly pulled cans and boxes from the grocery bags and put them on the counter. Lillian laughed. Obviously, Katherine was chattering to cover up her nervousness. If she let her talk long enough she'd find out what was going on. "I'm more of a dog person and..." she started and then she threw up her hands. "Oh, for Pete's sake. I don't have time for this. I have too much to do and not enough time to do it all. Patrick O'Reilly and his entire family will be here tomorrow night and expecting a celebration. My heavens, Lillian, what have I gotten myself into?"

"I don't know. You won't quit talking long enough to tell me," Lillian said with amusement. Then she frowned. "There used to be a Patrick O'Reilly I knew. I think we went to high school together. Maybe college," Lillian said, thoughtfully. For four months in 1962 she had attended Henry's Hair College before confronting a full head of lice and nits and dropping out. Now, at age sixty-something her "college days" were of great importance to her.

"Are you sure it's a real person and not one of your soap stars?" Katherine asked with a laugh. Lillian stared and she knew Katherine had caught her again.

"Lillian, you are getting too caught up in those stories. Why, you don't know what's real or what's TV!"

"Well, not all of us have a plush life in a big mansion like you do, Katherine. We depend on our stories to liven up our days."

"Oh, Lillian, you are such a delight! You think I have a lively life just because I live in this monstrosity? You know better. Before Letty arranged to have folks from the senior center come over, I sometimes thought I should start a day care just to get a little life back in the old place. I figured I could call it O'Malley Day Care and put little chairs and tables in the great room and fashion a slide down the main staircase. I swear, if it wasn't for Letty I think I'd have gone mad. I don't know what I'd do without her...or without you too, of course. Look at these tomatoes. Have you ever seen more luscious tomatoes?"

Lillian leaned forward and squinted at the tomatoes and then reached in the nearest bag and started pulling out cans and packages. "They had them on sale at the Safeway. Thirty-nine cents a pound," she said. Lillian was always one for a bargain. Katherine laughed shortly.

"I saw that ad. And I saw the tomatoes. They were green around the gills. In the summer the tomatoes at Polsky's are local tomatoes. I like that about Polsky's Market. Joe Polsky and his sons have always bought local produce and products. You know that, Lillian, since you've sold them crocheted pot holders for years. You should really buy more from them."

"I suppose you're right," Lillian said, as she unloaded the last can from the grocery bag. Picking up her bag, she settled down with her crocheting in the breakfast nook. After pulling three lengths of yarn high over her head and smoothing her project in her lap, her hook and fingers began to dance, in and out, back and forth, twisting and turning.

"So, tell me, if I didn't go to school with Patrick O'Reilly, who is he?"

Katherine poured two mugs of coffee and carried them to the table. Plunking the mugs down, she sat across from Lillian. While she doctored their coffee, three spoonfuls of sugar and a gurgle of cream in Lillian's and a scant teaspoon and tiny dollop in hers, she said, "All I know is that he spent most of his life here, working at the mills, and he raised his family here. They lived over on Park. His daughter, Connie Ames, said she walked by O'Malley House on her way to and from school. She's been away for quite some time. The family decided it would be a grand idea to have Mr. O'Reilly's birthday here in Danford."

"So, how'd you get involved in having this party?"

Katherine related the phone calls as Lillian crocheted. By the end Lillian had stopped the movement of her crochet hook and was staring open-mouthed. A puddle of spittle had gathered at the corner of her mouth. She sucked it in and lurched forward.

"That's the craziest thing I've ever heard. Katherine, you don't even know these people. Maybe it's a set-up to case the joint. Maybe they're after Paul Revere's silver or the gallery paintings. They are worth a fortune, you know. Or the jewelry! Katherine, your jewelry is priceless. Why, the pearls alone must be worth thousands. Call the police, Katherine, just call the police. There was a case like this one time on TV and someone was murdered, Katherine, murdered! Oh darn, now I've lost count again."

"Lillian, you are precious. If you had talked to Connie Ames yourself, you wouldn't worry one whit. Now, I'm going to start cleaning the silver. You want to help?"

"Help? Well, no, actually, I really don't like cleaning silver, no offense, but if you get it on your hands pretty soon you can taste that tinny taste in your mouth. I hate that tinny taste," said Lillian as she stuffed her crocheting into her bag and stood to her feet. She gulped the remains of her coffee and put down the cup firmly.

"Besides, I really need to get going, I'm having lunch with Sandra and her mother."

"Sandra?" Katherine asked in puzzlement. "Who's Sandra?"

"Oh, you know—Sandra from the sexy lingerie and candle shop. Pauline's daughter."

"I'd forgotten that Pauline, our new librarian here, was Sandra's mother. So, you're having lunch with Sandra? I thought you said that wasn't a wonderful experience, the first time you went into her store."

"Oh, well," Lillian said, dismissing her previous remarks with a wave of her hand. "I did feel like a fat old cow in the place but a group of us decided we needed to support her anyway. There was a regular parade going through there. They even had a list going to show when people would take their turn. Anyway, I went back in there and apologized for all the people traipsing through her store. She said she actually cried when Herb Clapper came in with Buddy Wilkes. She said they were charming. Imagine that. Calling Herb and Buddy 'charming.' She also said she thought they were going to have twin strokes when they saw some of the stuff she has in there."

Katherine waited patiently as Lillian paused to count stitches, peering intently at the marching rows of crochet work.

"Well?" Katherine said, throwing up her hands. "What happened next? How did this turn into lunch with her?"

"I guess she just wants to thank me. Pauline and Sandra moved here right after Sandra's father—Pauline's husband—died. Sandra had just gotten a divorce so it was good timing. Her mother had just sort of fallen apart. It had been over two years and she was still a mess. When Sandra saw all these seniors plowing through her store she saw what her mother could be like. So I started bringing Pauline to the Center with me. And then Letty got her doing the library work here. They're both doing very well and today we're having lunch. Sunday, you'll see them at church. I invited them to come and they said they would.

"Lillian, you are an amazing woman," Katherine said, shaking her head.

"I'd be even more amazing if I could figure out where I dropped a stitch," Lillian said, grinning. "After lunch I'm headed to the Senior Center."

"Will it be hard, going back after the election and all?" Katherine asked her with concern.

"I've been thinking about what you said and I decided I might as well just put it all behind me. Besides, you're right. I'll bet at least four of them come up today and whisper they voted for me. Besides, today's collage day. We're making collages out of doilies and leaves and anything we can find around the house or in the yard. I'm bringing yarn. Of course. I always bring yarn. I'm the yarn queen. And then after collages we're getting a lesson on, let me see if I can remember...Luring Worms to your Garden...by someone from that new garden center. I'm not much for worms but I'm thinking maybe some of the tips will work to lure a man to my bed."

"Lillian! I can't believe the things that come out of your mouth. Oh my, look at the time!" Katherine exclaimed, hopping up from the table. "You need to think about gathering your yarn for the collages. After all, you have enough yarn to start your own shop."

"You're changing the subject," Lillian laughed as she carefully folded the crochet work around the hook and tucked it into her bag. Settling the bag on her arm, she opened the screen door, then turned around and grinned. "I love shocking you. But admit it, Katherine! You'd love to have a man chasing after you."

"Go on, Lillian, you're going to be late," Katherine said, shutting the door firmly and waving from the window.

"Admit it!" Lillian hollered from the end of the driveway, waving back.

Katherine was frequently "horrified" by Lillian's frank discussions about worldly subjects. Truthfully, she wasn't all that shocked. With the right person she could be as blunt as Lillian. It was just that Lillian tended to rattle on and pass on what was told to her. It was easier to feign dismay than to discuss such things and worry they'd spread through town. If she'd admitted her loneliness and yearnings, the next thing she'd see was a trail of old men from the Senior Center lining up in the driveway. The thought made her chuckle. It was almost worth doing just to get a look at Marge's face. Poor Marge.

Chapter Thirty-Nine

Katherine quickly finished putting the groceries away, placing in the refrigerator things that needed to keep cool, and into the freezer things that needed to be kept frozen. The rest she left on the counter where they awaited Maxie's expertise.

The good silverware was kept in velvet-lined drawers in one of the huge cherrywood floor-to-ceiling built-in hutches in the butler's pantry. Katherine had learned from Maxie, who had learned from her mother, that the easiest way to clean it was to pull out the heavy drawers and haul them to the kitchen.

In the old days the silver was utilized so often that it rarely needed polishing. As she walked to the pantry, Katherine remembered the last time it was used was for John's funeral. That long ago? John's funeral seemed to be the end of a lot of things. Opening the first drawer, she bent over and breathed deeply. She loved that smell. It smelled of wood and spicy polish, of age and memories. The old ornate silverware glistened in the bed of green. It wasn't Paul Revere's silver—the Revere silver, twenty-six pieces in all, was hidden behind this, the 1890s silver, in a secret drawer that was accessible only by twisting a tiny latch nearly indiscernible in the ornate frontice carving of the middle hutch. Only Letty, and her lawyer, knew the secret.

Wearing rubber gloves, Katherine worked diligently on the silverware, which just needed a touch-up. Actually, it didn't really need cleaning at all but that was part of the process of entertaining. Order flowers, clean the house, cook the food, polish the silver.

She had just gotten silver polish pasted onto half the silver when the phone rang. Stripping off the rubber glove from her right hand and turning off the water, Katherine walked across the expansive kitchen to a little nook that held a small desk for writing lists and looking at recipes, and picked up the receiver. It was Lillian and she was excited. She always seemed to be excited about something, Katherine thought with a smile.

"So, what's up, Lillian?" Katherine asked.

"On the walk home I was thinking about your cat."

"I don't have a cat."

"Face it, my friend, you have a cat. A male cat without a name. I was thinking about that and came up with the perfect name. Lucille."

"I really don't want to name that cat, but if I did I don't think it would be Lucille. Lillian, the cat is quite obviously a male. Very obviously a male."

"Well, I know that. It's just that my mother's name was Lucille and I've never named anything after her. Well, except for a plant once, but the thing died two weeks later."

Katherine couldn't help but laugh. "You named a plant Lucille?"

"I know it's crazy. A plant named Lucille should be beautiful and feminine, and this one was pretty ugly. Stumpy. Big on the bottom. Before I went strictly to plastic, I had all my plants named: Ernest, Sophie, Tipsy, Harvey Wallbanger...."

"Tipsy, Harvey, and Wallbanger?"

"Tipsy, was a notorious drinker, always demanding more and more. Harvey, was this philodendron who went on a growing binge and slumped drunkenly all over one wall. So, what do you think? Can we call him Lucille?"

Katherine shook her head and covered her mouth to stifle

a snicker. Then she said into the phone receiver, "Sure. We'll name him Lucille. I'm certain your mother would be thrilled."

"We could call him Lou. It's perfect! And now that you've officially named him; you should admit he's your cat.

"OK, he's my cat. His name is Lou. And I have silver to polish. Bye bye, Lillian."

"Toodles," Lillian said in return, hanging up her phone.

Katherine chuckled all the way back to her silverware project. Outside the kitchen window she could see the cat sunning himself on the porch rail. She tapped the window and he opened one green eye and looked her way.

"Hey, you there! Cat! Guess what? I own you now and you have a name," she informed him. The cat jumped from the rail, and strode across the veranda, twitching his tail twice at the news.

"You're name's Lucille," she called after him.

Chapter Forty

The powder blue Lincoln Continental Town car glided through the beautifully ornate wrought-iron gates that had guarded Danford Cemetery for over a century. Sitting in the passenger seat, Nora Whitcomb pulled down the vanity mirror and checked out her makeup. After brushing a speck of dried mascara off her cheek, she snapped the mirror back in place and turned to her husband.

"I just don't understand why we had to come. Daddy's a big boy. Visiting Mama's grave could have been done without us. I don't know why the whole darned family had to be here."

Stuart sighed. "She's your mother, Nora. Dan and Connie just thought we should all pay our respects. I never knew her but I think it's a shame she isn't here to share this time with all of us."

Nora squiggled deeply into the pale gray leather seat and turned her head to look at the gravestones and manicured lawns floating by.

"If she hadn't been spending all that time volunteering in the hospital maybe she would be here with us today," Nora said sharply.

"Nora, she died of cancer. You don't catch cancer."

"Maybe not, but she still could have spent less time there and more time with us. Stuart, I was only twenty-three when she died. I was barely grown. Truthfully, I barely remember her."

Stuart shot her a quick glance before pulling in behind the big Ford van the rest of the family was stuffed into. He had wanted Brent to ride along with them, remembering what it was like to be fourteen and interested in big fancy cars. But Nora, typically, had firmly declined for Brent, saying he needed to be with his mother.

"I think you remember her far more than you're willing to admit," he said to his wife.

"Think what you want," she said, dismissing his remark. Opening the door, she got out in one fluid motion and then bent over to peer back inside. "Come on, Stuart, let's get this over with." Shaking his head and sighing, Stuart opened his door.

Danford Cemetery was arrayed in springtime beauty. Flowering plum trees were flocked with masses of delicate pink blossoms and birch trees were arrayed with baby, just unfurled, springtime green leaves.

It was a glorious day. The squirrels were chattering in the trees and birds flitted from branch to branch ahead of the mob of O'Reilly's breaking up the quiet peace.

Eleanor and Donny and Jessie Lou and Brent had broken away from the adults and were quickly striding from grave to grave.

"Look, here's another Eleanor," said Eleanor. "Eleanor Gates, b. April 1, 1923, d. Nov. 22, 1956. Rest in peace."

"Look at the angels carved into this one. Isn't it beautiful? I wonder how they did it so delicately." Jessie Lou, at fifteen, had an artistic soul and delighted in beauty.

Connie Ames walked up to the group.

"Come with me and I'll show you something," she said as she headed to the south end of the cemetery. The four young people followed behind.

Crossing the gravel road, Connie continued past ancient markers and gravestones, some of them dating back to the 1880s. Coming to a stand of tamarack trees, she stopped. This part of the cemetery wasn't beautiful. There were no ornate gravestones and the trees sapped so much moisture from the ground that the lawn was sparse and weed-filled. It was quiet here, more somber. Behind the trees, the ornate black iron fencing looked different, older and more settled.

Stopping just before the trees, Connie motioned to her right.

"Do you see them?" she asked. The children were puzzled but followed her gaze.

"Oh! Wow!" Jessie Lou said, as she walked to the marker and knelt down. The others followed.

"This is, like, really old," Brent said, running his fingertip over the carving.

The wooden cross had suffered time and weather. The crossbar, held in place by two rusted nails that had left a trail of dark tears on the wood, dipped to the right and the dates and initials were barely visible. "1870-1872. And the initials are A.J.," he deciphered. "It was just a baby. I wonder who A.J. was," he mused as he stood up.

"There are two more of them," Connie said. "At least there used to be. Over to the left of that big tamarack." The five of them walked that way, crunching on years' worth of pine needles. A squirrel raced up a tree behind them, scolding them for intruding on his territory.

The two graves were barely visible through the weeds and fallen branches and were discovered more from the mounded dirt than the wooden crosses. Jessie made out the names: "The left one says Ada Neal, 1849-1871. See? Whoever carved it carved an angel. You can just make it out. This other one says, B.A.B.Y. Neal. 1871. Baby Neal. It was her baby. It must have been her baby and they both died in 1871. Oh, how sad that is."

"When I was a little girl and we would come here for Memorial Day we would bring tons of lilacs and tulips. Anything we had in the yard that looked like a flower. We would meet at Aunt Jo's house and all the cousins would be there and we'd make bouquets in tin cans. We'd pile them in Aunt Jo's station wagon and come to the cemetery. It was like a carnival here on Memorial Day. Everyone with flowers and chatting and laughing. We'd fill up the tin cans from the water spigot and haul them to the graves. Grandparents, great-grandparents, aunts, uncles, friends. Dan and Nora and I have a baby sister buried over in the infant section. If you would like, I can show you her grave. They named her Diana. I didn't know about her until I was grown.

"Anyway, one year Dan and I discovered this section and we decided they were the very first graves in Danford Cemetery. We never found any that were older, or that had simple wooden crosses. I used to spend hours wondering about A.J. and Ada Neal and her baby. I spent a day in the library trying to discover who they were. It has always been mind-boggling to me that someone can die and years later not one soul has a memory or a tale about them."

"That is so sad," Jessie Lou said.

"I wonder why no one has taken the wooden crosses," wondered Brent.

"If they were more visible they probably would have disappeared years ago, I think," Jessie Lou said.

"I wouldn't take one," Donny declared. "Bad luck. Besides, what would you do with it? You couldn't take it to show and tell and you wouldn't want it in your room. Hey, race you back to the van!"

Donny and Brent sprinted back to the others while Connie and her niece sauntered back slowly, both of them thinking of young women and their dead babies.

Chapter Forty-One

By the time Connie and the children returned, the rest of the group had finished putting a bouquet of daisies and carnations on Edna O'Reilly's grave. Patrick was on one knee, brushing away twigs.

"It's hard to believe it's been so many years," Dan said. Connie went up and put her arm around his waist. "Sometimes I still want to call her and tell her some bit of news," she said.

"You do?" Nora asked, surprised. "It's been so many years. I did that for awhile but I haven't in a long time."

"Remember the time we dropped that gallon can of honey and she made us clean it up with spoons?" Connie asked Nora.

"And then she took a picture of us all sticky and gooey and laughing so hard we could hardly scoop it up," Nora said.

"Remember her catching moths and bees in the house with Kleenex and letting them out? She couldn't bear killing them. I've never known anyone so kind-hearted. But she could sure swat a nasty fly!" Connie said.

"I liked the times when she chased the cows out of the yard with her broom," Dan offered.

"Remember how mad she'd get?" Connie laughed. Turning to the kids, she explained, "The folks down the road had a bunch of cows. They'd move them from the high pastures to the lowlands and herd them down the road. A few would always escape and they'd come into the yard and eat her roses and rock garden plants. She'd fly into a fury, chasing those cows round and round the yard. But Grampa fixed that problem."

"What'd you do?" Donny asked.

Patrick slowly got back to his feet and smacked bits of plant debris off his hands.

"I put in a cattle guard at the end of the driveway so they couldn't get in. Thought Edna'd kiss my feet, she was so grateful. I remember she fixed a big old roast the next night and an apple pie with homemade ice cream," he laughed.

"I remember you dancing with her," Nora said quietly. Dan and Connie looked at each other, puzzled.

"Oh, you were both gone by then," she said, smiling. "It was in the summertime and there was a full moon. I got up for a drink of water and saw them outside, on the patio. They were dancing but there was no music. They came apart and laughed at each other and then Daddy swept her off her feet and twirled round and round. It was probably the most wonderful thing I ever saw."

Patrick turned away, embarrassed. "You shouldn't have been watching that, Nora," he said gruffly. "That was private."

"I know that, Daddy, and I'm only saying it now because I wanted you to know how it affected my life. I probably would have run off with that skinny Askelton kid and become a pot-smoking hippy in California if it hadn't been for watching you and Mom dance that night. I knew, then, that I had to hold out for true love—for that kind of love. And that's why I went through four years of college and landed a good job before I finally found someone worthy. Old Stuart, here!" She kissed Stuart on the cheek before turning to hug her father.

"Is that a compliment?" Stuart asked Dan quietly.

"I don't know," Dan said with a shrug. "Being as it's from Nora, I think it is. That was a touching thing she said, about them dancing."

"Didn't quite sound like her, did it?" Stuart asked.

"Nope. Sure didn't."

"She's acting a bit peculiar since we got here. Must be the memories or something," Stuart said pensively.

During the exchange, Connie had knelt to the ground. One hand was pressed on the grave and her head was bowed. "I miss her. I just miss her so much," she said to no one in particular. Dan reached over and touched her shoulder. "We all do," he said. "It'll never seem right, not having her in our lives." Connie lifted her arm and Dan took it and hauled her to her feet.

"Well, now. My goodness," Connie said. Nora gave her a quick hug, and kissed her on the cheek, startling everyone. Connie hugged her back, fiercely, then moved away and put her arm around her little sister's waist.

"Are we ready to hit someplace for lunch?" she asked.

Nora linked arms with Stuart and they and the children started ambling toward the van. Dan and Miranda and Connie followed. Patrick O'Reilly hung back.

"You folks go on and get loaded up. I just want to spend some time here alone," he said.

"You take your time, Dad," Dan said. "We'll move a bit down the road to give you some privacy."

"Thanks, Son."

Patrick removed his hat and held it in his hands as he turned to face the grave of his beloved wife. When he heard the two vehicles move away he knelt down and put his head in his hands.

"Edna, honey... I can't tell you how much I miss you. It's been so long but I still reach over for you at night. Isn't that crazy? I still hear your voice and I close my eyes and imagine you in the old house. It seems so strange not to be living there and living in a big city. I don't even know who lives in the old house anymore. Isn't that sad? Our old place, the one we built with such love, and now it's inhabited by strangers. I see you everywhere, Edna, in the flowers in the spring and the new snow in the winter.

"Sometimes I ache for you. And I wonder, sometimes, if I haven't wasted an important part of my life by being so faithful to you. If roles were reversed and I was the one in the grave I would have wanted you to find some dandy fellow and have a happy ever after. And I know you, deep down, would want that for me. Maybe I've messed up here. But it's a bit late now. I'm healthy as a horse but I'm nigh on eighty-years-old, and that's a bit old for finding a date. But sometimes I'm so lonely.

"I want to thank you for all the years we had together. We had some grand times, didn't we? And we have three good children and these dandy grandchildren that you never even met. I think, though, that you handpicked them in heaven and sent them down just for us.

"I miss you, Edna, and I doubt if I'll be back this way again to visit. But I trust you're with God and I will see you soon. I know you have a place saved for me up there. Sometimes I think back on how we decided to trust Jesus together and I think, no, I know, it was the best decision we ever made. It's always made things easier, knowing for certain just where you are right now."

Getting to his feet, Patrick brushed the tears from his eyes and then looked into the bright blue sky.

"God, please give her a hug from me," he whispered. Then he put his hat back on his head and turned to walk away.

CHAPTER FORTY-TWO

At 11 a.m. Maxie Bruce, arms laden with cookbooks and a bag of spices and herbs, banged through the kitchen door, shutting it with a hefty shove from her enormous hip. Dumping her load on the large butcher-block counter in the middle of the big kitchen, she took stock. Kitchen hadn't changed one whit, she thought. It felt mighty good to be back.

"Maxie, is that you?" Katherine's voice chimed loudly from somewhere near the dining room.

"Don't know who else it be," Maxie hollered back. A few seconds later Katherine pushed open the swinging door and grinned broadly. Placing her hands on her hips, she declared, "Maxie, you haven't changed one bit. Why, just looking at you I feel like I might be back in 1975. Maybe 1970. My heavens, it's good to see you." Crossing the kitchen briskly she gave the old cook a tight hug.

"Miss Kate, it's you who haven't changed none. Still scrawny. Not enough meat on you to feed a starving dog. Still got that long hair all bunned up like some virgin. Looks like you still full of spit and vinegar. But we getting' old, ain't we, honey? This fat old black body sure don't waddle fast as it used to."

"Oh, listen to you. You always did run yourself down. We aren't getting older, Maxie, we're getting better. Just the fact that we're both here and putting on this party proves that. Who else do you know who would get tangled up in such a thing?"

"Gotta admit it was right nice getting that phone call this morning, Miss Kate, even if you did call before the birds were up and forced me out of my warm bed."

Maxie looked around the kitchen and at her old friend and employer, her golden brown eyes warm with love and pleasure. "My, my, it's nice to be back in this old kitchen," she said softly, more to herself than to Katherine.

Katherine grasped a chubby black hand and squeezed. "It's like old times, isn't it, Maxie?"

"Sure is, 'cept a lot of what made them old times grand is gone. Lots of good folks gone up to be with the Lord, Miss Kate. Lots of good folks gone. Seems downright strange, knowing Mr. John ain't back there in his study. Last time I was here I was cooking up food for his funeral, tears drippin' all over the kitchen." Katherine felt her throat start to clog and gave way to indulge a bit of grief. Her eyes filled with tears.

"I know. I know," she said softly. "And your Walter is gone, too. Two good men who were loved. We're both old widow ladies. What woman ever thinks that someday she might be a lonely widow? Probably not many I'll venture. But right now, Maxie, we're old widow ladies with a challenge and I don't know about you, but I'm darned excited about it. We've got 10,000 things to do and only hours to do it. We have to be ready by 7 o'clock tomorrow night."

"Miss Kate, yesterday I was watching one of them talk shows on the TV and thinking what a miserable existence I had. Thought to myself, worms probably have more excitement and fun than I do. Today I feel like I could just bust a gasket. Got food to cook and people to feed. It surely is good to be back to work and feedin' folks," said Maxie as she tied a stiff white apron around her vast middle. "Miss Kate, you'd best get out of my kitchen and let this old woman get to plannin'," she said, as she reached into a cupboard to pull out a stainless steel mixing bowl.

"I'll leave for now but I'll be back to help," Katherine said. "We need to talk about the menu and times and all."

"We got time to do all that. Now I needs to just find my kitchen again and do some planning. First thing I'm gonna do is fix you some lunch. Come back around in an hour and we'll have one of them meetings like in the old days. Be a good girl and shoo now and I'll maybe let you peel potatoes tomorrow," Maxie promised.

Katherine was still laughing as she settled in her favorite chair in the great room and dialed the number for the florist. Waiting for it to be answered, she pulled out her notebook and pen, turned the pages until she found her list, and carefully crossed a line through "florist."

Letty came through the front door while the phone was on the third ring, and Katherine waved her in. Letty grandly blew her a kiss, motioning wide and smacking and, grinning, pointed to the dining room. A second later, Katherine could hear Letty in the dining room, singing softly as she clattered dishes. Katherine knew she'd probably have to correct the place settings and it was too early to set the table—the dinner wasn't until tomorrow evening, after all—but she was grateful for Letty's help. Things were coming together. As soon as she got off the phone, she could guide her more productively. She realized with amazement that Letty, who had been her steadfast companion for years now, had never taken part in one of Katherine's dinners.

On the fourth ring, what sounded to be a third grader, and could be either female or male, answered the phone at Danford Flowers and Gifts. Katherine carefully placed the order.

"I would like to order a centerpiece of flowers to resemble an English cutting garden with lots of roses, not too high and long enough and large enough to not look dwarfed and puny on a fifteen-foot table. Also a two smaller versions of the table centerpiece, one for a table in the entrance and another for a coffee table. Plus a small arrangement of pink miniature roses for a powder room. Also, one yellow rose boutonnière. Can you repeat that, please?"

"Uh, mmm, okay, let's see. A big centerpiece to be like maybe an English garden. It has to be long for a big table but it can't be too high. So people can see each other across the table, right?"

"Correct."

"Then, two more arrangements like English cutting gardens, one for a table by the entrance and the other one for a coffee table. And then you want a yellow rose boutonniere and a pink arrangement for a bathroom."

"Very good! They will need to be delivered to O'Malley House tomorrow morning before noon."

"O'Malley House? Like that big mansion place?"

"That's right. If Mr. Hobbins is still coming into the shop, please convey my regards."

"Will do. We'll get hopping on the order. Mr. Hobbins is, like, my grandpa. I'll tell him what you said. He told me once about the flowers he used to take to your mansion place."

"So, is Mr. Hobbins like your grandpa, or is he your grandpa?"

"He is my grandpa."

"Oh. And who are you?"

"I'm Danny Hobbins."

"You must be young Daniel's boy then."

"He's my father, but he isn't young. He's old."

"How old is he?"

"Thirty-nine."

"Believe me, sweetie, there will come a time when you think thirty-nine is so young you can hardly imagine it! I remember your father when he was probably your age. He would often help carry in the flowers. He was such a somber child, so quiet and shy. Ask him sometime about the accident with the bronze roses and lilacs."

"What happened?"

"Oh, I can't tell. He'll have to tell you himself. If you can get away from the shop, young Daniel, maybe you could help with tomorrow's delivery. I would like to meet you."

"Maybe I can. I'll ask Grandpa."

"Good, maybe I'll see you tomorrow then." Hanging up the phone, she smiled to herself. Why on earth had that old memory of the bronze roses and lilacs crept up through her memory banks? Odd how some things—important things like the sound of a person's voice—left you forever and other things, like a bouquet of roses and lilacs, just pop up out of nowhere.

"I wonder if Daniel even remembers," she murmured to herself as she settled back to let the memory fully flood her mind.

She and John were hosting a huge gathering. She couldn't really recall the occasion now, but remembered it was warm. Springtime, maybe. Young Daniel was just old enough to help deliver the flowers. His father was doing paperwork in the cab of the delivery truck and Daniel had placed the huge arrangement of bronze roses and lilacs on the bottom step of the porch while he went back to the old truck to get another bouquet. What happened next startled everyone in the house. Suddenly Daniel was screaming like a banshee. Katherine and Maxie and John came running from inside and Simeon could be seen huffing from the back orchard. Bert Hobbins flung himself from the pickup.

Daniel, shaking his fists and bellowing, was chasing a huge black Labrador retriever down the street. Bert had taken off after him.

"What on earth! Was he stung by bees? Why is he chasing that poor dog?" Kate was clearly perplexed.

"Got the devil himself after him, runnin' like that," Maxie said, shaking her head and wiping her dishwater-dripping hands on her apron.

It was John who first figured out the problem. Simeon, following John's stare to the sopping bouquet near his feet, figured it out next. They tried to stifle the chuckles.

"Watch your feet, Kate," John said somberly.

"What?"

"Got some dog dew on your flowers there," he said, nodding his head toward the bottom of the sidewalk. He and Simeon burst into laughter.

The grand bouquet, wrapped carefully in green florist's paper, was a drenched mess. The paper had dissolved down around the cut glass container and the roses and lilacs were dripping.

"Dog dew? That dog! That miserable cur lifted his leg on my flowers?" Kate was horrified.

"Get the gun, Mister John. Just get the gun. You and Mister Simeon can kill that brute. Fool dog shudda knowed we was having them flowers for a special gatherin'." Maxie feigned righteous fury but then joined the menfolk in a hearty laugh. Soon Kate was bent over in laughter herself. By the time a huffing and puffing Daniel Hobbins, followed by his father, joined them, they were all wiping laughter tears from their eyes.

Using a spray bottle, Maxie rinsed off the flowers and they were majestically set in their appointed place at the head table. That night, when anyone remarked on their beauty, John and Katherine would burst into laughter, much to the puzzlement of guests.

Chapter Forty-Three

Getting up from her chair, Katherine walked to the kitchen and pushed open the swinging doors. Maxie was resting her backside against the butcher block and leafing through a well-worn cookbook. She glanced over a pair of wire rim half-glasses and started a slow rumbling chuckle when she saw that Katherine was about to burst into peels of laughter. Katherine, holding the laughter in with one arm, flung the other over Maxie's ample shoulders.

"What's so funny?"

"Oh, Maxie, I was just reminiscing. Do you remember the dog dew flowers? The bronze roses and lilacs and young Daniel Hobbins?" Katherine dissolved into laughter. "Remember that stupid leg-lifting dog?"

Maxie joined in, her chuckles turning to loud guffaws.

"And them people saying how pretty them flowers were. I was refilling the punch bowl and that Hoskins woman—remember those snooty Hoskins people? She had two other women cornered and they was smelling them roses. They had their noses buried so deep you couldn't see their chins."

Maxie changed her voice into a flutelike tone, "She said, 'Oh, Alma, aren't they just lovely? Just smell that delicious scent.' I started chucklin' and spilled a drop of punch."

"That is so funny! That Effie Hoskins was a snob with a capital S," Katherine said, still laughing. "Serves her right, smelling that dog dew. What happened next?"

"Not much," Maxie said, sobering.

"She didn't say a thing when she saw you laughing?" Katherine had noticed the laughter die from Maxie's eyes and became alarmed.

"What did she say, Maxie?" Katherine said quietly.

Maxie turned and looked Katherine in the eye. She lifted her chin and recited the encounter as if was forever etched into her brain. "She said, 'Servants like you all don't need to be getting your noses into other people's business. Specially white people. Laugh at us again and I'll tell Mrs. O'Malley how disrespectful you are. Now you'd better get your big black hiney back in the kitchen where you belong.' "

"Oh, Maxie. I'm so sorry."

"Why you sorry? You didn't say it!"

"If I had known, I'd never have allowed that woman in my home. I'd have poured that punch over her head and publicly ridiculed her for her disgusting prejudice."

"Miss Kate," Maxie said, shaking her head and chuckling sadly. "You'd done that to her, you'd have had to have done it to near everyone there. They'd been lined up out the door. Them was different times, then."

"Do you think it's better now?"

"Mmm-hmm. My grandkids don't know the evils of racism and living in fear. My very own father, back home in Alabama, was whipped one night for saying howdy to a white woman. My grandson, Reggie has a best friend who's white as a linen pillowcase. They spend weekends at each other's houses. Reggie, he don't see that Nate is white and Nate, he don't see that Reggie is black. It's good."

"So, what about us then, Maxie?"

"What you mean?"

"Well, I am like Nate. I don't see that my good friend Maxie is black. But, my friend, Maxie, she sure sees that she's black and that I am white."

"Hmmm. Well, I guess that there's different."

"Is it so different, Maxie? If I were to ask you, would you go to lunch with me at La Bistro?"

"Miss Kate, I was raised in different times. Some things is just hard to overcome. Hard to forget."

"Do you consider me a friend?" Kate demanded. "Or am I just an employer?"

Maxie's eyes softened and gentled. "A friend," she said softly. "You've always been a friend."

Katherine clapped her hands merrily. "OK, then. We'll go to lunch," she declared. "We have a lunch date. As soon as you are ready, you just give me a ring and we'll be off for a grand afternoon. Lunch and shopping and maybe we'll stop by Danford Florists and get a couple of bronze roses for old time's sake."

Maxie stared. It was a frightful thought. Would people think she was uppity? Did she care? Thoughts, both positive and negative, ping-ponged through her brain. Katherine put her soft, tiny, pale hand over Maxie's larger, black hand.

"When you're ready, Maxie, call me. It'll be okay, I promise. I am your friend. And you can be sure I would have punched out that Hoskins woman's headlights if I had known. We haven't kept in touch for years and we have wasted too much time. We need to spend time together, Maxie."

Tiny tears gathered at the corner of Maxie's eyes. Pulling her hand from under Katherine's she wiped them away quickly.

"Miss Kate, don't you have something better to do than bother an old woman? I am trying to fix you a decent lunch here, you know."

Katherine, chuckling gleefully, glided out of the kitchen.

Chapter Forty-Four

Early in the afternoon, after a wonderful lunch of Maxie's famous corn chowder and bacon, lettuce and tomato sandwiches, Letty wandered through the mansion until she found Katherine, who had disappeared right after eating. As Letty walked down endless hallways and into different wings of the enormous building, she was, as always, struck anew with the beauty and vastness of the stately old place. Now, in a hurry, she didn't take time to explore or admire but wished she had a bike to make the journey speedier. Katherine was nowhere to be found. She'd checked her bedroom suite and all the rooms she generally used. Letty knew it was useless to open the dozens of doors to unused bedrooms and public rooms.

On the third floor she saw the door to the attic was open and knew that was where she'd find Katherine. Climbing the steep narrow staircase, Letty poked her head into the long room lighted by shafts of afternoon sunlight. It was four times bigger than Letty's apartment. Katherine had stirred up an amount of dust and it glittered and shimmered in the sunbeams.

If Katherine hadn't been moving her hands, it would look like an old master painting had been propped up against the wall, Letty thought.

Katherine was seated on an ancient wooden chair with a faded green velvet seat and back that were surrounded by brass studs. Sunlight streamed through one of the small overhead windows and pierced a stained glass window leaning against a thick support beam. The stained glass in the window depicted a country scene with fields of amber and a humble cottage hugged by richly colored flowers. Marring the beauty was a gaping hole at the bottom corner where the glass had been shattered. The sunlight streaming through the colorful window washed over Katherine, changing her hair to a glow of molten gold.

"So, here you are. I've been looking for a half hour!" Letty said. Katherine jumped. She had been so lost in memories she hadn't heard Letty's thumping footsteps.

"You startled me! I'm looking for the gift I want to give Mr. O'Reilly. I know it's here somewhere," she said, carefully putting the pile she'd accumulated on her lap back into the trunk. "Maybe in this old trunk," she said, scooting her chair to a large wood and metal trunk with a curved lid.

"What are you looking for?" Letty asked, as Katherine blew a layer of dust off the trunk, unlatched the lock and lifted the creaking lid.

"It's a book. It came out in the '40s. It's a limited edition on the history of the area. I think it was published by the historical society. It's full of old photos of the early buildings and the days when teams of horses skidded logs out of the woods and pulled enormous sleds piled with them. The men are all dressed in these very strange clothes with boots that lace up to their knees and hats of all sorts. The women look sturdy and unhappy and overworked. My husband is in there, along with his father and uncles, all of them looking so serious and dour. There are pictures, lots of them, of workers in sawmills and in blacksmith shops and stables. And pictures of early celebrations and grand houses. Even this house is in the book, and the newly planted trees are so small and look so weak. Since he spent a large part of his life here, I thought it would be a perfect gift for Mr. O'Reilly."

By the time she finished the description, Katherine, with Letty's help, had removed the top layer of fabulous velvet quilts and fragile linens and unearthed a mother lode of old books encased in richly-colored, embossed leather bindings.

"These are priceless!" Letty gasped. "Look at this. 'Uncle Tom's Cabin by Mrs. Stowe.' Doesn't even say Harriet Beecher Stowe, just plain old 'Mrs. Stowe.' And it's a first edition. Longfellow. Shakespeare..."

Holding the thin Romeo and Juliet volume to her heart she quoted, solemnly and eloquently, "But, soft! What light through yonder window breaks? It is the east, and Juliet is the sun." Opening her eyes, she smiled and said, "But you sitting there all golden, Mrs. O, I think right now you are the sun!"

"Why, Letty, you surprise me," Katherine exclaimed in delight. I wouldn't think you'd know Longfellow from a longhorn, let alone Mrs. Stowe's first name. And quoting Shakespeare?"

"Shocked you, did I? Let's just say that, like, there's more to me than meets the eye, and there's quite a bit that meets the eye."

"I'm going to have to do some exploring, I see," said Katherine, chuckling, as she dove deeper into the trunk and searched through the piles. Pulling out a thin book from near the bottom, she held it high and then bounced spryly to her feet. "I found it!"

As they walked through the darkened halls, Letty remembered her mission.

"I talked to Maxie about you sitting at the table and she agrees. Maxie's called her granddaughter, Elva, who is a real waitress and worked at Howard Johnson for years before she went to school and became a teacher. Elva is coming to help. And I'll be there to help, too, but you'd be better off with Elva, because you know how clumsy I am. I'd end up spilling hot gravy all over the birthday boy's lap and we'd be sued. 'Sides, I got this entertainment thing I'm in charge of. By the way, that Maxie's one great lady. You didn't say she was black."

"She's black? Huh! Well, I'll be darned. I hadn't noticed. Did she mention that little Elva started hanging around here and helping when she was just a child? My goodness, Elva...she must be in her thirties by now."

Katherine smiled at the memory, and then suddenly her eyes widened. "Oh, Letty, I haven't played hostess for nearly a decade. My social skills haven't just deteriorated. They're dead. It makes me a wreck to even think of presiding over a table of ten strangers."

"But, don't you see, that's why it'll be easy," said Letty as she tripped over her feet and stumbled toward an heirloom game table. "There's ten of 'em and they'll be so busy yakking and enjoying the food and atmosphere, you won't have to do anything but look pretty and smile!"

"Well, I don't know, Letty. Maybe if I wasn't alone."

"So, ask Simeon."

"I did. The other night he heard you leave and came over all worried something had happened. I told him about the birthday party and asked if he'd play host with me. He said he would."

"I think you can count on him, but maybe it would help if you talked to him and verify he's still coming. He'd be a great host. You know Simeon is a great talker, once you get him started."

"Oh, I don't know, Letty. It would be nice to have someone with me but Simeon can be so, well, he can be so..."

"Stubborn and ridiculously prideful and unyielding?"

"Yes! That's it exactly. It took me six months to get the man to actually sit in the kitchen and have a cup of coffee with me. He preferred the porch. Said he didn't belong in the Big House. 'The Big House' he called it, as if it was a cathedral built by the saints themselves."

"Tell you what. I'll talk to him. Make sure he's going to be here."

"Okay, be my guest. Just don't get him all riled up and thinking he needs to hide out for six months. He's spooky as a deer in a pea patch, Letty, and I'd hate to give up our coffee and lunch times together."

"I promise I won't scare Simeon," Letty said as she loped off toward the attic door. Katherine held her breath and closed her eyes as Letty stumbled down the stairs. The crash came at the end, just a few steps from the bottom. "I'm okay! Nothing's broken!" Letty hollered back up the stairs to Katherine. Rubbing her hip, she limped off, muttering, "dang feet."

Chapter Forty-Five

Letty let herself into the mansion well before seven o'clock Saturday morning and headed straight to the ballroom to finish the decorating she had started the night before. The past two days had been filled with dozens of phone calls, arranging entertainment, hauling decorations from storage rooms, testing the sound system and lighting, and hoping it would all come together.

A dozen times Letty had told herself that it was crazy the turmoil this simple birthday party was causing. Katherine could have settled on a simple dinner of lasagna, salad, and French bread and purchased a birthday cake from Polsky's Market and shoved in candles. And Letty could have dragged the cake upstairs to the ballroom and hooked up her boom box for background music. Instead, Letty had gone overboard with the entertainment and had arranged enough music and surprises for a full-fledged black-tie charity event. And Katherine had brought Maxie on the scene, coerced Simeon to be host, and was acting as if she was entertaining the queen of England.

Letty knew part of the plans included a tour of the mansion. Luckily, all the rooms were kept in perfect shape, especially since she and Katherine had spent countless hours the past year putting the rooms back to their original condition. Thankfully, that was one thing that wasn't on the list of things to do.

It really was quite strange—that they were leaping into this celebration so wholeheartedly. It was almost as if there was something else at play. As if this was a practice run for something bigger. It would be interesting to see just what God was up to.

The ballroom was almost ready and Letty had to admit it was stunning. She sat on the floor, untangling strands of miniature lights which were all plugged into a nearby socket.

When Katherine walked into the room she immediately wished she had her camera. Letty looked as if she was sitting in the middle of a thousand glittering diamonds. She had pulled a strand around her neck and the lights nestled in her long blond hair. She looked like a Madonna, surrounded by the stars of eternity.

"Having fun?" Katherine asked as she strode across the huge room.

"This is going to sound crazy," Letty said with a grin, "but I am having fun. At home I'm always the one who gets to untangle the Christmas lights. And I love untangling necklaces. I used to smush up Mom's necklaces into a wad just so I could disentangle them. Well, until she caught me." She stood up, unplugged the lights, and started across the room to hang them on a large silk weeping fig tree.

"Hang on for a sec and I'll give you a tour. I think you'll like it. But don't turn around and look until I tell you."

Katherine tagged along after her. She was amused. She had seen this room decorated hundreds of times and remembered the thrill of doing it. She was renowned for coming up with strange and exotic themes. No one ever really knew what to expect when they came to an O'Malley gala. One Christmas she had a live Nativity scene, complete with sheep and a miniature donkey and a real infant whose mother played the role of Mary.

"So," Letty said as she reached up to fix a light strand, "do you think it's odd that we're getting so carried away with this party?"

"I've been thinking about that," admitted Katherine. "And you're right. It is odd. Maybe it's because I haven't entertained in so long and I'm realizing how much I miss it. Maybe it's because Maxie is here and this is how we used to do things. Or maybe it's because the people are strangers and I want to make a good impression. I hope they don't think we're crazy with all this hoopla. Whatever it is, I agree. It's downright odd that I'm getting so extravagant with this party. For heaven's sake, it's just a birthday!"

"It isn't just you," Letty said, as she plugged in the lights and stood back to check out her work. "I'm not going to tell you because I want you to be surprised, but you won't believe what I've come up with for entertainment. I'm totally shocked it came together so easily and quickly. Like totally. It's almost like there's more to this thing tonight than we know. Like God's up to something again."

Katherine frowned. "Oh, my. I had sort of thought about that, in that it was a fleeting thought that zipped through my brain, but now that you're putting it to words it's alarming. My goodness, do you suppose...?"

"Mmmm-hmmm. I suppose. It seems like every time you start letting the grass grow under your feet, something happens to keep you moving. The last year we've been working on the rooms without knowing why. And now we're in the party business, without knowing why. You've gotta admit it's dang exciting!" Letty said, grinning.

Without waiting for an answer, Letty took Katherine by the shoulders and turned her around. "OK, you walk back to the door and don't turn around until I tell you.

"And no peeking!" she added as she took off running the length of the ballroom. Leaping on stage, she disappeared behind velvet curtains, turned on the lights, and then came off the stage and turned off the row of overhead chandelier lights. From there she went from one wall outlet to another, turning on the miniature lights that festooned dozens of fake trees.

Letty was out of breath as she reached Katherine's side. "OK," she said. "Turn around and look."

"Oh!" Katherine exclaimed in delight as her hand flew to her mouth. "It's beautiful. Absolutely beautiful. It looks like an enchanted forest. The tables, the arrangements. It is absolutely spectacular, Letty. I am so proud of you! I can't believe this. It's so sad that this old ballroom has been just sitting here all these years waiting, patiently waiting, to entertain again. For people to dance on its floors and to laugh and be happy. Why, Letty, I think I could just sit down here and bawl."

"Aw, Mrs. O, don't cry. I hate it when you cry."

Turning to Letty, Katherine took the younger woman's hands into her own. "You brought it to life again. Really, because of you, the whole mansion is coming to life again."

"It's nice, having all the seniors here working during the week and now this party going on, isn't it? Hey, do you suppose Maxie has anything to eat?"

"Knowing Maxie, she has a five-course lunch ready for us," Katherine said. "Are you done enough here to take a break?"

"It's all ready, except when the entertainers show up we'll have to do some tuning and maybe some adjustments on the sound. I'm not too good at that but one of the guys is a whiz, so I'm not worried."

"Oh, Letty, sometimes I think I'm too old for much of an upheaval and God is certainly turning things here upside down. First, all the work in the rooms, and now this dinner. I'm glad God always knows what's best for us."

Chapter Forty-Six

By the time Letty and Katherine reached the dining room they could hear Maxie's voice from somewhere beyond the kitchen. Katherine put a finger to her lips to warn Letty and the two of them tiptoed to the door to listen. They could hear a melodic whap of a dish towel on the back porch railing and the voice of Marge Reynolds next door. Maxie was clearly angry but Katherine was sure the vapid and divisive Marge wouldn't even be aware of it. Marge, leaning out her dining room window, was waging a vigorous battle.

"What is the matter with you? Can't you talk? All I want to know is if Mrs. O'Malley is all right. Who are you, anyway? I have asked you many questions and I demand that you answer them."

Maxie didn't answer. She kept her face passive and just continued to shake the flour from the towel. Marge leaned farther out the window.

"Perhaps I should call the police. Perhaps they can get some answers out of you," she hissed. Maxie shut her eyes for a few seconds and then carefully, deliberately, folded the cloth and wiped her floury hands on her apron. The golden brown eyes darkened to the color of cold, rusted iron as she set them on her adversary. Her voice was calm, polite, and severely deliberate.

"All you want to know, is none of your business," Maxie said evenly. "Cain't just open that window, Miz Reynolds, and demand to know what was in all them grocery sacks Miss Kate brought into the house. Cain't just open that window and ask what that little girl Letty was doing here so late last night. This here's a private residence, not some social club where you pays your dues and gets the right to know. Ain't none of your business who I am or what I'm doin' here. I think you'd best get back in your house so's I can get my work done."

Marge Reynolds was irate. "It is my moral responsibility to see to the welfare of my neighbor. Are you an employee? And how do you know my name? Why does she need you to cook? Perhaps I should call the police and they can verify that you're authorized to be there and she is safe. After all, I don't know you and I have never seen you before. Believe me, I know everything that happens in this neighborhood and you have never been in this one before. You're an outsider, and I demand to know why you are in that house."

"Miz Reynolds, you should know me from before. When I was helpin' Mr. John and Miss Katherine with the big parties? Them parties you and your husband used to come to over here at the mansion, all dressed up and laughing."

"I don't know you at all, and I think you made that up. You've never been here before in your life. I demand to know your name."

"Miz Reynolds, I come to this house to work in 1943. I was fourteen and I helped the cook and cleaned some. I was here in 1945 when Miss Kate and Mr. John was married right out in that parlor. Me and the cook stood in the back and dried our tears with our aprons. I was here when the babies started coming and dyin' and I was here through the death of Mr. John. My mama come to this house to work in 1925 when she was fifteen. She was one of the first black people in this part of Montana. She worked for the old folk O'Malleys. Out back by the old stable was where she met my pa, a black man straight from Alabama, who was delivering feed for the livestock. When they was married two years later, the old folks gave them $25 and a set of fine china. I still have that china, every piece of it.

"Miz Reynolds, you a newcomer to this here part of the country. Probably don't even know about the baby the Hollisters down the way lost twenty years back, or that old Mrs. Price's first husband died in a POW camp during the big war or that there used to be a swamp right down past the first intersection. Full of bullfrogs so loud they kept the old folks awake most of the summers until they got so elderly and deaf they couldn't hear 'em no more. Know what used to be sitting smack dab in the middle of where your house is now?"

Marge Reynolds, smitten to silence by the verbal barrage, shook her head.

"The outhouses. Stinkin' things they was. Fearsome. Three of 'em. Maybe four. Maybe more, now I think on it, cuz they was for the outside hands too. Some for ladies. Some for gentlemens. All of em' full of crap and maggots. Ain't no discrimination when it comes to crap and maggots. Back around 1934 the old folks O'Malleys was coaxed to sell off that hunk of land to some vagabond kin and he built the house you're livin' in. 'Fore that it was a like a park around O'Malley House. That relative built that house right over the top of them outhouses. Then he sold out 'thout giving the O'Malleys a chance to buy back the land. Kids back then used to laugh and joke about that house. Word was if you sat next to the inside wall in the living room you could still get a whiff of the stench from them outhouses. Always wondered if that was true. Is it true? Miz Reynolds, you live there now; can you smell them outhouses?"

Horrified by the vision and by being labeled a newcomer, Marge sputtered in fury. "This is absurd. I'll not stand here and listen to any more of this nonsense."

"Ain't nonsense. Ask anyone hereabouts who's got a history here."

"I'll not ask anyone about anything," she replied as she slammed shut the window. Maxie's voice rang out, following Marge across the room, following her as she flung herself into her chair and covered her face with her hands.

"My name's Maxie Bruce and Miss Kate is fine as fine can be and we're having us a grand old party here tonight," she hollered. As an afterthought she added, "Next time maybe I'll tell you the story about old Ned Beecham who shot himself in your garage back in the '50s. It was summertime. Hotter'n Hades. Didn't find the poor old coot for three days. He was ripe by then. My, my, it was a stinkin' mess."

Huffing back through the back screen door, which slapped shut with a bang, Maxie stomped to the butcher block, snapped up her rolling pin and began rolling out pie dough. After a few minutes she grabbed a spatula and scraped the dough into a heap and dumped it into the garbage can. "Old bat made me beat this dough so tough I could make hubcaps out of it," she muttered just as Letty and Katherine tumbled through the door and stared at her in shock.

"What you two gawkin' at?" Maxie demanded, angrily wiping the back of her hand across her broad brow. "You been eavesdropping?"

The two culprits nodded in unison.

"Danged old busybody made me ruin this pie dough," Maxie complained again as she tossed another bit of dough into the can. "I beat it half to death with that rolling pin. That pie be tougher'n shoe leather if I used that dough. You two quit that starin' and get outta my kitchen. I got pies to make. If'n you're hungry, there's lunch in the 'fridge. Ham sandwiches and fruit salad. "

"Maxie, you are a true treasure. I never thought I'd live to see the day when anyone got the best of Marge Reynolds," Katherine said as she held the door open for Letty. Maxie sifted a new pile of flour on the butcher block, the dark chub of her underarms swaying in quick rhythm.

"Don't like being mean to no living creature but, Miss Kate, that snoopy woman sure got my dander up," she said. "Now the Lord's gonna make me figure a way to apologize, I just know he is. The good Lord don't like it when we treat his children bad and I'm gonna pay for this, I just know I am. It'll start botherin' me something fierce until I crawl over there and ask that awful woman to forgive my blabbery mouth."

"She gets everyone's dander up but there's something so pathetic about her," Katherine said, sobering. "We used to be such good friends and I don't know what happened. When Bud died a few years back, she just sort of disappeared. I tried to talk to her but she basically slammed the door in my face. I gave up trying after awhile. I never did figure out what I did wrong or if I said something that angered her. It's very sad. She must be very lonely. In a way, I'm touched that she's worried about me. Maybe I'll give her a call."

"You're a better woman than I am, if you're gonna call her," Letty said. Turning to Maxie she confided. "That Marge Reynolds is always causing trouble. She calls the police to complain about trees dropping leaves in her yard, or my car making too much noise, or when the horses get too close. Sometimes she calls the police just to call the police. Just to cause trouble."

"Well, she surely was causin' trouble here today, but bein' lonely ain't no reason to be so high and mighty and unfriendly to others," Maxie said as she swiftly and rhythmically rolled out a perfectly round pie crust. Then she muttered to herself, "And being unfriendly ain't no reason for Maxie Bruce to be so hostile and nasty. I'm sorry, Jesus, that I treated one of your very own children so downright badly."

Chapter Forty-Seven

Opening the antique secretary in the elegant turret room she considered her sanctuary, Katherine took out a slim black address book. Running her finger along the raised alphabet along the side, she stopped at the "R." It was sad, she thought, that she had to look up Marge's number. It wasn't that long ago that she knew that number as well as her own and, if she didn't walk through the back gate to visit in person, called it several times a week just to chat.

"Raymond, Stella. Rayburn, Rex. Renfrew, Mike. Renfrew, Charles and Mary. I wonder whatever happened to them. Moved, I think. Here it is. Reynolds, Bud and Marge. Two-eight-three...No, I think that's a two. Two-eight-two. Two-eight-two-four. Darn it, I can't read this thing." Fishing under the papers, she found a pair of cheap, dime-store reading glasses and put them on. Sitting in her chair, she dialed the number. After six rings she was about to hang up when Marge picked up the phone. She didn't say hello. Just breathed into it.

"Marge. Is that you? Hello? Margery?"

"It's me." Her voice was low and quiet.

"This is Katherine. I'm sorry about the run-in you and Maxie had a few minutes ago. She's very protective. Didn't you remember her from when John was alive? She always helped with our big parties," Katherine closed her eyes and prayed for wisdom.

"I don't know that woman from Adam. I really can't talk now. I have a headache and I think I'm going to be sick. She had no right to talk to me like that." Marge could still feel her heart trying to beat itself out of her chest. She was way too overwrought about the whole situation. Why did she do it, anyway? Hanging out the window like a crazy woman. Besides, maybe she did know that woman. She realized halfway through her screaming that Maxie looked familiar.

"Maxie was being very protective of my privacy and you pushed her over the edge. She feels upset, herself, at how things went."

"She should. Talking to me like that. Like some...some minion. I was just worried about you."

"Why?"

"What?"

"I asked, 'why?' Why were you worried about me?"

"Well, I thought something was wrong, what with all those people coming and going."

"Why would that matter? Why would you care?"

"Well, you're my neighbor. My friend. Of course I would care."

"Marge," Katherine said softly. "I have tried for three years to talk to you. To help you. You shut the door on every attempt I made. Why do you care now?"

Marge started to cry. "I don't know. I just don't know what to do anymore. I saw that blond girl there last night, then Simeon was there until late and now this strange black woman is there... I thought maybe something awful had happened to you. That maybe you were gone, too."

"Well, if it took a battle with Maxie Bruce to get us talking again, it was worth it, don't you think?"

"I don't know."

"Well, I know. I want you to think it over and sometime next week come over for tea like in the old days."

"I can't."

"Why not?"

"I can't tell you. I just can't."

"Can I come visit you?"

"No. I'm sorry."

"Is this another door slamming shut?"

Marge started sobbing. "No. You just don't understand. I have to go."

Long after the phone clicked in her ear, Katherine sat holding it. When the beep-beep-beep warning tones interrupted her reverie, she carefully replaced the receiver. Marge was right about one thing. Katherine just didn't understand.

God, please help that poor unfortunate soul, she implored. Better yet, God, show me what I can do. Lord, help me to forgive all the times she has tried to hurt me, and help me to love her as you do.

Chapter Forty-Eight

By the time the florist's van from Danford Flowers and Gifts drove up the driveway late that afternoon, the smells of roast beef, plump potato rolls, and hot-out-of-the-oven apple and huckleberry pie drifted out of the kitchen. Katherine was at the sink peeling carrots and potatoes, and Maxie was deftly and methodically getting the salad ingredients ready.

Sitting in a box on the far left kitchen counter top was the birthday cake Josephine Grimm had dropped off earlier. As usual, it was a remarkable masterpiece. Josephine was known throughout the whole valley for her cake-decorating abilities and every few years taught a class at the community college. The most difficult thing about having a Josephine Grimm cake for a festivity was finding someone with the courage to cut into it. The first time they had used her services—for Katherine's birthday—John had stood over the exquisite cake covered with tiny pink and white and yellow roses, and the hand holding the cake knife quivered. Looking up at the guests he remarked, "It's sort of like cutting a hole in the Mona Lisa."

The air in the kitchen was festive as the two old friends chatted about the old days. Peels of laughter filled the kitchen, Maxie's booming and gruff and Katherine's chiming and melodic. They were so noisy they didn't hear the ringing doorbell.

On the fourth ring, Letty went to the door. A tiny elderly man with slightly crossed eyes and wearing a faded Dodgers baseball cap handed her a big bouquet wrapped neatly in filmy green florist's tissue. Standing in the middle of the sidewalk behind him was a young boy, about twelve, gaping up at the third floor of the mansion.

"I'm Bert Hobbins. Danford Floral and Gifts. Been a long time since I brought an order of flowers to O'Malley House. Miss Katherine entertaining again?" he asked. Letty smiled and nodded and reached out to take the flowers.

"Just a little ol' birthday party," she said, heading toward the dining room. "You can bring the rest in here," she called over her shoulder. She stumbled on an unseen enemy, and water slopped from the bouquet and dribbled down her arms. "Dang it," she muttered.

She was wiping off the spilled water when the florist brought in another arrangement and set it carefully on the rosewood sideboard. The young boy held his boutonnière box tightly as he looked around the room. Letty carefully dislodged it from his hands.

"It's nice to know there will be some celebrating again in this old house," Mr. Hobbins said, gazing around. "I've wondered about Miss Kate the past few years. I knew she'd stopped entertaining when her husband died. About the only time she ordered flowers was when babies came or people died or someone was sick." Just then a blast of laughter burst from the kitchen. The old florist raised his brows in question.

"She's not old and lost now. Come and see," Letty said, grabbing the old fellow by the arm and leading him toward the kitchen. Young Danny, eyes darting from left to right, from one treasure to another, followed behind.

Katherine and Maxie were still chuckling in amusement over some memory from the past when the kitchen door opened.

"Why Mr. Hobbins. Mr. Bert Hobbins!" Katherine exclaimed, wiping her damp hand on a towel and thrusting it out for him to take. "Are you delivering orders yourself these days?"

"Just this one, Miss Katherine," he said, shaking her hand firmly. "It's been so long since you ordered flowers I decided I needed to make sure they weren't for your funeral."

Katherine burst into laughter. Removing her hand, she used the back of it to move a runaway curl off her damp forehead. "Nope! I'm still alive and kicking. And you are, too, I see! I would think the flower business would keep a person smiling. Dabbling in all those lovely, sweet-smelling flowers all day." Katherine spotted the boy behind Bert Hobbins. Taking long strides and extending her hand briskly she smiled at him.

"Oh, ho! You must be young Daniel's son, Danny. I am so glad to meet you. I hope you have time, before you leave, to have a tour of the house. Letty can take you. She can show you where all the ghosts live," she said, shaking his hand. His eyes widened at the mention of ghosts but he managed to smile shyly.

"I see you've met Letty," she said, turning back to Bert Hobbins. "She's my right-hand woman and keeps me from taking myself too seriously. And surely you remember Maxie, don't you?"

Mr. Hobbins nodded. Then he lifted a shaggy eyebrow and smirked, revealing a darkened front tooth. "How could anyone forget the kitchen general? Meanest woman in any ten kitchens," he joked.

"And how could anyone forget the florist man who passes off dead shriveled flowers for fresh?" Maxie retorted, placing her hands on her ample hips.

The two grinned.

"Been a long time, Bert," Maxie said.

"Sure has, Maxie," he answered. "Nice to see you back doing something useful."

"Me, I'm surprised they still let you drive at your age. You got a license?"

"Nope."

"Didn't think so."

"You still know how to make that sweet potato pie?"

"Could be."

"Bet it's not as good as you could make fifteen years ago before the years piled on."

"Ha! Bert, you ain't gonna trick me into no sweet potato pie-baking."

"Can't blame a man for trying," he said sadly, shaking his head. "I never tasted anything in my life as good as your sweet potato pie. Now that my Mary's gone..."

"Well, I 'spose I could make one up in the next week or so," Maxie conceded. "But I want a bouquet in exchange—fresh flowers, none of them discards."

Bert thrust out a hand. "Deal," he said as Maxie grasped it firmly.

"If you get them flowers off-loaded before they's all dead, come on back and get a cup of coffee while Letty's taking Danny around the house," Maxie told him.

"Today's coffee, or yesterdays?" he questioned with a grin, motioning toward the half-empty pot sitting in the coffee maker.

"Tell you what. It's such an honor having you here today I'll brew up a brand new pot," Maxie said. "I'll even make it that gourmet coffee that costs an arm and a leg these days."

"There's just two more to bring in, so I'll be right back," Bert said.

Bert and Danny, accompanied by Letty, went out to the van to bring in the last two arrangements. Making no attempt to hide, Marge Reynolds stood in front of her living room side window and held the curtain aside with one hand. Frowning, she stared at the house next door. When Letty held her flowers aloft and waved gaily, Marge turned smartly and left her post, the curtain settling back into place. Letty felt a tug of pity for the stern-faced woman. How awful to be so lonely and so bitter and nasty to others that there wasn't a chance to rid yourself of the loneliness, she thought. Maybe there was something she could do. There had to be something.

Skillfully balancing an arrangement in one hand, Bert shut the van doors and turned the handle to lock them in place. The three of them turned at the shrill sound from down the street. Danny and Bert stared, and Letty chuckled.

"Yoo-hoo! Yoo-hoo, Letty!" Lillian Dip was aboard her ancient green bike and Petunia was hunkered in the basket, her eyes wide in fright. Lillian was traveling at quite a clip, one hand steering and the other holding down an ancient yellow sunbonnet with ribbons flowing gaily behind. She was outfitted in a bright green Lycra workout suit. Red socks peeked out from her dingy white tennis shoes.

"Wow," whispered Danny. "It's that crazy lady. I've seen her at Polsky's."

"Danny!" hissed Bert Hobbins. Even though he might agree, he was embarrassed at the description.

Letty chuckled as Danny's grandfather admonished him by the use of just his name. Her father could do the same thing.

"She's not really crazy," Letty said just under her breath. "She's really quite delightful. I hope I'm just like her when I'm nearly seventy." Raising her voice, Letty hollered, "Yoo-hoo back, Miss Lillian! You're just in time to help decorate!"

Lillian Dip zoomed toward them and made a right hand turn at the very last second, causing the flower-bearing trio to slam themselves against the van. They could feel the whoosh of air as she zipped past, bounced over the sidewalk and continued over the lawn. Making a large turn, Lillian headed toward them again, stopping just short of a giant elm. Leaning her bike against the tree, she dusted off her hands, tamped her hat down firmly on her head, scooped up Petunia and dumped her on the lawn, and jauntily bounced toward them.

"Well, now, that was quite a ride! I forgot to use the brakes. I keep doing that! So, how are the festivities coming along? How is Katherine holding up? My, what lovely flowers! Anyway, I guess they're lovely, underneath that paper. How many arrangements did she get? Friday at the big wedding on TV they had so many flowers you could hardly see the bride and groom. They were magnificent. Did any of you see the wedding?"

Danny and Bert stood open-mouthed and staring. Letty laughed gaily. Hugging Lillian to her side, she turned to the dumbstruck males.

"Lillian watches afternoon soap operas on TV. Friday on one of the shows there was a grand wedding. That's what she's talking about. It wasn't a real wedding here in Danford."

"It was more real than any wedding has ever been in Danford," Lillian said firmly. "And I should know. I've been to almost all of them."

"You might be right about that!" Letty said. Bert chuckled.

"Better get these flowers in the house," he said. "Come on, Danny. What're you standing behind the van for? Let's get things moving here."

Lillian, shaking her legs one by one, and hiking up her bra strap, strode sharply up the sidewalk to the front steps, her magnificent rump undulating in the green Lycra that had it in a stronghold. Danny stared at the sight until Bert caught him and gave him an unobtrusive punch.

"Ow," Danny said, rolling his shoulder.

"Mind your manners," Bert retorted quietly.

Chapter Forty-Nine

Opening the front door, Lillian quickly stepped inside. "Yoo-hoo. Yoo-hoo, Katherine. Where are you?" she bellowed.

Standing in the dining room, Katherine was deciding on linens when she heard the shrill voice. She rolled her eyes. "That's just what I don't need right now," she declared, lifting a pink damask tablecloth from the small linen closet in the butler's pantry off the dining room.

"In here," Katherine hollered back. Soon the parade of people, Lillian, Letty, and Bert and Danny Hobbins came trooping in.

"Put them all on the sideboard for now," she said to the flower bearers.

"I'd go with the pink tablecloth," said Lillian.

"That's what I thought, but Mr. O'Reilly's a male," Katherine said. "And he's the guest of honor."

"A real man wears pink," Lillian declared.

"That's true," said Bert Hobbins, his good eye fixed on her soberly. "I've been wearing pink for years." Three pair of female eyes turned to his diminutive stubby figure and his oversized ears and crossed eye and quickly turned back to the tablecloth issue. Letty looked at Katherine, her eyes smiling.

"Well, you three can figure it out," she said. "Danny and I are going exploring." Taking his hand, which was warm and sticky because he was, after all, a typical boy, she pulled him from the room and set off toward the ballroom. Katherine knew that they'd be deep in the attic within five minutes where Letty would regale him with all the mansion tales.

"Miss Lillian, can Petunia come along with us?" Letty asked as she and Danny left the room.

"Make sure she minds her manners," Lillian said. Letty gave a little kissing sound and Petunia ran to follow.

"You two are on your own," Bert said to Lillian and Katherine. "I'm heading to the kitchen for that cup of coffee Maxie promised me. I know flowers, but I know beans about tablecloths."

"We could go white, but that seems so formal," Katherine said with a frown. It was her thinking frown, the one that people closest to her recognized as being there just before a remarkable revelation. The grandfather ticked in the silence as Lillian waited.

"I know!" Katherine declared. "That filmy botanical cloth. It must be in here somewhere." Shuffling through layers and layers of linens she found what she was looking for.

"Eureka!" she said, pulling it out. It was long, as long as the table with two of its leaves, which were precisely what would be used, and made from material so light it fairly floated. Pale gold and pale green leaf fronds were imprinted on a buff-colored background.

"We can use this with a buff undercloth and a gold runner. White Spode dinnerware with gold chargers and the goblets that are rimmed in gold. It will be elegant but manly. For a true male look, we can pop some pheasant feathers—there are some in the decorating boxes in the attic—in the centerpiece. It will look lovely. Absolutely lovely!" Katherine was excited and delighted at the plan.

"Oh, it's going to be such a grand event for you," Lillian sighed. "Do you know that I have never been to a formal dinner like this one you're having?" she declared broadly. "By the time I moved to the neighborhood you'd quit entertaining." The words were spoken wistfully but tinged with a bit of accusation, as if Lillian's moving to the neighborhood may have had something with Katherine's change in lifestyle.

"Oh, and you missed some grand affairs, let me tell you," Katherine said, taking her up on the challenge and feeling the need to, once again, explain. "But after my John died I just lost the will to have a houseful of people. It didn't seem important at all anymore. Now that I am going through all this excitement for just a simple birthday party, I'm thinking I may have been mistaken in becoming a bit reclusive.

"Anyway, dear Lillian, I've been thinking about you. You can't, of course, come to the dinner, since it's a family thing for Mr. O'Reilly and, except for Simeon, who is my date, it will be just the O'Reillys. But afterwards...."

"Whoa! Just a minute here. Simeon is going to be your date?"

"Well, maybe not a date. He's just going to co-host the party with me."

"Simeon is going to get dressed up and come to the Big House? Now that's pretty amazing!"

"Actually, I would count it as a miracle. I'm thinking if he does, indeed, show up, I might travel to the Vatican and have an audience with the Pope to see if I can get it on the certified list of miracles. But, back to you, Lillian. I'm thinking that you could come over for the entertainment portion."

"Really? I can come for the entertainment?"

"Mmm-hmmm. Not the dinner, like I said, because that's just for the O'Reillys, but for the entertainment. Letty's arranging for that, and I have to admit I'm a little worried. The O'Reilly's are to arrive around seven, so we should be in the Ball Room around, say, 8:30. You can just come in. If we are still at the dining room table just go up to the Ball Room and we'll be there shortly."

"What should I wear?"

"I would imagine it will be semi-formal. I'm going to wear a long black velvet skirt with a white silk brocaded top. It's simple and comfortable and a way to show off that grand Trifari black and gold rhinestone necklace John gave me in 1952. I love that necklace."

"Why don't you wear your diamonds? Or your pearls?"

"Oh, they're too fussy. Too extravagant. Too show-offy. I like the costume jewelry just as well. I'd rather lose the diamonds, no matter what their worth, than the necklace John gave me in 1952."

"I suppose." Lillian frowned. She truly didn't understand. She had a jewelry box full of old brooches and necklaces and they didn't seem that valuable to her. But a diamond necklace worth five figures? Now that was something of value!

Lillian brightened when she thought of the evening ahead. "I'd better get home and figure this out. I need to take a shower and fix my hair. I wonder if it's too late to get it cut and permed," she said as she peered at her watch. "Oh, it is too late. It's already past two. Well, maybe I'll put it in rollers. I wonder if it's too short to get in rollers. Katherine, I'd better get going. I have to figure out what to wear! I'll see you around 8:30. Oh, this is so exciting!"

Rushing around the table to Katherine's side, Lillian enveloped her in a smothering hug. "Katherine, I love you. You are a dear, dear friend."

"Lillian, you're breaking my ribs."

"Oh! Sorry. Katherine, I'd stay and help with the table and all but I have to make myself beautiful," she said over her shoulder as she fairly galloped through the great room to the front door. "That's going to take some time!" As she walked through the front door, Lillian burst into a happy rollicking song.

"I hope that wasn't a mistake," Katherine muttered to herself, and then she chuckled brightly. "This might be a birthday party they'll never forget." Then she remembered something.

"Petunia! Lillian, you forgot Petunia!" she hollered just as the door slammed shut. Katherine shook her head. If Lillian didn't remember the little dog, she'd have Letty walk her home.

Chapter Fifty

By four o'clock in the afternoon Petunia had been delivered back home, Maxie had everything under control in the kitchen and Katherine and Letty had the dining room set to perfection. The botanical tablecloth was perfect, and the long gold runner lent an air of elegance. The chargers gleamed beneath the white china and the polished silverware glowed. In the center of the table the long, low arrangement did look like a small cottage garden with its masses of gold and pink roses, purple monkshood, frilly ferns, day lilies, Russell lupines in assorted colors, ranunculus and spiky stocks of purple statice. The pheasant feathers, which Letty and Lillian both doubted would work, finished it off beautifully.

The guests were to arrive at seven. Maxie, just like in the old days, had sent Katherine off for a nap. Now, settled on top of her silky gray damask bedspread and covered with a light down comforter, Katherine stared at the ceiling and ran through her mental list. Everything was on track, except for Simeon. His place was set, but she hadn't heard from Letty if he was coming to dinner.

Oh, well, she thought as she shut her eyes and rolled to her side. If he chooses to back out we can remove his setting and no one will know he was supposed to be there. No one, but me.

Katherine didn't know but after Danny and Bert Hobbins left in their floral van, Letty had jogged to Simeon Quest's house. As she looked around, she was impressed all over again. Simeon's house always made her heart melt. It was perfect, like something swept up out of the Old Country and settled right here in Danford.

It looked like a cottage, although it was as big as the average house. The roof was made of hand-split shakes that had weathered over the years and the stucco outside of the house was painted a pale buff. The bottom four feet of the house were covered in cobblestones. The mullioned windows had rounded tops to match the rounded front door. Simeon kept the windows gleaming.

It was the setting that made the house perfect. It looked as if it had been there for generations. English cottage gardens surrounded the outside and framed the curving pebble stone paths. In the summertime the lawn was thick and perfectly groomed and a fountain tinkled in the left hand garden and flowers bloomed in happy profusion in the rock garden.

Letty stopped at least three times to look at perennials peeking through the rich soil as she made her way to the front door. Once there, she banged the knocker. Simeon didn't answer. She walked around the back and he wasn't in the vegetable garden or out in his workshop. Nor could she see him out in the pasture land or down by the creek. She checked his garage and his car was gone. She wanted to leave a note but didn't have paper or a pencil. Picking up a handful of small pebbles from the driveway she fashioned the message: C.A.L.L. L.E.T.T.Y. on the back doorstep. Smiling at her cleverness, she walked back to the mansion.

A mile away, at Fodders Toggery, Simeon was burning with humiliation. Hugh Fodder, proprietor for some thirty five years, was crouched before him, tape-measure in hand.

"Just settle down, Simeon," Hugh prompted. "This isn't so bad. I just need to get a measurement."

"Might not be bad for you. You're the guy with the tape. I'm the victim, here."

"Just hold still," Hugh said as he tucked the tape close to Simeon's crotch. "There, got it. Thirty two inch inseam."

"I don't know why I couldn't just get it off the rack like when I buy a new suit," Simeon grumbled.

"Tuxes are different. There are two hundred pairs of pants in there and you can spend all day trying them on or spend two seconds getting a measurement. Believe me, it's easier to get the measurement."

"What all do I need to go with this monkey suit?"

"Hang on, I'll be back in a minute and show you." In less time than it took Simeon to seat himself on a plush green velvet chair, Hugh was back.

"I'd go with all black," he said, holding up the tuxedo. "Black tux, black cummerbund, black bow tie, white shirt. Here, try this on."

While Hugh fussed with the suit, Simeon stepped out of his khaki slacks. Slipping into the tuxedo pants and jacket, he found they fit perfectly. He looked very elegant, even if he was wearing a dark blue button down shirt underneath the jacket. He had just gotten a haircut and his hair, now mostly white, almost glowed against the black background. Despite his hair, he had the figure and face of a much younger man. He kept in shape, not through regimented exercise, or the Danford Athletic Club, but by working outside. Face it, Quest, you still cut quite a figure, he thought to himself.

"You know that you wear black socks and black shoes, too, don't you?" Hugh asked.

"I'm not that stupid. Of course I know that. I might have lived here most of my life but I'm not a hick, Hugh," Simeon said, pulling off the jacket and pants.

"OK, Mister-I'm-not-a-hick, do you know enough to take your date a corsage? And that you should wear after-shave so you smell good?"

"A corsage? Ahhh. No one said anything about a corsage. Where do you get those? Supermarket?"

"Not a supermarket. Never a supermarket. You stop by Danford Floral. Do you know her colors?"

"Colors?"

"The color of dress she's wearing?"

"Heck no. Should I call her?"

"Might be a good idea."

"You got a phone I can use?"

"In the office, door behind the cash register."

"Thanks. This is getting way too complicated for me," Simeon muttered under his breath

"Say, Simeon?"

"Yeah?"

"Maybe you should put your pants back on."

"Huh? Oh."

"So, who is this date of yours? She sure has you flustered."

"I'm not saying. Knowing the grapevine in this town, you'll find out soon enough. I just hope you're right about this tux thing. I really just wanted a new suit. It isn't like we're going to Carnegie Hall or something. It's just a birthday party." Zipping up his pants and fastening his belt, Simeon walked from the fitting area and headed toward the office. Settling in the chair behind the desk, he dialed the familiar number.

"O'Malley residence," the voice said. It was Maxie.

"Maxie. Man, it's good to hear your voice. This is Simeon. Do you know what Kate is wearing tonight?"

"Why is that any business of yours, Mr. Simeon?"

"Well, it's my business, Miss Nosy, because I'm supposed to help host this silly dinner and I just found out I should be bringing her a corsage."

"Oh, my! A corsage. How romantic."

"Cut it out, Maxie. I'm getting a little nuts here, what with getting measured and fitted. I just want to know what she's wearing."

"Measured and fitted for what?"

"A tux, Maxie. A tux."

"A tux? Oh my! I don't know what to say."

"That's something new. Just say what she's wearing."

"Can't tell you, and she's napping," Maxie said.

"Doesn't anyone know?"

"Let me holler at Letty. LETTY! DO YOU KNOW WHAT MISS KATHERINE IS WEARING TONIGHT?" Simeon had flung the phone from his ear at the first bellow.

"Mr. Simeon? Mr. Simeon? You there?

"I'm here but I'm DEAF now, thanks to you."

"She don't know."

"What?"

"Letty don't know what Miss Katherine is wearing. If I was you I'd just go with pale pink and white baby roses and baby breath. Goes with anything. Even if she wears red, the little baby roses would look good. And don't go buying one of them store-bought corsages. Go to Danford Floral and Gifts."

"Do you people get a kickback from that place?"

"What?"

"Never mind. I'll see you later, Maxie. Thanks for your help."

"Mr. Simeon?"

"Yes?"

"It's a mighty good thing you're doin' tonight," Maxie said.

"I hope so," Simeon replied.

"Oh! Wait. Don't hang up. Letty wants to talk to you."

Simeon heard a shuffling of the phone, then Letty's breathless voice.

"Simeon?"

"Yup."

"I just got back from your house and you weren't there."

"I know. I was here."

"Miss Katherine just wanted to know for sure if you're coming tonight. No, that's not quite it. I wanted to know if you were coming tonight."

"Yup."

"You are? You aren't going to back out?"

"I'll be there. I promised her, and I'm going to put on my fancy manners and a bow tie and be the best co-host I can be."

"Well I'll be...That doesn't sound at all like you, Simeon. Why the change of heart?"

"I think it has something to do with age."

"Oh. I don't know what that means, but maybe sometime we can sit down and you can explain it to me. Simeon, I gotta go. I've got this entertainment thing I'm in charge of and I have to set some more chairs up on the stage in the ballroom."

"You need any help?"

"Nah. I've got it covered. The biggest job was dusting off that grand piano."

"Well, I guess I'll see you tonight, Letty."

"Yup. I'll be the one with the tux," she said.

"You're wearing a tux?"

"Well, duh. The Master of Ceremonies always wears a tux, silly."

"Did they measure you, too?"

"Huh?"

"Never mind. See you tonight. I'll be the guy wearing Perry Ellis cologne."

"Oooh, Perry Ellis. How romantic. That's courtin' perfume."

"Oh, hush and go dust something."

Laughing, Letty hung up the receiver.

"He's coming!" she hollered to anyone within earshot. Pawing through cans deep in the pantry, Maxie lifted a can of beans and shook it in victory. Thank you Lord, she said to herself. She felt a quivering in her innards and excitement in her bones. Maybe those two were finally going to get together.

Chapter Fifty-One

Back at the Danford Hotel, the O'Reilly females had created a chaotic, but very nice smelling, scene. In each of the three rooms the O'Reilly clan occupied, beds were covered with panty hose, dresses, and silky slips as things were laid out in readiness. The males had wisely gotten ready beforehand and were all down in the hotel bar, watching football game reruns on a sports channel, gulping Coke and eating peanuts.

"You couldn't pay me to be in that room another minute," Brent said.

"Me, either," Donny piped in, although deep down he didn't know why anyone wouldn't want to be there since it was so fun and exciting.

"Well," Stuart added, "you sure wouldn't have wanted to be in mine. Nora's so excited about spending the evening at O'Malley House she's made herself sick. She must have eaten half a packet of crackers, trying to feel better."

"I'm just happy my old suit still fits," Patrick said happily. "Who'd have ever thought I'd be eighty years old, anyway?"

"I hope you live another eighty years, Grampa," Donny said, snuggling into him.

"That's my dream, Donny, to live to be 160 years old. My, I'll sure look good then, won't I?"

"I hope I look half as good as you, Dad, if I get to be that age," Dan said, tossing a peanut shell toward a small metal bucket. "If someone asked me I'd say you're around 72 or so. I'd never guess eighty."

"Truthfully, I don't feel eighty. Some days I feel ninety. The good thing is that I've been healthy most of my life, except for things like gallstones and appendectomies and broken arms and legs. No cancer. No heart problems. You didn't get my handsome gene, Dan, so I hope you got my good health."

"Oh! I forgot!" Donny said, jumping from his chair and spilling peanut shells on the floor. "I was supposed to stop by the front desk and ask for an iron. The one in our room doesn't work right. Mom's gonna kill me." He raced out of the room.

"Man, you couldn't pay me to go back up there," Brent said again, his eyes never leaving the football game.

Donny came back five minutes later.

"She wouldn't let me in," he said, "said it was going to be a surprise. She just grabbed the iron and slammed the door right in my face."

They came down in unison, Connie and Nora leading the way, followed by Eleanor, Jessie Lou, and, finally, Dan's wife, Miranda.

Dan spotted them first. "Wow, will you look at that," he said in a hushed voice. Brent and Stuart followed his eyes.

"Whoa! I think that shopping yesterday paid off," Stuart said. "What a bevy of beauties!"

Patrick, hadn't heard a word, and was still focused on the peanuts and ball game. Brent poked him on the arm with his finger and nodded toward the foyer. Patrick turned and stared. Then he smiled, his false teeth gleaming in the dim light.

"Well, look at them. What a bunch of beautiful women. The O'Reilly women. They clean up right nice, don't they?"

"Eleanor and Jessie Lou look about twenty years old," Dan said, frowning and looking around the bar to see if anyone was leering at his daughter and niece and feeling a bit disappointed when he saw that every male in the place was glued to the game on the big screen television.

"Well," said Stuart, rising from his chair and dusting peanut salt off his hands, "I don't know about you fellows, but I'm going to collect my date." Striding toward them, he stopped and bowed deeply.

"Ladies," he said to the assembled females, nodding his head in approval. "You are looking mighty fine this evening." He held out his arm, "Mrs. Whitcomb, may I have the honor?"

They were perfectly matched, Stuart in a dark blue suit, white shirt and handsome red tie. Nora's honey blond hair was fluffed around her face and her dark blue body-clinging evening gown perfectly matched his suit in color. She wore her diamonds around her slim neck and matching earrings dangled from each ear. She was beautiful, and her abnormally pale face enhanced her alabaster skin.

"How are you feeling?" he whispered in her ear, as he kissed her cheek.

"Better, but I'm so excited I'm still a bit queasy," she whispered back. "Don't tell Daddy or he'll just worry. And for heaven's sake don't tell Connie or she'll be calling a doctor. It's just nerves."

Miranda was fussing and nervous and wringing her hands. Dan knew from the conversations between Jessie Lou and Miranda that Nora and Connie had ganged up on his wife and convinced her to buy the dress she was wearing. Dan was overwhelmed. He was used to seeing her in sweatshirts and jeans or little Mother Earth get-ups. Dressing up, to Miranda, was wearing a blouse with a jean skirt and putting on earrings.

But tonight she was a different woman. Truly, if she hadn't been with the others he never would have, at a glance, known she was his wife. Her dark hair had been piled into a stylish mound of curls on top her head. Her dress, red satin with a low cut bodice and a slit past her knee, was stunning. A string of pearls and pearl earrings took it from sultry and brash to sheer elegance. She looked sort of like a combination of Sophia Loren and Audrey Hepburn and cocktail bar strumpet. Dan was floored.

"I don't know what to say," he admitted quietly, walking up to her and removing her fluttering right hand from her left.

"You don't like it, do you?" Her eyes fell to the floor.

"Don't like it? I don't think I've ever seen a woman more beautiful than you are tonight. You look like a movie star. You look better than a movie star."

"Really? You really think so?"

"Didn't you look in the mirror tonight, Miranda? Don't you ever look in the mirror? You're absolutely gorgeous. You always have been."

"I told her that, too, Daddy," Jessie Lou said. "Doesn't she look wonderful?" Dan turned to his daughter.

"And look at you! You look absolutely wonderful, too, Jess." She did. At Nora and Connie's direction she'd purchased a slimming skirt of dark purple with a matching, long, jacket. Glittering rhinestones completed the ensemble. She, indeed, looked much older than fifteen.

"And you! What happened to little Eleanor, the family tomboy? Has anyone seen Eleanor?" Dan said loudly.

Eleanor giggled. "She's still here, they just stuffed her in a dress," she said. Her simple flowered dress wasn't as elegant as the others and would work well for Sunday church.

Connie stood on the sidelines, smiling warmly at her family. She loved them so much but she wished Mitch could have seen fit to give up a few days of work and join the celebration. She would have been proud to take his arm and be his partner for the evening. She had almost decided that owning your own business meant disowning your family. If she had known the sacrifices she never would have agreed to jump in such a devious and family-threatening pool.

Chapter Fifty-Two

"Well, Pops, I guess you're my date tonight!" she said brightly, tucking her hand under Patrick's arm.

"And I couldn't be more delighted," he said, patting her hand. "You look just as pretty as a newborn calf tonight."

"Is that a compliment?"

"Sure is! Maybe you're prettier! What is this stuff anyway?" he asked, motioning to her elegant antique-looking dress.

"The material? Chiffon. The tag calls this dress a 'Flyaway Rosette Chiffon Tea Dress.' See, Daddy, there's a pale peach under-slip beneath the layer of ivory chiffon. This rosette just above my waist holds the layers of chiffon which sort of flow out in an upside down scalloped vee."

"Well, whatever it is, it's mighty pretty on you."

"It's a replica of a vintage dress from the 1920s."

"Ah! The 1920s. No wonder it looked familiar!" he said.

"Did you notice I'm wearing Mama's jewelry?"

Patrick looked closely. The coral necklace, earrings and bracelet had cost him a month's salary. He had given them to Edna on Christmas Eve, when all the kids were tucked in their beds and dreaming of sugarplums. He was swept back in time and the scene was instantly before him. They were lying on a pile of pillows, their heads almost beneath the decorated tree. She had tinsel in her hair and he had laughingly pulled it away and dangled it over her face, tickling her nose with it. She had sneezed and laughed and grabbed it from his hand and threw it behind her shoulder.

"Don't move," he said. "I want to give you your present tonight."

"But it's Christmas Eve. Christmas isn't until tomorrow."

"Tomorrow there will be all these kids yammering and hollering and tearing paper. I want this to be you and me."

"Well, okay, but you aren't getting yours until tomorrow."

Patrick laughed and got on his hands and knees. Reaching behind the tree, he pulled out a shell-shaped box covered in burgundy velvet.

"I'd have wrapped it but the Santa paper just didn't seem to fit," he apologized.

"Oh, Patrick, what have you gone and done?" Edna said, sitting up. She held the box to her heart for a full minute, then another. She closed her eyes. Patrick moved his head so close he could see the fine purple veins in her eyelids. He frowned.

"Aren't you going to open it?"

"I don't want to."

"Why not?" She opened one eye and looked at him.

"Because then it will be over. Because then I will know what is inside. This way it's still a wonderful exciting mystery. I don't think I'm ever going to open it." She closed her eye and resumed her statue-still pose.

"Open it, or I'll tell you what it is," he warned. Her eyes popped open and she hugged the box closer to her chest.

"You wouldn't!"

"Sure would. You have to the count of five. One. Two. Three."

"OK, I'll open it!"

Hunching her shoulders and taking a deep breath, Edna slid a finger beneath the lid and pried it open a half inch before letting it snap back in place.

"Oh, Patrick, I don't want to ruin the surprise," she said.

"It's just the Hope diamond and a few lesser necklaces," he said. "Nothing special."

"OK, here goes." She lifted the lid but kept her eyes closed for a few seconds before looking. When she did look, she gasped.

Nestled in the formed velvet box were a gold and coral necklace and matching earrings and bracelet. Each piece sat in its own sculpted place. Edna had never seen anything more beautiful.

"Is it real?"

"Yup. Came all the way from Spokane. I've been talking to a jewelry store over there. He described it but his words didn't do it justice. I knew you were partial to orange, so coral seemed to be just the ticket."

"I love it!" she said and started to wail.

"Why do you always do that? You always cry when I do something nice for you!"

"It's just a woman thing," she had said, rubbing her eyes with her hands.

Patrick smiled at the heart-warming memory. Now the necklace graced his daughter's neck and it was so very fitting that she had it. Nora had thought it was tacky-looking. "Orange is the color of insanity," she declared. As it had on Edna, it looked as if it had been hand-crafted just for Connie.

Patrick O'Reilly felt the swell of good memories well up in his chest. "She'd be proud of you," he said, hugging his eldest daughter.

"Are we ready to go yet?" Brent asked. He was uncomfortable in his new suit and his new shoes felt uncomfortable. He hated ties. Fourteen year old kids shouldn't be forced to wear ties, he thought. It ruins their childhood.

"We can go in, let's see, in another fifteen minutes," Stuart said, looking at his watch. "Nora and I thought it would be fun to travel in a limo. This one holds eight so Donny and Brent will have to ride up front, but that should be okay, shouldn't it?"

"A real limo. A stretch limo?" Brent asked.

"They had to bring it up out of Missoula. If you can believe it, they didn't have a limo in Danford," Nora said with a laugh.

"Wow," said Danny, which was the word all the adults wanted to use but thought too juvenile.

They all settled in the foyer to wait, smiling at each other and amazed at how wonderful they all looked. The women perched, rather than sat back in the cushy chairs, lest they muss their hair or wrinkle their gowns. Miranda, in her red satin, wasn't sure what to do with her legs but finally crossed them gracefully, revealing nearly the entire length of a perfectly chiseled leg. "Lordy, lordy," her husband muttered in admiration.

The excitement was palpable and each person had his own reason. Patrick, for his birthday celebration, his offspring for the opportunity to see O'Malley House, the young girls the chance to act like grown-ups and for Donny and Brent, the adventure of riding in a real stretch limo.

By the time the limousine arrived, most of the party was already on their feet and chattering gaily. They were much too excited to sit. When he booked the limo, Stuart, who had ridden in them countless times and knew the ilk of driver they might get, had been adamant that they not be stuck with some gum-snapping teenager dressed in jeans and a black tie. True to his word, the owner of the company had come through. The driver was very distinguished and dressed in a fine uniform with a black cap. To top if off he had a wonderful English accent. Stuart decided he would slip him a $50 tip for making the short journey so memorable.

Chapter Fifty-Three

At the same time the black limousine pulled out from the curb, a Delta Airlines 747 landed at Glacier International Airport fifteen miles away. Mitchell Ames had his seat belt unfastened before the wheels touched down. He was sweating underneath his black suit and tried to force himself to be calm. He ran his finger around the collar of his pale blue shirt and pulled at the dark blue tie. For the fortieth time he looked at his watch. 6:45 p.m. There was no way he could make it. The plane had been over an hour late leaving Seattle, delayed leaving Spokane and arrived in Montana nearly three hours past the scheduled arrival time.

As the pretty blonde flight attendant warned everyone to stay seated until the plane came to a complete stop, Mitch sighed and settled back. He ran his fingers through his brown hair and rubbed his eyes. Over the years people had commented many times on his startling blue eyes that seemed to twinkle when he smiled—which was much of the time. Tonight they just looked weary and worried. There was no use trampling people to get out the door, he decided. He'd just pull down his carry-on bag, scramble to the nearest bathroom to wash his face and comb his hair, and grab the first cab he saw and head to O'Malley House.

He'd seen it in previous visits, of course, but couldn't give a specific address. From what Connie said, anyone who had been in Danford more than five minutes could find O'Malley House. He'd be there at least by 7:30. Hopefully, his late arrival wouldn't cause too much of a ruckus and problem.

Chapter Fifty-Four

Elva Bruce was nearly forty-years-old and had never been married. She was one of those thin, regal, black women who seem to radiate efficiency and intelligence. Her hair was clipped short and she fancied dangly, colorful earrings and exotic clothing. She turned heads wherever she went.

She had been a waitress for years, ever since she was fifteen and worked at a high ceilinged, echoey, very dingy coffee shop off Broadhurst. By the time she was in her twenties Elva had become so skilled at her job, and at conversing with customers, that she was pulling in more money than anyone she knew with a degree. Her car was new, her apartment in the best neighborhood, her teeth were well cared for, and she was able to buy clothes her friends couldn't afford. She was a waitress who could pick her jobs, and her tips amounted to much more than her wage. The best part was that she didn't have to bring her work home with her. The most she had to worry about was making sure the coffee was poured as often as her smile. To top all that off, the work kept her trim and slim and in very good shape.

And then one day she looked at her life and saw its emptiness. She wondered what had happened to her childhood dream of becoming a teacher and realized it was still deep inside her, smoldering and waiting for her to bring it back to life. Within a month she had a plan and had registered for college. In three years she accomplished what others took five years to do. The day she walked into her first classroom, two weeks before school started, she ran her fingers over the tiny desks shoved into a corner and pondered the tubs of clay and stacks of books waiting to be put on shelves. For the first time she felt like a teacher; she knew she was a teacher. She was thirty three years old and felt like she was coming home. She sat at her desk and cried.

In response to her grandmother, Maxie's, request, Elva had agreed to be, gratis, the waitress for Katherine O'Malley's gathering.

Truthfully, Elva would have probably paid for the honor. Not because of her beloved grandmother, but because of Katherine O'Malley. The summer she was twelve, Miss Katherine had allowed her to work at the mansion. She was Katherine's fetch and carry girl, which, at first, she resented greatly. In the end Elva had gained a whole education in the art of entertaining—everything from choosing the right flowers, to setting the table, to engaging in idle and entertaining chitchat at a formal function. Elva was allowed to help serve and to set up. Truthfully, it was this education that had taken her as far as she had gone in her work as a waitress. It had given her the edge that made her far above what was considered a normal waitress. She even used that training in her classroom, teaching second graders manners and how to set a table.

Climbing the gaily-lighted steps to the massive front doors of O'Malley House, Elva grinned. This is just like coming home, she thought. She hadn't been in this house for years, probably since Mr. John died and she helped serve after the funeral. She held her finger to the doorbell for a few seconds and then turned around to look back over the grounds. The roses, underneath the ornate lamps lining the sidewalk, were just coming to life. In a few weeks they would be beautiful.

Letty threw open the door and looked at the woman standing before her and burst into laughter.

"I thought I'd be the only female here wearing a bow tie," Letty laughed. Elva giggled and reached up to her red bow tie, pulled it out and let it snap back into place. She looked efficient and had dressed perfectly for the evening's work: black skirt, white shirt, black leather vest and the red tie.

"Well, there are two of us, at least, who know how to dress," she said to Letty, who was garbed in tuxedo trousers, a flounced white blouse and a black bow tie. She planned to throw on the short jacket with the long tails just before the entertainment started.

Elva held out her hand. "I'm Elva Bruce. You must be Letty."

"You got it," Letty said, grabbing the proffered hand. "Come on in and I'll show you the ropes. Actually, from what I hear, you can probably show me the ropes." Letty started down the six broad marble steps that led into the great room.

"I doubt it, but I can tell you one thing, it's sure good to be back here again," Elva said, looking around. "The place hasn't changed a bit. Everything is the same," she said in wonder.

"I hope it always stays that way," Letty said. "C'mon, let's go find Maxie. Everything's pretty much ready. Katherine was taking a nap but I crept up there a few minutes ago and she's up and getting ready. The guests should be here pretty soon.

"Hey, Grandma," Elva said as she walked through the kitchen doors.

"Well, if you aren't just as cute as a bug's ear," Maxie said, hugging her eldest granddaughter. "You and Letty here could be twins."

"Well, except for a few minor differences," Letty said, throwing her arm around Elva's shoulder and laughing.

"So, what's the plan here?" Elva said.

"Nothing special. It'll be buffet except that the shrimp cocktails will be on the table. Letty's put ice in the goblets, but the water needs to be poured and the lemon dropped in.

I just finished slicing the lemons. The coffee's brewing. I fixed sweet tea and got some soda on hand for the kids. I guess, you just gotta make sure everyone's got everything they need. Miss Kate and Miss Letty decided the cake should be served in the ballroom during the entertainment. Miss Letty's going to have her people sing or something. You might want to run on up there and make sure everything's set up okay. Other'n that, it's a go."

"Gee, you didn't save me any work at all!" Elva said in mock complaint.

"Don't worry," a voice chirped gaily from the door, "We're going to work the daylights out of you tonight!" Letty, Maxie and Elva turned at the voice.

"Oh, my. Miss Katherine, you are lookin' goood! You are lookin' fine," Elva said, drawling out her words.

Katherine blushed. "Oh, go away," she said, flustered.

"Turn around," Elva insisted. Katherine made a slow turn. Her black velvet skirt was just short enough to reveal a fine-boned ankle swathed in dusky gray silk stockings and the oriental collar on her ivory brocaded jacket heightened the elegance of her upswept hairdo which was held in place by a pair of antique jet and rhinestone hair combs. As she had told Lillian Dip, the black and gold rhinestone choker necklace, peeking from under the collar, and the matching earrings, dangling from her tiny ears, was the perfect addition.

"You look like the Queen of England," Maxie declared.

"Better than that. Have you ever looked at the Queen of England?" Letty asked. "She looks more like Princess Grace of Monaco. She looks breathtaking. Simeon's going to drop dead when he sees her."

"Simeon's coming?" Katherine asked, her mascaraed eyes widening. "You talked to him?"

"Talked to him while you were napping. He was fussing a bit, but he said he'd be here. He should be here any minute. At least I hope he knows a host should be here before the guests."

Katherine didn't say anything but her eyes glowed and she her shoulders raised in excitement.

"So, Miss Elva, my dear," Katherine said, with a twinkle in her eye, "can you tell me why this meal will be served buffet style with all the food on the sideboard, rather than giving each guest a prepared plate?"

"Is this a test?" Elva asked, narrowing her eyes. Turning to Letty, she said, "This woman's been testing me since I was twelve years old.

"Well, let's see," she said, turning back to Katherine, "my best guess is this: You haven't met these people and they are probably as flustered as all get out to be coming to O'Malley House. If you serve plate-style they will be trapped in their places. But, if you serve buffet style they will be up and down and feel more free. It will make them feel more at home and get rid of the anxiety. Right?"

"Oh, you are a wise woman," Katherine said, laughing.

"I was taught by the best," Elva said, taking two long strides to her and giving her a quick hug. Maxie stood by, grinning, her eyes fixed on Elva and bright with fondness and pride.

"Speaking of teaching," Katherine said, keeping her eyes on Elva, "Before this night's over I want the two of us to sit down and you can tell me all about your teaching. I was so proud when you were named Teacher of the Year last year."

"Thanks, but there were certainly a lot more who were more deserving than me," Elva said modestly.

The sound of a step on the back porch sent Katherine's hand to her mouth. Elva, Maxie and Letty turned toward the door.

"Settle down," Maxie warned Katherine. "It's just old Simeon. No need to go messin' up your lipstick."

All eyes were on the door window. A shadow passed and when three quick knocks sounded, no one moved. Finally, Letty looked around and strode to the door. "Oh, for heaven's sake, like Maxie said, it's just Simeon. Big deal." She threw open the door. Simeon glided through and, not turning around, gently kicked the door shut with his foot. In his hand was a small plastic box tied shut with a dainty pink ribbon.

Four mouths fell open and looked him over thoroughly, from his shiny black shoes, to the satin-striped tuxedo trousers, to the black satin cummerbund, pristine white shirt, perfectly-fitted black jacket and to the black bow tie.

Simeon turned brilliant red. "Well," he prompted, "say something!"

"I think I'm going to faint," said Letty.

"My, oh my," Elva said, walking around him and staring at him from top to bottom, "you are one handsome fellow. If I didn't have my sights on someone else right now I'd tie you down Mr. Simeon Quest."

"Oh, Elva, Elva Bruce, that you underneath all that grown up talk," Simeon squinted at her and quipped. "I haven't seen you in years. What are you, about thirteen now?"

"Thirty-something and old enough to know handsome when I see it," she declared, her hands on her hips. "Grandma. Letty. You two should come over here and smell this man. He smells delicious." Letty and Maxie joined Elva and surrounded a distraught Simeon while Katherine beamed from the doorway.

"Get away, just get away from me, you clinging busybodies," Simeon said in consternation, waving his arms toward them. Then he noticed Katherine, standing quietly in the doorway and his arms fell to his side. He parted his way through the now-quiet women, and they moved aside as he made his way to her.

Taking her hands, he shook his head and simply whispered, "Wow."

"Wow back to you," she said quietly, laughing.

"You look ravishing," he said.

"You look pretty ravishing yourself there, Mr. Quest," Katherine said.

"Well. Hmmm. Gee..." Simeon stammered.

"You going to stand there all night, holding that box?" Katherine prompted.

"What? Oh! These are for you." Simeon thrust the box at her and Katherine slid off the pink ribbon and popped opened the lid.

"Oh, they are beautiful. Just beautiful. How did you know that baby roses and baby breath are my favorites?"

"A little bird told me," he said, looking at Maxie. "Why don't one of you ogling females get over here and help me get this thing on her."

As if on cue, the three walked toward the couple.

"You do it," Letty said, looking at Maxie. "I'd stick her and get blood all over everything. You might not know it, but I really am a klutz."

"Believe her," Katherine said. "Please don't let Letty stab me. Elva, I know you are a pro at this. Actually, we should make my handsome date put on my corsage."

"Not me," Simeon said, raising his hands and backing off.

In a matter of seconds Elva had the corsage securely pinned to Katherine's bodice. "It was just what you needed to be absolutely perfect," she declared.

"You're a sweetie," Katherine said, patting her shoulder. Turning to Simeon, she said, "Shall we go sit in the great room and wait for our guests?"

Elva and Letty sighed in unison as the handsome pair, arm in arm, went through the swinging doors.

"And you two moonstruck spinsters should get your hineys up to the ballroom to get ready for our guests," Maxie said.

"Yikes! We don't have much time," Letty shrieked as she grabbed Elva and dragged her out of the kitchen.

Chapter Fifty-Five

The O'Malley House ballroom itself was nearly big enough for a basketball court and, in fact, Katherine and John sometimes did bounce a ball back and forth, using metal bins held aloft by ropes, for baskets. The windows were long and narrow and the walls were covered in very ornate white wallpaper. Window seats with padded blue cushions were situated along the outside wall. The floor was of light oak and had seen countless hours of dancing. At the far end there was a small stage, covered with heavy dark red velvet curtains. Near the stage was a full-size black Baldwin grand piano. The piano was very old, having been installed in the room before it was completely finished. Even though no one ever played it anymore, Katherine faithfully had it tuned twice a year and twice a year had to hear the piano tuner's enthusiastic praise of the piano's beauty and superb tone...and his offer to buy it, should she ever decide to sell.

Letty had set up five round tables, each with six chairs, just in front of the stage. They were covered in pale green cloths and topped with colorful silk flower arrangements. The tables and chairs would stay in position throughout the evening. If people wanted to dance after the night's official entertainment, Letty figured three-quarters of the giant room was still available.

To make the table area seem cozier, Letty had skillfully placed the fake trees that were all a-twinkle with tiny lights. Overhead, the giant chandelier and lights along the ceiling would be muted to a soft golden glow once the entertainment started.

Along the wall opposite the outside wall, to the right of the seating area, Letty had placed a long table that held the coffee and water urns, the birthday cake, appropriate plates and silverware and small trays of hors d oeuvres and chocolate covered strawberries and sweetmeats.

"You have been busy," Elva said in admiration.

"Does it look okay?" Letty asked with apprehension.

"It looks grand. I love the twinkling trees. Let me check out the cake table. You have everything, I think…napkins, plates, silver, cake… That's so pretty it must be one of Josephine's cakes. I'll just have to whip the covers off the trays and pour the coffee and water and we'll be good. I'm wondering about something for the kids to drink. Do you have anything planned?"

"I was thinking of making a simple punch everyone would enjoy."

"Good idea. Letty, I think it's all ready, up here. So, what's the entertainment, anyway?"

"Sorry, pal. It's a surprise. My lips are sealed," Letty said, running a finger over her lips.

"Not even a small hint?"

"Mmphngrhr."

Elva laughed. "OK, then. Be that way."

Walking back through the ballroom, Elva stopped momentarily and then did a few pirouettes and twirls. "Sorry about that," she said to Letty. "Can't come into this room without my feet wanting to dance. I get in here and I turn into a ballerina."

"I know what you mean. Sometimes I sneak off to just come up here and take off my shoes and slide around in my sock feet. It sure must have been grand in the old days."

"It was like being part of a Cinderella story, except the clock never struck twelve and ruined everything," Elva said with a sigh. "The first dinner dance I helped at I was just a kid, not even a cocky teenager yet. I couldn't believe the dresses and the jewels. Grandma had sent me up from the kitchen with a loaf of sliced French bread for the banquet table. It was all wrapped in foil. I stood right over there in the corner and just stopped and stared. Mister John came up to me, all dressed in a blue tuxedo and his hair slicked back. He leaned over and said, 'Is it dead yet?' I said something brilliant like, 'huh?' He pointed to the long loaf of bread. I had hugged it to my chest so hard I'd squeezed the daylights out of it. From then on it was our joke. Years later he'd pass me in the hall, or out on the sidewalk and make some French bread joke.

"But the best part," she continued, "was that he took the bread from me and set it down on the table and then led me to the dance floor. It was the first time I had ever danced."

By then Letty and Elva had walked through the double French doors, sauntered down the wide carpeted hallway and were strolling down the massive curved staircase that was one of the highlights of the house.

"Sometimes I imagine them gliding down these stairs, all dressed up," Letty said. "Tonight I'll get to see a bit of what it was really like."

"I hope it's everything you always envisioned it as being," Elva said.

Chapter Fifty-Six

Katherine O'Malley and Simeon Quest sat quietly on a white brocade couch in the great room. The room actually contained four separate conversation areas but Letty, at Katherine's direction, had done some shifting and adding of chairs so that the area in front of the massive fireplace would be where the guests first lingered.

"So, Simeon, you look quite handsome," Katherine said.

"It's all a façade," he said. Picking up his hand, he held it under her nose. "See? Grass stains and a dab of motor oil under the nail there. I might look good on the outside but on the inside it's just old Simeon Quest."

"Well, I've got that beat," Katherine said, hiking her dress past her knees. "Lookee here. See that bruise? Got that falling off the step stool when I was chasing down a spider in the kitchen. Sometimes, Simeon, much of life is a façade."

"I don't know about this, Kate."

"You'll do fine. Just be yourself. These people aren't royalty, you know. They're just ordinary people. Just relax and enjoy them. By the way, I'm going to ask you to bless the food."

"What?!"

"Simeon, you say the closing prayer in church all the time. You'll do fine."

"That's different."

"Just shut your eyes and pretend you're in church, then."

Letty was hovering in the dining room and had one ear tuned to the doorbell. At 6:57 p.m., when it rang, she was on her feet and striding toward the foyer in an instant.

"You two just stay there," she commanded the couple sitting so elegantly on the couch.

"Bossy thing, isn't she?" Simeon muttered.

"Hush. And smile. The show is about to begin." Katherine answered as she gracefully got to her feet.

Ten O'Reillys were like fifteen, maybe twenty, of an ordinary family. They entered O'Malley House with an extraordinary amount of noise and exclamations. Katherine knew instantly which of the striking females was Connie Ames and walked directly to her, Simeon following behind.

"You are Connie," she declared brightly, taking the younger woman's hands in her own. Connie smiled warmly. The rest of the group, the boys shuffling in at the rear, watched the exchange silently.

"And you are the legendary Katherine O'Malley. Mrs. O'Malley, I can't tell you how excited and delighted we all are to be here."

"Please, all of you call me Katherine. Anyone younger than eighteen can call me Mrs. O, which seems to be a nickname Letty here has given me in the past year," she said, addressing the group with a broad smile and motioning to Letty.

"I'll take your coats," Letty said. Looking at Donny, she added, "You want to help me? What's your name?"

"I'm Donny. Sure, I'll help," he said.

There was a flurry of activity as the women removed sweaters and shawls. Nora handed over her mink stroller.

"Now, come into the living room and let's get acquainted before dinner. Simeon, why don't you escort Connie and I'm going to accompany the birthday boy. That is, if I can figure out which one he is. There certainly doesn't seem to be an eighty-year-old in this bunch!" Everyone laughed nervously. Donny, fifteen feet away with Letty, turned around and yelled, "He's the one with the white hair. The guy in the back!"

"Oh ho! Now I spot him. Thank you for your help," Katherine said to Donny's retreating back. She held out her hand and Patrick O'Reilly shook if firmly.

"It is very nice to meet you, Mr. Patrick O'Reilly. Happy birthday," Katherine said, tucking her hand under his arm and gently guiding him across the oversized blue-tiled foyer and down the four broad white marble steps into the great room. Simeon followed with Connie Ames and the rest of the group trailed behind, too busy staring to talk. Brent and Jessie Lou and Eleanor had stopped at the top of the marble steps and were gawking at the grand room, trying to take it all in. Nora was trying not to ogle, to act as if being in such a place was an everyday occurrence. She clung to Stuart's arm while, behind her, Dan continually muttered 'wow' under his breath, much to her consternation.

The room was akin to something out of a magazine—white marble floors covered with ancient faded Aubusson, Sarouk and Kirman oriental carpets and filled with brocade and silk covered sofas and vases overflowing with flowers. Instead of a fire in a fireplace so huge that Donny could have easily stood upright in it, there was a mammoth silk arrangement. Slowly the crowd assembled in the seating area and stood nervously, waiting for Katherine's direction.

"Connie, if you'll go slowly enough, maybe Simeon and I can remember everyone's names and then we can sit down and chat. First, I will introduce you all to Simeon Quest, who is my very good friend and my partner in keeping the grounds of O'Malley House presentable. Simeon kindly agreed to be my co-host this evening. Letty Vanesse, who let you in and took your coats and is now romping through the halls with Donny, is my right-hand woman and also a very good friend. Don't tell her I said so, but life would be very boring for me without Letty. She is dressed rather strangely tonight since she is in charge of entertainment. I must warn you, her entertainment might be quite unlike anything you have ever seen. I am a bit worried about that."

"I thought I saw a group of rappers climbing the stairs a while ago," Simeon joked, knowing Katherine's fondness for rap music.

"Really? Awesome!" Brent said.

Katherine turned to him and said with mock anger. "It would be awesome because you would get to see me kicking their behinds right out the front door!" Everyone laughed.

Connie said. "Whatever it is, I know it will be just wonderful. Just being here is wonderful. If we could have brought McDonalds and sat in this room it would be wonderful," she said and then stepped next to Katherine and Simeon. "OK, here goes. You know who Daddy is, Patrick O'Reilly, and as you know, I am Connie Ames. My husband, Mitchell, couldn't join us on this trip to Danford, but our children are here. This is Eleanor who is twelve, Brent is fourteen and Donny, who is off with your Letty, is six."

Katherine took the hand of each child and repeated each name. Eleanor and Brent muttered shy hellos. Donny, who had scampered back to the group, shook her hand vigorously. "Mrs. O'Malley, you got a really cool house here. At least what I saw is really cool. Mom says you have turrets. Are you really rich?"

"Donny!" Connie was horrified. Simeon snorted. Katherine was delighted. Nora only hoped the old woman was too deaf to have heard.

"Well, I admit that I do live in quite a grand house and there are turrets and I probably have more money than I need, but I'm not as rich as a lot of people in the monetary sense. Do you know what monetary means?"

"Nope. Wait! Is it like where those priests live?"

"No, that's a monastery. Monetary has to do with money. A lot of people are richer than me monetarily, which means they have more money, but few are as wealthy when it comes to friends and blessings. Does that make sense?"

"Huh-uh."

"Well, look at it this way. You have parents and a brother and sister. I'm sure you live in a nice house and have a lot of friends. Those things are much more important than having money in the bank."

"I have a dog, too. He's a Chesapeake Bay retriever."

"See? You're very blessed, too. You and I can talk more later, especially about your Chessie, because I used to have one, too. But now I really should meet the rest of your family."

Connie continued, introducing Dan's family. "This is my brother, Dan, who is actually the oldest of the three of us, his wife, Miranda, and their daughter, Jessie Lou, who is fifteen."

"I am so pleased to have you in my home," Katherine said as she shook hands with each of them. Jessie Lou muttered a shy 'hello' and Miranda gave Katherine a weak handshake. Why, the poor woman is shaking like a leaf, Katherine thought. She gripped Miranda's hand tightly and looked her in the eye and winked. The unspoken words Katherine relayed came through loud and clear. Miranda grasped the older woman's hand and stood taller and straighter. "Thank you," she said.

"You probably don't remember this," Dan said to Simeon, "but years ago, when I was just a youngster Dad and I got stuck out in front of the house here one winter. You and Mr. O'Malley pulled us out with an old tractor. Mr. O'Malley invited us in for hot chocolate to thaw us out, but Dad thought we should get on home to dinner. I've always regretted that and this night will make up for that past disappointment."

Nora mentally rolled her eyes. It was obvious that Dan had memorized this little speech.

"We still have that old tractor out back in the shed," Simeon said. "It still runs and I still use it to pull people out of the ditch. If it wasn't so late I'd take you out there and show you."

"Was it a John Deere?" Patrick asked. "I can't remember."

Simeon nodded his head. "I think it's about the first one made. It's a 1939 model. I don't think you can kill those John

Deere tractors. They're sort of like that pink battery bunny that just keeps going and going."

"Someday I'd like to have one but right now it wouldn't be practical. Not much use for a John Deere when you live in a subdivision and on a lot about the size of Auntie May's bed quilt," Dan said. Connie patted him on the arm.

"If we aren't careful, they're going to veer off into cars and football games," she said conspiratorially to Katherine. Motioning to Stuart and Nora to step closer, she said, "This is Nora, who is our younger sister, and her husband, Stuart. Dan and his family and Daddy live in Seattle. My family lives in Spokane, and Nora and Stuart live in Cleveland.

"They don't have any kids. They have jobs and work a lot," Donny added. Nora smiled brightly.

"Sometimes I think children like you are the reason for the old adage, 'children should be seen and not heard.' Mrs. O'Malley, it is truly delightful to be in your home. Like most children who grew up in Danford, I always dreamed of coming through those doors. And, like most children who grew up in Danford, whenever I got in trouble I vowed I was going to run away and live here."

"Believe it or not, we had many children who did just that," Katherine said.

"Really?" Nora was surprised.

"They'd ring the front bell and some of them even had little suitcases or paper bags of clothes and toys. I would bring them in and give them milk and cookies. If John was around, he'd talk to the boys and I'd listen to the girls. If John was gone, I'd talk and listen to anyone who showed up. I'd give them a tour of the house and we'd talk about family. Except for John, I didn't have any family and I was careful to point out how fortunate they were. These runaway wannabes always skedaddled back home with smiles replacing the tears."

CHAPTER FIFTY-SEVEN

"So," she said, clapping her hands and smoothing her velvet skirt, "enough about runaways. Let's sit down and get things back on track. We will dine in about fifteen minutes and that is enough time for all of you, children included, to give me a quick rundown of your lives. Connie would you and your family like to begin?"

"Sure. We live in Spokane. My husband, Mitchell, and I are starting an equipment rental business, which is going very well but is very stressful. Before starting the business, Mitchell was in sales, selling heavy equipment. Kids, will you go next? Brent?"

"Do I have to?" Brent muttered.

"Yes, you do," Katherine said, laughing. He smiled back at her.

"I'm fourteen and I like rap music. I want to be a rap star. My goal is to be a rap star. Just kidding. I like all music, actually. I get pretty good grades and I like snowboarding and Lacrosse, football, basketball and being in plays. I was in Fiddler on the Roof last year."

"Good for you! Your parents must be proud of you," Katherine exclaimed. She looked at Eleanor, who said, "I'm

Eleanor and I'm twelve. I would like to be a movie star or a famous country western singer when I grow up. If not that, a veterinarian at a zoo. I get okay grades."

Katherine poked Simeon unobtrusively, a poke that said, *Okay, buddy, do your share here.*

He cleared his voice. "You're pretty enough to be a country western star, but can you sing?" he asked pointedly.

"Not very well," Eleanor admitted. "So maybe I'd better be a veterinarian." Simeon and Katherine laughed and Eleanor smiled brightly.

"How about you," Simeon said to Donny.

"I'm going to be a super hero and save people," Donny said, crouching down and then jumping up as if he was leaping to a high building in a single bound.

"The world certainly needs more of those," Simeon said, laughing. "So, which super hero do you want to be?"

"Spiderman. If not him, the Incredible Hulk," he said, going into a crouch and growling.

Dan pulled Donny on his lap and cleared his voice. "I'll go next," he said. "Miranda and I and Jessie Lou live in Seattle and Dad lives in a basement apartment in our house. I started out waiting tables in college at this little restaurant and now Miranda and I own it. It's called, believe it or not, O'Reilly's. Great name, huh? It seats about eighty. Sometimes I think I'd like to sell and move back to the peace and quiet of Danford. Driving in Seattle anymore is pretty bad. It sometimes takes me over an hour to get home."

Before anyone could comment, Miranda started talking as if she had to get the ordeal over with. "If Dan would move to Danford, I would help him pack," she said. "I don't have much to do with the restaurant. I paint. And I like to cook. I really would like to move here where it's peaceful and not so busy." She averted her eyes. For all the world, Katherine thought, she was like a little girl who had to recite in class. She warmed to her instantly.

"We would love to have you live in Danford. The town, as you have all discovered this week, could use a good restaurant. And you're an artist!" Katherine was impressed. "Miranda, you and I will have to have a chat later on. You'll have to look closely at the paintings when we tour the house."

Leaning over Simeon to reach her, Katherine cupped her hand and whispered in Miranda's ear, "By the way, Miranda, I want to tell you that you look absolutely breathtaking in that dress. No! Don't blush and look down. Stand tall and proud. You own the world in that dress!"

Miranda looked at her and smiled broadly.

Nora, who had been trying to catch the words, settled back against the chair as Jessie Lou shared.

"I'm Jessie Lou and I'm fifteen. The oldest grandchild. I play flute in band and at church and I'm in the church choir. I don't know what I want to be when I'm grown. Just happy, I guess." She looked embarrassed that she didn't have loftier goals.

"Jessie Lou, I think that's the most admirable ambition of all. It takes courage to admit that what we want most from life is to simply be happy. I don't suppose you have your flute with you, do you? Too bad, I'd have enjoyed listening to you play."

"You go next," Nora said, lifting her head up to Stuart, who was standing next to the chair in which she was sitting, his hand casually on her shoulder. He smiled at the room at large, which made him look younger and more youthful. He was a person who enjoyed life, Simeon thought, and one I could be a friend with. Actually, I could be friends with Dan, too.

"I'm Stuart and I'm fifty one years old and I, too, want to be a rapper," he started out, much to the glee of the others. Most were surprised; they didn't think of Stuart as having much of a sense of humor. "Actually, I'm in banking. Boring old banking. Rapping would be more fun."

"He won't tell you, but he's president of a large branch of Wells Fargo in Cleveland," Nora said proudly. "He always makes it sound like he's the janitor at Liberty Loan." Stuart blushed, and the rest laughed at him.

"I'm Nora and the baby of the family. I'm the director of human resources for a large microchip manufacturing company. We employee around 920 people, so it keeps me busy. My hobbies are staying in shape, tennis and golf. Stuart and I are both into golf. And last year I won the Ladies Tennis Championship at our club. Lately I've been busy decorating our new, 4,600-square-foot house on a lake outside the city."

"I can't imagine keeping track of that many people," Katherine said. "Or working so hard to keep in shape. Do you enjoy it all?"

"Oh! Well, I never thought about enjoying it. It's just what I do." Nora was clearly puzzled and didn't understand what Katherine was implying. Katherine had spotted her and figured her out from the minute Nora walked through the front door. She was a frightened, lonely, insecure woman who covered it up with wealth, style, job status, and business. How sad, Katherine thought. She doesn't know her true worth.

"Patrick, that just leaves you," Katherine said, turning to the old man. "Tell us about yourself."

"Well, I'm wondering...what the hell's a rapper?" he said which brought a shout of answers from the youngsters.

"Hmm," he continued after being educated, "that sounds pretty strange. About me... Well, I was born here in Danford. My grandparents came to the state in the 1880s and settled on the east side of Montana. My dad came to Danford and met my mother and moved over here. There were four of us kids, and I'm the only one left. I lived here and raised my family here and moved after my Edna died. I love this old town and I still miss it. I'd like to live here again, someday. The town might have changed a bit but the heart is still here. I guess my roots are so deep they'll always be here in Danford."

Katherine reached over and touched Patrick's arm just as the quiet chime of a dinner bell could be heard coming from the dining room. "It is a grand old town, isn't it, Patrick? Especially for those of us who have decades of memories here."

Rising from her chair, Katherine smiled and looked at her group of guests. "Let's head to the dining room, shall we?" Taking Simeon's arm, she led the way. The rest followed behind, heads moving from left to right to take in the stupendous beauty of the mansion and its contents.

Chapter Fifty-Eight

"I would like Patrick to sit at the foot of the table and I will sit at the head with Simeon to my right and Connie to my left. The rest of you can sit anywhere you would like," Katherine said when they entered the enormous, extravagantly decorated room. She and Simeon took their places and watched the rest of the group as they were seated. Katherine was pleased that the children weren't bumped to the end in a clump but were seated between adults.

By the time the shuffling had ended, Maxie and Elva had slipped into the room and were standing quietly. Katherine turned to them.

"Everyone, I would like you to meet Elva and Maxie Bruce. Maxie, here, has been my good friend and entertainment partner for decades and she cooked up this wonderful meal we'll be enjoying shortly. Elva is her granddaughter, who has also been a good friend for many years and started helping at O'Malley House when she was, what, twelve? In real life Elva is a teacher, quite a renowned teacher here, actually. Maxie and Elva will be serving tonight and if you need anything, please just ask. I have also asked them to join us after dinner for the entertainment and cake."

Patrick beamed and said he'd be proud to share his cake. He didn't, in fact, even know he had a cake. Dan and Connie smiled and greeted Elva and Maxie warmly. Nora didn't say anything but looked at Stuart in surprise.

"This is going to be a rather informal affair," Katherine said apologetically. "We're going to eat buffet style and the food is over on the sideboard. I thought that would be easier, especially with the children, than having individual plates. We'll start with the shrimp cocktail that's in front of us and Elva and Maxie will bring our salads, and after that we can dish up."

"Simeon," she asked, reaching over and taking his hand and, with her left hand, taking Connie's, "could you please ask the blessing and we can get started. I'm starving!"

As everyone around the table held hands, Simeon cleared his throat and bowed his head. "*Gracious Father, we thank you for the blessings that you continue to shower upon us. We thank you for old friends and new. We especially thank you for the laughter of children in this old house tonight. Please bless the food and the hands that prepared it. May this night be a special tribute to Patrick and the eighty years he has lived on your earth. Thank you, Lord, for bringing these special people into our lives. Amen.*"

Everyone echoed a murmuring 'amen' except for Donny who said the word very loud, making the group, except for his mother, laugh.

Within seconds everyone was discussing the jumbo marinated shrimp ringing footed bowls filled with ice and small crystal containers of cocktail sauce.

Five minutes into the appetizer, the doorbell chimed and Katherine shuddered inside, sure it was Lillian who had "accidentally" misjudged the time. Mentally, she adjusted for the addition and within seconds had a plan for adding an extra plate setting. A slight frown crossed her face so quickly that Simeon was the only one who noticed it.

"Who do you think it is?" Simeon whispered.

"I don't think it can be Lillian. Surely she wouldn't be here this early. Besides, if it was Lillian the whole house would know she's here by now," she said in a low voice.

Within seconds Letty was standing in the dining room. Her eyes were twinkling and she was smiling.

"May I have your attention," she said loudly. Everyone stopped eating and looked at her expectantly.

"I have a special surprise for your guests," she explained to Katherine.

"You do?" Katherine looked puzzled.

The O'Reillys all looked at each other, equally puzzled.

"Mrs. O', if you'll come here for a minute I'll explain and you can do the presentation," Letty said. Simeon got up instantly and pulled out Katherine's chair and helped her to her feet.

"Don't look at me," he said, sitting back down. "I don't know what's going on!"

"I think it's a surprise," Donny said in a stage whisper.

"I think so, too," Simeon said in an equally loud whisper, "and it must be a big one if Katherine O'Malley didn't know about it. She knows everything."

A few minutes later Katherine strode back into the room and stopped in the doorway, smiling gleefully. The men stood up upon her entrance.

"Oh, please sit down," she said. "We have an addition to our party. One I think you'll all approve of."

"You can come in now," she said loudly, turning toward the door.

Mitch Ames came and stood beside her for a scant second before spotting Connie and rushing to her.

"Mitch!" Connie squealed, leaping to her feet. "What are you doing here!?" She hugged him fiercely, closing her eyes and hanging on as if he was an answer to prayer, which, of course, he was.

The room went into instant pandemonium as everyone got up from the table and met Mitch with hugs and loud exclamations. Connie sniffled quietly, a few joyful tears wetting her husband's rumpled suit, while their three children circled him excitedly.

Simeon held Katherine's hand tightly as they watched the family reunion. Both their eyes glittered. "Makes you wish you'd had a big family, doesn't it?" he said huskily, his voice catching. Katherine could only nod her head.

Within five minutes the seating was adjusted to put Mitch next to Connie, and everyone went back to eating as Mitch told the tale of his decision to put family first and his bad luck with airlines and schedules. His arrival had dispelled the tension and the mood was fun-loving and frolicsome. By the time dinner was finished, everyone at the table was relaxed and jovial and the banter difficult to keep up with.

By then Katherine had garnered enormous amounts of information about the O'Reilly family. She discovered she had worked with Edna O'Reilly on numerous hospital guild committees and Simeon recalled working on some of the community 4th of July fireworks shows with Patrick. As time went on, they were amazed at how much the little town of Danford had given them in common. They had dozens of mutual friends and shared hundreds of memories. Patrick had even worked for several years for O'Malley Lumber Company.

The most fun was the sharing of Danford memories. Everyone, except maybe Nora, had a deep-seated love for the little town.

"Remember when someone shot off the cannon right down Main Street?" Dan asked before stuffing a forkful of roast in his mouth.

"I'd forgotten all about that," Simeon said in surprise, resting his fork on his plate.

"Me, too," added Katherine.

Nora frowned. "I think I was too young." She picked up a goblet and took a drink of water.

"Tell us, Uncle Dan!" Donny begged around a mound of mashed potato in his mouth.

Using his fork to gesture, Dan related the story. "There used to be a strip of green grass in the middle of Main Street, down at the end. Now it's a turn lane, I think. There was an old World War I cannon there and we used to play on it when we were kids. I think it was in the 1960s or 1970s when a bunch of high schoolers got the bright idea of shooting it off. The ammunition was right there—a pyramid pile of cannon balls. I don't know what they used to shoot it, gunpowder probably, but they blew a cannon ball clear down past Kelly's Bar and almost to the railroad tracks. I heard it shook the ground and roared tremendously."

"What happened next?" Brent said, curious.

"The kids took off running and they never did find out who did it. I was still in grade school and no one was talking. That week the firemen mixed up cement and stuffed it in the cannon. Afterwards, everyone was most surprised by the fact that no one else had ever shot it off."

"Do you remember when the bank burned down?" Nora offered as she tore off a tiny section of homemade roll and daintily popped it in her mouth. Katherine had noticed that Nora wasn't eating much, just nibbling on the roll. She also seemed quieter than her sophisticated demeanor would warrant. Something is wrong here, she thought to herself.

"I remember," Connie said aloud as everyone else nodded in recollection. "I can't remember how old I was, but I was still at home. We had been visiting friends and it was really late and Daddy was driving. The whole sky was pink when we came over the hill into town. Until we got right downtown we didn't have any idea what was burning. I remember crying. Everyone was crying. I think that bank was one of the first buildings in Danford, wasn't it?"

"That was an awful night," Katherine said, shaking her head. "John's grandfather had started that bank around 1889 and John was on the board when it burned. There was a lot of family memorabilia there. Photos, items in display cases from the original bank and that sort of thing. When we got the call we went down and John just wept. I think the whole town was there that night, watching the fire. I remember it was cold outside and the fire was so hot, but I was still freezing. Shock, maybe. The weeks after were a mess, trying to get accounts straightened out. Luckily, most of the safety deposit box contents were unharmed. It took weeks of investigation, and the fire marshals finally decided it was probably from faulty wiring."

"Well, that wasn't a very happy memory," Nora apologized. "Maybe I can come up with a better one. How about the time the streaker zoomed through the basketball game?"

"Darn, I missed that one," Simeon said.

Donny set down his glass of milk and looked at Nora. His upper lip was decorated white.

"What's a streaker?" he asked. His mother and father, holding hands under the table, looked at each other and smiled as if sharing a private memory.

"It was one of those 80's fads," Nora said, looking at him. "Streakers take all their clothes off and run through a crowd. This time he ran out during halftime at a basketball game. Everyone screamed and laughed. He had on a mask so no one could see who it was."

"He was completely naked? That's a dumb thing to do," Eleanor said. Jessie Lou giggled and nodded her head in agreement.

There was a momentary silence. Donny had patiently waited for such a time to impart the important knowledge he had learned in school. As the meal wound down and people settled into that comfortable camaraderie of a good time, he found the perfect lull.

"Mrs. O, I learned something in health class," he said importantly. Connie stopped mid-fork and stared. Health class, she knew from sitting in on Brent's sexual education classes, could be...oh, good grief.

Katherine leaned toward him expectantly. "And what did you learn in Health Class, Donny?" she asked.

"Well, I learned all about fatulance," he declared.

"Fatulance? Do you mean flatulence?"

"Yeah, that word. You should have fatulance fourteen or sixteen times a day and it means you're healthy," he declared.

Nora was horrified. Miranda ducked her head and blushed. Connie could almost feel the heat of her face singing her arm. Dan and his father continued shoveling food. Donny beamed proudly and the other children had stopped eating and were watching the scene unfold. Katherine, used to all sorts of social blunders, gracefully breezed through this one.

"I think that is absolutely fascinating," Katherine said, looking at him with utter delight. "It's amazing what you can learn in school, isn't it? You are very lucky. We never got to learn things like that when I was in school."

Everyone burst into relieved laughter.

"So, what did you do around here that was fun?" Brent asked. So far he couldn't see where there was much to do in the diminutive town.

"In the summer we swam in the lake and in the winter we skied. We had toboggan parties and ice-skated on the ponds and on the river. We rode our bikes endless miles. We fished and hunted and played hide-and-go-seek in the summer," Connie said.

"There wasn't TV in the early days," Patrick added. "I remember we got one of the first television sets, Edna and me. An old Sylvania with this little tiny oval screen. It was in the 1950s and the whole family came to see. I hauled a big antenna nearly to the top of a ponderosa pine in the back yard and we could pick up a signal from Spokane. By the time the kids came along nearly everyone had television. Now people have two or three or even four sets."

"That's sort of sad, isn't it?" Katherine said, looking at him. "Fifty years ago there were kids biking and hiking along this road all the time. They'd sometimes play ball out in the field if the cows were in high pasture. If you drove to town you had to watch out for the kids and dogs and bikes. Nowadays you don't see many kids outside playing. I guess they're all inside playing those games."

"X-Box," Simeon added. "They're all playing X-Box."

"What do you know about it?" she asked mischievously. He blushed brightly.

"Simeon! Do you know how to play that game?" Katherine was shocked.

"Bought myself one a couple years ago."

"What?"

"I read that video games keep your hands and your mind limber. I have to admit, I'm pretty good. I could take you on, Brent!"

"Hey, if you had your game here I'd take you up on that challenge," Brent said. The girls noisily joined in, both claiming they could beat any male at the table, and everyone started boasting about scores and game specifics.

"Can I ask you a question," Nora said quietly, leaning toward to Katherine. She had waited until both Maxie and Elva had left the room.

"Well, sure, ask me anything," Katherine said, smiling.

"I'm just curious about your servants. They're more like friends or something. Do they always join the after-dinner entertainment?"

"Oh, my dear. They aren't servants. They have been good friends for decades. The fact that they sometimes get paid has nothing to do with it. And tonight there isn't money involved. They're just helping out, just like I'd help out at one of their parties if they asked me. As far as joining the festivities, I'll have Simeon tell you. Simeon, tell Nora about the circus."

Simeon was still laughing over the raucous banter with the O'Reilly children about Nintendo.

"What circus?" he asked.

"You know, the circus we hired for John's birthday."

"Oh, that circus," he said, frowning. "I've been trying, all these years, to forget that mess."

"C'mon, tell us!" Connie pleaded.

"It was a dark and gloomy night," he started in a low voice. "Actually, I made that up. I didn't get there until late. I wasn't going to come at all but I heard all the hollering and laughing and curiosity got the best of me. I'm not much for big parties."

"It wasn't much of a circus," Katherine cut in excitedly. "'Weevil Brothers Famous Circus and Daring Acts' was how it was billed. They showed up in a huge old truck with an elephant, a rattletrap van and a low-slung, peach-colored Cadillac, which must have been fifteen years old. They all piled out, a group of seven or so very strange people. They had a dog act where the dogs—poodles, I think—were all dressed in skirts and hats and turned circles to music. The high wire act was on a low wire they'd strung between the van and the truck. It wasn't four feet off the ground. The fellow's name, I'll never forget it, was 'Roscoe Verlinda, of the famous Verlindas.' He was all dressed in a sequined jacket and a white leotard with funny ballet-like shoes. That was before men wore leotards. Actually, I don't think men have ever worn leotards. Well, maybe they did around the time Shakespeare was alive. Anyway, this particular leotard showed every hair on Roscoe Verlinda's leg it was so tight and set all the females to snickering. I was very embarrassed. Roscoe Verlinda climbed on the bumper of the truck and climbed up a small ladder and stepped out on that wire. He was really pretty good, even considering he wasn't much more than a few steps from the ground. But no one could get past the leotard. Oh, Simeon, tell them about the elephant!"

Everyone was still laughing at Katherine's description when Simeon rolled his eyes and set down his fork. "The elephant. I had just gotten to the corner of the house when I could feel, not really hear, but feel, the thumping of something huge. You know how you can do that, sort of feel things in the ground? I could hear screaming around the front of the house. I just stepped around when here it came. A huge elephant with a monkey on his back. The monkey was dressed in a red and white cowboy suit and was screeching, making this horrible noise and his yellow teeth were all bared back. It was a frightful vision, this monkey. He was beating the elephant's head with his big white cowboy hat, and the elephant was on the loose. His eyes were bulging and he looked terrified. Behind him came the so-called trainer, a man with a quirt who looked like he drank at least a bottle of Cuervo every night before bed. Behind the trainer came the rest of the troupe: Roscoe Verlinda, two middle-aged women dressed in bulging, scanty outfits who claimed to be trapeze artists, even though there wasn't a trapeze, the young woman who handled the dogs, and a couple of other sleazy-looking people who just seemed to be lurking around doing nothing."

"What happened?" Jessie Lou and Dan asked simultaneously. They looked at each other and smiled. Miranda was laughing softly at the story as if she could envision it all in her head and could paint it on canvas. Simeon used his hands to show a big circle.

"Potholes. That elephant made the biggest potholes all over the lawn. And messed this huge pile of elephant manure. Trampled a couple of young trees and went through the rock garden like an Army tank. The beast ended up a couple blocks away. They dragged him back and even though they had promised everyone could have a ride, the thing was so agitated they just heaved him back onto the truck," Simeon said.

"One good thing, you have to admit, Simeon, was the elephant manure. The flowers never looked better than that year."

"Maybe so, but the potholes are still there, if you know where to look. I never could get them completely filled in and each spring they settle."

Katherine turned to the rest of the guests, "The best part was Maxie. She was helping with the party and had brought her kids and grandkids, including Elva, to see the circus. She made her younger girls turn around during the trapeze act, which she declared was obscene, and once the poor shabby elephant started going mad she herded the whole bunch of kids, including most of the other children who were here, onto the front veranda. They all hid behind the outdoor furniture and she had the front door open, ready for them to jump through if the beast started climbing the steps."

"That was a wild party," Simeon admitted.

"John, after he quit laughing, said it was the best party he'd ever been to," Katherine said with a soft, triumphant smile.

Chapter Fifty-Nine

By now everyone had finished eating. The men were sitting back in their chairs, trying to ease their uncomfortably full bellies. Donny was shuffling his feet on the floor and was clearly getting restless. Eleanor and Jessie Lou wanted to keep listening to the memories and stories.

Maxie and Elva came in and quietly began smothering the flames of Sterno cans beneath serving chafing pans. When Maxie walked past Patrick O'Reilly, he reached out to touch her arm.

"Did you cook that roast?" he asked.

"Yes sir, I sure did," Maxie responded.

"Well, I've never had anything that was as tender and juicy. How'd you do that, anyway?"

Maxie laughed. "It's a salt jacket roast," she explained. "It's really easy to do. Just cover a baking pan with tinfoil and put in about a quarter inch of rock salt. Rock salt is the stuff you use to make homemade ice cream. You should season the roast with Worcestershire sauce and pepper. Then spray the rock salt you put in the pan with a bit of water and set your roast right down in the middle. Cover it totally with rock salt—it takes three or four bags for a big 'ol roast. Spray this mound with water and bake uncovered at about 475 to 500, for about twelve minutes a pound. When you take it out, put it on a newspaper. The salt will be hard as a rock and you'll need a hammer to break it loose. Just take out the roast, brush off any excess salt and it's perfect! It tends to be pink, no matter how done it is, because the juices are sealed inside."

"A salt jacket roast," Patrick mused. "I've never heard of such a thing. You'd think it would be salty with all that salt, but it wasn't. It was delicious."

"If you'd like I could write the recipe down for you," Maxie offered.

"Please do," Connie spoke for him, "I can copy one off for myself. It really was wonderful. Nora, would you like me to copy it for you?"

Nora looked ill at the thought of a hunk of bloody meat being slathered with Worcestershire sauce and covered with salt. She just stared.

"I would sure like a copy," Stuart said quickly.

"Well," said Katherine. "I believe everyone is finished eating, so let me give you a tour and then we'll head up to the ballroom."

"Can I use the rest room?" Nora asked, getting to her feet.

"Of course! I apologize, I should have told you all before. There's a bathroom just down the hall to the right and if you go further down, there's one just off the library. Maxie can show you, Nora, and then you can catch up with us. We'll wait in the library for you."

Nora walked to Maxie and the two left the dining room and began walking down the hall.

"The ballroom? Is it really a ballroom," Jessie asked breathlessly, looking at Eleanor and then at Katherine.

Katherine laughed merrily. "It really is. It's nearly the whole third floor of the house. Letty has been up there organizing and getting things ready. I don't know if you've heard the commotion coming in and out but that was her surprise entertainment. At one point I thought I heard elephant footsteps. Did you hear that, Simeon?"

Simeon chuckled. "If that elephant's back, I'm getting my rifle," he joked.

Elva came quietly into the dining room as everyone started to rise from their chairs. "Elva, just leave the dishes if you don't get them done. The grand tour will take about twenty minutes and I don't want you and Maxie to miss any of Letty's entertainment. I might need you both there for moral support," Katherine said. "I wish I knew what that girl was up to."

"She wouldn't tell me, either," Elva said, laughing. Then she lowered her voice and crouched toward Katherine menacingly and said, "Maybe we should be afraid. Be very afraid."

"Oh dear!" Katherine said in mock horror and then she remembered Donny. "But why should we be afraid when we have a super hero in our midst?"

Everyone in the dining room laughed jovially and then turned as they heard a high voice calling from the great room.

"Yoo-hoo, Katherine! Everybody. Oh, I can see I got here just in time," Lillian Dip exclaimed, clapping her hands. Eyes widened in surprise at the unannounced guest.

"Lillian! My!" Katherine exclaimed.

"Oh, good Lord," Simeon muttered behind her.

Everyone else simple, openly, stared.

Chapter Sixty

Afterwards, long after everyone went home, Katherine and Simeon marveled that Lillian, in less than seven hours, could so elaborately outfit herself.

"Really, you have to admit, she was rather breathtaking," Katherine chided.

"She looked like a demented pink hippo, and you know it," Simeon laughed.

"Well," Katherine said, unable to think of anything polite to answer in return.

Admittedly, Lillian Dip had looked like a demented pink hippo. Her short steel-gray hair had been covered with a long elaborate blond wig—a tremendous stripper-like wig—of small curls and fat curls and cascading waterfalls of curls. Perched on top and held in place with a jeweled hat pin, was a black sequined hat that had probably belonged to her mother and last worn in 1939. Lillian's face, normally unadorned except for lipstick and rouge when there was a new widower who started easing his misery and loneliness at the senior center, was aglow with color. Turquoise eye shadow reached from eyelids to eyebrows. Her eyes were heavily lined with black liner and her eyelashes coated with mascara. Bright lipstick, an orangish red which unfortunately made her teeth look yellowish, coated her lips and two red circles of blush were carefully placed on each cheek. At the bottom of one was a penciled-in beauty mark.

While the rest of the group stood like stupefied statues, Katherine quickly took hold of the situation. Marching to Lillian, she grabbed her arm and said, "Why, my goodness, didn't you just thoroughly dress for the occasion!"

"I like that dress. It looks swirly," Donny said in admiration. Lillian, eyes brilliant from the praise, turned a quick circle for him. The dress—Katherine learned later she'd picked it up that very afternoon from Value Village—was heavy pink taffeta with a fitted bodice, huge flaring skirt and a massive bow just above Lillian's rather large rump. On her feet, and displaying surprisingly slim ankles, were black high-heeled shoes with sequins at the toes. Everyone noticed, as she made her circle, that she, unfortunately, wore knee-high hose. She was as bejeweled as the Queen of England with many huge, ornate rings with adjustable bands. Around her neck, both wrists and at her ears, were fake pearls. She looks, Katherine thought to herself, like a pink Christmas tree. She even, with the sequined hat, had an ornament on top, not quite an angel with twinkle lights, but an ornament nevertheless.

"This," Katherine said with much ceremony, "is my good friend and neighbor, Lillian Dip. She lives just down the road. Lillian has been much interested in all the excitement of Patrick's party so I invited her to join us for cake and Letty's show. I hope none of you mind."

"Of course not. We're very glad you could join us, Miss Dip," Connie said while the others just nodded. She stared pointedly at Dan, who cleared his voice.

"The more the merrier, Miss Dip," Dan said, jovially.

"Call me Lillian," Lillian said grandly.

"Well, I for one am glad for another person in the 'more mature' category," Patrick said charmingly, obviously much enchanted by Lillian's overblown presence. He stepped around his children and grandchildren and plowed his way up to her. Bowing slightly, he held out his arm. "If you will do me the honor, I will escort you to the rest of the festivities."

"You must be Mr. Patrick O'Reilly!" Lillian exclaimed, batting her sultry black lashes and majestically linking her plump arm through his. "Well, sir, I would be delighted to have the handsomest man in the room escort me."

"Tell me, Lillian," he said, patting the jeweled hand dangling off his arm while looking her in the eye and turning slightly to face her, "is there a Mr. Dip?"

Lillian lowered her eyes. "Not for the past seven years," she said. "He was a wonderful man who died of cancer."

Patrick looked at her with compassion. "I lost my Edna to cancer," he said soberly. "Over twenty years ago." Then he brightened, "Well, Lillian, it looks like we're both fancy free, then!"

"And the night is young!" she replied with flirtatious charm.

Nora and Connie looked at each other. A tinge of alarm covered their bland smiles.

My goodness, all she needs is a fan! Katherine marveled. She looked at Simeon who was staring at Lillian as if he'd never seen her before.

"We're just starting the tour," Katherine explained to Lillian after she had been introduced to everyone. "One of the group, Patrick's daughter Nora, is using the facilities and will be meeting us in the library so we might as well head that way."

"We read the Visitor Guide write-up in the motel room. It was amazing. I never knew any of that about O'Malley House," Dan said.

"Good!" Katherine said. "Since you read that, we can save a lot of time on tedious details. They did a fine job on writing about the house."

Chapter Sixty-One

By the time Maxie and Nora got to the large, high-ceilinged bathroom down the hall off the kitchen, Nora was shaking and very pale.

"I'm sorry. I think I'm going to be sick," she said.

"Don't be sorry. That's just something you have to go through. You just go right ahead and be sick, honey, and then you'll feel better," Maxie said, taking her hand and leading her into the bathroom. "You just sit here on this chair and I'll get a wet cloth for your head." Opening a tall cupboard, Maxie pulled out a hand towel and two washcloths and walked to the sink. Maxie turned the old-fashioned porcelain knob marked H, and quickly soaked one of the washcloths in the frigid water, rung it out and took it to Nora, who had her arms wrapped around her stomach.

"Do you want me to leave?" Maxie asked her as she gently placed the wet cloth against Nora's forehead.

"No, please stay with me," Nora said, putting her hand on the washcloth so Maxie could move. Maxie returned to the sink and held her hand under the still-running water. She knew from years of experience that it would be at least three more minutes before warm water made its way through the ancient pipe work snaking through the house and found its way through the faucet. A few feet away, Nora had tossed the washcloth to the floor and now knelt on an ancient Afshan oriental runner, her head close to the toilet bowl. She quickly threw up three times and then went back to the chair.

Maxie handed her the warm washcloth and Nora wiped her lips.

"Well, that was certainly a waste of a perfectly wonderful meal," she said.

Maxie laughed. "It was like that with my second one," she said. "I called him the backward baby. I never did have morning sickness. It was all at night."

"Morning sickness!" Nora was dumbstruck. "You get morning sickness if you're pregnant. I'm not pregnant. I can't be pregnant. This is just the flu or something."

"Oh! And how long you had this flu or something?" Maxie asked, pulling out a small stool from under a vanity and sitting heavily.

"It has to be the flu. Or excitement. What else could it be? It comes at night when I get excited about something." Nora was frowning, mentally putting facts together.

She looked at Maxie. "I've had it for probably two weeks now. It's just at night and crackers or something salty helps."

"Well, I think you're pregnant. I thought so when I saw you and I have a sort of second sight when it comes to these things. I can always spot the pregnant ladies, sometimes long before they know. I got friends, who if they see me lookin' at them funnylike they start keepin' away from me. When's the last time you had your monthly?"

"I haven't missed."

"You have one that was short?"

"Last month. Two days was all. I thought that was strange because I'm usually like clockwork. Now I'm about three days late."

"I had two of my babies like that. Didn't miss, just sort of slowed down that first month," Maxie said. Then she grinned. "Yup! Girl, you are pregnant!" she declared.

"Pregnant," Nora said in a whisper. "I won't tell Stuart until I get a test. I'll get one of those kit things tonight." She started to cry.

"Why are you crying?" Maxie said, hugging her. "This is a happy time. A new baby in your life. A brand new life. What a precious gift from God."

"I've always wanted a baby," Nora said, blubbering and sniffling. "Stuart and I have tried for years. I've had tests. He's had tests. We've done all sorts of things and nothing worked. Three months ago we just gave up and decided we weren't meant to be parents."

Maxie reached over and pulled a four-foot hunk of toilet paper from the brass stand and ripped it loose. Taking it, Nora dabbed her eyes and laughed crazily. "A baby!" she exclaimed. Then she frowned and her eyes teared over again.

"They've always thought, Connie and Dan and all of them, that we were too stuck in our careers to want kids. We never told them differently,"

"Why not? They're nice folks. They would have understood, it seems to me."

"I don't know why. At first we were sort of embarrassed and then we were going through all those tests and it just never seemed to be the time to say anything. It's like if we brought it up we would have to admit to ourselves and to each other how much having a baby—a family—meant to both of us. It would make it more painful somehow."

"I can sort of understand that," Maxie said. "You feel like joining the others?"

"I feel....I feel just wonderful!" Nora said. "Thank you so much for helping me. Please don't tell anyone, okay?"

"Ain't my news to tell, honeybunch," she said, squeezing the young woman's hand.

Chapter Sixty-Two

By the time Maxie led Nora to the rest of the group she hadn't missed much of the tour. They were assembled in the library and Katherine had allowed the children to glide sideways on the moveable ladders that allowed access the top shelves some fifteen feet overhead, had given the rundown on the family history, and was talking about the contents of the house.

Nora slipped in and found her way to Stuart's side.

"You okay?" he whispered.

"I'm fine," she said, looking at him with complete adoration and taking his hand.

"You sure?" he asked, looking at her sideways and noting her tear-reddened eyes.

"Absolutely sure," she said, pulling his arm close. Looking around she was amazed at the proliferation of antiquities in the room. It was as if nothing had changed for nearly 120 years. The great room seemed more modern, despite numerous Kirman, Kerohan Sarouk, Hadje Jallil and other antique oriental carpets on the floor and priceless tables, china cabinets and an exquisite harpsichord and miniature harp.

The library had hundreds, perhaps thousands, of ancient books reaching from floor to ceiling on three walls. In one corner stood a globe that had to have been several hundred years old. In fact, Nora had seen one that was similar at Mt. Vernon in George Washington's study. The desk in the opposite corner was huge and very ornately carved and covered with priceless accouterments such as inkwells, quill pens, blotters, and the like.

The deep oversized dark red leather furniture was worn and looked invitingly comfortable. Beneath the massive window with a curved top was a long chaise lounge upholstered in a flowered pattern of taupe and mulberry and burgundy. In the middle of the floor was a large, dark oak table neatly piled with 100-year-old games and toys. The children were busy exploring and discovering the room's many treasures, to their mother's consternation.

"Believe me, these things have gone through generations of people. I don't think they can hurt them," Katherine said, adding, "Besides, they're being very careful."

Picking up an object, she showed it to Donny and Eleanor. "This is a stereoscope," she explained. "These cards go on it. See how there are two scenes, side by side? When you put it in the stereoscope and look through the viewfinder, the scenes go together and it looks three-dimensional. See?" The children took turns looking through the whole pile of views, mostly scenes of cities in Europe, and marveled at the horses and buggies and old-fashioned vehicles.

Turning to the rest of the group, Katherine began to enlighten them more on O'Malley House. "Most of the objects in here belonged to John's great-grandfather," she said. "It was our good fortune that none of those O'Malleys ever threw out a thing. It all went into out-buildings or up in the attic. The attic is a virtual museum, but we won't have time to explore it tonight. When the house was built, the O'Malley's rejected most of the furnishings that had been in Beatrice's side of the family for generations, preferring to buy everything new. Some of those old pieces, such as the globe in here, are around the house, but most are in the attic.

"For some reason," she continued, "I have this urge to make this place into what it was eons ago. With Letty's help and the help of a whole fleet of Danford senior citizens, we have gone through a lot of the mansion, restoring rooms to what they were originally. For instance, we took all the old Reader's Digest books of the month out of the library here and anything else that was younger than 100 years, and brought back in things like the ink wells, the round game table and the like.

"Letty and her group have been busy cataloging things, room by room, and this spring we have arranged for a curator from a museum back east to come and spend a month and help us date and value the items.

"Right now, the only rooms that aren't restored are my bedroom suite, which we will start to restore as soon as I move into the attached maid's room, and the kitchen. I simply don't need three rooms. A place for a bed and dresser are just fine." Everyone laughed.

"One thing that has made things easy is that none of the woodwork or walls or the outside was ever changed," Katherine continued. "The wallpaper you see throughout the house is what was put on originally. That is the benefit, I suppose, of having the house stay continuously in the family. If the place had ever been purchased by strangers, they may have felt the need to 'make it their own' by painting rooms and knocking out walls. For the O'Malleys, keeping it the same was keeping the family tradition the same and preserving the family heritage. The only exception to this is in the kitchen. It was remodeled in the 1920s, updated in the 1940s after a small fire—which, incidentally, also resulted in the addition of two modern bathrooms—updated again in the 1960s and new linoleum put down in the 1970s.

"Before we are done, that will also be remedied. The original cook stove, which is beautiful porcelain over cast iron and complete with a water reservoir and warming ovens, is in the old carriage house. It's a little rusty in places, but otherwise, good as new. Since I don't remember how to cook on a wood stove, I'll keep the microwave but I'll hide it somewhere. From what we can gather from photos, the original wood flooring is in good shape and we will strip off the '70s linoleum. When I say 'we,' by the way, it means a crew, not Letty and me. I'm not going to get down and pull up linoleum. Does anyone have any questions?"

Donny raised his hand. Mitch put his hand on the boy's back, as if he could clamp a hand over his mouth if needed.

"Donny. What would you like to know?" Katherine asked, ruffling his hair.

"Have you ever been on Antiques Road Show?"

"No, I haven't." Katherine said, laughing merrily. She was quite enchanted by little Donny Ames.

"Well you should go on there. Some of this stuff you own is probably worth a lot of money," he declared knowledgeably.

"Well, Donny, this is going to sound really strange, but somehow I don't feel like I own any of it. It's like I'm a caretaker. God has blessed me with the job of taking care of everything. I wasn't born an O'Malley and, sadly, I'm the only one left alive out of the whole bunch. This is their history, even though I had a small part in it."

The next dozen rooms were looked at quickly: the billiard room, the fernery, which had all the women oohing and exclaiming over. "I don't think I'd ever leave this room, if it was mine," Connie said as dangled her fingers in the burbling fountain. Katherine had Simeon tell the story of the flagpole while they walked the broad curving staircase to the second floor.

"As you can see from up here," Katherine said, "this house was really reaching to the future with the open railing that looked over the great room. This narrow room along the railing wasn't really used for anything at all, except to hold the long row of family portraits as you can see. It's really just a very wide hall. At the time it was an incredibly novel idea to have this open view to the room below, and it garnered the architect from back east great accolades. In the journals and diaries of the original O'Malleys they remember as children sitting up here and watching the parties down below. One little girl wrote about sitting up here all Christmas Eve, waiting to see Santa Claus."

"Did she see him?" Eleanor asked.

"Nope. Somehow Santa delivered everything and she didn't even know it."

Chapter Sixty-Three

The adults were all rapt and simply looked at each and shook their heads. The inside of the mansion was far beyond anything they had ever dreamed of or believed possible. Katherine was used to this reaction. Most people were dumbstruck at the overwhelming beauty and sheer numbers of exquisite items in the mansion. Sometimes there was a whispered, "Will you look at that!" but usually she played tour guide to a totally attentive group.

"Another innovative thing about the house is the fact that it is light and airy. The wall coverings are in pastels, for the most part, which was quite against the Victorian tradition of dark woods and somber settings. There are six bedrooms on the second floor and three suites. Each suite has three rooms: a sitting room, dressing room, and bedroom. Since we're short of time I'll just show you one suite and one of the bedrooms. If the doors are open, however, feel free to peek inside any room. I hate to rush everyone, but I know Letty is waiting.

"This is by far the most opulent of the suites and Letty and I fondly call it Cleopatra's digs. The ceiling is incredibly ornate and the gold does a lot to make it look like a room in a palace. The crystal chandelier was given to Beatrice from Franklin, when electricity was added to the house in 1920. This room has never changed, as far as furnishings, for the most part, except for the little rocker, which belonged to Beatrice's great-grandmother on the Livingston side and dates back to the 1770s. Everything is French provincial and purchased when the house was built. The little things on the dresser, such as the silver vanity set, the compacts, jewelry cases, hand mirrors, perfume atomizers, clocks and the like, were found in Beatrice's trunks in the attic, and Letty and I placed them throughout the room. Jessie Lou, would you be a sweetheart and open the wardrobe door."

Jessie Lou, who was overwhelmed by the gold and blue beauty of the room walked across the muted Persian carpets and walked to the huge white and gold French provincial wardrobe. The wall covering behind it, as in the rest of the room, was silk with blue and gold vertical stripes. She had the oddest desire to jump on the bed with its coverlet of pale ivory silk and a pile of gold satin and blue velvet pillows.

The dangling knob on the wardrobe was actually a tiny gold figure of a woman. Jessie Lou pulled it and was immediately enveloped in the wonderful aroma of age and wealth, a sort of pungent, spicy smell with a tinge of mustiness and an almost indiscernible whiff of mothballs. Gasping, she quickly pulled open the other door and stood back.

The wardrobe was filled with ancient silk and satin gowns, silk chemises, daytime dresses, housecoats, fur and velvet capes and any number of related items. The shelf above held hats of all sizes and shapes, and a hook to the side of the ball gowns held handbags, some of them velvet, some gold and silver mesh.

"Can I take one out?" Jessie Lou asked in a whisper. Katherine nodded. Carefully, Jessie Lou removed a pale green ball gown, with a slim-fitting, low-cut bodice that came to a vee below the waist. Long sleeves ended in a froth of flowing cream-colored lace, as did the bottom of the gown. It was sumptuously beautiful, breathtakingly beautiful, and in perfect condition.

"The drawers in the dressers all contain things like corsets, silk stockings, linen nightgowns, and the like. The small traveling trunk in the corner is full of shoes," Katherine said. "It was all in trunks belonging to Beatrice, who, by the way, is buried in the Danford Cemetery." Jessie Lou carefully put the gown back in the wardrobe and shut the doors.

The group left the room and continued down the hall. Walking beside Jessie Lou and Eleanor, Katherine said, "The next time you come to Danford, call me and come over and we'll play dress-up."

"Really?" the two girls said in unison, looking at Katherine and then at each other.

"Can big people come too?" Connie asked in anticipation.

"You can all come," Katherine said, laughing. Reaching a room on the left, she walked in. "This was a guest room, but sometimes guests stayed for months, even years. One of these men was apparently a musician because we found an old banjo, a mandolin, a violin and several harmonicas in the closet. Plus, there's an old gramophone in the corner. Like in the Cleopatra suite, the chiffarobe—the piece of furniture along the side wall that is like a wardrobe with drawers and mirrors—is full of period clothing and the drawers are full of items that we found in the attic."

"Look at these things," Dan said, peering at a wooden tray filled with small musical instruments. "I've never seen anything like these." There were many regular harmonicas, both large and small, but also a Reed-o-phone with a horn attachment, a small tambourine, and a harmonica with five brass trumpet horns. The "Beaver University Chime Harmonica," according to the box, featured two bells and 96 reeds.

"Do you play?" Katherine asked.

"A little," he admitted, as he carefully studied a Hohner Tremelo, turning the silver harmonica over and over in his hand and then putting it carefully back in the box.

"He's really good but he's too shy to say it," Donny piped up as he picked up one engraved as Celestial Echoes. "He has three harmonicas. He plays them a lot when we go camping."

"My John used to play harmonica when we went camping, too. I haven't been camping in years," Katherine said wistfully.

"You can take my place anytime," Connie said.

"Miranda, do you like to go camping?" Katherine asked. Miranda hadn't said six words since dinner ended.

"Actually, I do, because I can sketch," she said so quietly Katherine could barely hear her. "But I guess I don't like the smoke, or the bugs. Or the tent. Or using an outhouse or a bush. Now that I think about it, maybe I don't like camping." Everyone laughed and Miranda blushed to her toes.

While Miranda had been talking, Katherine had carefully secreted the harmonica Dan had picked up and held it behind her back. Holding it so only Simeon could see it, she slipped it in his pants pocket. He looked at her inquiringly. She winked.

"Patrick, do you like to go camping?" Katherine asked, continuing the conversation. Patrick and Lillian, one tall and stooped, the other short and pudgy, were standing by a window, admiring the view of the gardens below.

"I'm sorry. What did you say?" Patrick asked.

"She wanted to know if you liked to go camping," Nora said, loudly. She knew it was obvious she and Stuart weren't the camping sort and wouldn't be asked the question.

"Camping. I haven't done that in years," he said.

"We went camping just last year, at Lost Lake," Dan said, reminding him.

"That wasn't camping. We took that Airstream of yours."

"I think if you have a campfire and sleep in the woods, with or without an Airstream, it's camping," Dan said, laughing in defense.

Katherine turned to Simeon. "How about you, Simeon?"

"I guess riding herd is sort of like camping," he said thoughtfully. "I haven't missed helping move cattle to the upper pasture in the spring and moving them back down in the fall in something like twenty-six years. It takes two days, sometimes three or four. At night we camp along the creek and build a big campfire. For some reason things taste better there, even if it's Hamburger Helper. After dinner we sit around the campfire and talk and toss in empty peanut shells and make 'smores. We bed down on mats on the ground and look up at a ceiling of stars, if we're lucky, or under a tarp and a puddle of rain, if we aren't. It's probably two of my favorite times of year." Like Miranda, he blushed.

"I'd like to do that sometime," Katherine said, with a wistful look and a yearning in her voice.

"You would? That surprises me," Simeon responded.

"There are a lot of things about me that might surprise you," she said quietly, not telling him that for years John had urged her to come on the cattle drives but she had always been too busy. It was something she had always regretted.

"Well," Katherine said to the group, "if we don't get up to the ballroom, Letty's going to have me camping out in the back forty! But first, we have to take time to see Connie's turret room. Follow me!"

Katherine opened the door to the turret room and stood aside so Connie could go in first. "It's perfect. Absolutely perfect," Connie said in wonder, holding her hands to her face. The rock walls were untouched and the long tall leaded glass windows seemed to have been carved into them. The rosewood sleigh bed was very high and covered in a white watered silk coverlet. A small set of stairs was at the side of the bed, put there to help people in and out of the bed. It was a canopy bed, with intricately carved posts. Above, inside the carved rosewood was a fringe of long elegant lace.

The walls of the room held delicate oil paintings in pastel colors with ornate gold leaf frames, while ancient carpets of the softest, most muted colors covered the floors. There was a highly decorated rosewood chiffarobe, the top covered with cut glass atomizers, gold and velvet jewel cases and toilette sets befitting Queen Victoria herself. A fireplace was on the wall to the side of the windows, its elaborately carved rosewood mantle covered with old photos in silver frames and small objects d'art. Of all the rooms they had seen, while the smallest, it was the most perfect.

"Go ahead, go on in," Katherine said to Connie, laughing. "It isn't haunted!"

"Wow," Connie said as she entered, followed by the rest of the group. She was unable to find a more suitable word. "I knew it would look like this. I just knew it!"

"It's too bad you hadn't knocked on the door when you were a child," Katherine told her, "To a child this room would look like something out of a fairy tale."

"It still does, to this adult," Connie said.

As everyone filed out Connie lingered before finally, reluctantly, closing the door. She walked behind Katherine and the older woman, as if thinking of something, turned and said, "I'll catch up." Moving back to the turret room Katherine quickly went to the top drawer in the dresser. Dumping the jewelry from a velvet case, she re-crossed the room and fiddled with the doorknob before joining the others. Catching up with Simeon she surreptitiously showed him the case and patted her hip. He took it from her and slipped it in his pocket. She gave him a wink and a smile.

Chapter Sixty-Four

The stairs, two sets of them, to the ballroom were located at one end of the vast billiard room, which was located at the end of the second floor hall. Both sets of stairs, identical with one to the left and one on the right, were open and very wide to accommodate large numbers of people coming and going. Between the sets of stairs were huge mullioned oval-topped windows with dozens of panes. The windows overlooked the backyard with the stables, Simeon's cottage and the creek beyond.

As they went through the billiard room and began climbing the stairs Katherine apologized to the children. "I know you would love to stay here and play billiards, but Letty has something special planned for us and she'd be disappointed if we weren't all there." Brent trailed his fingers wistfully along the worn burgundy felt on the ancient gold-embellished billiard table before running to catch up.

Letty had put on the short-waisted, long-tailed jacket to her tuxedo and she was standing near the French doors, waiting for the guests. Elva and Maxie were puttering around the dessert and hors d'oeuvres tables.

Two tables to the right of the stage held an assortment of people who were quietly and politely observing the guests. The entertainers, Katherine correctly guessed.

The ballroom was resplendent in beauty. Letty's ingenious placement of trees covered with tiny twinkling white lights and the round tables at the stage end of the room made the area seem cozy and intimate and absolutely luxurious. The stage was lighted for entertainment, the thick velvet outer curtains pulled to the side. The tables were covered in green cloths and decorated with flowers and candles.

Lights in most of the ballroom, except for the end they were using, were kept dimmed. The long windows along the wall were night darkened except for moonlight, starlight, and a few lights from the town and neighboring buildings. The burnished wood floors glowed in the muted light.

"Oh, my," Nora said, clinging to Stuart's arm. "Don't you just want to start dancing?"

"Just call me twinkle toes," Dan answered before Stuart could say anything. "Our senior prom in the Danford High gym was nothing like this!"

Katherine, overhearing, laughed. "I can almost guarantee Letty has dancing on her menu," she said. "That girl can't come in here without dancing."

"If there's dancing later, will you do me the honor, Miss Lillian?" Patrick asked Lillian Dip, who was standing near him.

For some reason Lillian was minding her manners and being very un-Lillian. Lowering her eyes demurely, she said, "I'd be happy to dance with you, Patrick."

"Letty, we're all yours," Katherine said to a smiling Letty, who was nervously standing on the fringe of the group. Brent was eying her with appreciation and hoping he'd get a chance to dance with her later. He'd taken a class in swing and was eager to try his steps outside a classroom.

"Well," she started nervously, "I thought we'd..." She realized no one was listening, everyone was looking around and chatting excitedly about the ballroom. They had been pretty much overwhelmed by the whole evening and hadn't had much of a chance to let loose and discuss it all. And now, topping it off, they were in this room that was so magnificent it was the stuff of Danford legends.

Letty put two fingers between her lips and let out a shrill whistle. The chatter stopped instantly.

"OK, listen up everyone!" she said loudly. "Welcome to entertainment, O'Malley style. If everyone will follow me I'll show you to your tables."

Mitch took Connie's hand and gave her a quick kiss on the cheek. She looked at him with eyes filled with pure love.

Jessie Lou, with Dan and Miranda on either side, followed. Eleanor, Donny and Brent followed behind with Patrick. Eleanor and Donny each held one of his hands. Behind them were Nora and Stuart. Stuart had his arm around Nora protectively. He was worried. There was something wrong with Nora. No one should have the flu for such a length of time. He was terrified it was a cancer of some sort.

Katherine and Lillian brought up the rear behind the parade of guests. Lillian took a deep satisfying breath and smiled broadly at Katherine. Katherine grabbed her hand, feeling the metal of at least five rings.

"Lillian, can I talk to you a minute?" she asked.

Lillian looked alarmed. "What's wrong?" she asked.

"That's what I want to ask you! What's wrong?"

"Why?"

"You aren't acting like Lillian Dip. You're much too quiet and polite and reserved! I don't know the person beneath that pink satin dress. You haven't said twenty words all night. "

"I'm trying to act like a sophisticated lady. Like someone you'd be proud to claim as a friend. I don't want to embarrass you."

"Oh, you old silly. I don't want you to be a sophisticated lady. I want you to be my friend Lillian Dip. I'm proud of you just the way you are, crochet hooks, Beidecks and all."

"You are?"

"Absolutely!"

"Do you care if I run down and grab my crocheting bag? I left it in the foyer and it makes me much more at ease with strangers if I'm crocheting."

"Well, of course. Run and get it, but hurry back." Lillian smiled and turned to leave, then thought of something and grabbed Katherine's arm.

"That Patrick's one hot guy, ain't he?" she said in a low purring voice.

"Oh, get out of here," Katherine said, laughing and giving her a gentle shove.

"Back in a flash," Lillian said as she strode toward the ballroom doors, the huge pink satin bow above her rear end bobbing up and down as she went.

The seven O'Reilly adults found seats at two of the six-place round tables in front of the stage, leaving room for Simeon and Katherine and Lillian Dip. The four children sat at a table behind them and would be joined by Maxie and Elva. Before the evening was over, the arrangement would be changed a dozen times.

Simeon reached over and took Katherine's hand. "So far, it's been a whopping success," he said softly. "I never knew half that stuff about O'Malley House."

"It has been fun, hasn't it Simeon?" Katherine asked. "I just hope this part goes as well as the first. Wasn't it wonderful the way Mitch came all that way and surprised Connie? It just made my heart melt."

"The whole night has been pretty wonderful," he said. Then he looked around. "Where's Lillian?"

"She went to get her crocheting. Said she can't be herself with out it."

"Did you get a load of that dress?" he asked in a low voice.

"Simeon, you hush." Katherine whispered.

"I saw the tag. It's an original. By Omar the Tentmaker."

"Simeon!"

"Why? No one can hear."

"I can hear. You just shouldn't talk about people like that. Besides, it isn't an Omar, it's a Jezrood."

Simeon burst out laughing.

"What's so funny?" Lillian asked, coming in and settling into the chair next to him.

"Oh, this woman. She's wild. She's wise. She's witty. She's beautiful," he said expansively, motioning to Katherine.

"She's going to hit you," Katherine said under her breath.

Chapter Sixty-Five

Letty climbed the three steps to center stage and looked out shyly. "I probably don't need to use this microphone since there aren't that many of us, but it's here so what the heck. Besides, some of our entertainers can't entertain without a microphone. I hope you'll enjoy what we have planned for you. About halfway through we'll break for birthday cake and snacks, then more entertainment, and then we can do some dancing." Looking beyond the first tables, she spotted the young people. "Brent, you gonna dance with me?" she called out.

"Do you know how to do swing?" he called back, flipping his silky honey-colored hair out of his eyes with an adept toss of his head. His green eyes sparkled in the candlelight.

Letty laughed merrily, "Do I know how to do swing! I can probably teach you a thing or two!" she said, giving a twirl to everyone's delight, and then laughter as she tripped over her own feet and stumbled to catch herself.

Turning her attention back to the group, she cleared her throat and lowered her voice theatrically. "Ladies and gentlemen and special birthday guest Patrick O'Reilly...tonight you will be bedazzled, enchanted, intrigued, befuddled, amused, and delighted," she said, and then added in a normal voice, "I hope. If not, well, I tried.

"First off, let's get in the mood by talking about birthdays. Lucille Ball said the secret of staying young is to live honestly, eat slowly, and lie about your age. You can't lie about your age, Mr. Patrick O'Reilly, because everyone's already told us how old you are. I think the whole town, from all those phone calls trying to find a party place, knows how old you are!

"You were born in the year 1925 and these are some of the other things that happened that year: Calvin Coolidge was president, Lawrence Welk started a new band, F. Scott Fitzgerald wrote *The Great Gatsby,* Adolph Hitler wrote *Mein Kampf*, flagpole sitting became a national fad, television was invented, and a guy named Earl Wise invented the potato chip. And where would we be without potato chips?

"Actually, that wasn't the most important of all," Letty continued, "...the most important event, to your family tonight, was that you were born in a tiny little house on Hill Street.

"Bob Hope said you know you're getting old when the candles cost more than the cake, and middle age is when your age starts to show around your middle. Maurice Chevalier was more practical, saying 'Old age isn't so bad when you consider the alternative.'

"I know this one is true, because my grandmother says it to me: 'Inside every older person is a younger person wondering what the heck happened.'

"Designer Coco Chanel said, 'Nature gives you the face you have at twenty, but it's up to you to merit the face you have at fifty,' and Mark Twain added, 'Wrinkles should merely indicate where the smiles have been.' Mr. O'Reilly, it is obvious that you have smiled your way through life and your face doesn't look much past seventy and still shows your rugged handsomeness. Your countenance, and your family, is your testimony to a life well lived and loved.

"Katherine Hepburn said, 'If you survive long enough, you're revered—rather like an old building.' Well, we're doing that tonight, revering your eighty years in a building that is older than you by at least fifteen.

"I will end with this wonderful quote by Susan B. Anthony: 'Sooner or later we all discover that the important moments in life are not the advertised ones, not the birthdays, the graduations, the weddings, not the great goals achieved. The real milestones are less prepossessing. They come to the door of memory unannounced, stray dogs that amble in, sniff around a bit and simply never leave. Our lives are measured by these.'

Raising an invisible glass in salute, she sang, to the tune of "Sing a Song of Sixpence":

Sing a song of Birthdays
Full of fun and cheer
And may you keep on having them
For many a happy year

By the end of the second singing of the short song, everyone in the room was standing and at its finish, they all applauded and cheered a blushing Patrick O'Malley. Brent gave a shrill whistle and Donny, attempting to do it himself, managed to spit all over Eleanor's arm.

Eleanor frowned and glared at him while wiping her hand on her thigh. "Gross. That was just gross, Donny," she hissed.

"All right, then," Letty continued when everyone had settled back down. "Let's bring out some talent here. Before Misty Purvis comes up to play her harp, I would like to tell you that the first three performers here tonight take a turn at the Muddy Waters Coffee House, which is a sort of jumping off point for local musicians. Some of the musicians who started out there have gone on to be professional. If you have time, you should pay it a visit. The coffee house is at the end of Main Street in an old rambling house and is stacked from floor to ceiling with books and games. People come and spend the day playing checkers and chess, or just quietly reading. Four nights a week there is entertainment.

"Misty, come on up," she said, looking at the side table filled with an assortment of artistic-looking people.

Even young Donny could have picked out the harp player by her long flowing wispy muslin gown and her long, limp blond hair. She wore wire rim glasses and hesitantly and shyly came to the stage and walked to where her harp was set up.

Misty blushed and fluttered her eyes, then said in a soft voice, "I'm going to play two songs for you, a rendition of 'Morning has Broken' and a combination of two songs: 'All is Well with My Soul' and 'Jesus Loves Me.' "

From the minute Misty's fingers floated to the harp, to the last haunting pull of the strings, the entire room was enchanted. A long minute of silence endured as everyone let the beautiful music settle in his soul.

Lillian finally broke the silence by saying, "Oh, my!" and everyone clapped politely. Letty bounded back on stage, tripping on the top step and catching herself before she fell.

"I know what you mean," she said. "The first time Misty played at the coffee house everyone just sat there. She thought we hated it, but we were too stunned and too struck with the beauty of the music to do anything. Applauding seemed to take away from what we had just heard. Isn't she just wonderful?" Letty motioned to Misty Purvis, who blushed shyly as she put the harp back in place. The audience applauded wildly. "Thank you," she said in a hushed voice.

"Next Allen James is going to come up and regale us with something a bit livelier," Letty announced.

Allen James was a thin man with a short beard and a moustache and hair pulled back in a ponytail. He was dressed in jeans and cowboy boots and a blue cowboy shirt with mother-of-pearl buttons. A red neckerchief was tied at his throat. The crowd, expecting to hear cowboy music, was surprised when the young man played a medley of tunes from the '50s and '60s including "Earth Angel," "In the Still of the Night," "Why do Fools Fall in Love," "Peggy Sue" and "Long Tall Sally." By the time he finished, with the Beatles' "I Want to Hold your Hand," everyone was singing along with him raucously. When he finished, they gave him a standing ovation. Letty bounced back on stage and gave him a hug.

"Allen James!" she said loudly, drawing out the name, "and you can see him nearly every Friday evening, at the Muddy Waters Coffee House." Then she said more quietly, "Now I know you can probably smell the huckleberry pie and birthday cake and coffee so let's take a break. But before we do, Allen, can you lead us in singing happy birthday to Mr. O'Reilly?"

Everyone sang loudly as Allen played accompaniment on his guitar. Patrick O'Reilly was surrounded by his children and grandchildren, all of them touching him, either by holding his hands, or by patting his shoulder. Donny sat on his lap.

"I don't know what to say," he said with a sniff at the conclusion of the song.

"Well, we do... 'Happy Birthday!'" Katherine said grandly, then turning to the rest of the group and the table of entertainers she added, "Everyone line up at the tables and get some refreshments. You too, all of you wonderfully blessed musicians."

Chapter Sixty-Six

A shuffle of chairs ensued as everyone got up and made their way, laughing and chatting, to the long table of food.

Stuart helped Nora up and took her hands in his. "All you all right?" he asked.

"Why?" she said, grinning.

"Because you've been smiling ever since you got up here," he said. "I know you don't feel well and you're still pale as a ghost. Given all that, I don't think I'd be smiling."

"Gee, can't a girl smile if she wants to?"

"Sure, but what are you smiling about?"

"It's a secret, at least for now."

"But we don't have secrets."

"Can you wait until later?"

"I suppose so, but whatever it is it must be good."

"I hope it is," she said, enigmatically, and gave him a quick hug.

"I'm starving," she added.

Connie Ames, with Mitch by her side, stood in front of the table and stared. There were three huckleberry pies, three apple, an incredibly decorated birthday cake, and trays of fancy hors d'oeuvres.

"Are you all right? What's the matter, Connie dear?" Katherine asked with great concern, when she noticed that the younger woman was a little distraught.

"It's too much," Connie wailed. "What you've done for us. I can't believe you did all this for us. The dinner, the tour and the music and now this. You don't even know us!"

Katherine laughed quietly, and hugged her close. "Let me tell you something. I can't tell you what this has done for me, planning this party. Since John's death, I haven't done much of anything socially. I've let most of my old friends go and have simply sat in this rambling old house and stagnated. It started a while back with Letty bringing in all the people to help in the house but this party for you has been the finale of the changes in my life.

"Within the last three days my whole world has changed. Maxie's back in my life, and Elva, and I have all of you as new friends and I hope we'll stay on contact for many years to come. Really, this has been a time of miracles. Just look at Simeon here, all dressed up in a tuxedo and looking so fine and handsome."

Connie laughed and looked at Simeon.

By then all the O'Reilly's had gathered and were listening. Katherine continued, looking at all of them with fondness. "You've taught me a lot about family. Mitch, when you walked through that dining room my heart just melted. You O'Reillys are a fine family. Dan, you have a lovely—no, a stunning! —wife and a charming daughter. Nora and Stuart, you are such a beautiful young couple, so vivacious and alive. Patrick, it has been an honor to host this party for you and it has been a true pleasure learning how many people and events we have in common. Brent and Eleanor and Donny, you have been a delight all evening, especially you, Donny."

Then she turned back to Connie. "But you, Connie, I fell in love with you over the phone when you asked if I thought things happen for a reason. You have all happened to me, for a reason. I have hosted hundreds of parties in this room and all of them have been fun and festive. But none, not one, has filled my heart to overflowing like this one. Thank you. Thank all of you."

She started to sniffle and walked away before anyone could see. Simeon followed her, and when she finally stopped, by the windows, he quickly pulled her into his arms.

"Oh, Simeon," she said. "I just hate crying. I've cried more in three days than I have in three years!"

"Well, it gives me a good reason to hug you," he said, chuckling.

"You don't need a reason," she said.

Chapter Sixty-Seven

The thought of huckleberry pie was too strong for the adults in the party to remain maudlin for very long. The children had already loaded up plates and were headed back to the tables. Maxie handed a slice to Patrick, the cooked berries flowing out over the plate in a pool of sumptuous purple. No one wanted to cut the birthday cake for the moment, being content to just admire its beauty.

"Huckleberry pie!? I haven't had huckleberries for years. Edna used to make the most wonderful huckleberry pie in the world," Patrick O'Reilly said.

"What are huckleberries?" Donny asked, looking at his mother. Connie lifted her eyes to the heavens and shut them in angelic repose.

"I think God placed them in the Garden of Eden and, somehow, after he closed it off, a little bush escaped. They're sort of like blueberries except that's like saying skim milk is like ice cream," Connie told him.

"Hmph. That's a good description," Simeon said. "I'll have to remember that."

"I can't get over this pie," Connie said to Maxie. "Not only the huckleberries, but the crust. It is by far the best crust I have ever eaten."

"I'll tell you a secret. There's always been a bit of an argument over who makes the best pies, me or Miss Katherine. The truth is, she makes the best pies by heredity. The pie crust recipe is one her grandmother used, except they probably used bear or pork lard instead of Crisco. The trick is half, and half, and half," Maxie said, conspiratorially.

"Half and half?" Connie asked, leaning in.

Maxie beamed and crossed her arms, as if she was privileged to one of the best kept secrets in the universe, but was willing to share.

"Everything is halved," she explained. If you use six cups of flour, you cut in half that amount—three cups—of shortening, and half that—a cup and a half—of water. It makes the flakiest crust you'll ever eat."

"I know that," Connie said around a mouthful of pie. "I'm eating it!"

"It's a simple recipe but just so's you don't forget I'll go fetch some paper and a pen and write it down for you," Maxie told Connie. "I'll be back in two shakes."

When the O'Reillys had gone through the line, the musicians filed through and then Lillian and Elva, Simeon and Katherine. The last four chatted and jibed from one end of the table to the other, Elva making smart remarks about Simeon coming out of his hole and Simeon teasing her about just coming out of puberty.

Katherine put down her fork and sat back and watched the people she loved bantering and trading jabs. It was one of those flawless moments in life, one of those times so rare and heart-huggingly perfect that you wished it could go on forever.

Suddenly Simeon frowned and took Katherine by the hand. "Excuse us," he said, pushing back his chair and helping Katherine to her feet just as Elva was mid-sentence in what would surely be a clever and witty remark. Katherine felt a shudder of unease that turned to alarm as she looked toward the ballroom door, toward which Simeon was hauling her in long loping strides.

Maxie stood, grim-faced, in the doorway. She was flanked by two sheriff's deputies.

Before Katherine and Simeon reached the doorway everyone had ceased talking and eating and watched, puzzled, at the scene taking place before them.

Deputy Johnny Thunder Cloud ducked his head in embarrassment and didn't bother to hide his annoyance. "I'm sorry, Miss Katherine, Mr. Simeon," he said, taking off his hat, "but we got another anonymous call about the noise here and vehicles parked in the road."

"Oh, that old battleax," Katherine cried, shaking her fist. "It was her, wasn't it, Johnny? The 'anonymous' person was Marge Reynolds?"

"Katherine, you know he can't tell you that," Simeon said, patting her hand. "Johnny, did you think there was excessive noise?"

"No, sir, I sat in my car for a bit and didn't hear any noise. Then Miss Maxie here let me in the house and even then it was pretty muffled."

"Are there any cars in the road?"

"No, sir, there aren't any cars out there at all."

"I hope you put that in your report," Katherine said. "It's a sad day when a person can't have a little party in her own home without a disgruntled, jealous old woman next door complaining needlessly."

"I'm sorry, Ma'am. I'm just following up the complaint," the deputy said, looking around. "What kind of a party you having here, anyway?"

"An eightieth birthday party for Patrick O'Reilly. You might remember the O'Reilly family from when you were a youngster. Patrick's family brought him back here to show him the old town."

"Sure, I remember them. Connie graduated the same year I did. Are they all here? Danny, too? And the younger one. Nelda, I think was her name?"

"Nora," said Simeon.

"Oh, yeah, Nora," the deputy said, shaking his head as he remembered.

"Would you like to come in and say hello?" Katherine asked, reaching for his hand.

"Sure would! Man, me and Danny used to have some great times together out on the football field." He started walking across the floor toward the guests who had politely quit staring and were quietly chatting and finishing their dessert.

Dan jumped to his feet and bellowed. "Thunder? Johnny Thunder Cloud?"

Johnny Thunder Cloud grinned. "Danny, I can't believe it's you! I've always wondered what happened to you!"

Before he finished his sentence Connie had gotten to her feet, sidestepped Dan, and flung herself into his arms. "Johnny! I can't believe this. Look at you. I always figured you'd end up on parole somewhere, and here you are a sheriff's deputy!"

Johnny gave her a big hug and then held her away from him and looked at her. "Connie. You're more beautiful than ever. Man, I always figured you'd grow up and become some dismal housewife with a bunch of kids, and here you are looking like a movie star. What are you doing these days?"

"I'm a dismal housewife with a bunch of kids!" she said, bursting into laughter. Turning to Mitch she saw that he was staring open-mouthed, as were her children.

"This is my family," she said, "the ones with their mouths open. This is my husband, Mitch, who is by far the best husband in the whole world. Mitch, this is Johnny Thunder Cloud. We all went to school with him." Mitch stood to his feet and shook hands.

After introducing her children, Dan introduced his family. Miranda, clearly intimidated by the handsome good looks of the newcomer, lowered her head. Nora, pulling Stuart along by the hand, approached the group.

"I'm Nora, and I sure remember you," she said. "I thought you were the most handsome boy in school, even if you were a lot older. A lot older.

"I remember you, too," he said, laughing. "Always hanging around and being a little pest."

"But, you have to admit, a cute little pest," Nora said, cocking her head and giving him a sideways look.

"I have a feeling you can still be a pest," he said, looking at Stuart for confirmation.

"I'm Stuart, the pest's poor berated husband," Stuart said, extending his hand. Nora pretended to kick him.

Katherine, noticing Letty standing patiently on the stage, interrupted the reunion by asking Johnny Thunder Cloud if he and the other deputy, a chubby balding fellow still standing in the doorway, would like to join the party. He declined since he was on shift, but he and Dan exchanged cell phone numbers and made plans to get together the next day.

"Don't worry about your anonymous complainer," Johnny told Katherine, giving her a quick hug. "I'll give her a call and get her calmed down. I'll tell her I came over here and raised Cain and threatened to haul the whole lot of you to jail." Katherine laughed at the absurdity of the situation.

"I appreciate it and I apologize for my earlier, very uncharitable and very unkind, outburst toward her, the poor soul," Katherine said. "Would it be bribery if I had Elva fix plates for the two of you to take with you?"

"Heck no! I think it would be just caring for a couple of starving deputies, especially if we can have a piece of that huckleberry pie."

"You've got it!" Katherine said, beckoning to Elva to join them.

Chapter Sixty-Eight

A few minutes later, back on stage, Letty resumed the entertainment by declaring to Patrick that it was pretty cool to have such a wild eightieth birthday party that the sheriff's department had to come quiet things down.

The entertainment following included a short skit by a comedian who had everyone howling with laughter, especially when he outlined Patrick's history. And then Letty got back on stage.

"Mr. O'Reilly, I have a question for you," she said, looking down to where he sat at the table.

"Fire away!" he said. He was enjoying himself immensely. This had been a night to end all nights.

"Better yet, you come up here and I'll ask you in front of everyone." The old fellow got up and walked to the front of the stage. Taking her extended hand, he climbed the three steps. Once he was beside her, Letty nodded to Allen James, the guitarist, who came forward carrying a gleaming saxophone. Letty put it in Patrick O'Reilly's hands.

"Does this look familiar?" she asked quietly.

"It looks like my old sax, but it can't be," he said, frowning. "I sold it years ago. But, look there, it's got a dent on the side just like mine had."

Dan and Connie and Nora looked at each other. They didn't know their father had owned a sax. They knew he had once played in a band, long before they were born, but they didn't know what he played.

"Who did you sell it to?" Letty asked him.

"I believe it was Gilly Washburn."

"How did you know Mr. Washburn?"

"Gilly and me and Boots Franklin and Harley Regis had a little band. Fellow by the name of Kenny Jeems played drums. Called ourselves the Starlight Boys. We played around town during the '40s."

"What happened then?"

"The war. Off we all went. We all came back except for Kenny. He died in France. We tried to start it back up when we got back, but it just wasn't the same."

"Actually," Letty said, turning from Patrick to the guests, who were listening attentively, "I learned all that from my father, who is involved in a hundred different civic groups and knows every band that's ever played in the state I think."

To the side, the musicians were smiling in expectation. They knew the secret and, as musicians, they were greatly touched by what Letty was doing.

"Patrick, this is your saxophone. It's been in its case for at least the last twenty-five years."

"How did you get it?" Patrick asked, puzzled.

"I found Gilly Washburn!" she said triumphantly. "He still lives in Danford. Gilly, come out."

A wizened little old man with black horn-rimmed glasses and a head so bald it gleamed in the overhead lighting came from behind the back curtains. He needed a cane to walk and his dentures were too big for his face, giving him a naked horsy look. He wore an old-fashioned, powder-blue leisure suit, a black bolo tie, and cowboy boots, which were fitting because of his bowed legs.

"Gilly?" Patrick asked, striding toward the little man.

"You don't look much different at all," Gilly Washburn exclaimed. "I'd-a knowed you anywhere!"

The two old friends clapped backs and started reminiscing.

"You can catch up later," Letty broke in. "Through Gilly's help I've located the others, too. Boots Franklin, who lives in Missoula, and Harley Regis, who lives down by Dillon with his daughter. They both drove up to be here tonight. Harley brought his great-grandson, Shawn, who is a drummer."

The two oldsters, followed by a teenager with long brown hair and leather pants and vest, came out on stage. There was a flurry of activity.

"Did you know he played in that band?" Dan asked Connie.

"I knew he played in a band but I didn't know it had a name. He never has talked much about the early days and hardly ever talks about the war."

"Well, I'll be," Nora said. "Imagine Daddy playing a saxophone!"

Within ten minutes Shawn had his drum set up and the foursome of ancient musicians were assembled in front of him.

"We've had the opportunity to practice a bit this afternoon," Gilly said to the crowd, "so I hope we don't hurt your ears too bad. Paddy, do you remember how to put that thing on?"

"Paddy?" Connie said, looking at Nora and Dan. They all three laughed. Patrick was grinning like a monkey as he slung the saxophone strap over his head and settled the instrument against his side. Licking his lips and the saxophone reed, he gave a few trial notes, a few of them loud squawks which caused Lillian to squint her eyes. She wished she'd brought her bongo drum.

"We'll play some of the oldies," Gilly said, but we'll start slow. "Paddy, if you can remember to read music, we'll do 'Blue Moon' first." Patrick nodded, and smiled around his mouthpiece.

The familiar song started out crudely, with much squawking and squealing. Gilly, who still performed occasionally, had brought his digital piano and adeptly guided the group. Boots played acoustic guitar and Harley played steel guitar, both of them out of practice but showing that they knew what they were doing. Shawn, obviously talented, tried to tone down his drums and get the slow, casual, rhythm.

Patrick closed his eyes and tried to place himself back in time. He was never much for reading music. If he knew the song, after the first note he could just play along.

They played a multitude of songs, "As Time Goes By," "Begin the Beguine," "I Only Have Eyes For You," "Stars Fell on Alabama," and "Brother Can you Spare a Dime?" Everyone danced, even the other entertainers, taking turns and switching partners, and laughing happily. Letty proved herself to be an accomplished dancer, which surprised Katherine, given how clumsy the girl was. If the song had any sort of a quick beat, she and Brent twisted and turned and swirled, to the amusement of everyone.

"Hey, we're pretty good!" Patrick said in astonishment when the band took a few minute break after playing "I Only Have Eyes for You." "I can't believe I remember how to play this thing."

"Guess it's like riding a bike," Harley said.

"I think it's because we're all deaf," Boots said. "We can't really hear ourselves. But nobody's left yet."

"You fellas mind if I sit out the next few?" Patrick asked.

"We planned on that," Gilly said. "It's your party and I see a woman in pink out there that's had her eye on you all night. Letty said the new guys can join us, but I doubt if that harp can keep up. By the way, you can have your sax back. I haven't played it in years and I always felt it was yours anyway."

"I'll pay you for it," Patrick declared, running his hand lovingly over the gleaming brass.

"No, you won't," Gilly retorted as he peered at Patrick through lenses that made his eyes look like they belonged to a koi goldfish. "It's a birthday present."

“I don’t know what to say,” Patrick said.

“You mama never taught you any manners? You say, ‘Thank you, Gilly.’”

“Thank you, Gilly!”

Katherine was astounded at what Letty had put together in just a few short days. The party was a surprising success, an astounding success. She wished she could have invited a hundred people to hear this music and enjoy this time. Walking up to Dan as the musicians started to rally for the second set—this time including Misty the harpist, and Allen the guitarist—she held a burgundy leather box out to him.

“I was going to give this to you as a keepsake of this night just before you left, but I think now is a better time,” she said. Dan took the box and beamed in amazement.

“You’re giving me the old Hohner Tremelo? I can’t believe it!”

“It’s yours. Take it and get up there and play. Just pretend you’re sitting around the campfire,” she told him. He shook her hand effusively, and then hugged her. Then he rushed off to show the treasure to Miranda and Jessie Lou before jumping, with one leap, to the stage. Katherine wondered how he would ever play around that grin.

Chapter Sixty-Nine

Lillian was on her fiftieth sigh of the evening when she saw Patrick coming her way. "Can I get you anything?" he asked her.

"Oh, I'm fine. Just perfectly, wonderfully, fine," she responded. "They're starting to play, shouldn't you get back there?"

"Nope. I promised a beautiful lady I'd dance with her tonight. Will you do me the honor," he said, bowing and holding out his arm.

The band was playing "I'm in the Mood for Love." Patrick swept Lillian to the dance floor and began dancing. He, to the surprise of his children and Lillian, was a ballroom dancer, making beautiful, broad sweeping turns and grand moves. His three children were chagrined that they never knew he could dance, his daughters that they had never danced with him.

Lillian felt like a queen. She quickly settled into his style and they made an attractive couple, he tall and fit in a black suit with his thinning hair glowing white in the muted light, and she, garbed in flowing pink satin with her jeweled rings and her blond curls bobbing to the rhythm.

"You play a mean sax," she complimented him at the end of the dance.

"Pardon?"

"I said you play a mean sax," she said more loudly.

"I used to. I was surprised that I remembered the fingering. I still can't believe all the guys from the band are here, well, except for poor Kenny. You want to sit the next one out?"

"Do we have to?" Lillian asked. "Do you know I haven't crocheted a single inch since I've been here? I brought my crocheting but there just doesn't seem to be time to do it. Usually I need it if I'm nervous, but I haven't been a bit nervous tonight."

"My Edna used to crochet. I think I have at least six afghans around the house, including two with orange from the sixties."

"Good for her! Crocheting is a sign of intelligence, you know," Lillian said.

"I didn't know that. Well, makes sense, Edna was pretty smart."

"This isn't my real hair," Lillian confessed after a few minutes of silence.

"Oh, I know that," Patrick said, amused.

"My real hair is short and brown and gray."

"Wash and wear hair," Patrick said with approval, "that's the best kind. Makes it easier to get up and go."

The band played a heartfelt version of "Over the Rainbow" and part way through the song Lillian sighed deeply. "This reminds me of the wedding Friday," she said.

"What?" Patrick asked.

"I said this reminds me of the wedding Friday," she said.

"What wedding?" Patrick asked near her ear.

"Oh, never mind. It was just something on TV," she said, alarmed that she had brought it up. She had promised herself that she wouldn't bring any television stories to the party.

"It wasn't the wedding between Eleanor and Bart, was it?" Patrick asked with interest.

They danced through the next three songs, totally captivated with each other.

By 12:30 a.m. Donny and Eleanor were drooping and Lillian and Patrick were the only ones left on the dance floor, although Patrick had danced with his daughters and granddaughters and charmed them quite thoroughly.

The last song came to an end as they were discussing the tragedy of losing a spouse to cancer. They were surprised to discover Elva and Maxie had quietly removed all the food.

Letty went back to the stage and everyone watched her. Behind her, the musicians were quietly packing away their instruments.

"This has been quite an evening," she said. "Before we go our separate ways, I would like to try to sing a song, and I'd like all of you to join me." Reaching down, she pushed the play button on a small boombox and the orchestra on a sound track started. After the musical intro, Letty closed her eyes and started singing, "O Danny Boy," her voice high and sweet and pure. The entire group joined in, holding hands all around, and singing with all their might. The notes faded away and the silence ensued, until Letty quietly said, "Thank you, good night, and, Patrick, happy birthday."

Everyone in the group applauded and cheered. Donny, jolted awake, looked around and said, "What'd I miss? What'd I miss?"

Patrick spent a few minutes with his old friends, and they made arrangements to meet the next day for breakfast and to catch up on each other. The younger musicians pumped his hand and wished him the best, saying it was a night they'd never forget.

Chapter Seventy

Within a few minutes all that remained were the O'Reillys, Katherine and Simeon, Letty and Lillian. They slowly walked down the stairs to the second floor and then on into the great room where Elva had their coats waiting.

Connie and Dan and Nora were effusive in their gratefulness, and Patrick surprised everyone by tearing up when he tried to say thanks.

"It's been quite a birthday," he said, blowing his nose loudly. "Quite a birthday. Man, I hope I'm not getting a cold."

Katherine, with Simeon at her side, handed him her gift and he opened it quickly. He exclaimed in surprise at the old book on Danford history.

"I was going to give it to you earlier, but there never seemed to be a time," Katherine said apologetically.

"This is wonderful," he said. "I was telling the kids that I can't remember what happened to some of the places, and where the new buildings are I can't remember what was there before."

"I do that all the time, and I live here," Simeon said.

"I gave Dan the old harmonica and Nora, I want you to have this to remember tonight," Katherine said, handing her a small jewelry box. Inside was a tiny locket of gold, obviously meant for a child. Nora's face crumpled but she kept the tears at bay.

"It's beautiful," she said quietly.

"I don't know why I was meant to give you this one," Katherine said, still puzzled. "I had another one picked out but I just knew this tiny locket was the one you were to have. It belonged to Beatrice O'Malley when she was a child. The initials B.O.L. stand for Beatrice Olivia Livingston." Nora held up the locket and the light danced off the gold.

"Connie, this is for you," Katherine said, as she handed her a dark green velvet-lined box. Inside was a large, very old-fashioned, very ornate key made of steel and decorated with brass. Connie took it out carefully and held it up.

"It's the key to the turret room," Katherine said. "I hope you will come back soon and use it."

"I just don't know what to say to you," Connie said in a choked voice. "A key to the turret room?"

"Now don't start crying again," Mitch said, giving her a squeeze and muttering he wished he had stock in a tissue company. Turning to Katherine, he said, "I promise I'll send her back soon. The new business is taking so much of my time, and you would do her a world of good."

"But she has to bring the kids, too."

"Hey, you can keep that bunch for good!" he said jovially.

Katherine stepped back a few steps and said, "All of you are invited here, anytime. I hope we can do this again—well, except for the birthday and the lavish entertainment—very soon. Maybe we could all go camping with Simeon when they move the cattle. We'd have to borrow a few horses but wouldn't it be a fun time?"

"Really?" Brent said, echoed by Jessie Lou.

"I love horses. I absolutely love horses," Jessie Lou squealed.

"Then I think we should just all do it," Simeon said, warming to the idea of spending a few days with this group. "I'll let Katherine know the dates and she can get together with

Connie. I hope all of you can make it. Stuart, could you and Nora come out?"

"We could sure try," he said. "I don't see why not. I'd love to see Nora on a horse."

"I've been on a horse," Nora said to him. "We had a horse when we were growing up, didn't we, Connie? Rounding up cattle sounds like loads of fun, but right now we really need to let you poor people get some sleep," she added, giving Simeon and then Katherine a hug.

The group reluctantly moved out to the front veranda and then settled into two cabs that Elva had summoned. The limo was long gone. Lillian was in the front seat of the lead car since they would drop her off at her trailer just down the street. The taxis drove off, taillights twinkling in the dark of the night.

Chapter Seventy-One

In the kitchen, Maxie and Letty and Elva were laughingly putting the last of the silverware away when Simeon and Katherine joined them.

"Sure don't feel like one o'clock in the morning, does it?" Maxie asked.

"I feel like I could use one more dance," Elva said, grabbing up Simeon.

"Get away, you little twerp," he teased. She flicked him with her dish towel.

Katherine looked at Letty and shook her head.

"What?" Letty asked.

"You are the most amazing person," Katherine said, settling back against a counter top. "I can't believe what you pulled off tonight. It's beyond comprehension. And your song. I've never heard anyone do a better job on 'Danny Boy.' The whole evening has been just amazing. Maxie. Elva. The dinner. The pies. Everything. I don't think you could go anywhere in the world and pay any amount of money for an evening like tonight. It tops anything I've ever had a part in. And Simeon! Just look at you, and you were so charming to everyone. All of you were just...just perfect! Even Lillian was perfect!"

"And that's saying a lot," Simeon said.

"I haven't had this much fun in ten years," Maxie said, adding wistfully: "I wish we could do it again soon."

"Actually, I've been thinking about that," Katherine said to Maxie, pushing herself away from the counter. "Simeon and I attend First Baptist, you and Elva and your family go to Free Will Baptist and Letty goes to the Four Square Church. Between the four of us and Lillian we know everyone over the age of sixty-five in town. We could have a Golden Agers party—make it a potluck so we don't have to do a lot of cooking. Gilly and the rest of the Starlight Boys said they want to start getting together again, and I'll bet there are others who would like to dust off their instruments and play in a band. We could dance and eat and laugh and get to know each other."

"That's a great idea," Elva said. "I know a lot of waitresses who would help just to get a chance to be in O'Malley House. It could be a lot of fun."

"You can count on me," Letty said, fishing a piece of pie out of the tin and putting it in foil to take home.

"Let's plan on it. Simeon, you in or out?" Katherine asked, looking at him.

"I'm not much for parties, Kate," he said, frowning. Then he cocked his head and added, "But, like Maxie, I haven't had this much fun in ten years. Make it twenty years. I'm in. But do I have to wear a tux?"

"You do if you want to catch a hot mama," Elva said.

"Isn't it past your bedtime, little girl?" he jabbed.

"Well, I don't know about anyone else here, but I'm tired," Maxie said, putting on her jacket. "Elva girl, you gonna sit here yakkin' all night or take me home?"

"Right behind you, Grandma," she said, sliding a slim arm into a sweater.

"And I'm ahead of both of you," Letty said, hugging everyone and heading out the door.

Maxie opened the kitchen door to leave and then turned to Katherine. "You plan on bein' home tomorrow after church?" she asked.

"Should be. Why?"

"God's been talking to me about that Marge next door. He won't let me rest until I pay her a visit. Figured I'd do it after church."

"Come over afterwards and tell me how she is. I'm worried about her." Katherine said, adding, "You want me to go with you?"

"No, I think the good Lord wants me to do this myself," she said.

Shutting the door behind Elva and Maxie, Katherine turned to Simeon.

"Well, Mister-oh-you're-handsome-in-a-Tux, you were certainly the life of the party tonight. You danced with every female there. I didn't even know you could dance."

"I don't know how. I just sort of stand there and move back and forth."

"Well, it works very well. It was quite a night, wasn't it?"

"Sure was."

"Would you like some tea?"

"I'd better get on home. I have to usher at church tomorrow and I'd like to do it awake."

"I'll see you tomorrow, then. Simeon, thank you so much for helping me tonight. I really appreciate it."

"I didn't do anything. I was just sort of there."

"That's what I needed from you. To just sort of be there."

They moved outside to the veranda. In the background the rush of night winds could be heard in the treetops.

"It's going to be dawn soon," Katherine remarked, shivering in the chilly night air. Simeon moved toward her and put his arm around her.

"Do you mind if I kiss you goodnight?" he asked softly.

"It has been such a perfect night I would be disappointed if you didn't," she said, turning to face him and snuggling close to his chest. She lifted her face. He bent down and kissed her softly, gently. Katherine was surprised to find that he was quivering.

"I didn't do a very good job. I need to try that again," he whispered. Katherine chuckled. He kissed her again, this time longer and not quite so gently. Then he held her close. She could feel his heart beating. He smelled good. He felt strong.

Simeon could also feel her heart beat. She felt so petite. She felt soft and warm and…right.

"I'd better get home," he said huskily.

"Good night, Simeon," she whispered.

"Good night, Katie," he whispered back.

"I'll see you tomorrow," she said as he walked across the back veranda.

"Tomorrow," he said back. His single word was a promise.

Chapter Seventy-Two

Marge Reynolds had been in agony all night long. She knew Katherine and Letty were having a party, and that troublemaker Maxie person was also there. She had counted. There were over a dozen people there and cars lined the curving drive. She had seen Lillian walk up the sidewalk all dressed up like she was attending her first prom, and her heart ached. She missed her old friends, but how could she ever tell them what was wrong?

Marge felt left out and so very alone in the world. Tonight she refused to cry and, instead, settled on methodically beating herself up. She was good at self-inflicted blows that were carefully aimed at her conscience and her heart.

I have never been like other people, she thought to herself. No one has ever understood me. All my life I've said things that don't make sense and people look at me funny. No one ever gets my jokes or laughs. People just walk away while I'm talking. Not that there is anyone to talk to or even to walk away now that I'm trapped in this house. I'm so alone.

About a year before Bud died, Marge had decided that she was becoming an invisible person. She could walk through a whole mall and not one person would make eye contact with her. She might as well be a trash can or a mop bucket or a poorly dressed, aging mannequin. People bumped into her and didn't apologize, like she was a post or a bench.

When Marge talked about it with her older sister, who had died a few months later of a massive heart attack, her sister had thought about it and then her eyes grew big with wonder. Stella felt that way, too! She was also invisible. It must be an age thing, Marge thought.

Marge talked about this with Bud, almost ranting, saying that when you use a parking garage you can have your parking ticket validated by a store clerk so you don't have to pay the parking fee. Any store representative can validate your parking ticket. That simple stamp declares that you are a genuine, valuable customer and your spot in the garage was taken for an important reason.

"People need to be 'existence validated,' she told him with much feeling. "Not by family, who are only too aware of our existence, but by strangers and passersby we encounter in our daily lives."

In the end she decided people are like the roses, not the modern tight versions that don't smell, but the big old-fashioned full-bloomed roses that have such a delightful scent they send your head spinning. In the spring, when they first bloom, people run around smelling every bloom. They declare they have never seen such glorious roses. They can't smell them deeply enough, or touch their velvety petals often enough. But after three days the wonder of them wears off.

The wonder of us as incredible individuals wears off also, she thought to herself with pity at the time. We should learn to be more aware of one another. Not just the gorgeous people, the striking, well-groomed people who invite stares simply because of their beauty. I mean the ordinary, the frumpy, the elderly, the homely, and the impaired. The world is filled with people who need a few kind words and the encouragement and hope those words can give.

It is so sad, she thought; for old people the glory days, where the bloom of youth touches us with beauty and energetic splendor, are over. Most of us have settled into the staid puddle of matriarchy and patriarchy. But that doesn't mean we don't exist.

The revelation changed her attitude toward others. Marge started keeping track, looking around in stores. She saw them everywhere, invisible people you wouldn't glance at twice. People who were so nondescript they sort of blended into the shelves. She talked to them, chatted with them, touched their arms and remarked on the day, or their clothes, or their faltering smiles. At every opportunity, she attempted to bring a bit of sunshine into another life. She actively sought out other invisible people. In return, she found herself becoming more and more visible.

And then she started getting sick. And then Bud died. And then her world crashed in around her. Her world imploded and turned into a black ugly knot of nothingness. Now she lived in an abyss so deep she didn't know how to climb out. She had no hope.

God, why won't you help me?

There was no answer.

Chapter Seventy-Three

Maxie Bruce fidgeted all through church, knowing what was to come afterwards. She frowned during "Blow the Trumpet in Zion," cheered up during "Celebrate Jesus," and went back to frowning during "Draw me Close to You." When the altar call came she inched past three grandchildren and two children and made her way to the front. Hanging onto the railing, she eased herself down onto her arthritic knees, pulled her suit jacket down over her ample hips, and bowed her head.

Oh, Lord, I know you want me to go over there and talk to that Marge Reynolds and I don't know why I'm so nervous. Maybe because I know I wasn't acting in love or like a follower of you when I got all carried away with her. I want to make it right and I feel you want me to go there for a reason. Father, I pray that you will give me the words to say and that you will start right now to soften her heart. Lord, I ask you to send your angels to protect her, and me, so that your will can be done this day. Please take away the fear I have and replace it with love. Please let me see this woman the way you see her. Thank you, God, for your son Jesus, and for what he did on the cross for me, for Marge Reynolds, and for all of mankind. Amen.

Getting back up, Maxie noted that Sister Sadie Stephens was eyeing her with much interest. Sister Sadie couldn't bear when someone went to the altar to pray and she didn't know the reason why. She was one of those pious Christians, those meddling Christians. One time she announced to everyone that she was praying that God remove the troublemakers from the church. Sister Sadie was sicker than a dog the next three Sundays and had to stay home in bed. She never considered that she might have been an answer to her own prayer.

Settling back in her pew, Maxie felt at peace. Little Henry slipped a hand in hers as they rose and sang a rousing rendition of "Family of God" to end the services.

Instead of riding back home with a child, or grandchild, Maxie had driven her old Studebaker to church. She'd told Elva where she was going, and to make her apologies that she couldn't join them for breakfast. In the Bruce family they took turns hosting breakfast after Sunday services.

The inside of the old car was warm from sitting in the spring sunshine. It was a glorious day, a day for just sitting and enjoying the outdoors. Maxie, who hadn't gotten to bed until after 2 a.m. the night before, was tired. She knew if she put her head back on the plastic seat she could go to sleep right there in the church parking lot.

Marge Reynolds was sitting in the living room when Maxie drove up. She wasn't doing anything, just quietly watching the wind fluff the leaves of the elm tree in the front yard. It was Sunday, she knew, because her favorite radio station was broadcasting services from some mega-church back east. She listened to the opening music, which sounded as if the choir must have at least a hundred members. Then she pushed the off button.

As she gazed out the widow, a tan and black Studebaker, an old car that was polished to within an inch of its life, glided up in front of the house. Marge sat up in alarm. No one, in the past two years, except for the fellow from the church who shopped for her once a week, had visited. Well, that wasn't true. Some people came and rang the bell but she never let them in. She just closed her eyes and didn't move until they quit ringing and knocking and left. The rest of the day afterwards was spent hiding out, usually in her bedroom or the kitchen, in case they returned. She was always terrified they would come back.

When Marge saw Maxie Bruce emerge from the car she wasn't truly alarmed, figuring that the woman was visiting next door. Odd, though, that she parked in front of her house.

Maxie Bruce looked impressive and surely must have just gotten out of church services to be so elaborately dressed. She wore a beautifully cut red dress with a long matching jacket. A black and white patterned scarf was at her neck and black dangling earrings hung from her chubby earlobes. She wore a broad black hat with a sweeping black feather adding an air of sophistication. Maxie walked a few steps from the car then turned around and removed the hat. Opening the passenger door, she placed it on the front seat and shut the door again. Using two hands she sleeked back her hair, braced her shoulders, and looked right at Marge's house before coming toward it on the sidewalk.

Marge quit breathing. Surely that harridan wasn't coming to visit her, after all that she had said. The woman was hateful!

Maxie continued her determined walk, turning left onto Marge's sidewalk, up the front porch steps and right to the front door. She knocked boldly, and rang the doorbell. Marge, who was sitting a mere ten feet from the door and was barely breathing, didn't answer.

Maxie rang the doorbell again. A few seconds later she knocked. Marge closed her eyes. She opened them when she heard the click of high heels. Marge, who had walked to the front window, was looking right at her, hands on her hips.

"Miz Reynolds, I need to talk to you," she said, bending over and peering in. Her voice through glass was muffled. "You need to let me in."

Marge shook her head violently.

"Please? I need to talk to you."

Marge put her hands to her face. Maybe if she was still enough the woman would leave. Maybe she hadn't seen her sitting there

Maxie walked back to the front, opened the screen, and turned the handle on the front door. She opened it a foot and poked her head in.

"Miz Reynolds, I need to talk to you," she said firmly.

Marge, her hands covering her face, didn't move. Maxie, suddenly realized something was very wrong and went inside. Walking to the couch, she stood in front of her.

"Well, you poor dear, you're scared to death of me, aren't you."

Marge kept her hands to her eyes and didn't reply.

"Why, you don't have to be scared of old Maxie. I ain't gonna hurt you. I just wanted to come over here and say I was sorry for talkin' to you like that. I had no call to be so disrespectful and so hateful. The good Lord has been really chiding me over my actions that day." Reaching over, Maxie gently took her hands and moved them. Marge looked panicked.

"I think I'm going to be sick," she said.

"You don't feel well?"

Marge shook her head.

"Is it because I'm here?"

Marge nodded.

"Can we talk about it?"

Marge didn't respond.

"I've been praying a lot about you the last few days," Maxie said, sitting down and gently taking Marge's hand, "and I think the Lord has been talking to me."

When the thin, attractive, but very agitated older woman didn't pull away, Maxie was encouraged.

"I met you a half dozen years ago, just before your husband died, but you must not remember me. I've been talking to

Katherine and Lillian and neither of them can remember when they saw you at Polsky's last or even when they last saw you a-diggin' in your garden. I pondered on that some and during the night God gave some thoughts. God speaks to me a lot at night. I just sort of wake up with ideas about this or that. My idea this time is that you haven't been out of this house for years. Is that true?"

"I don't want to talk about it," Marge said in a low voice.

"Well, we have sort of a problem here, then, because God wants me to talk about it, and since he's the boss I'm sorry but you're going to have to hear me out," Maxie said, looking at her watch. Then she added, "By my watch it is 1:15. I promise I'll be finished up in less than a half an hour. Then you can kick me out."

CHAPTER SEVENTY-FOUR

"There is no God," Marge said. Her voice was so full of resentment Maxie was startled.

"Now, how on earth can you say that?" Maxie asked. She had been a believer since she was seven years old and God had performed miracles in her life and showered her with blessings. She could no more imagine life without God than she could imagine life without air or water. She lived for serving Jesus, and her life was kept in constant excitement as she went about his business.

Marge was instantly transformed from a fearful, meek, docile woman to a rigid, tormented soul full of naked bitterness and fury. Yanking her hand away, she stood up. She was shaking. She had evidently forgotten her previous feeling of illness and was riding along on a track of vicious, unvented rage. And it was moving fast.

"How on earth can you say there is?" she demanded. Her lips were smashed to a thin line and her eyes blazed. She pulled her blue sweater tight, overlapping the sides, and clamped her arms over them. Her graying hair was sleek and attractive in a long pageboy. A long tendril on the side fell forward and she pushed it behind her ear angrily.

"Let me tell you about your God," she said to Maxie, bending over and staring at her. She talked through gritted teeth. "Your God took my husband away, the only person in the world who cared for me, despite my faults and oddities. The only person who understood and loved me anyway. Without even a warning 'God' just up and let him die. And let me tell you about my daughter. My beloved daughter. She didn't want a thing to do with me. She wouldn't even come to the funeral. Bud wasn't her dad, she said. So, here I was without anyone. Not one person in the world."

"But that's not true. You had lots of friends. Katherine told me. You just shut them out," Maxie said tenderly.

"We aren't talking about friends here. We're talking about God. You're right about me not leaving. I haven't been out of this house in nearly four years. And that's given me a lot of time to think about God. And to ask him to help. Do you know how many times I have asked him to help? A hundred times, was it? Two hundred? He has never answered. Not once. He has never once answered. Do you hear me? Not one time," she said, ending on a sob.

She sank back down on the couch, seemingly depleted, and once again hugged her stomach. Maxie handed her a tissue out of a box on the coffee table. She had noticed there were tissues handy all over the room, no fewer than six boxes. Maybe eight. They were like knickknacks. Marge decorated with tissue boxes.

Maxie closed her eyes in prayer. The clock on the mantle ticked softly and a car whooshed by outside.

"What did you pray?" Maxie asked softly.

"What do you mean, what did I pray? I asked for help. I asked him to talk to me. I needed him!"

"Did you ask him to forgive you?"

"Forgive me for what? I didn't do anything wrong. I was just a pitiful sickly old woman whose husband died."

"Let me tell you about God, and his son, Jesus," Maxie said, settling back. "First of all, talking to God is like talking on the phone. You can't just lift up the receiver and talk to whoever you want to; you have to do some things first. Like get the phone line put in, pay that pesky phone bill every month and then you have to have the correct number to punch in. Right?"

"I guess," Marge said.

"God's the same way. You have to do some things first before he can talk to you."

"That doesn't make a lick of sense. I thought God was supposed to be omniscient—knowing all things all the time. Well, if that's true, he should have heard every word I ever said to him," Marge said, a sneer in her voice.

"He probably did hear. Maybe you weren't listening. Maybe you were too stubborn and too angry."

"What was I supposed to do? Cry a little harder? Beg a little more?" The anger was receding from Marge's eyes and she was starting to display the despair she had felt over the years.

"Getting to God is easy. And if you are honest and think on it, he probably answered all your prayers. He never abandoned you. He sent Katherine. He sent the man from the church every week to bring you food and other things. He sent a lot of people. But you didn't see God in them and your heart was hardened."

Marge didn't respond, and Maxie sat quietly, waiting. God gave her peace and she knew he wanted her to be still while he did a bit of heart surgery. Finally Marge spoke, quietly and with wonder.

"They were all answers to prayer? They were, weren't they? All of them?" Marge slumped in her chair and put her hands over her eyes. Maxie patted her shoulder and gently took her hand in hers.

"Marge, do you really want God to be a part of your life? If you do, first you have to admit you are a sinner. And we all are sinners. We are born in sin. Did you know that most of the agony of Jesus dying on the cross wasn't from being nailed there, or from being whipped and tortured? It took so long and was so agonizing because he had to soak up every sin from every person ever born and ever to be born. All those black sins, from murder to rape, to lust to envy to theft. Every sin was placed on him. That's what he died for, for us, and for our sins.

"I was told once like this: a man who liked ants found an anthill in a field. He'd watch the little ants moving leaves, or bits of rock, and even their dead. Sometimes red ants would come near and the black ants would swarm out and fight for their hill. The man learned that a subdivision was coming in and the field would be excavated. He didn't know what to do. He tried telling them, even yelling and hollering, but they didn't pay any attention. The only thing he could imagine that would save them would be if he could become an ant himself. Then they'd understand.

"We're like those ants. Jesus, the Son of God, became one of us so he could tell us about the dangers of hell. Then he died for us. Because of that we have been cleansed of sin and we are guaranteed a home in heaven forever. So, to become children of God, and to receive his blessings and eternal life, we have to admit we're sinners, and ask for forgiveness and believe in Jesus. We have to ask him into our heart. And then God can listen to us and hear us. It's as easy as that. Let me tell you some Bible verses. God talks a lot about this in the Bible.

"In John 3:7 Jesus says to be saved we must be born again. The Bible in Romans 3:23 says: 'For all have sinned and come short of the glory of God.' John 3:6 says, 'For God so loved the world that he gave his only begotten son, that whosoever believeth in him should not perish but have everlasting life.' And Romans 10:13 says: 'For whosoever shall call upon the name of the Lord shall be saved.'

"I know that's a lot to swallow and there's a whole lot more I could tell you. To give you the Maxie condensed version, 'God loves you and his son died so you could be saved,'" Maxie concluded.

"Our lives here are just temporary. We're just visitors on earth. Our real home is up there in Gloryland, in Heaven.

God created us for one purpose, for his pleasure. We're 'sposed to worship him and to do his will. We're just here on a sort of temporary assignment. We're like them missionaries in a foreign land. I don't know why he chooses some good people to bring home early and why he allows some seriously evil people to live until they're near a hundred. My baby granddaughter was only three years old when she was hit by a car. The man was drunk. Went out of control and smashed right through the fence around their front yard. Her mama and daddy cried and wailed and had a hard time forgiving God, but they did. That was six years ago. Know where that man is today?"

"In jail?"

Maxie laughed. "Nope. Right about now he's probably in church praying for the Sunday evening service. He did go to jail for what he done, and he found more than just other prisoners in there. He found Jesus. He'd been drinkin' and druggin' all his life and had to go to jail to find out how to be free. Isn't that something? Now he's assistant pastor at the Baptist Church down on Hughes Street and he has a big ol' prison ministry. Maybe my baby granddaughter was sent here just for that very purpose, to bring Ned Beach home to God. That's the way I see it, anyways. She was on assignment, just like I'm here talking to you. Just like I'm on assignment.

"Everything, from the flowers blooming to the volcanoes erupting to birthing and dying, happens in God's time."

"Do you think, if I do all that you say, all that asking forgiveness and everything, it will fix my life?" Marge asked hesitantly. The question was pitiful in its quest for hope.

"Can't guarantee it," Maxie said merrily. "Some folks think once they's Christians they get a new Caddy in the front yard and a yacht in the back and three bank accounts full of money and everything's happy ever after. Sometimes bein' a Christian ain't that grand. When we accept Jesus, God don't declare we'll be rich and successful and own the world. We aren't supposed to own the world. What he does declare is that we'll always have him to go to, that we can have peace and joy and be content. That if we live our lives with faith he will bless us abundantly, but that might not be in material things. If we believe, he can heal our sorrows and our broken hearts and broken bodies. The best thing is that we get life eternal in heaven with him. The alternative is a life of torture in hell. We are made to be God's. We are truly his!"

"That's a lot to think about," Marge said. "But I can't imagine anyone powerful enough to fix me. There's too much too wrong."

Maxie chuckled, the sound coming deep from within. "God was powerful enough to make the mountains and the oceans and all the creatures of the earth. Believe me, Miz Reynolds, he can fix little old you," she said, patting Marge's knee.

Marge shook her head sadly. "I just don't see how," she said.

"I'll tell you what. Will you trust me to make that first step? Forget about the healing, about him fixing you. Forget about a future in heaven and all the rest. Do you want him to listen to you? To hear you in the night when you need someone to cry out to?"

Marge began to cry softly. She nodded her head, as if she couldn't really believe that a few simple words would allow God to listen to her. Was he really waiting for her?

Maxie took a deep breath and silently asked God to be with her. She knew that this moment was fragile, that the wrong words could keep this poor woman forever chained to a life of agonizing misery. But the right words could bring her a freedom she had never before known.

Get on your knees so she remembers this time.

Taking Marge's hand, Maxie slid from the couch, kneeling in front of it. Marge, without hesitation, followed.

"Marge, do you believe God is real?" Maxie asked softly.

"Yes, I do," Marge said. It was so soft she Maxie could barely hear her.

"Do you believe that Jesus Christ is his son?"

"Yes."

"That Jesus came to earth to die for our sins?"

"I believe that."

"Do you admit that you are a sinner and you want to repent of those sins?"

"I am a sinner and I do want to repent."

"OK, then, repeat after me. Dear Lord...

"Dear Lord...

Marge quietly repeated Maxie's prayer: "I know I have sinned and done wrong. I am willing to turn away from those sins and do whatever you ask me to do. I know that you died on the cross for me and I know that you were raised from the dead. I ask you to come into my life right now and take control. Please forgive me of my sins and help me turn completely toward you. I receive you as my Lord and Savior right now. If I died today, I know I would go to heaven to be with you. In Jesus' name, Amen."

Maxie had to crawl to the arm of the couch to pull herself up. Marge, who was in very good shape, considering her age and other problems, reached down and helped her.

"My gettin' up muscles just aren't what they used to be," Maxie said, panting from the exertion. "Do you have any tea?" she asked Marge. "Could we go in your kitchen and have a cup of tea?"

Marge nodded and walked toward the kitchen, Maxie following and rubbing her hip.

After getting settled at the kitchen table, Marge talked at length about her many illnesses and, finally, her agoraphobia. "I'm just a mess. I sometimes get enough nerve to get to out the front door and then I feel breathless and like I'm going to suffocate. I feel safe in here but then I start to worry about what if I have a heart attack and have to leave."

Maxie was overwhelmed with compassion. She had asked God to show her Marge Reynolds through his eyes and she was filled with love and concern.

"Marge, I want to ask you something," Maxie said.

"All right," Marge said. She was agitated. It was disturbing to talk about everything and she was terrified that it would bring on another panic attack. If she kept quiet and calm, and crept about the house carefully, sometimes they would leave her alone. Today she hadn't been quiet and calm.

"Can you tell me what we did this afternoon?"

"Of course. I accepted Jesus Christ as my Lord and Savior."

"Do you feel differently?"

"I feel safer, somehow, and I feel like he's going to listen to me."

"After listening to you the last couple of hours, I want to tell you about something else. Do you know what spirits are?"

"Do you mean like ghosts?"

Maxie laughed. "No. Good spirits are the spirit of love or the spirit of compassion. Evil spirits are like resentment, bitterness, anger and fear. If it's okay with you, I'd like to pray for you."

"You think I have those spirits in me?"

"At one time or another, all of us have evil in us. We just have to root the bad stuff out. But God's a gentleman. He can't do anything to us without our permission. Prayer is sort of like giving him permission. If you have a Bible you can look up in Ephesians and it tells you how to battle evil."

"I'd like you to pray for me."

"Good," Maxie said, placing gentle hands on Marge's shoulders. She waited a few minutes for God's words to settle in and then began: "God, I ask that you be with us right now. I ask that you be with Marge and give her peace. Father, just fill her to the brim with your peace. Father, we ask that you remove all the panic and fear from her. Satan, you have no control over this woman and by the blood of Jesus I demand you leave. You have no right to stay here and you must leave now. Dear Lord, this precious child of yours has accepted you today and asked you into her life. I ask that you restore her joy and her contentment and that you take this empty life and make it whole. I ask that you make her path narrow and deep so that she can't veer off of it and that you make this path known to her. I ask, Lord, that you listen to her cries at night and her questions during the day. I ask that you give her strength to leave the house and the knowledge that she can do all things through you. God, I ask that you make her aware at all times that you are right there, standing beside her and that if she needs comforted you will hold her close. We pray all these things in the name of your perfect son, Jesus Christ. Amen."

Marge had crumpled down from her chair sometime during the prayer and was on the floor, Maxie beside her. For many minutes after the prayer Maxie continued praying silently, her lips moving and emitting little whispers of sound.

Marge looked up. "I don't know what you prayed. I didn't hear," she said.

"Most times I don't know what I prayed either," Maxie admitted. "I just sort of open my mouth and the Good Lord stuffs in the words. I heard myself on tape once and I whispered over and asked my daughter who that person was, I didn't hear them in the prayer service and my daughter said, 'Why, that's you, Mama.' Me! Why, I sounded like one of them college graduates."

Maxie helped Marge to the chair. "How you feel?" she asked.

"I feel like I've been run over by a truck. I feel like I've been drained out. But, Maxie, I feel free. I feel...I don't know how to explain. I feel totally at peace."

"Truthfully, you look like a different person. Your whole face looks different. I think you've been delivered from evil and left in God's glorious light."

Marge smiled. It was a smile of perfect contentment.

"You doin' anything tomorrow afternoon?" Maxie asked.

Marge laughed, the sound tinkling like the chimes of angel harps. "I haven't been outside this house for nearly four years and you're asking if I have plans?" The thought was ludicrous.

"I'm going to leave my Bible with you today. You just read the highlighted parts throughout the New Testament, I'll show you where that starts, and it'll give you something to think about. Then tomorrow afternoon I'll bring you a new Bible. Think you can do that? Go out for a bit? Maybe just a ride in the country?"

"The way I feel right now I can go anywhere. I'll give it a try," Marge said.

"Good girl," Maxie said, getting up to leave. Marge hugged her tightly. "God, please bless this, your child," Maxie whispered. Then she made her way through the living room. At the door she stopped and turned around.

"By the way, I made that up about the outhouse smells in your house," Maxie said.

Marge looked at her and gave a tentative smile. She wasn't used to smiling but it felt good. She let it grow a bit.

"I knew that," she replied.

Chapter Seventy-Five

Across town, everyone in the O'Reilly clan was packing. "I don't know how five people can make such a mess in a motel room," Connie complained. "Brent, look under the beds to make sure we got everything." Brent grumbled, but fell to his knees and bent over to peer underneath. He pulled out a white sock.

The rental van had been turned in and they were all flying out early in the evening. Dan and Connie and their families and Patrick were all on the same flight. Stuart and Nora were leaving an hour earlier, headed to Cleveland.

"Eleanor, open the door," Connie said from the bathroom when she heard the triple knock. Nora came in and looked around the room.

"You aren't all packed up yet?" she said in surprise.

"We're still looking for a lost tennis shoe," Mitch said. "It didn't wander down to your room, did it?"

"Haven't seen one," Nora said, smiling. Mitch smiled back. He'd never really cared for his sister-in-law but last night had shown a new side of her to him. He suspected she wasn't as hard and sophisticated as she wanted people to think.

"You might want to have Brent go down to Dan's room," Connie called from the bathroom. "Nora, come in here and talk while I'm packing up in here."

Nora stood in the doorway to the bathroom.

"Do you want to walk to the drugstore with me?" she asked Connie. "I need to go pick up a few things for the flight."

"Honey, I'd give anything to leave this chaos. Just wait one sec," she said, dumping makeup into a makeup bag and wiping shower water off the shampoo and conditioner bottles before putting them in her bag.

Walking into the room, she hugged Mitch from behind. He was packing and watching a TV rerun of "Bonanza" at the same time. She stepped on her tiptoes and kissed him on the back of the neck.

"You care if I walk to the drugstore with Nora? We'll only be gone a few minutes."

"And leave me here in this chaos?" he asked. Turning around he swung an arm loosely around her neck. "Sure, go ahead. You two aren't going to see each other for a while."

"Can I come to the store?" Donny asked.

"Sorry, buddy, but you have to find your shoe," his dad told him.

After walking down the hall, Nora and Connie stepped into the elevator. It was so quiet, so muted. "Listen to that," Connie said to Nora.

"Listen to what?"

"Quiet. Absolute quiet," she whispered.

It was a brilliantly sunny day and they slowly walked the two blocks to a Walgreen Drug Store, soaking in the bright Montana sun. It was always a surprise, each time they visited Danford, to realize how clear the air was here. While Nora shopped, Connie looked through the tourist sections and chose some huckleberry cordial chocolates to take back and give to the elderly neighbor lady who was keeping an eye on their house.

Nora kept an eye on Connie and slipped up to the checkout stand when she wasn't watching. Handing the pregnancy test kit to the gum-snapping, overly made-up middle aged woman handling the till, she said, "Can you put this in a separate bag for me? I don't want my sister to see it."

The woman smiled knowingly. All sorts of people came through her line with test kits, some as young as fourteen and some as old as mid-fifties. Some were bubbly and happy with husbands, others were sullen and secretive and scared. All of them willingly doled out money to find out their future.

The clerk was counting back change when Connie stepped into an adjacent line. They finished at the same time and, each carrying small bags, opened the door and stepped back out into the sunshine.

A youngster on a skateboard plummeted down the sidewalk just as they got outside and glanced off of Nora, sending her bag skittering to the curb.

"Watch it, kid!" Nora yelled, grabbing onto Connie to keep from falling.

"Sorry!" the boy hollered as he continued on his way.

Scattered along the sidewalk were Nora's purchases: a newly released best-selling paperback novel for the trip home, a package of peanuts and a candy bar. Lying naked in the middle of the walkway was the pregnancy test kit. Nora grabbed it up and stuffed it in the sack, but not before Connie spotted it.

"You want to tell me why you need that?" Connie asked. Suddenly the mysterious night sickness made sense. She felt like a complete dummy for not figuring it out. She had been pregnant three times and surely should have recognized the signs.

"I don't know, but I might be pregnant. Maxie said last night when I got sick at O'Malley House that I was, and told me about nighttime morning sickness. I haven't told Stuart. I wanted to do this test thing first."

"Pregnant! Wow. Nora, would it make you happy?"

Nora closed her eyes and gave a rueful smile. "Nobody knows this, but Stuart and I tried for years to get pregnant."

"I had no idea. I thought you didn't want children. We all just assumed that you wanted just your careers."

"We've both been tested and the doctors can't find anything wrong. We've tried everything under the sun. We've just sort of given up. A few months ago we just decided we weren't meant to have children," Nora said with a shrug.

"I am so sorry. I didn't have any idea. I feel awful that you didn't trust me enough to tell me," Connie said.

"If we'd lived closer I probably would have, but it's hard to tell about stuff like this over the phone."

"If you are pregnant, what will Stuart say?"

"I think he'll be the happiest man in Danford. He wanted six children. Please don't say anything, okay, Connie? If it isn't true I'd just as soon no one knew I'd even taken the test. If it's negative I won't tell Stuart."

The sisters chatted about babies and pregnancies all the way to the motel. Connie walked Nora to the door of her room and hugged her fiercely before she went inside. "I'll be praying," she whispered to her.

"Thanks," Nora said.

Chapter Seventy-Six

"Did you buy me anything?" Donny asked as Connie entered the room. Everything was packed and her whole family was stretched out on the bed, watching TV.

"Nope," Connie said. "Did you find the shoe?"

"It was in the closet behind the ironing board," Eleanor said.

"Dan and Miranda want all of us to go to that restaurant down at the end of the block for lunch," Mitch said. "We have to be checked out before noon. The front desk said we could store all of our suitcases downstairs and then the courtesy van can take us to the airport when we're ready to leave. Dan figured we could have lunch and then the kids could play in the park for awhile. He was going to check with Stuart. Said he'd knock on the door when they're headed out."

"Sounds good to me," Connie said.

A half hour later Dan rapped on the door. Donny ran and opened it. He and his uncle Dan were good buddies.

"How you doin', Sport," Dan asked him as he picked him up and tossed him in the air. Donny squealed. "You all ready to go?" he asked Connie.

"Can we wait just ten minutes until this show is over?" Brent asked.

"Sorry, Charlie," Mitch said. "On your feet. You can help haul suitcases."

Dan, Stuart and Mitch used a hotel cart to ferry luggage to an elevator and then to the storage room. The rest of the clan followed in another elevator. During the ride down Connie tried to catch Nora's eye but Nora was ignoring her. Connie didn't know if that meant good news or bad news. She was in the bathroom when the men left, so didn't see Stuart to see if she could read anything from his face.

The stroll to the restaurant was boisterous as the children romped together ahead of the adults. Connie was sometimes amazed at Brent. He seemed to be two people, one a child who still liked to horse around and play, the other a sullen fourteen-year-old who tried to be mature and scoffed at anything he considered juvenile.

The restaurant was busy and they had to wait a few minutes for the waitress to push tables together so that they could all be seated together. Ordering was a fifteen-minute ordeal, with Donny changing his mind between the macaroni and cheese and the mini hot dogs kids' meals. Brent ordered a T-bone steak but when everyone stared at him, especially his mother, he decided to go with a cheeseburger.

"Well, it's been quite a weekend," Dan said. Everyone nodded.

"It's been the most amazing weekend I think I've ever spent," Connie agreed.

"We got to go to O'Malley House and I don't think I'll ever forget the entertainment Letty had for us."

"I've never had a birthday like it," Patrick said, adding that he might turn eighty again next year.

"Tell them who you called twice already this morning," Dan teased him. Miranda poked her husband in the ribs. Patrick blushed.

"Who?" Connie asked, as if she didn't know.

"Lillian," Patrick said boldly, as if daring anyone to say anything further.

"That's nice," Nora said. She said it as if she'd been drinking, the words coming out in a sort of slow slurring contentment. Everyone looked at her. She was gazing at Stuart and smiling. He nodded his head and took her hand.

"Stuart and I have an announcement to make," Nora said, taking her eyes off her husband and looking around the table.

Connie's eyes sparkled. Under the table, she grabbed Mitch's hand.

Nora blushed, and continued, "We didn't think it could ever happen. We've tried for years and been to doctors and had all these tests..." She started to cry. "Daddy, can you hear me?"

"What? Sure I can hear you. I'm not deaf," Patrick said. "So, you're crying. What's this all about?"

"Well, I guess I'll just say it. I'm pregnant. We're going to have a baby."

Connie was instantly on her feet, hugging her younger sister. Dan pumped Stuart's hand while Mitch clapped him on the back. Brent looked disgusted. Jessie Lou looked rapt; it was so romantic. Donny wished he'd ordered the macaroni and cheese. Eleanor was imagining holding a brand new baby; a brand new cousin.

Patrick just sat and grinned, his dentures gleaming in the restaurant light. His baby girl, Nora, was pregnant. Soon another member would join his family. Life was good.

Chapter Seventy-Seven

Simeon, considering the lack of sleep from the party the night before, was pretty chipper during church services Sunday morning. At the end of the service he caught up to Katherine, who was just pulling on her coat in the coatroom.

"You look pretty sprightly for a girl who partied half the night," he teased.

"You don't look half bad yourself, considering. Your feet must be tired from all that dancing," she teased back.

"Katherine, can I stop by after church?"

"It is after church."

"Well, I know that. Can I come by? I need to talk to you."

"So mysterious!" she said, cocking her head and squinting her eyes a bit as if she could ferret from his mind what he wanted to discuss. "Tell you what. I'll fix us lunch. There's a ton of leftovers in the fridge. Even with what Letty and Maxie and Elva took, I could still feed the whole church today on leftovers. Give me fifteen minutes to change clothes and come over. If I'm not in the kitchen just come in and wait."

A half hour later, both of them dressed more casually in slacks and sweaters, Simeon was helping Katherine pull things from the refrigerator. They would have, she decided, leftover salad with some of the marinated shrimp added, hot roast beef sandwiches, and apple pie.

Simeon was nervous, almost fretting. Finally, as Katherine was pouring sweet tea into glasses filled with ice cubes, he took a deep breath, stood up and started to talk.

"OK, let's have this out. I'm going to try and say it so you can understand. Just give me a chance here." Simeon cleared his throat and looked Katherine in the eye. "You and I not getting together did have something to do with all the money you have. But now I'm thinking I'm over seventy-years-old, and that's too old to worry about what people think. In actuality, people would probably be surprised at how much money I really do have. Your John was very good about sharing stock tips and I've done very well. I could have left years ago and bought a grand house but this was my home and, in a way, you were my family."

"I didn't know that about John giving you advice," Katherine said in surprise.

"He was a good man. You were a good couple. There was a time when I was very jealous of what he had."

"Those were the years when you closed yourself off. I knew. Simeon, I knew."

"I thought you might have. It probably wasn't hard to figure out why I never wanted to leave."

"So, why then, after John died, didn't you pay attention to me?"

"The money, the way people would talk. Men are very proud, sometimes, Kate. And sometimes it's that pride that gets in the way of happiness. Last night I was up all night long, praying and asking God what to do. Being with the O'Reillys showed me how I've just thrown my life away. Life is too short to continue doing it. I've decided to heck with what people think. It simply doesn't matter anymore. I don't know why, maybe talking to God half the night and praying, but suddenly everything seems very clear and nothing matters but you and me. I guess I'm trying to say we shouldn't waste another minute. If you'll have me, we should just get married."

"Married?" Katherine stammered. She was stunned. She fell into her chair. She could feel the blood draining from her face. A sort of whooshing sound was going through her head. She couldn't quite capture the word, as if its meaning had suddenly been lost, as if was a foreign word or one he'd just made up. When she was a child she learned if she said the word "brush" over and over and over, it would suddenly cease to have meaning.

"If you'll have me. I'm old and I've never had a wife. I'm probably not the best fish you could reel in, but no one could love you more," he declared firmly. By now he was agitated and needed pacing room.

"Did you really say that—that you want to marry me?" Katherine asked, dumbfounded. "Two days ago, I couldn't get you to sit and eat cookies and have tea without having to hogtie you, and today you want to get married?"

"Hmph," Simeon said. "I talked this all out with God last night and I thought maybe he'd go ahead of me, like he does sometimes in the Bible and sort of pave the way. That you'd sort of know."

"God never told me anything!" Katherine said.

"Well, you think about it and let me know," he said, and started toward the door.

"Where are you going?" Katherine asked.

"I don't know. I just thought you should think about it."

"Come back and sit down. Right there. Take a drink of tea and just calm down a little. This whole thing has come as a bit of a shock."

The two sat in silence for a few minutes, not looking at each other. Simeon gulped his tea and thumped his mug on the table. He drummed his fingers. He wanted to look at Katherine but was afraid to. He was afraid of what he'd see there. He'd wanted her so long and now, now! to think it was all out in the open and she had the power to turn him down. He'd curl up and die if she did. Just curl up and die.

Katherine reached out and took his hand in hers. "Simeon, look at me," she asked gently. He looked up. She took his other hand and captured both of them in hers. "Do you know how many times in the last three years I wanted to march to your cottage and throw myself in your arms?" she asked.

"Do you know how many times I hoped you would?" he asked back softly.

"What would you have done?" she wanted to know.

"I don't know," he admitted. "Maybe our lives would have been different. Maybe we wouldn't have wasted all these years." He hesitated for a full minute and then looked her fully in the face, blue eyes to green eyes.

"Katherine," he said, using her full name, "I want you to know that I have loved you since the day I first saw you with your red hair hanging down your back and the sun shining on your face. You were like the glory of Ireland, come right here to Montana. You were a blaze of laughing perfection in a very gloomy world. I can close my eyes and see you just as you looked that day."

"I didn't know," she whispered. "I didn't know it was that soon."

"Well, now you do. You know my darkest, most well-kept secret. John suspected years ago. The year before he died he came to see me and stammered and hem-hawed and finally got around to saying that if anything ever happened to him he would appreciate it if I would take care of you. He mentioned the summer we added on the room to the cottage and how we seemed to, quote, 'get along like a house afire.' I think he knew all along."

Katherine was stunned.

"I don't know what to say," she said slowly. "For my part, I've always loved you. Of course, as a friend and someone to trust, until after John died. After that it became something different. It grew. These last years I have so enjoyed your company and the friendship has deepened into something much more. I love you, Simeon."

"I love you, Katie. After all these years, it is a relief to finally have things out in the open," he said, reaching across cupping her face in his hand. "I don't know what the future holds but if you will marry me I will promise to always try and make you happy."

Putting her arms on the table and lowering her head to them, Katherine started to cry. In an instant Simeon was at her side. Hauling her up, he held her close and nestled his face into her neck. "Don't cry, sweetheart," he murmured. Lifting her chin, he kissed her sweetly, softly.

"Oh, Simeon, I have loved you for so long," she whispered.

"What?" he asked. "You'd better say that louder, Katie. You know I'm hard of hearing!"

"I said, 'I have loved you for so long!'" Katherine said, her voice gruff from crying. She laughed.

"And I love you, too," Simeon said loudly, hugging her tighter and smacking her on the lips. He rocked her back and forth. Katherine chuckled as she burrowed into his sweatshirt. She found a perfect spot just below his breastbone and she smelled deeply his familiar smell.

"So, will you say yes? Will you, Katherine O'Malley, become my lawfully wedded wife?"

"I will say yes. I will become your lawfully wedded wife."

"Oh. Wow!" he said, and then frowned. "Does this mean I have to wear that tux again?"

"You can wear a white leotard for all I care," Katherine said, laughing happily. "I'm sure glad you're also partly blind so you can't see how bad I look," she added, wiping a finger under her eyes.

"It's too bad you're so deaf you can't hear my heart pounding like a teenager's," he teased and then had a thought.

"Hey, if we're going to be married, maybe we could save money by sharing Geritol and liver spot medicine. You could borrow my hot pad and I could use your reading glasses."

"For a date we could watch the grass grow or go to a lecture on cleaning dentures or learn walker and wheelchair maintenance," she quipped.

They laughed and he moved her out of his arms. Stepping away, he took her hands and looked at her with such a tender look, such a loving look, that it took her breath away. She said the first thing that came to her mind.

"Thank you, Simeon," she said.

"You're the one to thank," he responded, and a cloud of regret passed across his face. "Maybe you should have gotten angry years ago. Maybe we should have found people like the O'Reillys years ago."

"Would it have worked then?" she asked.

"Maybe not. Probably not. Things just sort of happen in their own time, I think. At our age everyone's dying and you start to realize how precious life is and how short it is. I've been thinking about that a lot the last few months."

For long minutes they just stood quietly together, relaxed and content in each other's arms. He kissed her on the neck, the soft part under her earlobe along the jawline. "Kate," he said quietly, "I hate to break this up, but I'm starving."

She moved away and smiled at him with such love that it caught at his heart.

"Typical man," she said.

"After lunch do you want to go to Polskys?" he asked.

"Polskys Market? Why? You want to go shopping?"

Simeon chuckled. "I figure we might as well get the rumor mongering started and there's no better place than Polsky's. We'll have all those old ladies whispering in the aisles."

Chapter Seventy-Eight

Before they went shopping they called Letty who screamed and yelped and carried on and said she'd be over that night. Maxie wasn't home. Elva, who happened to be there, said she was still with Marge Reynolds. Elva cried at the wedding news and promised she wouldn't tell her grandmother. Simeon and Katherine wanted to share the news themselves. Lillian, like Letty, had jumped and hollered and said she was coming right over but Katherine asked her to wait until that night; she and Simeon had some planning to do. Upon hanging up the phone, but not before telling Katherine that Patrick O'Reilly had called her twice already that day, Lillian started crocheting a wedding afghan.

After calling the rest of their friends, huddled together with the receiver between them, Katherine and Simeon talked about when to get married. They called their pastor to see when he would be available. It would be a small wedding, they decided, with just a few close friends and a reception for everyone at the mansion. They laughingly decided it would have to be planned around their doctors' appointments.

While they were still laughing, Maxie called to tell them about Marge. Katherine and Simeon were both astounded and a bit horrified to learn that the woman had been housebound all that time.

"I can't believe I didn't realize," Katherine said, her voice filled with regret. Katherine agreed to accompany Maxie and Marge on Marge's first outing the next afternoon. After thoroughly discussing Marge's condition, Katherine told Maxie about the proposal.

"And people say God don't answer prayers," Maxie bellowed. "I been praying for this day for nigh onto five years!" She started to say goodbye and hang up the phone because she wanted to spread the good news, but Katherine remembered something. "Wait, Maxie!" she said, "I forgot to tell you something. I don't know what it means, but Nora called this morning and said to tell you the answer is 'yes.'"

"Oh, my," said Maxie. "I knew it. I just knew that girl was pregnant!"

"Pregnant! This is a day for good news," Katherine declared.

Late that afternoon Katherine and Simeon sat out on the veranda on a porch swing. The sun was starting its downhill slide and a few robins were rehearsing their night song. The grounds of O'Malley House were lovely, perfectly trimmed and pruned with masses of spring flowers just coming up. They both loved this place.

"Look," Simeon said, pointing toward the creek. A deer had come into view and was standing near his cottage. The cottage was beautiful in the ebbing sunlight. It looked like it had been scooped up from an estate in England and settled lovingly into this perfect spot. Simeon kept it looking like an English cottage, too, with flowers and walkways, perennial and herb gardens and banks of roses. Few people knew that in back he'd surrendered to modernity and put in a pool and a hot tub.

Simeon sighed almost discernibly. Cocking his head, he looked at his cottage, and then he turned and looked at Katherine.

"Tomorrow I'll get some boxes and start packing," he said.

"I was just thinking the same thing!" she said.

"Why would you need boxes?" he asked, puzzled.

"Oh! We haven't talked a bit about where we'll live. Do you want to move to the house?" she asked curiously.

"Do you want to move in with me?" he asked hopefully. Katherine laughed. She shook her head as a wonderful thought lighted its way through her mind.

"Simeon, do you remember what I said during the tour last night, about O'Malley House not really being mine and how Letty and I are getting the rooms all put in their original condition? We've been working on this for the past year and a half. I never knew why it was happening, but I think it's all coming together now. I think God had all this planned, long ago."

"Really? Do you think so? That's amazing, if it's true."

"Just think about it. I've been happy here since I was in my twenties and now I'm getting ready to move into a maid's room and put in the old wood cook stove so the place will look authentic. More and more, I've felt O'Malley House should be opened for the public to see. Can you imagine school children going up and down the halls? That's been sort of my plan. That I'd have a little maid's room to live in and cook on a microwave in the pantry. Like I said last night, I'm just a caretaker of this old place. Simeon, God's been making a lot of changes, you have to admit."

"Sometimes it's hard to comprehend that he has elaborate plans for our lives and that he cares that much. It's when we look back that we can see how all the pieces fit together. Restoring the house certainly must be part of his plan," Simeon agreed, and then he thought of something. He shook his head and snorted.

"What?" Katherine asked.

"You won't believe this," Simeon said, laughing. "Six months ago I bought a new bed. I had just a twin and the thing started killing my back. After what, thirty years, the thing starts killing my back? I bought a king sized monstrosity and I've been thinking I'm crazy all this time. I don't need a bed that big. The thing's all brass and takes up half the room. Not only that but I got talked into buying one of those doohickies that go around the bottom, one of those skirt things, and a white down comforter and even some of those pillow things."

"Pillow shams?"

"Yeah, those things. Every time I crawled into that bed the last six months I've been thinking I was getting a little bit too close to my feminine side. Now I'm thinking maybe that was part of his great plan, too."

Katherine was laughing so hard the swing was shaking. "God is so good to us," she said through her laughter.

The voice in the kitchen brought about more peels of laughter.

"Yoo-hoo! Katherine! Simeon! Are you two lovebirds out there?" Lillian hollered, peering through the window in the kitchen door.

Simeon groaned. "Don't answer. Pretend we aren't here," he whispered. Katherine swatted his knee.

"We're out here on the veranda, Lillian," Katherine hollered back.

Then she turned to Simeon. "Love me, love my friends," she said, giving him a kiss on the cheek.